ON ALL FRONTS

On All Fronts

BRYAN SCHARF

AUTHOR'S NOTE

This project began in the beginning of 2019, and as I sit here typing at my desk next to my mask and bottle of hand sanitizer near the end of 2020, I can't help but be grateful to my wonderful friends who joined me on this journey. Not just because of the adventures we've had and the progress made, but because writing these books has given me a glimmer of hope for our future. As I type, the west coast is in flames because someone decided to use explosives at a gender reveal party, political books are dropping like the leaves soon will, and anger, frustration, and hate are festering in my country's open wound.

And here I sit. Writing the tales of heroes. Of a knight who charges forth to do battle knowing no other result besides victory. And he is a friend. Of a healer who offers caution and level thinking at a time when I fear to lose my own head. And he is a friend. Of a girl who appreciates the beauty of the strange, concrete world covered in nature's bandages, willing to fight tooth and claw to protect them. And she is a friend. Of a man so determined to do what's right he will bear any storm the world may throw at him. And he is a friend. Of an old curmudgeon who begrudgingly takes up arms against the evils of the world because he knows it is the right thing to do. And he is a friend.

At a time when I see nothing but evil and corruption and hate, I get to spend my days recording the tales of mighty heroes who are willing to stand up against these plagues.

And they are my friends.

I do not know when this book may find you or what evils have befallen the world since I've penned these words, but remember this: There will be heroes.

And they may well be your friends.

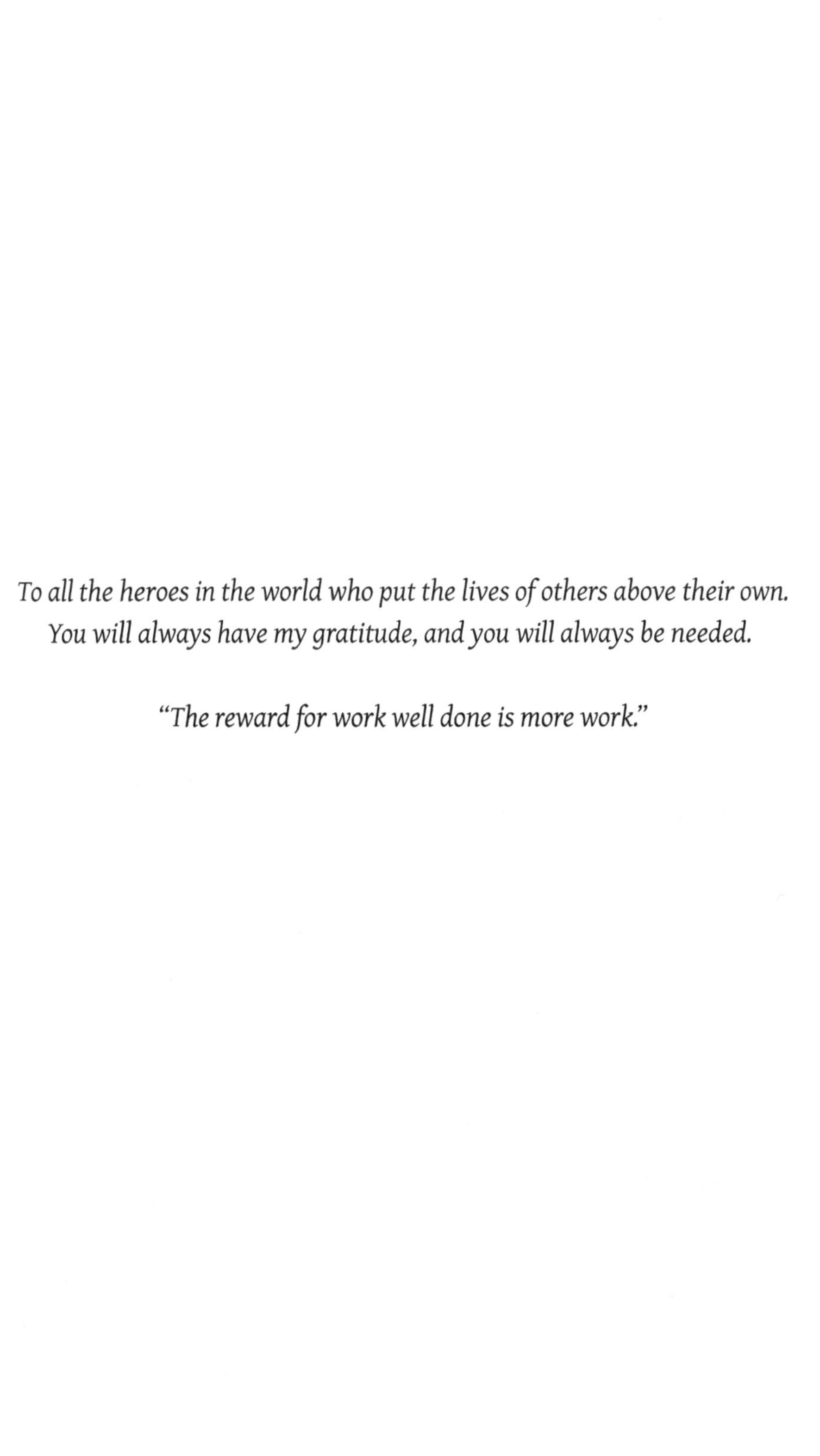

To all the heroes in the world who put the lives of others above their own. You will always have my gratitude, and you will always be needed.

"The reward for work well done is more work."

~ 1 ~

MORGAN

"Seriously, I gave you one job," Smithers said grumpily, barely audible from behind his coffee cup.

The stubble on the old man's face was growing in much coarser than Morgan had ever seen it before. When they had first met, he seemed sharp and alert, if a bit surly. This morning all he was really giving off was surly. His thinning, white hair was tossed and rumpled, some of it falling in front of his bloodshot eyes. He wore a pair of denim jeans and a loose button down that hung open over a dark tee shirt.

Sure, she had only known him a few days, but the same could be said for just about everything in this world. It was hard to believe that she and the others had woken up only a couple days ago in St. Augustine hospital here in Boston, rather than the world they had originally come from. Morgan pressed her hand to her head as she tried to draw any memory of where she was from. Images of the dense, lush forest, her family among the trees, but when she tried to draw out their names, pain shot through her skull. Shaking her head, she changed her focus.

Smithers was leaning against the counter of the cantine of the Cathedral of the Holy Cross where they had been staying the past few days. It was sparsely decorated, with blank walls and motley furniture that did not match any aesthetic. Currently, she was sitting on a padded stool that was probably older than she was.

Fidgeting with the foreign clothing she was wearing, Morgan nervously began looking around, trying to ignore the heat in her face.

Opposite Smithers stood Luis L'Hopital, arms crossed and jaw clenched. His short cropped black hair was slightly rumpled, though at the length he wore it that did little to offset his proud demeanor. Luis was a holy knight of Nike, Goddess of Victory, and wore his devotion proudly. He had a sour expression on his face that had come when Smithers had told him to leave his sword downstairs and not to carry it openly. Luis was of the opinion that a knight should always be armed and ready to defend the weak, so Morgan knew he had his friction lock baton close at hand in the pocket of the leather jacket he was wearing. However, that did not change the glower he shot towards the older man.

Next to him, calmly sipping at a cup of tea at the table was Lee Errapel. The two had formed a sort of brotherly bond through their divine natures, though Lee was practically Luis' opposite in every way. Scarred and tattooed, the priest of Goibniu, god of the Forge and Hospitality, looked every bit the grizzled warrior Luis did, though Morgan knew how Lee detested violence. His long, silver hair was pulled back neatly in a smooth tail, nary a hair out of place, cutting a distinguished figure, seemingly at ease, though his eyes were actively scanning the room, sharp and acutely aware of his surroundings. Morgan had a difficult time understanding Lee, whose sharp mind was constantly taking in and processing his surroundings. While Morgan liked the priest well enough, knowing he was probably dissecting her actions just as much put her slightly on edge.

The final figure in the room had his torso sprawled out on the table, precariously close to knocking over a bowl of cereal. His legs dangled off of a stool that he balanced unconsciously on two of its four legs. Morgan could hear the light snoring from the figure they called Timm, because it was a lot easier than trying to pronounce his full name.

"Timm!" Smithers said, sharply. "Wake up! We're plotting!"

"Huh?" Timm's head shot up and he opened his eyes blearily, looking around at all of them.

Morgan had to suppress a giggle or else draw Smithers attention upon herself. The side of Timm's face was bright red and sported an indented line from where his head was resting on the sleeve of the newest shirt provided to him by the church's thrift shop. Timm had a habit of making his clothing unwearable and Morgan realized she hadn't seen him in the same outfit twice. Usually that was because the clothes he had been wearing at the time got torn to shreds or covered in blood. More often than not, both.

His mop of brown hair fell across his eyes and he drew an arm across his mouth, wiping away a faint line of drool. Morgan didn't blame him for being a bit out of sorts. In the past twenty-four hours he'd been stabbed, sent to the hospital, attacked wearing nothing but a hospital gown by two men trying to kill a child, and then shot at by the Irish Mob. If anyone had earned a rest, it was Timm. But here he was with the rest of them planning their next move.

"What did you expect us to say?" Luis asked Smithers, irritation in his voice. "Patrice is in trouble, and Father Mitchell needs our help protecting her."

Smithers sighed heavily. "Of course we're going to help the kid. But could you have at least told us before you agreed to getting us up at this ungodly hour?"

"You needed your rest," Morgan interjected, trying to calm the situation. "We didn't want to bother you with it after what happened last night."

"So you decided to wake me up at the crack of dawn after what happened last night to tell me we have more dangerous work to do?" Smithers asked, coffee still not having worn down the harsh edges of sarcasm in his voice as he said it eventually would.

"Father Mitchell said that the reward for work well done was more work," Luis said.

"Ain't that the truth," Smithers muttered, sipping at his cup. "Fine, we do this, what is the plan exactly?"

"Latoya and Patrice will be heading to Austin, Texas via something called a 'train'." Lee explained, looking at a sheet of paper Father Mitchell had printed out for them, making them swear to burn it after they were done. "We take them to the 'Amtrak' station where they will board the 11:15 to Austin and we make sure that nothing attacks them as they board. Father Mitchell informed me that he had friends at the next couple stops that would board and watch over them."

"Sounds like a solid plan," Smithers said, nodding. "I've just got one question for you."

"What is that?" Lee asked.

"Why the hell did you assholes wake me up at six in the morning to help them catch an eleven o'clock train?" Smithers asked, gesturing at the analog clock on the wall.

Morgan had been practicing trying to read it recently. She had been spoiled by the digital clocks that were available on many screens around the city and in the vehicles they'd been traveling in. As she counted back the minutes on the big hand, she realized that it was precisely six o'three.

"Ooh!" she exclaimed. "That means we have about five hours until the train leaves!"

"Yeah, we do," Smithers said, getting up from the counter. "And I'm going to spend those five hours cleaning my guns and napping. And if anyone wakes me before nine, I'm going to shoot them."

Father Mitchell walked in as Smithers was heading out and eyed the older man with an amused look.

"Please don't shoot anyone in my church. I know you all could probably survive it, and even heal from it overnight, but still, it will cause a ruckus," the priest called after Smithers, who was stomping down the stairs.

"No promises!" the old man called back.

Morgan chewed her lip as the old man descended. She had wanted to speak to the group about another matter, however Smithers' nerves had seemed quite frayed and she did not want to address another matter that may create tension until this one was settled. She turned back to her breakfast and caught Lee's stare. That feeling of being dissected overcame her again, and then quickly pulled her eyes away from his, glancing down at the soggy mush of what remained of her cereal.

"Morgan," Lee's voice asked, though she knew it was not a question. "Do you have something to tell us?"

"I'm not sure what you mean," Morgan answered, using her spoon to stir the congealed corn and rice concoction. "You described the plan thoroughly."

"Not about the plan," Lee pressed. "You seem uncomfortable, as if you want to say something but are afraid that it may cause issues."

Morgan clenched her jaw. Damn he was insightful. Or maybe she just couldn't help but wear her emotions on her sleeve. He sat there, stone faced, giving nothing away while easily reading anyone in the room. He must have known before Smithers left, but waited until he did to be sure Morgan would be more open to telling him.

She sighed, knowing that he may not pursue the issue terribly hard, but that there would be subtle means of attempting to draw the information out later. She might as well get it over with.

"It was about the ghost battle," Morgan said, still stirring her cereal, which was beginning to resemble more of a stew. "But it didn't seem relevant at the moment, so I figured I could wait on bothering you all with it."

"You heard Smithers," Timm said, groggily. "We've got five hours to kill."

"And you're our comrade," Luis added. "If you have concerns then it should never be a bother to share them with us."

Morgan chewed her lip slightly, knowing they were right. "Okay then, back at the park, when we were fighting the ghost, I looked out over the frozen lake and saw an elk."

"That is unusual," Father Mitchell said, sipping at his coffee. "While we do get them in the northeast from time to time, they usually steer clear of the cities and keep to wilder territories."

"But this one wasn't alive," Morgan said, her voice straining slightly. It was only then she noticed just how badly this had been affecting her. She felt her heart beginning to race as a sudden, unknown fear gripped at it. Taking a deep breath, she tried to calm down. "It was standing, the fur and flesh rotting off of it, glowing with an eerie green aura around it. It felt somehow malevolent. Like it was angry at me."

"You specifically, or all of us?" Lee asked.

"I'm not sure," Morgan confessed. "It was looking at me, but I suppose I could be wrong about that, considering its eyes were gone."

"That's a lovely image," Luis said, taking the others slightly off guard. Sarcasm was a new color on him, but Morgan smiled. It did suit him.

"Well, thankfully, it didn't last long," Morgan continued. "Once I looked away it vanished. I couldn't find a trace of it."

Luis pursed his lips in thought. "Something like that..."

"Sounds undead," Lee finished the thought. "Similar to what we were fighting. Undeath attracts its own. Could have been called from our battle."

"This is true," Luis nodded in agreement with Lee before turning to Morgan. "If it happens again, tell me immediately. I can see if I can sense the creature, figure out where it is, perhaps what it is. And it won't escape twice."

Morgan nodded. "Thank you, I will do that."

"Very well, now that that's settled," Luis said, pushing off from the counter he was leaning against and starting for the stairs down to where Smithers had disappeared earlier. "I am planning on going for a run. If any of you would like to join me, feel free, but try to keep up."

"I would be happy to," Lee said, standing. "Based on how our luck seems to go, it would be wise to warm up my muscles before heading to the train."

As Lee caught up with Luis, Timm's head popped up from where he had dozed off again at the counter.

"I'll come too!" he practically shouted.

"Aren't you injured?" Lee asked. "Would it not be best for you to stay here and catch up on some rest?"

"More sleep will just make me lazy and sluggish," Timm said, smiling. "Nothing wakes you up like brisk air and a pounding heart!"

Morgan watched the three descend the stairs to prepare for their run. She didn't quite understand the need to run around for the sake of running. In the forest, it was best to conserve your energy while you had it rather than burn out and be tired when running was needed. She sighed and chalked it up to a difference in culture before starting in on her mush of a breakfast.

She heard a similar sigh to her own followed by Father Mitchell chortling slightly on the other side of the room. Looking up, Morgan saw him sipping at his coffee and watching where the three had just been with amusement in his eyes. He looked over and caught her stare, smiling at her.

"To be young and energetic," Father Mitchell said, wistfully. "Though I doubt even in my hay day that I would have been able to keep up with you lot."

"You seem rather fit," Morgan said, feeling her face go warm. She turned back to her meal and stirred it a bit. "I mean, you look like you can take care of yourself. You should be able to keep up."

Father Mitchell laughed. "A mere mortal such as myself? Hardly. What you all can do is amazing. I'm no slouch, I agree, but I'm also not superhuman."

Morgan gave him that one. It seemed as though their abilities put them apart from the people of this world. She didn't understand why, though. She never had difficulties drawing on her magic in this world, except for that time at St. Augustine's, however that was due more to the poison the false physicians had been pumping into their bodies than access to the power. She could draw upon the power of this world, so it made no sense that others could not.

"I don't know if we're superhuman, as you say," Morgan said, slowly working over her breakfast and her thoughts. "We have access to something that is here, something that permeates the entire world around you. Perhaps we could show you how to do it too? Perhaps there's a way for the people of this world could have access to the same power we have."

Father Mitchell shuddered. "That is not a prospect I find comforting."

Morgan turned to him, confused. "Wouldn't it be better for this world if there were more people like Luis and Lee who could pull the poison and sickness from people with a touch?"

"It would," Father Mitchell said, getting up. He walked over to her and put his hand on her shoulder, and Morgan felt a warmth surge through her that felt familiar. Looking up at him, for a moment she saw the shadow of a man framed by thick green foliage, glowing orange with the warmth of the setting sun.

In a blink of her eye, the image was gone, replaced with Father Mitchell again.

"However, I think of the others in this world and what they might do with it. Those like the ones you fight against. It is not enough to merely have power, you must also respect it."

Morgan smiled, remembering her own father saying something similar to her when her powers were first drawn out of her.

"Now, if there's nothing else," Father Mitchell said, stepping away from Morgan and heading to the door. "I have quite a bit of work to get to."

"Oh!" Morgan exclaimed. "Since we have time, is there any place I can practice my dulcimer?"

"You... have a dulcimer?" Father Mitchell asked. "I thought you said that the people at St. Augustine destroyed all your things?"

"All our weapons and armor," Morgan corrected him. "But my dulcimer is pretty small and was wrapped in an oilskin in my bag, so it's been pretty safe."

"You know what," Father Mitchell said, smiling. "I really should know better than to ask at this point. There's a small chapel we use for small blessings that don't require the grandeur of the main building. It has excellent acoustics."

"Thank you," Morgan said, wolfing down the rest of her breakfast, no longer caring about its taste or texture.

Soon after, Morgan found herself in the small chapel Father Mitchell had directed her towards. The ceiling towered about twenty feet over her head and it looked like three dozen people could comfortably sit within. She was unsure what Father Mitchell's definition of 'small' was, however she was fairly confident that it did not match her own.

She took her time setting up the instrument, small as it was, and treated tuning and caring for it like a small ritual. The scent of wood from the forest back home... wherever home was... lingered on the instrument. She ran her fingers gently over the light carvings across its face. Soon she drew them over the strings, feeling them hum at her touch.

Slowly she began to run the tips of her fingers across each in turn, then in light rhythms, and then into more intricate patterns. While her mind could not draw the names or lyrics of any of the songs she was playing, her fingers seemed to remember the path home without any hesitation. She sat and played, allowing herself to be taken deep into the forest of her youth, but rather than fight for the memories she could not grasp, she rode along the currents of the ones that came naturally and smiled.

The hairs on the back of her neck stood on end causing the fluid movements of her fingers to shift into harsher, more deliberate strokes. Her eyes snapped open, ripping her consciousness from the forest back into the chapel to find the being that had triggered her instinctual reaction.

Standing by the open doors of the chapel was a man dressed similarly to Father Mitchell's Sunday wear. He had the black, button down shirt with the white collar, and it was difficult to tell where his shirt ended and pants began as the black was pristine and unfaded by time. Around his neck he wore a cross, much like Father Mitchells', though unlike the wooden one around the young priest's neck, this man's was made of gold.

He was staring at her, piercing blue eyes staring over his hooked nose. There was no hair on his face, nor hint of stubble, but the thinning grey hair on his head was slicked back with some kind of grease or oil that only accentuated his hawkish features. When Morgan locked eyes with him, her playing stopped.

"I'm sorry," Morgan said, hearing the tension in her own voice. "I was told I could practice here."

"I'm sure you were, it seems you have the run of the place," the man said, and as soon as she heard his voice, Morgan remembered him. Father Pearson, the man who had been arguing with Father Mitchell about opening the church to 'strays' as he had called them. She felt her grip tighten unconsciously on the dulcimer.

"Beautiful song," Pearson continued, either not noticing the tension he had induced in her or choosing to dismiss it. "I don't believe I've heard that one before."

"It's from my home," Morgan said, knowing that if she were to try to draw the name of her home from her memory, it would only cause her pain. "Far away."

"I'd imagine," Pearson said, though his tone gave little away of his meaning. "You're one of the... individuals... Mitchell has brought in, no?"

"Yes, I am," Morgan said, her voice turning hard. "*Father* Mitchell is a good man to be so kind to strangers. One of the tenants of your church, as I learned. From him, as a matter of fact."

Her harsh emphasis of Father Mitchell's title was clear, but again, Pearson acted as if her own inflections were as toneless and bland as his.

"Yes, the man does have many good intentions when it comes to strangers," Pearson said, his gaze intense.

"And we have only good intentions for while we're here," Morgan returned the gaze.

"I see," Pearson said. He slowly blinked, but Morgan felt no victory. This wasn't the battle of wills between two wolves asserting dominance. His was the blink of a well fed cat who wanted you to know that the only reason you weren't being skewered by its claws was because it had better things to do.

"The road to hell is paved with those, I'm afraid," Pearson said, turning for the door. "I'll leave you to your practice."

Morgan held her breath as he left, feeling more threatened by this old priest than she had by the mob. With them the threat was clear, a gun in your face or a knife in your back. This man was dangerous, though Morgan was unsure how she knew.

"One more thing," Pearson's voice cut through her thoughts.

She looked up to see him holding the door in his hand, staring back at her from the hallway.

"It may behoove you to start looking for other accommodations," Pearson said. "As much as it would Mitchell."

Silently, he closed the door, leaving Morgan alone in the uncomfortable silence.

~ 2 ~

SMITHERS

After tossing and turning in his cot for nearly three hours, Smithers finally decided to give up on sleep. Between the coffee, the clomping of those idiot's feet as they returned from their run, and the PTSD reruns that came from being in another goddamned shootout, Smithers just could not manage to find any quality rest. Nine on the nose he was sitting up in bed with one of the multiple guns they had taken from the Irish Mob laid out in front of him.

It was a decent AR, though nothing to write home about. Hadn't been modded to go full automatic, which surprised Smithers more than a little. He would have thought that something like legalities wouldn't have bothered the Irish Mob that much, though when he found the serial number filed off he assumed that more than likely they hadn't gotten to this weapon yet. He took it apart piece by piece and watched carefully as Luis, Lee, and Timm drew lots for the showers.

Luis won and went in, while Lee sat down on his bed and began flipping through one of the bibles that was lying around the place. Timm flopped down on his cot and passed out immediately. At least the boy would be quiet while he finished his work. By the time Luis had finished his shower, Smithers had finished the AR. By the time Lee had finished, Smithers had finished the 9mm.

They were about to wake Timm for his shower, when Father Mitchell descended the staircase and walked over to where Carl and his family were sleeping. The three women were still piled on top of the man, whose arms wrapped around them tightly, even in his sleep. *He might be a fool of a man,* Smithers thought, *but at least he knows the value of the people around him.*

Father Mitchell checked on them, smiled slightly, and then walked over to where Smithers was putting the pistol back together.

"Any problems?" He asked.

"Since I met these assholes, tons," Smithers replied. "But I'm guessing you meant with the Clan of Carl. That would be a hard no. They've been sleeping like the dead since last night. Not even this lot traipsing around down here has made them stir in the slightest."

"That's a relief," Father Mitchell said, and Smithers could see that it wasn't just an expression in the priest's case. Tension he had been holding in his shoulders relaxed and Smithers could see immediate physical relief wash over the man.

"Everything okay, there padre?" Smithers asked, checking the slide. "You look a little tense."

"I could say the same for you," Father Mitchell smiled, but relented. "I have yet to make transportation options for Carl and his family. It seems they will be with us for another day. With the mob looking for them, and by extension, you, it has been quite difficult trying to arrange anything."

"I don't think you need to worry about our names and faces getting out and getting in your way," Smithers said, loading a magazine and chambering a round. He ejected the magazine and loaded an extra bullet before replacing it.

"Based on the amount of blood on Timm last night I dared not hope for such a stealthy extraction," Father Mitchell said, raising an eyebrow.

"Lemme tell ya about the difference between 'stealth' and 'Russian stealth,'" Smithers said, holstering the pistol and taking out his shotgun to clean.

"I cannot help but think I don't want to know the difference," Father Mitchell replied.

"Probably not," Smithers said, breaking open the barrel and putting his cleaning brushes to good use. "That being said, few if any are going to be able to identify us, so today's festivities should still be on."

"I sincerely hope for a distinct lack of 'festivities' in this juncture," Father Mitchell said nervously. "Is everyone ready?"

"Lee and Luis seem good to go," Smithers nodded at them, then hooked his thumb at Timm who was still snoring loudly, face down on his cot. "The kid went and burned himself out with that run and I have half a mind to leave the liability that is his ass here."

"There may be wisdom in that," Father Mitchell said, observing Timm's deep slumber with something of a smirk on his face, as though laughing at a private joke. "And I suppose Morgan has not yet returned from the chapel yet?"

"Chapel?" Smithers asked. "What on earth was she doing there?"

"Not normally a question I have to answer in a church," Father Mitchell said, a snarky tone to his voice. "However, in this case I suppose it is a bit out of character. She was looking for a private place to practice her dulcimer."

"Okay, so I have a question about the dulcimer," Smithers asked, confused. "Where the hell has she been hiding that?"

"I was going to ask the same question, but the girl did become a bear once, as I've been told," Father Mitchell said.

"Yeah, she does that," Smithers said, nodding.

"Does what?" Morgan's voice came from the stairs, and both Smithers and Father Mitchell turned to see her in surprise, then looked at each other.

"Nothing," they said simultaneously.

"Oh, okay," Morgan said, clearly confused. "Well, is everyone here? I... I feel I should talk to the group about something."

"Saw another ghost already?" Luis asked, a wry grin on his face.

"What?" Smithers asked, confused.

"I'll fill you in on the drive over," Father Mitchell said, patting him on the shoulder. Smithers blew out a sigh and just continued scrubbing at the inside of the second barrel. One crisis at a time, he supposed. There was no point in borrowing trouble from later.

"Well," Morgan started. "Actually, I was thinking that it probably would be best for everyone if we stopped staying here at the church. Maybe after we finish the mission today, we should start looking into other options."

"Is something wrong with the accommodations here that brought this on so suddenly?" Father Mitchell asked, clearly concerned. Smithers didn't feel the priest was offended by the statement, but as much as he also wanted to stop living like a church mouse, the request was fairly sudden on Morgan's part.

"No, nothing is wrong here," Morgan said, scuffing her shoe against the carpet slightly. Smithers recognized the action. His daughter used to do the exact same thing when she wasn't telling the whole truth. "I just don't want us to be putting further burden on you, Father Mitchell."

"Oh," Smithers said, holding his hand up to tell Father Mitchell to leave this one to him. Mitchell read the sign easily and swallowed any question or remark coming. "And where exactly did the idea of us being a burden come from?"

Morgan's foot scuffed uncomfortably again.

"Who's kicking us out?" Smithers asked, pretty sure he was on the mark.

Morgan blinked, "N... no one..."

"Pearson," Father Mitchell said, with a sigh.

"Was he not the priest you were talking to the other day?" Lee asked. "The older man?"

"Yes, older and more... traditional," Father Mitchell said, with a sigh.

"Unbaptized babies go to hell and gay people make hurricanes kind of traditional?" Smithers asked, loading a couple shells into the barrels of his shotgun before stowing it away for safekeeping.

"Crudely put, but not inaccurate," Father Mitchell sighed. "Sometimes I feel I was placed in this church specifically to counter his... zeal for the old ways."

"By God or by the people above you?" Smithers asked.

"Yes," Father Mitchell replied, grinning at Smithers before turning his attention to Morgan. "I will not allow Pearson to kick you out, and in fact I will be having a word with him about overstepping his bounds. He may have seniority here, but there's no rank earned for being born earlier than another."

"But..." Morgan began.

"If you do not feel comfortable remaining here, and I would fully understand that after Pearson's behavior, I would be more than happy to help you all find a place to stay," he continued, and Smithers could see that he had an amazing talent for putting others at ease. "However, for the moment, I do need to speak with Pearson about other matters. I'll leave you all to your discussion and meet you outside with Latoya and Patrice in twenty minutes."

"Oh! Before you go!" Morgan said excitedly, holding out her hand. Smithers could see a small handful of berries cradled in her palm. "You should take one of these."

"Uh..." Father Mitchell said, looking at the berries that seemingly just appeared in her grasp. He reached out and picked a single berry up. "Thank you, I'm not overly hungry right now, so I'll save it for later."

"Just be sure to eat it within twenty four hours," Luis said, with a knowing smirk.

"Ah," Father Mitchell said, raising his eyebrows. "So it's like a boysenberry."

Luis' mouth twitched as confusion overtook the smirk on his face. "A what now?"

"Just go with it," Smithers said, waving the priest off. "We'll be ready when you are."

"Very well," Father Mitchell nodded and climbed the stairs.

"Do you lot always need to be so weird?" Smithers asked.

"I just offered him a berry," Morgan said, slightly dejected.

"Is it a magic berry?" Smithers asked.

"Yeah!" Morgan answered. "If you eat it you won't be hungry all day and…"

"Then it's weird," Smithers said, not wanting a lesson on magic fruit. "Anyway, we need to figure out a plan for the day. Timm seems to be out of commission and I don't feel like dragging dead weight around with us if we're going to the train station and apartment hunting all in one go."

"He's dead?" Lee asked, looking up from his book with an expression of concern on his face.

"No, dead weight," Smithers said, not exactly feeling the love from Lee. For a man whose job it was to care for others he sure had shit bedside manner. "Basically, Timm's useless today. Though we should cut the kid a break I suppose, with all that happened yesterday."

"Besides, we're merely escorting a woman and child to transport," Luis said. "Should be something we can easily handle."

"Now why'd you have to go and do that?" Smithers asked, groaning.

"Do what?" Lee asked, nose still down in the book he was reading.

"Tempt fate," Smithers said, pressing his fingers to the sides of his temples.

"I do not tempt fate," Luis said, smiling as he got up and walked over to where Latoya and Patrice were sitting. "I challenge it openly and walk away victorious."

He sat on the bed beside Latoya for a while, talking with the woman and her daughter. Patrice had really taken a liking to Luis, and Smithers felt that had a non-zero percent chance of being because she thought of him as her own personal guardian angel. While he packed his bag, the knight regaled the little girl with stories of victories and battles, of monsters and heroes, and Patrice laughed and smiled and gasped in excitement and fear.

Smithers smiled as he watched this. He couldn't help it. Surprisingly, Luis was far more charismatic than he let on about himself. And the kid loved him. As frustrating as these weirdos could be, they all strived to be decent people. Strange as hell, but Smithers could not deny that they were decent.

"Alright, if yeh ain't unconscious or being hunted by the mob, git yer butts upstairs!" Smithers called out. "Apparently we're spending the day challenging fate!"

~ 3 ~

LUIS

They hadn't bothered to wake Timm when they'd left. Luis did not feel the young man's help would be necessary to escort Latoya and her daughter Patrice to a station. If Timm had managed to fight off the two assailants who had come for Patrice in her hospital room by himself as well as managing to keep her from harm while he himself was injured, the knight felt that four of them could manage a small army of them.

He could tell that Smithers was somewhat annoyed at leaving Timm behind, but he felt that had more to do with being woken up early himself and having to go while Timm got to sleep further, but he bit his tongue. Currently, Father Mitchell was driving the church's van while Smithers sat in the front with him. Morgan and Lee sat in the middle row, while Luis sat in the back row with Latoya and Patrice, making light conversation.

Luis had taken to telling Patrice stories from his homeland and the great heroes of Nike. Trying to recall their names only caused him to get flashes of headaches and stumble over the tales, so rather than prod his thoughts for what he expected would be impossible to grasp, he would simply refer to the warriors in the tales as 'sir or lady knight.'

"There were lady knights?" Patrice asked, excitedly. "I thought only boys could be knights!"

Luis laughed. "Where did you hear that? Some of the fiercest soldiers in my battalion were women. There was one, her name escapes me at the moment, but she carried a sword longer than I am tall! She had the strength to cut a man in twain with a single swing, even through plate armor."

Patrice knitted her brow and turned to her mother, "Mommy, what does 'twain' mean?"

"Cut him in half," Lee's voice came from the seat in front of them, though his eyes never left the copy of the Bible that Father Mitchell had lent him.

"Yes, well, maybe we should change the subject?" Latoya asked, though Luis could sense that it was not as much of a question as she was making it sound like. "There's enough violence in the media and I don't think it's healthy for Patrice to be hearing all of this."

"But I want to hear about the lady knights!" Patrice protested.

"I'm confused though," Lee said, looking up at Latoya. "You are part of this religion, are you not?"

"Well, we're not Catholic," Latoya said. "But we are Christians."

"I do not understand the difference," Lee said flatly, before continuing. "You do not want her hearing of violence, but you let her read this book?"

"While the old testament is rather bloody and violent, the new testament is all about peace, love, and treating one's neighbor as oneself," Father Mitchell said from the driver's seat. "Just wait until you get to that point."

"I did," Lee stated. "And is it true that your god flipped over a table and beat men with a whip to drive them out of a temple?"

"Uh, I mean they were desecrating the church by using it as a means to make money," Father Mitchell explained.

"What about him cursing the fig tree because it did not bear fruit?" Lee asked. "That sounds rather petty."

"That one... I..." Father Mitchell sounded a bit off guard to Luis, though the stories Lee was telling endeared Luis more to the idea of thumbing through this holy text at some point. It seemed to have some interesting tales in it to be sure.

"You're right, that's not exactly violent," Lee muttered.

"Except against the tree," Morgan mentioned, her tone stern.

"This is true," Lee said, flipping through pages. He paused, read something, and seemed to confirm he found what he was looking for. "Ah, here it is: 'But these enemies of mine who did not want me to reign over them, bring them here, and slay them in my presence.' It does not seem as though this Jesus individual is much of a lamb."

"That's in the bible?" Latoya asked, seemingly surprised.

"Luke 19:27," Lee confirmed. "And once you get to the last book, Revelations I believe, it gets substantially more violent."

"How many times have you read that?" Father Mitchell asked.

"I'm on my second read through," Lee said. "The first was for overall impressions, the second is for detailed knowledge."

"Didn't I give that to you like two days ago?" Father Mitchell asked.

"Approximately," Lee answered, then returned to his reading.

Destroying desecrators and slaying enemies. Luis pondered this god of Father Mitchell's a little more. Perhaps the religion was not as weak as he had initially thought. It was most definitely not going to convert him, but he felt he could respect it a bit more now. So long as the values were upheld.

He reflected a bit on Father Pearson and the thinly veiled threat he had presented to Morgan earlier that day. Two different priests within the same order of the same church seemed to Luis to be vastly different in their interpretation of their holy text. Father Mitchell approached it much like the lamb he had told them their god was. However, looking at what Lee had presented and the underhanded methods of Pearson, he had a feeling he knew what parts of the bible both men focused their study on.

Luis shook his head. It was foolish to have such a complicated book with so many conflicting stories. Nike did not require a massive tome in need of a herd of shepherds tirelessly trying to interpret her words. Her words were simple: Honorable victory by any means necessary. No interpretation needed there, and that was why he never need question his goddess. Luis looked up at the driver's seat and saw Father Mitchell gripping the steering wheel tightly and wondered if the priest ever did.

"So why is it called 'Amtrak'?" Morgan asked, apparently trying to break the tension in the air.

"Stands for American Tracks, I think," Smithers answered.

"What's that?" Luis asked.

"Tracks are the things the trains travel across," Smithers explained. "And trains are like giant, metal wagons latched to one another."

"Not the trains," Luis said. "What is an American?"

"Me, for one thing," Smithers said. "I'm from America."

"I thought you were from Boston," Luis said.

"For one thing, no, I'm not from Boston," Smithers explained. "I'm not from anywhere in Massachusetts at all."

"I'm confused, are we in all three of those places at once?" Luis asked.

Smithers sighed deeply. "Okay, America is the country. The country is made up of fifty regions known as states. Massachusetts is the state we're in now. There are cities and towns all over the states, and the one we're in is called Boston."

"Ah, so like territories of an empire," Luis said, finally understanding the breakdown that Smithers was explaining to him.

Smithers pondered the question for a moment. "You know, now that you mention it..."

"Smithers, we do not live in an empire," Father Mitchell said, sourly.

"If that's true, mind explaining the status of Puerto Rico and Guam to me?" Smithers asked, smugly, though Luis did not know what he had to be smug about. "Or can we discuss the 'procurement' of Hawai'i?"

"You know something, my life was so much simpler before I met you all," Father Mitchell grumbled as he pulled the van into an alcove beneath a red and blue sign that said 'Amtrak.' "Here are the tickets, I assume you know how to find the track, and I'm going to pull the car around to the parking area. Come get me when you're done."

"Will do," Smithers said, then turned to the rest of the van. "Alright, everyone pile out. Luis, you're on them like flies on..."

Smithers turned his eyes to see the bright little face of Patrice smiling at him.

"Poop," Smithers finished. "Like flies on poop."

"Interesting metaphor," Luis said, clambering out of the van and checking the duffle bag that concealed his sword before tapping the pocket where the friction lock was stowed away. Patrice and Latoya followed him out, bags in tow.

Waiting for Smithers to exit the vehicle, Luis took the right flank as Lee fell into place on their left. Morgan, not really knowing much about military operations, moved in to help Latoya with her bag and chatted amiably about the upcoming trip and if they had packed enough to eat, offering each of them a single berry, to Latoya's confusion.

Luis smiled at this, but snapped to attention as soon as Smithers took point and waved for them to follow.

Inside the station there was a mass of movement and sound. Luis felt like he walked inside a human sized beehive with all the people moving haphazardly in different directions, but all with purpose. Moving staircases brought people up and down different floors leading to one 'platform' or another and Luis began to wonder how anyone could manage to navigate such a cluster of confusion.

Smithers, however, did not seem to have a problem. With ease he read the ticket and marched off in the direction of the necessary platform. Luis' stomach rolled as Smithers led them onto one of the moving staircases and he gripped the sliding rubber handrail tightly as they ascended. It surprised Luis that the people of this world managed to create two methods of replacing stairs, and that they were both horrific.

He was beginning to weigh the differences between these moving stairs and elevators in an attempt to determine which was worse, when Smithers stepped off and led them to where a mass of metal boxes with windows sat with doors wide open emitting a constant, heavy rumbling and gouts of heat and steam. They were dull and grey, but painted red and blue with the 'Amtrak' symbol plastered on the side. Through the windows, Luis could see row after row of plush red and blue chairs lined up at tables. It seemed a more comfortable means of transportation than a car or van, but Luis still felt he would prefer a horse to all this nonsense.

"Alright, we can't board with you," Smithers was saying to Latoya. "Ticketmaster won't allow for that, but you should be good once you're on board. We'll stay on the platform until you're all out of sight. Your next escort will be meeting you at the next station. Got it?"

"I think so," Latoya nodded, her lips pressed tightly together. "I would much rather have you all escorting me, but I know you have other things that need taking care of. And other people."

"You will be safe," Luis said, nodding. Then he looked down at Patrice. "Take care of your mother, Lady Knight."

Patrice's face lit up as she smiled at Luis. He couldn't help but smile back at her. The young girl would make for a fine warrior someday. She had already faced harsher trials than Luis had at her age and came through powerfully. While he may be concerned for her life, he did not fear for her spirit.

Smithers went over the plan with Latoya a few more times just to ensure that she had the whole thing memorized. Father Mitchell had insisted they burn all non-essential paperwork before leaving and adamantly refused to let Latoya write any of it down. He warned leaving a paper trail could make it easier for these men to find her and her daughter again. With this knowledge, Latoya answered every question Smithers posed quickly, confidently, and with the professionalism of a soldier, and once again Luis was impressed.

As they boarded the train, Luis scanned the crowd, searching for anyone who fit the description of the men Timm had faced the night before. He had not been as detailed as Luis would have liked, however he could not fault the man, what little detail Timm provided seemed to be all the detail these individuals had to offer the senses.

The train had begun its departure. Patrice was at the window, waving to Luis and the rest. Luis turned, smiled at the girl, and returned her wave when a sudden flurry of activity on the platform caught his eye. Four exceptionally indistinct men were making their way towards the moving train. Without hesitation, two jumped and disappeared into the space between two of the train cars. The other two leapt forward and grabbed onto a pair of ladders fastened to the sides of the train itself.

"Smithers, two inside, two going high," Luis said, already breaking into a run. "Get to them. I'm going high."

"Wait, boy, what?" Smithers called back, but Luis was already moving.

He saw the last car of the train pass him and was still picking up speed. Missing was not a luxury he had. Summoning his will, Luis ground his teeth and jumped for the back of the train where another pair of ladders were fused. Reaching out, Luis felt his fingertips brush against the rung of the ladder, but he knew that he was not going to make the jump.

Suddenly, a massive blow to his back forced him forward. He scrabbled for a moment as the rungs came back into reach and he gripped tightly as he felt something heavy grappling him from behind.

"Oh!" Morgan cried out. "I'm so sorry, I thought you were going for the other one! I didn't mean to land on you!"

Luis grit his teeth and grinned. Was it dumb luck that had sent her flying into him? He looked up at the sky and smiled. He had never been one to put much stock in luck. It seemed that Victory here today would require her by his side.

"Don't worry about it," Luis said, gripping the ladder tight. "You climb up first. I'll be right behind you."

Morgan obliged, using a combination of the ladder and Luis to clamber to the top. Luis secured his duffle bag and hauled himself to the top of the moving train. At the top, Morgan stood, wind whipping wildly around her as she stared hard at a pair of men holding swords staring back at her.

Luis grinned as he came to his feet next to her, the images of the city flying by them. He reached into his duffle bag, excitement pounding in his heart.

"Finally," he said, drawing the short sword from within the bag. "Now this is the kind of fight I've been looking for."

~ 4 ~

LEE

Lee watched Luis and Morgan leap for the train and felt his stomach drop as he saw them collide in a tangle of limbs on the narrow ladder at the back. They began to climb, but Lee didn't have the chance to track their progress as Smithers grabbed him by the arm and hauled him hard.

"Come on!" the old man shouted, running far swifter than Lee would have expected a man of his years to be capable of. "We gotta get to Latoya and the kid!"

"How are we supposed to do that?" Lee called back, bewildered by the lack of plan Smithers seemed to be following.

Without answer, Smithers crossed the platform and leapt into the space between cars. Lee heard a slight howl of pain as his leg made contact with a metal pole that ironically seemed to serve some safety purpose.

"Are you insane?" Lee called out, feeling his composure slip.

"It's only getting faster!" Smithers replied.

Not wanting to be left behind on his own in this strange city, especially after encountering the gunmen a few nights prior, Lee grit his teeth and made a run for the spot between the cars where Smithers was standing. Putting all his strength into the leap, Lee did not notice the platform beneath his feet ending until after he had gotten airborne. Panic gripped his chest as he flew through empty air, sudden doubts plaguing his mind.

His feet found purchase on the metal flooring and Smithers' tight grip kept him upright as Lee steadied himself against the wall. He could feel his heart pounding like a blacksmith's hammer in his chest.

"See," Smithers said, patting Lee on the shoulder. "That wasn't so bad."

"That was horrible," Lee answered.

"Well it's only going to get worse," Smithers grinned at him, pulling open a narrow door and slipping inside the car.

Lee followed and soon found himself surrounded by a sea of plush, uncomfortable looking seats and indifferent faces. If anyone looked up at them at all, it was simply in recognition that another living thing was moving toward them. Most didn't even acknowledge that much. Lee was astounded that a people who were so comfortable in their surroundings that they ignored basic survival instincts could even still be alive.

Smithers stopped short in front of Lee, almost causing him to crash into the older man. He nudged Lee and gestured at a pair of unoccupied seats. Lee looked at Smithers, puzzled by the instructions. Rolling his eyes, Smithers leaned in and whispered to Lee.

"Latoya and the kid are about three rows up," Smithers explained. "We can watch them from here, but we don't want to start the scene."

Lee slid into the seat, still not sure why they weren't actively attempting to protect their charges and said as much to Smithers, though he took the cue from the older man and kept his voice down.

"Listen," Smithers said, putting a duffle bag on his lap. "I don't know how they do things where you're from, but proactive heroics tend to be labeled as 'trouble making' or 'vigilantism.' It's safer for us to try being reactive heroes."

"End the fight, or prevent it, rather than start it," Lee said, attempting to paraphrase what the old man was telling him.

"Precisely," Smithers said, slipping his hand into his bag as he leaned back in his chair. "Though there's nothing that can be done about us having the unfair advantage of knowing it's coming."

Lee looked down at Smithers' hand and noted the metallic sheen of one of the hand guns he had procured from the mob hide-out the night before. The priest's stomach turned slightly, looking at the weapon that had filled him with so much dread. He knew that Smithers would be using it on the enemy, but that was no guarantee that the enemy would not have a few of their own. He began breathing deeply, trying to keep his emotions in check.

Smithers began tapping furiously at Lee's leg, breaking him out of his concentration. He turned to see the old man's face turning bright red, his eyes bulging as they locked keenly on where Latoya and Patrice were sitting. Lee turned his gaze and saw a pair of men standing next to Latoya. One had his hand on her shoulder, while the other had his within the folds of his jacket. Lee's mind wandered to the gun Smithers was concealing in the duffle bag, and instantly felt sick.

"We gotta divert their attention," Smithers said, his voice barely a hoarse whisper. "But if we stand up and start shooting, those bastards could kill them!"

Lee looked at the men looming over the terrified mother and child. He had long ago accepted death as an inevitability, and accepted that the loss of innocence was not beyond the universe, as it cared little for what mortals held sacred. There was little reason to allow such inevitabilities to drive one to rash action or fruitless ends. Smithers was clearly getting to the point of doing something stupid and drastic to ride in and save the day. That would not end in a worthwhile gain.

Though, Lee supposed, if one could manage to spit in the eye of the universe's plans while being of sound mind and cunning plan, there was also little reason not to at the very least try.

Lee's hand raised to touch the sigil that hung around his neck, a wheel whose spokes created the image of a hammer laying horizontally as though in the motion of striking an anvil. Taking inspiration from the act, Lee reached into the aether and pulled upon the threads of divine energy that lingered there. Weaving them together in the space of a moment he released his spell with the whisper of a word, and summoned the spectral image of a warhammer behind the man with the concealed gun.

Out of the corner of his eye, Lee saw Smithers turn to look at him, fear on his face replaced with utter shock. Lee had never been one to gloat or brag, but in this moment he could not contain the slight smile that tugged across his mouth. This was no parlor trick the man could lightly deny.

With a flick of his wrist, Lee brought down the hammer, striking the man with the gun with the ferocity of a blacksmith shaping steel.

The man did not have the fortitude to match his partner in this analogy, and staggered under the blow, falling to his knees and crying out in pain. His partner turned in shock to see the floating weapon poised and ready to strike again.

"Well," Smithers said, as shocked silence held the train car suspended in its moment of confusion. "That's one way to start a fight."

People began screaming and clawing to pass each other in the aisle, desperately trying to make their way through the backdoor away from the ghostly hammer. Lee sat calmly in his seat, knowing there was little he could do to aid these people in their escape. He only hoped that the panic would not draw the gunman's attention to them.

He flicked his wrist again, sending the hammer in a sideways swipe at the gunman making his way to his feet. The sickly crack that came from the impact made Smithers wince next to Lee, and a pair of teeth clattered from the man as he was sent reeling into the side wall, barely managing to stand upright. His beady eyes scanned the train, clearly ignoring the weapon assailing him until his eyes locked onto Lee.

"Caster!" the man called, shocking Lee.

From what Lee could tell, magic was completely unknown to the people of this world. Unless of course, it was only an unknown to the mass majority of people of this world, and particular individuals were in the know. From the holy book that Timm had recovered, it was possible that these men were part of an organization that had ready access to the knowledge and practice of divine power. Lee braced himself for some kind of divine retribution.

The window next to him shattered as the man he'd been beating with the spectral warhammer threw out his hand and let off a shot from a tiny pistol concealed, not within his coat, but up his sleeve. Icy fear gripped Lee's chest. Divine retribution would have been something he at least understood, but it seemed beyond this man's grasp. Unfortunately for Lee, the simplicity and brutality of firearms was well within it, and seemed to be his method of choice for dealing out pain.

Perhaps then, it was fortunate for Lee, that Smithers felt the same way.

"Drop your weapon!" The old man shouted, leaping from his seat and pulling his pistol from the interior of the duffle bag. "Drop it or I shoot!"

There were cheers coming from behind Lee, and finally it connected for him. Smithers held back, creating the illusion of the hero riding in to save the day. Lee had goaded the fight, but until a shot was fired, the people of the train were unsure of who the bad guy in the situation was. It was in their favor, then, that Lee had attempted to disguise where the initial assault had come from. This allowed Smithers to take control of the situation and dictate the roles their inadvertent audience assigned them.

"Clever," Lee muttered to himself, impressed with the old man's ability to manipulate others' perception of the situation.

The one with the gun turned it on Smithers faster than Lee could mutter the word, but Smithers had been prepared for him. The handgun barked out, releasing a single shot into the assailant's shoulder. He bucked from the impact, but still managed to level a shot at Smithers.

A shot he never managed to take. Smither released a second bullet, and Lee watched in awe as the tiny gun the assailant carried arched through the air, clattering to the ground five feet behind him. Gripping his hand in pain, the once gunman fell to his knees in agony.

Seeing that his ally was now essentially out of the fight, the other man turned to look at Smithers, hate burning in his eyes. He reached into his jacket, and fearing they would be dealing with another gun, Lee willed the hammer to swing out at him, but the man seemed to predict the attack, ducking under the blow and coming up in front of Smithers with the gleaming blade of a short sword.

Smithers reeled back out of the way of the blow, though the blade caught the casing above them that housed four long glowing tubes. With an explosion of sparks and fine white powder, the lights flickered out above them. Their fight, now only illuminated by the dim, ambient light filtering into the car through the windows.

Recovering from the attack, Smithers closed the distance rather than trying to escape, and pressed the barrel of the gun against the man's exposed chest. Lee heard the consecutive muffled barks of a pair of gunshots. Such a devastating weapon at such close range should have meant immediate and horrible death, but their assailant only staggered back a step. Lee watched in amazement as the burning holes in his clothing from where the bullets had struck him ended abruptly in plates of metal hidden beneath his clothing.

Staring in shock, Lee realized that these horrible weapons had in turn caused the creation of armor whose specific purpose was to stop them. He had never seen such monstrosities forged before, and thought that this must have been some kind of waking nightmare, to see the craft of his god and his church to be bastardized in such a way. While swords and axes too were weapons of war, and armor was needed to fend off their blows, these machines of horror were so efficient a child could land a killing blow. And here he stood, draped in armor built to withstand the chaos.

Lee grit his teeth and shook his head, clearing away the thoughts of these horrific machinations. He could debate the morality of war and weapons within his craft once Latoya and Patrice were safe. The killing blow may not have landed, but he could tell by the man's weakened posture that the attack did have some effect. Lee motioned for the warhammer to close the distance as well and brought the weapon down on the back of their assailant's head. He crumpled to the ground in a bloody heap at Smithers' feet.

"Check on the women folk," Smithers called to him, before the body had finished slumping over. He leapt over the downed assailant to the one that was writhing on the ground. With a swift blow from the back of his gun, the first gunman stopped moving.

Waylaying Smithers' order, Lee fell to his knees in front of the man he had bludgeoned into the ground. While the man had been trying to take the lives of innocents, Lee did not feel comfortable being the end of his. He pressed his hands against the sides of the man's head and reached out with his divine power. The fleeting thread of this man's life was quickly being pulled away, but Lee would not allow it. Reaching out with his power, he snagged the thread, bringing it back and tying off the man's escaping essence. With a jerk, breath pulled its way into the dying man's lungs before the effort overwhelmed him and he passed out again, slumbering until further medical treatment could be found.

"Hey, Lee!" Smithers called, and from the tone of his voice, Lee assumed it was not for the first time. "I said check the women folk! Ah forget it, check his pockets, we need to see who these assholes are."

Lee began rooting through the man's pockets as he listened to Smithers calmly addressing Latoya.

"Take Patrice," Smithers was saying, shushing Latoya as she tried to argue. "Take her to the back, you didn't see, you don't know us. If you say you do then they're going to hold you up in questioning for a while and that's going to give these guys another chance. Lee and I are going to give them something to chase."

Latoya tried to argue further, but it seemed as though the logic of Smithers' argument finally got through to her. She grabbed Patrice, and abandoning their bags, she ran to where the rest of the passengers were hiding in the cars further back.

"Anything good," Smithers asked, going over to check the other fallen gunman.

"Sword, gun, some kind of armor, and another bible," Lee flipped through the pages and nodded. "Annotated in a style very much similar to the other one we've got."

"Take it," Smithers said. "And the armor. Check and see if he's got that same tattoo."

"How do I..." Lee asked, curious as to how he could possibly remove the armor that seemed fitted to the man's body. He watched as Smithers tore at straps that came apart with a ripping sound.

"It's called velcro," Smithers said, pulling the armor off the gunman. "It fits right back together. And yup, here it is. Right above the hip. Another tattoo, just like what Timm drew for us."

Lee followed suit, removing the armor and rolled the unconscious man over. Sure enough, right where Smithers had found the first tattoo, Lee saw its twin inked into this man's hip.

"It's as though they're twins," Lee stated, bewildered by the lack of individuality between the two men. It was as if their own personalities were unimportant, even to themselves.

"We can worry about the Misters Smith when we get out of here. First we need to find Luis and Morgan," Smithers said.

Lee heard a scream and turned in time to see a third man matching the description of Smithers' 'misters Smith' go flying past the window. A few seconds later there came a heavy crunching noise of breaking bones and glass. A siren alarm began to blare, but faded into the distance quickly as they sped away.

"Well," Smithers said with a sigh. "I suppose at least *one* thing had to be easy today."

~ 5 ~

LUIS

Tension filled the air as Luis and Morgan stared down the pair of men standing on the rooftop of the train. Luis felt uneasy as the slick metal beneath his feet rumbled and clanked as it moved over unsteady rails. The men across from him seemed unperturbed as they shifted their weight along with the motion of the train. Luis noted their hands close to their weapons and inched his own a little closer.

Blaring through the air, a sharp whistle bellowed out from the train, breaking the silence and Luis' concentration with it. The men moved suddenly, and Luis drew his sword in anticipation of the attack, only to realize too late that the enemy was not in fact charging him, but running away.

"We're not their quarry," Luis muttered. He bolted forward on unsteady feet and gave chase, yelling over his shoulder at Morgan. "They're going for the girl! Don't let them escape!"

Morgan nodded at him and he watched her form rapidly meld and change, growing larger as hairs bristled out of her arms and face. Luis was confused as to why she would take the form of a bear on top of a moving train. There was no way that she could keep her balance, and the bulk of the creature would only serve their enemies' superior agility in the situation.

Luis then watched in horror as he realized his error in judgment. Morgan was growing larger and sprouting thick hairs, yes, but she was not becoming a bear. Her form bulged and expanded, forcing her to fall forward on her thinning arms. Two pairs more sprouted from her chest, lifting her up and granting her better balance. Her bottom jaw split vertically and spread open wide, the two halves hardening and twisting into pointed mandibles.

But it was the eyes, the eyes that would give Luis nightmares. They inflated, almost popping from her skull, turning black as they did, before splitting in half and reforming as four eyes. Luis felt his stomach roll as they repeated the process again, leaving Morgan's now arachnid face with eight gleaming black eyes.

Morgan, now a spider the size of a horse, hissed and charged forward, half on the roof and half climbing along the side as she raced after the men who were after Patrice. Biting back the bile that threatened to force its way out of his stomach, Luis tried to appreciate the tactic that would allow Morgan steadier footing on top of the train.

Luis moved forward, doing his best to keep his eye on the enemy and not the horrifying visage that Morgan had donned. She began to gurgle at the... throat? Did spiders have throats? With a quick side step he evaded her large form as she spun around and pointed her spinnerets at one of the fleeing men. A shot of fluid erupted from the back of the spider, engulfing the running man from head to foot with what Luis could only assume was webbing, pinning him to the spot.

The man turned, confused to see what had happened. Luis watched as his eyes grew wide and the color drained from his face. The knight was thankful for the loud clacking of the rails and occasional whistle blasts. He had heard men screaming in battle before, however this was something wholly different. This was a fear he had never known before. He rushed past the screaming man, and came up behind the other runner.

The second runner must have heard the screams and turned just in time to see Luis approach. He drew a sword and took a wild swing at Luis, who ducked easily underneath the scything arch. These men may have had enough training with a blade to teach them how to not cut themselves while wielding it, but Luis grinned as he felt his own superior training take over.

Planting his feet wide to gain sturdier footing, Luis pulled the hilt in close to his side and twisted his body at the hips to generate torque. He didn't need to draw power from his arm for a hearty strike, and he knew that. All the power from a blow came from the core. And, of course, from his faith.

Luis arched his blade tightly at the man in front of him, landing a solid blow between where he calculated the bottom two ribs were located. As he suspected, the man was wearing armor, otherwise the blade would have cut clean through to the spine, but Luis had taken that into account as well. Reaching out to the divine power of his goddess, offering a quick prayer for victory, his blade exploded in holy light, sending the man he struck staggering backwards.

Bringing his blade back into a defensive position, Luis grinned at the would-be assassin of a child. Barely able to stand before the superior foe, the man's eyes slid in and out of focus, and the grip on his own sword was weak. This was not a fight anymore; this was clean up.

The spider hissed in anger, and Luis turned to see the webbed man slide his blade through his bindings, tearing out of the cocoon that held him. He shrugged off the silks and shuddered in disgust, but steeled himself, squaring up against the giant spider. While he could not bring himself to respect an enemy that would set itself against a child, Luis did manage to grant the man credit for standing against such a horrific enemy.

A sloppy lunge from his opponent brought Luis back to focus. The blade tore at the leather jacket he wore, and Luis snarled slightly at his own carelessness. His attacker stumbled, and for a moment, Luis feared he would go tumbling over the edge. But the man managed to catch himself and turned on his heel to face off with the knight. Luis stepped back, creating distance and deflecting another poorly aimed attack.

Feeling a need to end the battle as swiftly as he could, Luis stepped in, bringing the point of his sword level with the man's throat. Steel clashed against steel as his opponent reacted with a speed the knight would not have given him credit for a moment ago. It seemed that the man had recovered from the initial strike and was rallying back.

Luis grinned, happy to see that the fight was growing more interesting. Nothing was worse than a hollow victory.

Screams erupted from the man Morgan was fighting, drawing Luis' attention away from his own battle. The knight felt his stomach roll again at the sight of six inch fangs being driven into the man's throat. He screamed, veins turning black as spider venom pumped into his blood, and Luis watched in horror as the man's face began to swell and bulge, turning red, then purple, then black. As the body slumped forward Luis prayed to Nike that it did so because life had left him before he saw it topple over the side of the train.

Morgan shot out another strand of webbing, presumably to catch him before he fell on the unsuspecting populace below. However, Luis did not have time to find out. Another strike of his enemy's sword drew him back into his own battle.

"Who do you work for?" Luis snarled, parrying the strike, sending another spray of sparks flying into the air. "Why do you want the little girl?"

"*In Nomine Dei!*" the man shouted, his voice brassy and strong with conviction. Luis threw his blade up to block the incoming attack, managed to catch the blade against his own...

Then a flash of holy light erupted from his enemy's blade, blinding Luis with searing pain. He cried out in agony, stumbling back a step. As he stepped back, Luis found no purchase under his left foot and lost his balance. Looking back, Luis saw the streets of Boston flashing by him, thirty feet down.

"No!" Luis snarled, dropping the weight on his right leg and falling into a crouch. He followed through on the momentum, turning the fall into a sideways roll, dodging out of the way of the dropping blade.

Catching his balance again, Luis positioned his feet under him and launched forward before he was even fully upright. Driving his sword forward, Luis turned his entire body into a thrusting spear, driving the point of his blade into the stomach of his attacker. The enemy knight's armor may have been impressive, but it was not as strong as the steel Luis had worn back in his world. His momentum carried them both to the ground, and Luis struggled to keep his grip on the sword.

A pair of spider legs as long as Luis was tall slammed to the ground on either side of Luis, keeping him and his now slain opponent from sliding off the side of the moving train. Luis let out a sigh of relief that turned into a shudder when he saw the horrific mask that was currently Morgan's face.

"Please turn back," Luis said, looking away. "I thought you could only turn into real animals. Not enormous nightmares."

"But these are real," he heard Morgan's human voice say. Praying that it was not her voice coming from the spider's clacking mandibles, for that sight would leave him sleepless for weeks, Luis turned and felt a flood of relief wash over him as the image of the spider was gone, and Morgan's two green eyes looked back at him curiously.

"I cannot imagine what nightmarish hellscape a creature like that would come from," Luis said, pulling his sword free and cleaning the blood from it with the tattered remains of his opponent's jacket. The armor was ruined, but Luis felt they didn't have time for such ghoulish work anyway.

"They're from my home," Morgan said, her voice sounding a bit sad. Luis looked away from her and scorned himself for speaking so harshly.

"Are they creatures you're fond of back home?" Luis asked.

"Well," Morgan said apprehensively. "Not so much fond of as afraid of, but I figured they would be the most useful form for our current situation."

Luis looked at the wind whipping her auburn hair around and felt the train shifting under him. He could not fault her assessment of the situation, but shuddered again at the memory of such a horrible creature.

"You were not wrong, and your help was greatly appreciated," Luis said, cautiously. "But may I request that you not take that form again? I found it... quite unsettling."

Morgan laughed. "I'll be honest with you, I kind of did too. Something about your skeleton being on the outside... blech."

Luis filed that away as another nightmare he'd have to be concerned about later, however the now belonged to Patrice and her mother. He shook his head and started forward, looking for a space between train cars that they could use to descend and enter the vehicle. The more time they spent exposed on the outside, the more danger he assumed they'd be in.

"Come on," Luis said to Morgan. "Let's get inside and find the others. We need to reconvene and discuss the plan."

$$\sim 6 \sim$$

SMITHERS

"The plan?" Smithers asked, his voice feeling strained and much more high pitched than usual. "The plan is to take what we can from these guys and get the hell out of here."

"Why is there a giant hammer floating in the air?" Morgan asked, pointing at the spectral warhammer floating above Smithers' head.

"Lee! Would you get rid of that thing?" Smithers barked, then taking a deep breath, he added, "Please?"

"Very well," Lee said, and with a wave of his hand, the hammer disappeared into vapors.

Smithers had never been on a mission that had gone *this* FUBAR *this* fast. Sure, he'd gotten into a shoot out with the mob because of these people, and nearly stabbed at a bar, but this was supposed to be an escort mission. Get the women on the train, go home, and crack a beer. Then these 'holier than thou' assholes showed up and now they could be looking at twenty-five to life if they were lucky. Smithers had to resist the urge to kick one of the unconscious fanatics they'd managed to down. Didn't want to add aggravated assault to the list of charges, though he was plenty aggravated already.

"We got the armor, but I feel we should leave the weapons," Lee said, ever the calm head in the storm. "To take them would leave the authorities to believe that they were unarmed at the time of the assault."

"So I assume this is another time when we will not be speaking to the authorities?" Luis asked, though Smithers could tell that this time he was more on board with the idea than the last time and was not trying to pick a fight over it.

"Yeah, that's the plan," Smithers said. "Probably best if no one knew we were even here. So we're going to want to am-scray before any of the other passengers decides to get brave and see what's going on up here."

"How are we supposed to do that?" Morgan asked. "We're moving too fast and are up too high to jump."

"Well, let's fix one of those problems, shall we?" Smithers said, walking over to a panel on the wall. "Hold on to something,"

Pulling down on the emergency break, Smithers felt his weight shift as the train began to slow down. Not waiting for a complete stop, he walked over to the pair of sliding doors and began forcing them apart. It took a bit more effort than he anticipated, and Lee had to step in and take the other door, but eventually the two got it open.

"Alright," Smithers said, pointing below them. "It's probably only about a twenty foot drop from here. There's a tree there we can aim for. Jump, grab onto the tree, and shimmy down. With what you lot can do that shouldn't be too hard for you, should it?"

They all looked at him, shaking their heads, and Smithers decided that was the best he was likely to get.

"Well then," Smithers said, taking the initiative. "No time like the present."

Feeling twenty years younger, or at least twenty years dumber, Smithers jumped out into the empty air. That brief second of free fall reminded him of those times he'd been doing something similar from a hell of a lot higher up, but the trip down was much shorter this time around. The branches came quickly and he managed to snag one of the thicker ones. Not waiting to see three far younger bodies hurling themselves at him and getting knocked ass over teakettle, Smithers began working his way down. He heard two other mild crashes in the branches above him, and looked up to see Lee and Luis following his path down. Good to see something going right today.

"Now," Smithers said, dropping the last five feet to the ground and looking up. "Where's Morgan?"

He needn't have asked. Not a moment later he saw Morgan's thinner frame launch herself from the train. He guessed she wanted to give the others time before she jumped out and turned into a monkey or something. Then they would be wandering the streets with a chimp or spider monkey or something. That would be a hell of a thing to explain to people on the street.

Morgan's tinny scream filled the air as she slammed bodily into one of the upper branches. She proceeded to hit just about every single other branch in the tree on the way down, finally dropping those last five feet to land on her ass in front of Smithers.

"Well," Smithers said. "I suppose that's enough monkey business for today."

"Monkey," Morgan said weakly. "That would have been a good idea."

Smithers helped her to her feet, brushing away broken twigs and leaves that clung to her. There was a slight trickle of blood coming from her lip, but she waved him off.

"I've had worse," she said, and made her way over to where Lee and Luis were waiting.

"Tough kid," Smithers said, with a nod of approval before following her over. "Alright, let's keep moving. We want to be gone. Now."

They walked for a few blocks, and Smithers was thankful to find that the day was a bit warmer than the past few days had been. It was still cold, considering this was New England in winter time, but Smithers was able to enjoy the cold weather without the wind biting through his clothes and making the arthritis in his knees act up, especially after jumping from an elevated train.

"We need to contact Father Mitchell," Luis said once they had gotten a good distance away from the scene of the crime. "He needs to know what's happening to coordinate with the other guardians on the route."

"You know, it's fascinating hearing you talk sometimes," Smithers said. "I can understand what you're talking about, in spite of you using that old-timey, Renaissance Faire language all the time."

"You still haven't explained what one of those is," Morgan pointed out.

"Priorities," Lee interjected.

"Right," Smithers agreed. "Well I don't have his cell number, do any of you?"

They all looked at him blankly.

"Right," Smithers sighed. "Look who I'm talking to."

Smithers wandered around for a bit, the other three in tow, but warded off any further questions with deflections about how he was working on it. He knew it was kind of cruel to do to them, as they were just trying to be helpful, but Smithers didn't feel like spending the entire walk explaining the details about his plan or the technology required to pull it off.

Finally, a convenience store on the corner of a sketchy road had exactly what he was looking for. For way more money that he thought appropriate, Smithers managed to buy one of those throw away phones loaded with a hundred minutes. With any luck, he'd never have to talk to anyone that long.

Tossing the packaging into a garbage can as they passed, Smithers fiddled with the device until it finally got turned on and activated.

"What is that?" Morgan asked.

"Burner phone," Smithers said, checking reception.

"What's a burner phone?" Luis asked.

"A phone you use when you don't mind losing the phone," Smithers said. "Basically, your heart don't break when you gotta throw it in a fire."

"Is that the technical definition of burner phones?" Lee asked.

"Not even close," Smithers answered, dialing the phone. "But it's the best explanation you're going to get for the moment."

"Four one one," the voice on the other end of the phone answered after only a couple rings. "How can I help you?"

"Hi there," Smithers said, taking a pen he snagged off the counter while the clerk wasn't looking and testing the ink against his palm. "I need the number for the Cathedral of the Holy Cross here in Boston?"

He scribbled down the number as best he could before thanking the woman at Information and hanging up. A moment later, the phone for the Cathedral of the Holy Cross began to ring.

"Hello?" a woman's voice answered.

"Ethel? That you?" Smithers asked. "They got you answering phones now?"

"One of my many jobs," Ethel answered. "How can I direct your call?"

"Looking for Father Mitchell," Smithers said. "You got a number we can reach him at?"

"I'm sorry, Father Mitchell is out with some folks at the train station saying goodbye to friends," Ethel responded. "I can take a message for you."

"We're the ones he was here with, but we got separated," Smithers explained. "I've got a new phone that doesn't have his cell number in it. Any chance you could give it to me so I can get in contact with him? He's our ride back and my knees ain't feeling all that great today."

There was a slight pause over the phone and Smithers worried the old man card wasn't going to come into play this time, but then he heard Ethel sigh.

"You got a pen?"

"Hello?" Father Mitchell's shaky voice answered the phone a few minutes later. "Who is this?"

"Smithers," Smithers answered him.

"How did you get this number?" Father Mitchell asked. "And what number are you calling from?"

"Burner phone, called information, begged Ethel. Any more questions before we get to the important stuff?" Smithers asked, giving Mitchell less than a second to respond before continuing. "Good, so we got jumped, but the girls are both okay, should still be en route if they move the passengers onto another train like I think they will. That many cops around I don't think these guys are going to try again. At least not today."

"That's something of a relief," Father Mitchell said, sighing heavily. "People were screaming and I was trying to follow in the car, but got caught in traffic, and almost got into an accident. Thank God nothing terrible happened."

"Well, I wouldn't go that far, padre," Smithers interjected. "There's a few fanatics that are unconscious, but at least one that's dead. They may be able to ID us, but honestly things all happened so fast. You still in the area? I don't want to be roving the streets with this group and two trigger happy organizations hunting us down."

"Give me your cross streets," Mitchell said. "I'll come get you."

After twenty minutes of nervously waiting on a corner and jumping at every siren they heard, the white van from the Cathedral of the Holy Cross rolled up and swung its doors wide.

"Get in," Mitchell said.

They all piled inside, Smithers claiming the shotgun seat again.

"Sorry, Father," Morgan said, glumbly.

Smithers looked at her and realized that she looked ashamed. Turning to see the other two, Luis wasn't meeting the Father's gaze either, and Lee suddenly seemed very interested in his seat belt.

"What's going on with all of you?" Smithers asked. Then turned to look at Father Mitchell.

The man was obviously furious, though Smithers was unsure at who that anger was directed at. The men who attacked his wards would make the most sense, perhaps himself for not being able to do more, but then again, there was the chance...

"Are you pissed at us?" Smithers asked.

"I am not, as you said, 'pissed,'" Father Mitchell replied, putting the van in drive and pulling away from the curb.

"But you're upset with us," Smithers pressed.

"I am," Father Mitchell replied, curtly.

"What the hell?" Smithers asked, getting irritated himself. "We protected them just like we said we would. Not our fault those assholes showed up and..."

"No, it isn't," Father Mitchell replied, and Smithers was shocked to find himself cut off mid sentence. The priest hadn't raised his voice or changed his tone, but managed to cut through Smithers' thoughts with a word.

"It isn't your fault," Father Mitchell repeated. "But my friends, and my flock, they were endangered today. Your actions were rash and violent, and now there are bodies stacked up and attached to my name."

"There would have been bodies regardless..." Smithers started to say.

"Yes," Father Mitchell cut him off again. "And probably far more had you all not been there. But I am still entitled to my feelings, am I not?"

Smithers couldn't argue with him there. The priest wasn't taking out his anger on them, but it was palpable. The man simply wanted peace and his world was being turned into a war zone. Perhaps Morgan was right about them needing to find another roof to sleep under. If they kept staying at the church, they were just as likely to be the cause of it burning to the ground.

"Well," Smithers said, shifting uncomfortably in his seat. "I'm getting the feeling our reward for this work is not going to be more work."

~ 7 ~

LUIS

Watching out the window, Luis surveyed the madness of the city as it passed them by. It did not seem to him that the battle had followed them from the train, but rather the madness was the same the city dealt with on a regular basis. He was fascinated at how different it was from his home, but how familiar the movements were. People flitted from place to place, seemingly with purpose, but accomplishing very little. They worked themselves into an early grave with little more to show for it than a weathered corpse. It was in his faith that he knew his actions had purpose.

And it was in the same faith that their enemy today did as well. Luis felt his grip tighten around the hilt of his sword. When he fought, he could draw in the concentrated power of his Goddess, and Nike would lend him the strength needed to reach his victory. Father Mitchell's faith seemed strong, but his god seemed false, contradictory. Preaching peace while his followers sought war. Today, Luis learned that they were well outfitted for that war.

"Can we at least put some music on?" Smithers asked, fiddling with the radio. "I've had enough of this tense silence. It's going to drive me insane."

Luis watched as Smithers hit a few buttons and spun the dial, and soon a voice filled the van.

"Witnesses were shocked today when what authorities are calling a terrorist attack struck in the heart of Boston. Individuals of indeter-

minable origin were seen fighting on the roof of a speeding train. Reports are stating that state of the art robotic units shaped like enormous spiders aided the foiled attempt, and police say that they have the suspects in custody. In other news..."

Father Mitchell silently reached across and flipped off the radio, plunging the van once again into awkward silence.

"Well," Father Mitchell finally said, his voice dull and without emotion. "At least you were successful in one aspect of the mission."

"Stealth was never part of the mission," Luis said, his annoyance finally getting the better of him.

"By making things this public you endangered Patrice and Latoya," Father Mitchell argued.

"We didn't make things public," Luis said, his tone growing hotter. "Those men with the guns did."

"I will concede that point, but a giant robot spider on the roof of a speeding train... Where did you even get that?" Father Mitchell said, exasperated.

Luis felt his stomach roll and tried very hard not to look at Morgan who was sinking slowly deeper into the seat next to him.

"I do not know what a robot is," Luis said. "But the spider was Morgan."

There was a long, silent pause that permeated the van. Luis could practically see the frantic thoughts flying about Father Mitchell's mind as he attempted to process the information presented to him.

"I'm starting to get the feeling I should never ask any of you questions ever again," Father Mitchell said, though Luis could sense the dark humor in the man's voice.

The knight realized that he should not get so easily frustrated with the priest. They had brought into his world some of the most terrifying and unusual experiences that one could possibly have, and Father Mitchell had gotten no warning or advice on how to handle them. The only one who he could turn to was his god, but Luis doubted this god gave answers as easily as Nike did.

"Father Mitchell," Luis started, seeking the words he needed to properly portray his thoughts. "When you speak to your god about the trials you face, how does he answer you?"

"What do you mean?" Father Mitchell asked. "I suppose in a similar way as your gods speak to you."

"My god froze time in the world surrounding my body and pulled my spirit into his domain while he was working the forge in order to remind me of my duties and position within his church," Lee said plainly, flipping idly through one of the bibles they had taken from their assailants.

"That's..." Father Mitchell stuttered, looking back at Lee through the mirror that hung off the windshield in front of him. "Was that your calling into the church?"

"No," Lee said, turning a page and tracing his finger over the assorted notations in the margins. "That was last night, during the shootout."

"Nike sends her messengers to me," Luis added. "She is more of a guiding hand in my life, leading me to victory. We've never directly spoken, but her words to me and the path she lays at my feet is clear."

"That must be nice," Father Mitchell muttered. "However God requires his flock to walk their own path, interpreting his Word and acting as we see fit in the world that He has provided us."

"Seems inefficient," Lee said.

"No offense, padre," Smithers interjected. "But I understand why these fellas might see your religion as less concrete than their own. They can do some pretty amazing stuff I've only ever seen faith healers fake doing on T.V. so a bunch of gullible old folks will send their life savings in."

"Except there are those in your religion who can do such things," Luis said.

The van grew silent once more.

"Come again?" Smithers asked.

"The man I fought on the roof," Luis explained. "He empowered his blade with holy light, the way I do. Nike grants me a portion of her power to aid me on my path to victory. This man, this knight, he did the same."

"I wouldn't go so far as to call him a knight," Smithers commented. "Don't you need to have some kind of honorable code or something?"

"A code, yes," Luis nodded. "But what is honorable to one is inexcusable to another. If he was trying to protect the church by any means necessary, then he may be able to rationalize killing a child."

"But that goes against the Laws of God," Father Mitchell said, earnestly. "One of our Ten Commandments, 'Thou shall not kill.'""

"Historical records show that your church makes a habit of ignoring that particular commandment when it suits them," Lee interjected, turning to a specific page in the bible he was holding, leaving one finger pressed between the pages he had been reading in order not to lose his place. "In fact, right here it states the best ways to prepare for war."

"Again, I will reiterate," Father Mitchell said from behind clenched teeth. "The difference between the Old and New Testament..."

"The point being that these men seem to follow your god and ignore such an oath," Luis stated, trying to bring the conversation back. "Yet he still managed to call upon your god's power to perform a feat that should only be accessible to holy warriors of great faith."

"That is true," Father Mitchell pondered. "But you manage to do the same thing, and you have used your power for great healing and great violence."

"I have," Luis agreed. "But 'not killing' was never one of my oaths."

"I'm almost afraid to ask," Father Mitchell said, turning to meet Luis' gaze in the mirror. "What was your oath?"

"Honorable victory," Luis stated, hearing in his mind the hundreds of voices of those he served with reciting the pledge as one almost as if he had been standing at attention in the training yard as he spoke. "At any cost."

Luis and Father Mitchell watched each other for a moment. Luis could feel the spark of faith in this man and knew him to be good. However, the knight feared that Mitchell's faith had been misplaced. These men worshiped his god in a way that granted them great power to do evil acts. Mitchell did not seem capable of either the act nor the power, which led Luis to believe that perhaps Mitchell was not worshiping his god in a way the god saw 'proper.'

The fear in Father Mitchell's eyes told Luis that the thought had crossed the priest's mind as well. And if this god was not a shepherd for the weak and lost, but something else entirely, what had Father Mitchell been praying to his whole life.

"These markings make no sense," Lee said sharply, breaking the tension of the moment. Father Mitchell returned his eyes to the road and said nothing further. Luis would need to meditate more on these thoughts in the future, but for now he needed to keep his eyes on his footing, not the finish line.

"What's the problem?" Luis asked.

"The lettering is different from the rest," Lee explained. "Here there are clearly common words. English as you call it here. And even these notes in Latin, while I cannot determine what they say, I can determine the language. My assumption is that they are prayers. '*Dei*' appears frequently, and from what Father Mitchell has translated for us before, it is simply a mentioning of their god. But these letters... they make no sense."

Smithers turned around and looked at the page Lee had the book open to, looking it over. "Huh, now I speak a few languages, but I couldn't tell you what that one means. It's all Greek to me."

Luis looked over at what Smithers was talking about and nodded.

"Yes, that seems accurate to me," Luis agreed with Smithers.

"Guess we'll have to find someone who can read it," Smithers said, nestling back into his seat.

"Why?" Luis asked. "You identified the language."

"That's just an expression, Luis," Father Mitchell explained, though his voice was beginning to sound tired.

"That may be," Luis said, pointing at the book. "But that's Greek."

"How could you..." Father Mitchell started to say, then laughed. "Of course. Nike, Greek Goddess of Victory."

"Wait," Smithers said, turning around in his seat. "You speak Greek?"

Luis held his hand out to Lee who surrendered the book. Looking over the pages, Luis recognized most of the words, though it seemed the dialect was a bit different than the one he had been taught. Reading some of it outloud, the knight began dredging up the memories of language and pieced together what was being said.

Most of it was nonsense, though Luis expected as much. The mind of a fanatic did not improve due to a simple change in language. Talk of fire and death were commonplace, and talk of the righteous taking their place at the right hand while sinners burned made Luis a bit uncomfortable, but one particular phrase was coming up frequently enough to catch his eye.

"*Adelfótita ton Ankathión,*" Luis read aloud before translating the words to their shared tongue. "Brotherhood of Thorns."

He turned to look at Father Mitchell.

"Does that mean anything to you?" Luis asked.

Father Mitchell pursed his lips, shook his head, and kept driving an expression of deep concern evident on his face.

"Damn," Smithers said, sighing and putting his hands behind his head, stretching as much as he could in the confined space. "Seems like one clue forward, five million questions back."

"There must be someone who would know more about this Brotherhood," Lee stated. "If they're not an official part of the church, that may make them some kind of outlier we can hunt down from a different direction."

"Ooh!" Morgan bounced up in her seat, hitting her head on the roof of the van as she did. "Ow! Ow ow ow... Ooh! I know!"

"Easy there kiddo," Smithers said, trying to hide a smile as he did. "You need to go to the bathroom or something?"

"No," Morgan said. "Well, actually yes, but that's not what it is. Why don't we go see Arbuckle?"

"The crazy college professor?" Smithers asked.

"Yeah!" Morgan said, excitedly. "He's always researching all that weird stuff and shady organizations. Maybe he's heard of them before."

"Hmm..." Lee pondered, scratching at his chin and looking over the notes in the bible he'd taken back from Luis. "That may not be a bad plan. Arbuckle seems well versed in a multitude of areas of study. Perhaps he can help us."

"Well, I'm not hearing any better plans," Smithers said before turning to Father Mitchell. "Okay, padre, we're heading back to school."

~ 8 ~

MORGAN

The last time Morgan had been on the campus of Boston University, the entire area had been bustling with activity. People were dressed in what Smithers had called 'business attire' since they were attending the job fair in hopes of finding means for making a living. Thus far, Morgan felt it was a rather silly process since they were making decent enough money with street performances and getting by just fine.

Today, however, there were far fewer people. There were still some people milling about or moving from place to place, most of whom were carrying green and white cups of 'milk with coffee in it.' Smithers had gone into more colorful descriptions, but Morgan had stopped listening after a while. She was far more interested in trying to retrace her steps back to where Professor Norman Arbuckle's office was. She led their way to the rundown building with the cold, steel letters that decreed it to be for math and science. And also, to the rickety old elevator, which sat forebodingly within.

She hesitated upon coming to the elevator. While Arbuckle's office was on the top floor, approximately twelve floors above her, and the climb would be exhausting, the last elevator ride up had been quite unnerving. The image of men with swords leering viciously at Patrice and Latoya flickered across her mind. This Brotherhood was still out there, and they were still after Latoya and her baby girl. Morgan steeled her nerves and pressed the button on the elevator marked 'up.'

"This will be unpleasant," Lee lamented quietly under his breath. Morgan turned to look at him and saw a queasy expression cross his face. Luis said nothing, but Morgan could tell that he was also less than pleased at the prospect of needing to ride the horrific device again.

"Oh, come on, you big babies," Smithers said, leaning against the wall as the elevator hummed to life. "It's not *that* bad."

"You all will run into a building filled with mad gunmen and have sword fights on the roofs of moving trains," Father Mitchell said, cocking his eyebrow at them. "But you draw the line at elevators?"

"Elevators aren't so much the problem," Morgan explained. "This particular elevator is quite... disconcerting."

At her words, the doors parted and they all began to file begrudgingly inside. Morgan saw Father Mitchell give Smithers a curious look, to which Smithers just rolled his eyes.

"They're just being a bunch of pansies," Smithers said, hitting the button for the top floor. Morgan braced herself against the side of the elevator as it lurched and began its long, grinding journey.

Mitchell looked at all of them as the elevator rose and then back to Smithers. Morgan clung to the railing that wrapped around three of the four walls around them, hoping it would help her keep balance. She saw him turn his attention to Lee, who had his head bowed as if in prayer, though Morgan thought that perhaps he was trying more to keep himself from vomiting. Finally, Luis stood, feet spread and hands clenched tightly in front of him, as though standing at attention, preparing to present arms. Father Mitchell turned back to Smithers.

"Every time?"

"In this one, yeah," Smithers said, shrugging as he leaned back against the wall behind him, seemingly completely at ease. "They were fine at the hospital. Probably because that was a newer model and actually gets safety inspections done on it."

Mitchell relented and leaned back against the far wall of the elevator, in much the same way Smithers had. Morgan felt her stomach roll and wished for a moment that she still had eight legs to steady herself.

Luis had expressed to her how that particular form did make him uncomfortable, and Morgan had to admit she was kind of relieved to hear it. Inwardly she shuddered at the thought of how the spider perceived the world. Eight eyes that never blinked, staring coldly out in all directions, the thick chiton that locked her limbs and held swirling pools of ichor that made up her innards, keeping them from pooling out, and the drifting air that vibrated with the screams of the dying pierced by her fangs.

The worst though, the worst had been what the others did not know about her transformations. It wasn't just the form of the animal she took, but part of their essence. Their instinct, their mind, bubbled just below the surface of her own. The simple demands of the bear or wolf were easy to justify: fight, hunt, flee, or you will die. But the spider... the mind of the spider had been alien, horrific. It was a mind she never again wanted to feel mingling with her own.

She would happily grant Luis' request considering it would mean she would never have to voice the doubts and regrets she had at taking that form in the first place. And never have to share her mind with that alien force again.

The elevator came to an unsteady halt and its doors slid open with a terrible metal on metal sound. Morgan was unsure if it was just her imagination playing tricks on her, but the scent of burning and ozone seemed to drift ever so slightly on the air, tickling her nose. They piled out of the car and began making their way down the hallway to the office door of Professor Norman Arbuckle.

Morgan knocked rapidly on the door.

"Go away!" Came an annoyed voice from inside. "I'm busy!"

"Professor Arbuckle," Morgan called back. "It's us!"

From within, Morgan heard the heavy sound of wood grinding against wood as Arbuckle pushed his chair away from his desk. Feet pounded across the floor and soon the sound of metal clicks indicated that Arbuckle was undoing the assorted variety of locks he had installed on the door himself. The door opened only a crack, enough to see Arbuckle's face behind a thin chain still connecting the door to the wall, though looking at it, Morgan felt it was more for show than function. A swift kick from Luis would be more than enough to remove that particular barrier.

Arbuckle himself was also less than impressive to look at. His wild brown hair was a tousled mess of curled locks so unkempt Morgan could not tell if he had just woken up or had never gone to sleep. The wrinkled vest and trousers he wore made her believe it had been the latter, unless he's slept in the clothing as well. His dress shirt was open at the top two buttons and his tie barely clung to its form from how loosely he wore it. His tired eyes were framed and magnified by the thick spectacles he was constantly pushing back up the bridge of his nose.

"How do I know it's you?" Arbuckle asked from behind the chain.

"Uh..." Morgan looked over her shoulder at Smithers, who seemed to be trying very hard not to laugh. She turned back to Arbuckle. "Have you been watering that plant I fixed for you?"

Arbuckle stared for a moment at her, seeming to mull what she had asked him over in his mind before slamming the door. Morgan was about to call out to him when Smithers put his hand on her shoulder.

"Hold on a sec," he said, holding his finger up.

He flicked it down, pointing at the door almost in time with the sliding of metal on metal and the sound of a chain clattering down. Arbuckle appeared again in the doorway, this time opening the door fully.

"Come in, come in!" Arbuckles said, ushering them quickly inside, looking nervously around. "Get inside before they see!"

"Before who sees?" Mitchell asked as they all crowded into Arbuckle's small office.

"It doesn't matter who 'they' are," Arbuckle said, closing the door and reengaging the locks. "'They' will go off and tell 'them,' and then the whole thing is... "

Arbuckle trailed off as though lost in thought. He turned around to face Father Mitchell. "And who, exactly, are you?"

"My name is Father Franklin Mitchell," Father Mitchell said. "I'm a Catholic priest over at the Cathedral of the Holy Cross."

"I see," Arbuckle said, going over to sit at his desk. "The cross you wear, is it made of... *silver?*"

"Uh... wood," Father Mitchell responded, clearly confused. "I don't go in for expensive things. A priest's life is to be one of piety and service, so precious metals are a waste of money that could be put to better uses."

"Hmmm..." Arbuckle mused, looking over the priest with interest before making a few notes in a black and white notebook on his desk. "Interesting indeed. I'll have my eye on you, *'Father.'*"

"Uh... You alright there, Arbuckle?" Smithers asked. "You're acting kind of... well, I'd say weird, but let's be honest, I should just say *weirder.*"

"Ah, that's because you may not be up to date on the current paranormal happenings in the world," Arbuckle explained excitedly. "You see, just last night, there was an assault on a warehouse known for illegal activity. The craziest thing is, the men taken to the hospital were claiming they had been attacked by a *werewolf!* Can you believe it? An actual werewolf sighting. Before meeting you all I'd say the lads were most likely just seeing things, but your very existence makes what I believed impossible *possible!*"

"Now how bout that," Smithers said, clearly amused, and Morgan could feel his eyes burning into the back of her head.

"You don't think that he's talking about..." Lee started.

"Me," Morgan said, sheepishly.

"What?" Arbuckle asked, confused.

"The werewolf, it was me," Morgan said. She looked up to see Arbuckle's eyes grow wide with fear, darting between her and his desk, then her and the door, as though trying to determine the best course of action.

"But I'm not a werewolf!" Morgan added, quickly. "I'm a druid. Like how I healed your plant? It's because my people are very in tune with nature. Some of us, so much so, that we can take on other forms."

"Druids?" Arbuckle said, his shoulders relaxing slowly. From the way he was speaking, Morgan could tell that he was also short of breath. "Like the Celts of old? That's phenomenal."

"There are druids in this world too?" Morgan asked excitedly.

"Well, there were," Arbuckle said, cocking an eyebrow at Father Mitchell who shifted uncomfortably in his chair. "At least before they were deemed heretics and exterminated."

Morgan deflated. "Oh..."

"Speaking of aggressive acts by an unjust holy organization," Smithers said, slamming one of the bibles they had taken from the Brotherhood members on the train down onto Arbuckle's desk. "We were hoping you'd be able to tell us a little something about this."

Arbuckle looked at the book on his desk then back at Smithers.

"Wouldn't he be better suited for such a task?" Arbuckle asked, gesturing to Father Mitchell.

"The book contains annotations in several different languages including Latin and Greek, written by a fanatical order known as the Brotherhood of Thorns," Father Mitchell explained. "As they are not an official order of the Church, I know nothing about them. I was told you were an expert on such things."

"Ah," Arbuckle said, taking the book and beginning to flip through the pages. "That makes a lot more sense. Good idea to get an outside force to investigate the wrongdoings of an organization rather than the organization itself."

"As I said," Father Mitchell repeated, his jaw tight as he spoke. "They are not an official part of the Church."

"They never are," Arbuckle said, waving his hand dismissively at Father Mitchell, not looking up from the book. "Except when they are and then it was just a couple of bad apples, or if it wasn't that then you just misunderstood the action, or the words, or look at the jingling keys as I move this pedophile to a church in some hole in the wall nation no one's ever heard of where he can retire and live the remainder of his life out in peace. I need a reference book, hold on a moment."

Arbuckle rattled off dates and locations under his breath, seemingly ignorant of the aura of rage coming from Father Mitchell's tense, quaking body. Morgan was concerned that he would clench his teeth so tightly that they would crack. Before she had a chance to check on him, Arbuckle returned.

"Here we are, from the ancient annals! Not an original mind you, not on a teacher's salary," Arbuckle said, setting a large tome down on the table.

He flipped through the pages with purpose, though Morgan could not trace what that purpose was. She doubted the words and letters would have made much more sense to her even if they had been facing right side up.

"Huh, seems your unofficial chapter of the church is not only official, it's also ancient," Arbuckle stated, flipping the book around to show the group.

Morgan looked down at an image, a circle with curved thorns coming from both the inside and outside of the circle. It was the same image they had seen tattooed on the men who had attacked both the train and the hospital. The language around it confused her, but looking at Luis, she could see the knight's eyes flickering across the page.

"Loosely translated, they seem to be some kind of secret order," Luis said, thoughtfully. "Though there's not much information here on them."

"When you're the Vatican's secret police, you tend to keep histories of yourself to a minimum." Arbuckle murmured as he leaned over the book, pointing out a particular passage to Luis. "My ancient Greek is a little rusty, but it seems that they were also quite a fanatical group."

"What do you base that off of?" Father Mitchell asked, tersely.

"The fact that it's written in Ancient Greek," Arbuckle replied. "They seem to have been using Greek at a time when Latin was the primarily spoken language, much like the way whack-a-doodle cults today use Latin to make themselves sound more impressive than they are."

"But why is this particular group after Patrice?" Morgan asked, curiously. "What could she have done to possibly anger a religious cult? She's just a child."

"Probably nothing," Arbuckle shrugged. "But didn't you say you lot used your ability to cure her of cancer or something?"

Luis nodded. "I removed the affliction from her."

"There you go," Arbuckle gestured to Luis and sat down as if that had explained everything. Morgan looked between Luis and Arbuckle curiously for a moment.

"You wanna be a bit more specific there, prof?" Smithers asked the question that had been burning in all their minds.

"What? It's not obvious?" Arbuckle looked at their confused faces. "I suppose not, though I'd expect the locals to be able to put two and two together on this one. Christianity, the Catholic church in particular, hates competition. There's the issue of Islamophobia in this country alone that proves that."

"To be fair to the Catholic church," Father Mitchell cut in. "That's mainly propagated by Evangelicals and political parties that use them as a means for advancement."

"To be fair, your qualifier 'mainly' means that your Church's hands aren't white as the driven snow on this matter," Arbuckle countered, causing Father Mitchell to tense again. Arbuckle continued as though he hadn't noticed. "Odds are, if they have access to the power you've described, Luis, then they may have access to powers beyond that. Perhaps powers similar to your own."

"If they have the power to heal, why do sicknesses like this still exist?" Morgan asked. "I mean, we thought your world was without magic and sicker for it. If they have the power..."

"There is far more profit to be gained from treating a disease than curing it," Arbuckle said flatly. "The church relies on donations from those who turn to God for answers. Give them vague hope, they give you money for more every Sunday until they die. Give them a cure, you get a one time payment and you'll only ever see them again on Christmas or Easter."

Morgan did not understand the significance of the days mentioned, but when she turned to look at Father Mitchell, she saw anger on his face, but something else. He wasn't looking at Arbuckle and his eyes showed... shame?

"So you all come walking in, free as you please, throwing your healing around willy-nilly. You performed a miracle in the eyes of the church as if it was as easy as tying your shoe. Something they've been claiming is a rare occurrence for thousands of years. How does that make them look?" Arbuckle continued. "So they need to be sure that they sent a message. Two to be exact. Firstly, that the 'miracle wasn't real. The girl died after all, probably complications from the tumor, the tests were probably wrong. Whatever, she's in the ground now, so stop asking questions.' Very Catholic Church-like."

"And the second message?" Luis asked, his steady voice cutting through the obvious tension growing in the room as Mitchell's hands gripped the arms of his chair tighter.

"The second message seems to be for you, specifically," Arbuckle pointed at Luis. "Roughly translated: 'this is our territory, back off or we'll kill you too.' The Church makes a habit of that. Slaughtered the Celtic druids, slaughtered Muslims in the crusades, led literal witch hunts and burnings throughout Europe, all the while having their own magical bruisers in the wings. Prime example of 'do as we say, not as we do,' which is again, common practice in the church..."

"*Enough!*" Father Mitchell shouted, jumping to his feet so violently that he sent his chair flying backwards and tipping over. Smithers jumped back out of the way to avoid being hit by it, but the priest did not even seem to notice. "We came to you for information on the Brotherhood, not for your editorial on my religion!"

The room was silent for a moment. Morgan sat, tensely pressed against her chair, afraid of what was to come. She saw Luis and Lee trade a look with one another, but it seemed to be such that only soldiers of faith could understand. Smithers' eyes were darting between both Father Mitchell and Arbuckle. The former was shaking so badly, his fists clenched tightly at his side, that Morgan worried he may launch himself at Arbuckle. Almost a perfect contrast to him, Arbuckle sat calmly behind his desk, watching the priest with cool, calculating eyes. Morgan got the impression that this was not the first time Arbuckle had faced off with an irate religious person.

"Morgan," Morgan heard Smithers say her name, very softly. "Would you be so kind as to walk Father Mitchell down to the van? Maybe stop and grab a coffee on the way?"

"I thought you said that stuff was coffee flavored milk?" Morgan asked, her confusion keeping her from moving as her eyes stayed pinned to Father Mitchell's enraged form.

Smithers gave her a flat look. "Then get him one of those."

Morgan realized what Smithers was asking her at that moment. They needed more information, and the obviously volatile interaction between Arbuckle and Father Mitchell would only serve to impede their progress. Luis, Lee, and Smithers were all armed, wearing armor under their clothing, and would feel like a forced removal. Morgan, however, could help Father Mitchell out of the situation with a more gentle hand. She did not think the man capable of violence, but Smithers clearly trusted her ability to manage the priest's wounded pride.

Not much different than dealing with a scared, wounded animal, Morgan thought to herself as she stood up. Placing a gentle hand on Father Mitchell's arm, she spoke aloud. "Come on, Father. I wouldn't even know how to order in that place."

Father Mitchell's breathing was fast, and his eyes never left Arbuckle, but after a moment his shoulders noticeably relaxed. With a nod, he followed Morgan to the door, never once looking away from the flat, bland expression Arbuckle wore.

*   *   *

Morgan found the decorations of the coffee shop off putting. The green was deep forest colored, the floors were a dark wood color though clearly were not made of wood, and the harsh white created a contrast that was as jarring as the beverage she was sipping on. Not wanting to expose herself to the sugar and caffeine that she had once seen ravage Timm into a mania, she had ordered some kind of fruity tea, except the fruit had been overly sweetened by excess sugar, making it so viscous that it tasted more like she was being force-fed fruit pulp mixed in honey with every sip.

Across from her, Father Mitchell sat, stewing in his anger, gripping the paper cup of plain coffee and milk in front of him a bit tighter than he probably should have been. He had taken the lid off to allow it to cool faster, though still had not taken a sip. Father Mitchell had muttered darkly to himself while they had walked down the stairs from Arbuckle's office, but when she had asked him what he was saying, he only responded:

"Just praying for strength."

Now they sat in the coffee shop, and Morgan was unsure of how to approach him. Arbuckle had said some horrible things about his religion, but it almost seemed to her that Father Mitchell had no arguments against the actions allegedly taken by the Church. He just seemed angry that it was brought up. Was the church really guilty of such horrible things? How could he associate with them after that? Was he really as kind as he acted, or was it just pretend?

"All of it," Father Mitchell said, suddenly, in a low, quiet voice. Morgan was startled, afraid for a moment that he could read her thoughts. "All of it was true."

"You.. knew?" Morgan asked. "About the Brotherhood?"

Father Mitchell shook his head. "No, that was new information to me. But I can believe that it was true as well. Especially with everything else he was saying."

"The wars? The genocides?" Morgan asked, carefully. "They all happened?"

"They did," Father Mitchell nodded. "Some of it for the 'glory of the Holy Roman empire,'" he said, and she could hear the scorn in his voice. "Some for the Christian Kings. Some for the men who claimed that God had come to speak with them in their dreams. But always for power, and never for faith."

Father Mitchell shook his head angrily. "It was *never* the faithful who started the wars. Never the *faithful* who wanted them. It was always those who sought to use the faithful to expand their own power. Charismatic leaders who said God spoke through them and conveniently demanded that the people do exactly what the leader wanted in the first place, but this time because God said so. And the people, a lost flock needing guidance, followed the wolf because it carried a shepherd's crook."

"So Arbuckle was right that the Church did those awful things," Morgan said. "But he was also wrong because the Church was led astray?"

"In a manner of speaking," Father Mitchell said, looking up at her and smiling for the first time she'd seen since the morning's breakfast. "Sometimes the organization of the Church leads the people astray as well. Politics, fear, hate... they all poison us, regardless of how faithful we are. We are still human, still fallible. But it falls on us to rise above that. Each of those examples Arbuckle gave, they were the most extreme examples of the times we as a Church failed to rise above. Change takes time, and we're improving, but every time our mistakes are thrown in our faces we stumble because we're just reminded that there is still so much hate and fear that keeps us from being able to offer some people love without getting spat on."

Morgan considered his words for a while, stirring her drink idly as she did. She watched the syrup congeal at the bottom of the cup and grimaced. Smithers was right to say that the drinks here were not worth the cost. Looking back up at Father Mitchell, she finally understood the problem.

"Have you ever had a dog?" Morgan asked Father Mitchell.

"What?" he asked, clearly confused.

"Have you ever had a dog?" Morgan repeated.

"When I was a boy," Father Mitchell nodded. "Yes."

"Did that dog ever bite you?" Morgan asked.

"No."

"Why not?"

"Well," Father Mitchell thought for a moment. "Why would he? I treated him well."

"And you do the same with your flock," Morgan said, nodding. "You have a hard time imagining why anyone would be so averse to you, so aggressive towards you, as you've never wronged them. But, though it wasn't your hand that held the switch, they were beaten by your kind just the same.

"Imagine you're a puppy. You're fresh into this world and the first person you meet abuses you. Doesn't feed you, hits you when you do something wrong in their eyes that's natural in yours. You're hurt and scared, and then you're passed to a new owner. That one treats you the same, or perhaps even worse. And so your life goes, being passed along and beaten and starved and treated like dirt, until finally you come to find yourself in a room with a kind person. One who freely offers you food, who offers you love instead of scorn. They offer you all the kindness the world holds. And that puppy, now a dog, bites. Do you blame the dog?"

Father Mitchell shook his head.

"No, of course not. It's a learned behavior, and it takes a long time for a dog to unlearn that kind of abuse. Patience is required." He looked up at her and smiled faintly. "I feel you're talking in parables to me. I am the dog and those who scorn the church were those who beat me?"

"No," Morgan shook her head. "You're the kind man who gets bitten. Arbuckle was the dog. I've seen that look in the eyes of wounded animals before. Arbuckle doesn't hate you. He doesn't know you to hate you. But he has experienced pain from those in your position before. His eyes were filled with cold detachment, a lack of emotion, because to allow himself to get emotional means he'll get hurt. He ripped into you with facts you could not dispute, because to give you the chance to argue would be to hand you a switch. He didn't trust you because of your attachment to the church. You were the kind man, there only to seek knowledge, but you were bitten by a dog who has known no other treatment from men like you in the past. How can you blame the dog?"

Father Mitchell paused. His hand reached up to the holy symbol he wore around his neck. Plain wood hung on a humble cord. He ran his fingers over it for a few moments, deep in thought. Then, with a smile, he lifted his coffee and took a sip.

"You would make a fine woman of the cloth one day," Father Mitchell said, grinning. "Granted, the church will have to allow women to become priests before that could happen, I suppose. Seems maybe Arbuckle had a few fair points in his analysis."

"Perhaps he did," Morgan said, returning his smile. "Though I think I'll stick to animals. They're far less complicated than people are. Add in religion and it just makes things more confusing. I'll leave the faith to the faithful."

"I think you have more faith than you know," Father Mitchell said, standing and donning his coat. "Though your faith is placed more securely among mortals than the divine. Come on, let's go warm up the van for when the others come down. I'd rather learn what they know in comfort."

Morgan stood, happily disposing of her vile excuse for tea and followed Father Mitchell out into the cold Boston air. There was a slight spring to her step as she walked. Joy filled her chest as she watched Father Mitchell walk, his posture strong and tall of a man whose faith had been restored.

Finally, Morgan thought to herself. *Finally I got the chance to pay him back. If only just a little.*

$$\sim 9 \sim$$

LEE

Lee shifted uncomfortably in his seat as he watched Father Mitchell leave. Casting his glance over to Arbuckle, who was sitting calmly behind his desk, face an unreadable mask. There was no smug satisfaction, no glee at the anger of his verbal sparring partner, and no sense that he'd enjoyed ripping into the priest the way he did. Lee could appreciate that in the man, though it was Luis who voiced the concerns Lee had been struggling with.

"What was that about?" Luis asked, an edge of anger in his voice. "Father Mitchell is a good man, you didn't need to upset him like that."

"He's only upset because I'm right," Arbuckle said, coolly.

Luis looked ready to argue when Smithers stepped forward and placed his hand on the knight's shoulder.

"Listen, Luis," the old man said. "The Catholic church has done some absolutely horrible things in the past. And some of them are still being done today. The Vatican is a city, a sovereign nation, in the middle of a country thousands of miles away. With the money and power they've established, they're bound to make enemies."

Luis sighed. "Probably why the Brotherhood exists in the first place."

"That's more of a chicken and egg scenario," Arbuckle interjected. "Was the retribution for their heinous acts what caused the creation of this Brotherhood, or was the Brotherhood the hand holding the sword the church plunged into the neck of the world that called for retribution?"

"Your language is colorful," Lee noted, turning his full attention back to Arbuckle. "I fear your feelings may color your findings."

"Hardly," Arbuckle waved his hand dismissively. "The Vatican is an entity so bloated on its own power that you'd be hard pressed to find someone outside of the organization that has a good thing to say. They usually pussy-foot around the issue because it's taboo to put the clergy's feet to the coals."

Lee raised an eyebrow at him.

"A figure of speech," Arbuckle said, rolling his eyes. "No one civilized does that anymore. Just as no one civilized sends goons to kill a little girl in her hospital bed."

Arbuckle had a point there, and Lee could not deny that he'd been having some reservations about Father Mitchell's religion himself. Having read the Holy Book presented to him, there had been many instances of hypocrisy and disturbing imagery that Lee would have normally affiliated with a much worse religion. One that worshipped an evil god, perhaps.

There were moments of clarity, passages that focused on love, kindness, and brotherhood, but they came much later in what Father Mitchell called the "new" testament. But even there Lee found passages that shook his core slightly. Father Mitchell had said that many parts of the bible needed 'interpretation' and that the book was written at a time when people believed things differently than they did in the modern time. Before he could truly decide which side of this fence he belonged on, Lee resolved to do more research.

"So you feel that their actions are cruel?" Lee asked.

"Don't get me wrong," Arbuckle said, hooking his thumb at the door Father Mitchell had just exited through. "Guys like that mean well. Good souls who wanted to do good work in the world, and joined an organization that promised to help them do just that. He's not at fault for buying their crap hook, line, and sinker."

Lee did not understand the metaphor from which Arbuckle drew, but he nodded as an indication for the professor to keep going.

"The church promises people that their life has meaning, even in suffering, and that people who suffer in life will be rewarded in death," Arbuckle went on. "Can you imagine that? Getting people to pay you, when they're dirt poor, because you're selling them paradise at the expense of throwing their one and only life away? It's despicable. Life should be lived, the world should be explored, and people should be happy now, not hoping that they'll get to be happy when they're dead."

Lee was somewhat taken aback. It seemed that Arbuckle was speaking from experience here, though what experience that was he was wary to prod. The man was passionate and excited over the discussion, and Lee was hesitant to have that passion turn to anger at a memory.

"Is that not what Father Mitchell strives for?" Luis asked. "He has taken us in and protected us from the dangers of this world, and we have done the same for him."

Arbuckle sighed. "As a Cretan it is for me to say that all Cretan's are liars."

"Wh... what?" Luis asked, confused.

"It's a paradox," Lee explained, following Arbuckle's logic. "He's saying that a good man in an evil system is still a good man, though the actions the system puts him through will inevitably be evil."

Arbuckle nodded. "He's going to be faced with a choice one day, either ignore the evils of his organization and become just as corrupt, or buck them and leave. They're too ancient to ever change. Weak minds will always follow because they appreciate the normalcy that being led grants them."

"Shepherded by a crook," Lee agreed.

"A more accurate statement than you realize," Arbuckle smiled. "But the paradox is created when you ask a logical question to an illogical system, and that's why he got angry. Because he knew I was right, but me being right meant that there was much more wrong than just his philosophy."

"Considering this paradoxical enemy we're facing, and their relation to our ally, what course of action do you recommend?" Lee asked.

"None," Arbuckle answered. "I hate the church and the horrid things they do, and I'm happy to mouth off about them, but the church is a dangerous enemy. And I'd have said that before I knew about the magical hit squad they had up their sleeve for the past thousand years. My recommendation, don't get involved."

"That ain't exactly an option," Smithers said.

"They attacked us, and they attacked those we protect," Luis said, nodding in agreement. "That type of action cannot be ignored."

Lee looked between the two men, noting the resolution on their face. He felt a slight smile tug at the corners of his mouth. Their resolve was impressive, and their bravery bordered on stupid, but Lee could appreciate the dedication of the men he found himself standing beside.

"I suppose that's the answer to that," Lee said, turning back to Arbuckle. "What would your second opinion be?"

Arbuckle sighed deeply. "Well, if you're going to ignore sense, then maybe you'll listen to logic. You're spreading yourselves a bit thin. You've got me looking into DIARD for you, and now you want me looking into the Brotherhood. If I try to do both, you'll get a little information about both and I'll have twice the number of targets on my back. So, choose one and I'll focus on that. Who's more important?"

"I've kind of got a bone to pick with DIARD," Smithers piped up.

"But the acts of this Brotherhood cannot go unpunished," Luis countered.

"So," Arbuckle said, turning to Lee. "I suppose that makes you the tie breaker."

Lee pondered on the issue for a moment. Much like preparing metal at the forge, you don't want to rush the process or it may become brittle and all your hard work would have been for naught. Instead, he laid his tools out on the workbench that stood before him in his mind.

On the one side of the argument, Smithers had a point about DIARD and their direct connection to Lee finding himself in this strange new world. They had woken up in a facility run by the organization, taken against their will, their property stolen and destroyed, and now he and the others were living in fear of the retribution brought down by those who may well be hunting them. The emotional gut reaction was that DIARD was their personal enemy, and the more information they had to take them down the better.

However, Lee rarely reacted to anything solely based on emotion. Unlike Luis, who looked at the Brotherhood through eyes clouded in anger, Lee could see that these men were dangerous in their own right. While none that they faced were as skilled in holy magic as he himself was, and none of them managed to match Luis' skill on the battlefield, they were numerous and well funded. Their coffers were deep and their connections crossed oceans, if Arbuckle was to be believed, and Lee had no reason to doubt that.

In the end, Lee made his decision based completely on logic, as men were meant to.

"Keep your eyes trained on DIARD," Lee nodded before turning to Luis. "They have kept themselves mostly in the shadows. This Brotherhood has made no effort to hide themselves from us. It is more likely that we'll be able to gather our own intelligence in the field against them. By putting Arbuckle's skills to work on hunting

DIARD we are more likely to come away with useful information about both entities."

Luis pursed his lips, but did not say anything. Lee was under the impression that the knight was not pleased with the decision, but understood the logic. He gave Lee a curt nod and then turned his attention back to Arbuckle.

"Alright then," the professor nodded. "I'll keep my ear to the ground and see what I can dig up for you. I haven't found out much yet that you didn't already know, but I do suggest you don't ask too much about them outloud. Ears everywhere, you know."

The three said their goodbyes to Arbuckle and showed themselves out. Out voted, Smithers grumbled the whole way down the stairs as Lee and Luis walked silently in unison, as though marching along to an inaudible drummer. Lee spent the walk back to the van pondering the information Arbuckle had given them. It seemed to him that this world was filled with more dangers than he'd originally given it credit for. The arcane and divine threats, seemingly nonexistent when they arrived, were instead so well hidden that the everyday citizen was left blissfully unaware of the threats surrounding them. How such a thing could be kept secret was beyond him, but he made a note to do more research on the topic.

Upon returning to the van, the trio found that Morgan and Father Mitchell were already inside and had warmed it comfortably. Father Mitchell sipped on a cup of coffee while Smithers kicked Morgan out of the front passenger seat. When they'd all settled in, Father Mitchell drove the van forward and out of the parking lot.

Smithers filled them in on the rest of the information that Arbuckle had provided them with, and Lee interjected here or there with details he felt relevant. When they got to the part where Arbuckle asked where to aim his focus, Morgan seemed noncommittal to either side, whereas Father Mitchell's jaw grew visibly tight.

"Do you disagree with my decision?" Lee asked him.

"It's not that," Father Mitchell said, his throat a bit hoarse. "It's just... there's so much going on, and I was hoping to get more answers about who these men were, turning my faith into a false idol."

"The golden calf?" Lee asked.

Father Mitchell smiled. "Precisely."

"I do not believe that they have," Lee stated, bluntly. "Your religion is one of violence, intolerance, and blind obedience by nature."

Lee saw the anger flash in Father Mitchell's eyes and decided that an explanation would be better sooner than later.

"The difference is what you made of it," Lee added quickly. "You cannot deny the hypocrisy that your book preaches, however you can choose to toss such evils aside and interpret your religion the way you feel best. As a means to help others."

Father Mitchell seemed to relax as he thought over Lee's words. "You have something of a point there. I suppose we have evolved as the centuries have marched on. The church isn't the same creature it was a thousand years ago."

"Unfortunately, it seems that this Brotherhood disagrees," Lee noted. "And they wish to interpret the book quite literally indeed. The danger they pose is based more on ancient lore than modern interpretation. That lore I can research myself, or question you about, DIARD is an unknown entity that will not show itself willingly."

"You may have a point there... GAH!" Father Mitchell's response was cut short as the windshield in front of him fractured into thousands of pieces, held together by little more than the pressure of its frame. A perfect hole sat in its center, and Lee reached up to wipe away the splash of warmth he felt hit his face. His fingers came away red with blood.

Father Mitchell's blood.

The roar of an engine caught Lee's attention as he looked out the window to see the Black Rider appear beside the van. At first, Lee thought that perhaps he'd been the one to have shot Father Mitchell, but rather than wielding a weapon, he slammed his fist against Smithers' window, waved emphatically at them. Before they could react, he rushed away through the street on his strange mount as though fleeing. Turning to see what could have possibly sent the Black Rider running, Lee saw two black vans, similar to the one they were in, emerge from the traffic behind them.

Hanging out of either side of the vans were men holding guns as long as Lee's arm. All of which were pointed directly at them.

$$\sim 10 \sim$$

LUIS

There was a gasp of pain from the driver's seat, and Luis turned to see Father Mitchell grasping his arm. The shot only seemed to graze him, but the amount of blood pouring down his arm was alarming. Luis reached forward and clamped his own hand down over the wound. With a flash of holy energy, the wound sealed and the tide of blood stemmed.

"Drive!" Luis called out harshly.

"I... I can't see!" Father Mitchell cried out, his voice pitched high with panic.

Luis contorted himself, twisting his body so that he was precariously balanced between the two front seats. Kicking out with both feet, his boots caught what remained of the windshield and sent it flying out of its frame onto the street below.

"Now drive!" Luis snarled again.

Something in his voice must have kicked the priest's mind into gear, because suddenly Luis was thrown back into the seats as the van jerked forward violently. Seeing their quarry getting away must have also stirred the gunmen into action, because not a moment later, Luis heard the angry buzz of gunfire as bullets shattered glass and ricocheted off the van's frame.

They were catching up, and soon Luis saw one of the vans level up next to them, a pair of gunmen pointing long guns braced against their shoulders into the unprotected side of the church van. With no cover, they were sure to be mowed down. He took up as much of a defensive stance as he could and braced himself for death.

The Black Rider's mount roared behind Luis, and the knight turned in time to see him pull back in line with the van. Producing a pistol much like Smithers' from the folds of his jacket, the Black Rider braced his arm against the hood of the moving van and let off a shot, not at the gunmen, but at the driver of their van. The glass next to the driver's head shattered, and though Luis could not tell if the bullet had made contact, the effect was immediately apparent. The driver swerved, throwing off the aim of the gunmen, making their shots go wild.

"Don't aim for the shooters!" Smithers yelled, pulling out his shotgun and lowering what was left of the passenger window. "Take out the drivers or the tires!"

"What's a tire?" Morgan yelled.

Instead of answering, Smithers reached through the window with his shotgun in hand and unloaded the first barrel into the wheel directly under the driver. The wheel exploded into a hail of smoking rubber and buck shot, giving the driver even greater difficulties controlling the van.

"Tire is wheel," Luis answered. "Got it."

Not waiting to lower the window, Luis pulled the gun he had taken from the Irish Mob and pointed it at the van opposite the window.

"Wait!" Smithers shouted. "Open the window first!"

Luis had already pulled the trigger. Instead of the sound of an explosion erupting from its barrel like when Smithers fired his gun, all sound ceased. An incessant ringing in his ears began, blotting out all sound. It was off-putting enough that it caused his hand to jerk at the last moment. He watched as his shot went wide of the driver he'd been aiming for and sent sparks flying from the frame of the enemy's van.

Hissing in disappointment, Luis reached back and grabbed Father Mitchell's shoulder. Saying a quick prayer, he asked Nike to grant the man her protection as a means of ensuring their victory. A warm, radiant glow came from his hand and wrapped around Father Mitchell's body. Luis saw the priest ask him a question, but with the ringing in his ears, the knight had no idea what he asked and decided to just point at the road in front of them as if to say, *"Don't ask, just drive!"*

Father Mitchell seemed to get the message as another hail of bullets cascaded against the side of the van. The sudden inertia of the van caused Luis to fall back into the seat behind him. Beside him, Lee sat, his expression as calm as though nothing were happening around him, though the knight could see his chest heaving with deep, heavy breaths. Lee's eyes went dark as he reached his hand out towards the driver of the van beside them. The ringing in Luis' ears intensified and the knight clutched them in agony.

The ringing stopped, and all Luis could hear was the screeching of metal being warped and twisted and the shattering of glass.

"That van is no longer a problem," Lee said, though his voice came out more as a tired sigh.

Luis turned to look and saw the crumpled mess of steel and glass that had once been pursuing them reduced to smoking rubble against the side of a building. For just a second, Luis thought he saw the driver of the van slumped over the steering wheel, blood streaming from his ears, but Father Mitchell swerved around a corner and the visage was gone, leaving Luis to wonder exactly what Lee had done to save them.

The back window shattered as more bullets pelted the van. A burning pain erupted from Luis' shoulder, but he ignored it.

"Get down!" Morgan shouted, pushing Luis out of the way and throwing up her arms.

Luis tried to grab the girl to pull her back down so she wouldn't present such an easy target, but his right arm gave out from under him, forcing him back. The smell of lavender began to mix with the acrid, oily scent filling the air. Luis turned to look as the asphalt between them and their pursuers cracked open. Thick, twisting brambles shot out of the ground, wrapping themselves around the wheels and underside of the approaching van.

Luis grinned excitedly as smoke began to plume from the bottom of the black van, but the loud cracking of splintering wood soured his expression. The smoke poured from the van profusely, egged on by the crackling flames that came from the kindling it had turned Morgan's spell into. The men within leaned out again to take another shot.

One caught a round from Smithers in his shoulder and careened back, falling from his perch inside the van.

"Wear yer goddamn seatbelt, asshole!" Smithers shouted back from the front seat. Luis thought he heard a rhythmic ringing coming from Smithers and rubbed at his ears.

"What the hell?" Smithers asked, pulling out his burner phone. As he did, the ringing got louder and Luis was relieved to see the damage to his hearing had not returned. Smithers tossed the phone into the cupholder beside him. "I don't need my auto warranty renewed."

Luis leveled his gun through the now empty back window and let off another shot, though this time with his left arm. It went wide as well, but he watched two trails of sparks fly off the hood of the van as he struck. Turning, his gaze met the blank expression of the Black Rider, who had taken his shot the same moment Luis had.

For what seemed like an eternity on the battlefield, the gaze held, and Luis felt a sense of trust for this Rider. It was not something he could ever explain to anyone who hadn't experienced it for themselves, but a kinship is born between those who stand together on the field of battle, and no words need ever be exchanged. No language need be common between them. This Rider fought with them, and so, Luis would continue the fight.

Lee pressed his hand against Luis' wounded shoulder, and for the second time in as many days, Luis felt the eerie sensation as the bullet in him slid back out, expelled by the flesh that was knit together by divine will. Feeling the strength return to his arm, Luis flexed his fingers and tested the newly restored limb. He transferred the gun to his now good hand and he, the Rider, and Smithers began unloading their own hail of bullets into the smoking van.

Outnumbered and outgunned, the van began to pull back, disappearing into its own smokescreen. Feeling the gun click empty, Luis lowered it and turned to see a shaken Father Mitchell clutching the steering wheel so tightly that his knuckles had turned white. Luis reached up and gently put his hand on the man's arm.

"You did well, Father," Luis said as softly as he could manage, as though talking to a lost child. "Focus on the task at hand, feel your fear later."

Father Mitchell nodded, though Luis was not sure if the priest managed to control his fear as well as he'd have hoped. They continued to rumble down the streets as the Black Rider pulled up alongside the passenger side of the van. He held his hand to the side of his helm in a fist, then extended his thumb and small finger while nodding at Smithers. Without a word he sped ahead and took the point position in front of the van.

A moment later, Smithers' burner phone began to ring again.

"Persistent warranty," Luis said to Smithers.

"Just once," Smithers said, picking up the phone. "I want something to be easy."

"The only thing easy in life is death," Luis said, leaning back in the seat to catch his breath. "And even that I intend to make as difficult as possible."

~ 11 ~

SMITHERS

"**B**urner phone," Smithers said, answering the call coming in from a blocked number. "How may I direct your call?"

"You the guy following the motorcycle?" A voice asked. If he had to peg it, Smithers would say it was a kid barely out of his teens, deep enough to think he's a man but too young to really be considered one.

"That's me," Smithers said.

"Keep following," the voice said again. "He'll lead you to a warehouse where we can talk."

The line went dead.

"Watch a few more thrillers, kid," Smithers muttered to himself. "You'll get the creepy, cryptic voice down someday."

He then turned to Father Mitchell and saw that Luis was whispering to the priest, seemingly trying to calm the man down. Smithers wasn't sure exactly how successful a venture that was going to be, as the poor man was shaking like a leaf and white as a ghost. The sleeve of his shirt was soaked in blood, though the black barely showed it. With the wound healed, Mitchell could probably play it off as having been ripped on a piece of sharp, oily metal. Got plenty of damaged van to blame it on.

Smithers looked around at the planetarium of bullet holes around him, sunlight streaming through them like so many stars. Mitchell would probably have a harder time explaining the van

86

than the shirt, though it seemed fruitless to attempt any explanations at this point. Hell, even the truth doesn't make any sense.

"You alright, padre?" Smithers asked Father Mithcell. The priest didn't exactly answer, merely gave Smithers the barest of nods. "Okay, then just focus on the biker there. We're following him to a warehouse where we're going to 'talk' to him and his partner."

"I don't like the way you said the word 'talk,'" Morgan said nervously.

"Well, we're either going to have a nice conversation with the guy," Smithers said, fixing his seat belt more out of habit than for any measure of protection the damn thing could give him at this point. "Or we're about to get sniped from the roof and thrown into shallow graves. Either way, I'm pretty much done with today."

Morgan made a sound that was something between a squeak of dismay and a growl of displeasure, and Smithers neither had the time nor intention of deciphering what it meant. Luis saved him the effort.

"The Rider could have slayed us on the battlefield," the knight said, relaxing back in his seat. "He fought alongside us, and that earns him my trust. At least in this matter. I do not believe he nor his partner will harm us."

"Unless they're in opposition with whomever was in the vans," Lee added. "And they want what information we have before they kill us so their rivals cannot get it from us later."

Now it was Father Mitchell's turn to make the squealing noise. Smithers rolled his eyes and turned to the group.

"This is getting us nowhere," Smithers barked at them. "Either they're our enemy or they're not. We ain't gon' find out by bickering or from speculating. We play this right, we get out alive no matter what their intentions are. Since none of you are mind readers..."

Smithers trailed off for a moment as icy fear gripped at his chest. *Oh dear god,* he thought to himself. *Please don't let any of them end up being mind readers.*

"Point is, guessing gets us nowhere," Smithers said, shaking the terrible thought from his head and turning around to face out of the hole where the windshield used to be. "Best we can do is hope for the best but be prepared for the worst."

It took nearly fifteen minutes worth of driving to arrive at their destination. Smithers calculated that they probably could have gotten there by a more direct route, but that would have meant driving a van full of bullet holes through several rather populated areas. Considering the number of police sirens he heard in the distance, he was quite content with taking the extra time.

The biker led them up to a chain link fence that encircled a large, though shabby looking, warehouse. He got off the bike, engine still running, and opened the gate for them, waving at Father Mitchell to bring the van through. The priest was running on autopilot at this point and followed directions without question. Once they were through, the biker walked his motorcycle through the gates and closed the fence behind them.

A bay door on the side of the warehouse began to open, and now on his mount again, the biker drove his way through. Father Mitchell, for his credit, shot Smithers a worried look before following. The man was scared and hurt, Smithers noted, but not stupid. That was always a good trait to have.

They got inside and killed their engines. Smithers took a slow breath and opened the door, stepping out into what could either be a great opportunity or an early grave. He sighed a little as he thought about that. There were too many times over the past couple days when he could say that he was about to do something that could put him into an early grave. It was the kind of thing that made a man reevaluate his life choices.

Smithers looked around at the inside of the warehouse he found himself in. The space was open, and though it was two stories tall, most of the 'second floor,' if it could be called that, was made up of assorted catwalks. A couple other cars were visibly in different states of repair on the first floor, and the biker walked his motorcycle over to what looked like a service station. Several large windows ran the length of the walls just above the catwalks, though they let in very little sunlight as they were all boarded up. Against the back wall was the only portion of the warehouse that had a solid floor up top rather than interconnected metal frames, and it was easy to see why.

Computer monitors of assorted sizes were set up around what looked like the kind of system you'd get in a fancy hacker movie. A few of them looked to be nothing more than smart televisions reimagined as monitors, and each one was showing feeds from different news stations and websites. The largest of these clearly showed the shoot out they had just participated in from the perspective of a grainy security feed.

"That one catch your attention?" called a familiar voice from the desk in front of the monitors.

Sitting in a chair at the desk was the figure of a young man who looked exactly as Smithers had imagined him. Short, brownish-blonde hair was cropped fairly close to his head, though left shaggy on top, making it hard to determine a specific color at this distance. If Smithers had to guess, it looked like a home job. A pair of glasses framed his blue-grey eyes, which were a stark contrast to the hair. He wore a wry smile, but neither turned nor stood up, so Smithers had a hard time getting any further details of what the boy looked like.

"I'm guessing that was you on the phone," Smithers said, not quite a question. "Why don't you come down here if you want to talk?"

"No can do," the boy responded. "Take it up with my secretary."

"I'll give you secretary," the biker muttered, walking over towards Smithers. He held out his hand to Smithers. "Pleasure to meet you."

Smithers looked at the man's hand, but didn't take it.

"I tend to look a man in the eye when I shake his hand," Smithers said, eyeing the biker. "And usually take a name along with it."

"Oh, sorry," the biker said, seemingly genuinely surprised as he reached up to remove the helmet. "I practically live in this thing, sometimes forget it's on."

As the man pulled his helmet off, Smithers instantly got the sense of deja vu. His dirty blonde hair hung longer than the other boy's had, and the shaped beard that reminded Smithers of that snarky guy from the super hero movies marked him as older, but the blue-grey eyes sparked with mischief were dead ringers for the boy sitting up at the computers.

"My name is Damian Meeker," the young man introduced himself, offering his hand again to Smithers. This time, the old man decided to take it. The boy had a good grip, but wasn't trying to impress anyone with his strength. Smithers could appreciate that. "The troll up there is my brother, Simon."

"Yo!" Simon called down, his back turned to them as he continued tapping away at his keyboard. Smithers felt a twinge of irritation.

"Yeah, don't mind him much," Damian said. "I was always the more social of the two of us, but no one can beat Simon on a computer."

"Is that why he's the guy in the chair and you're the wheel man?" Smithers asked. Damian seemed to shift a bit with discomfort.

"Uh, one reason," he responded, dropping his voice. "But not the main one."

"You can tiptoe around it," Simon called down. "But you sure as hell know I can't. Come on! Get them up here!"

Damian laughed and shook his head. "Yeah, he's also the blunt one of us. We can head up top and make introductions if you like."

"Of course," Luis said, stepping forward. "I am Luis L'hopital."

"Ah, a Frenchman?" Damian asked.

"No," Luis said plainly and made his way to the metal stairs towards Simon, leaving a very confused Damian behind.

"Well, that answers... nothing," Damian said, turning to the rest of them and flashing a smile that Smithers would have thought would be reserved for movie stars and the like. "Best not to keep them waiting I suppose."

Lee and Father Mitchell began to follow, and Smithers took a step forward before looking back at Morgan to find her standing rooted to the spot, her mouth hanging agape as she watched Damian ascend the stairs.

"Stay like that and you're liable to attract flies," he said, unable to resist teasing the girl a bit. "And yeh ain't a frog right now, so I'm guessing that's not going to be pleasant."

The girl's mouth snapped shut as her face burned a light pink. Smithers laughed to himself, but decided it was best not to embarrass her any more than he already had. He clapped her on the shoulder and started making his way up the stairs. A moment later, he could hear her hesitant footsteps follow.

Up top he got a better view of Simon and the brotherly resemblance grew even more apparent. The difference was, where Damian clearly worked with his hands and had the frame to prove it, Simon was frailer looking and had the complexion that Smithers would have attributed to vampires had he been confident enough to say that such creatures didn't actually exist and he could avoid potentially insulting them. However, up close, Smithers noted another key difference. Simon gave him a smile.

"Okay, so now that you've seen both, who's wheels are nicer? Damian's or mine?" Simon asked as he pulled himself back from the computer.

Smithers now caught the full view of the motorized wheelchair Simon sat in. Though he wore jeans, he didn't bother to cover his legs with a blanket or anything and it became clear that the muscles in them were all but gone.

"Now I see why you didn't want to come down to talk," Smithers said, trying to mask his surprise with the same casually blunt tone Simon used. .

"Figured you guys were athletic enough to go toe-to-toe with those DIARD agents, you could handle some stairs," Simon said, cracking a grin. He didn't have the movie star looks Damian did, but Smithers could tell he didn't miss the mark by much. "Plus, wiping security footage of you guys has been keeping me busy. It's in your best interest if I stay by the keyboard."

"Well that poses quite a few questions," Lee said, leaning against a railing to the catwalk. "You both know about DIARD and wish to help us keep them off our tail."

Smithers gave him a look.

"How in the hell do you know what security footage is?" Smithers asked him.

The priest shrugged. "You realize that I've been reading just about everything I can get my hands on, right?"

"I don't remember the Bible talking about security cameras," Smithers said.

"I don't remember the bible being the only book in your libraries," Lee retorted, and Smithers relented. The man had a point.

"I take it from that particular tit-for-tat not all you guys are from this world?" Damian asked.

"Raising even more questions," Luis said, a hint of suspicion in his voice.

"Tail these assholes long enough and you start to notice a pattern," Simon explained, tapping away at his keyboard. "There have been energy spikes in different areas around the world. People like you show up, DIARD shows up, people like you disappear."

"There are others like us?" Morgan piped up, and then seemed to catch herself, returning to her more reserved position by the stairs.

"Not that we've gotten the opportunity to meet," Damian said, turning to look directly at her and for a moment Smithers thought the girl went a shade darker. "But we've seen some pretty suspicious footage of... well, Simon?"

Simon, midway though eating some kind of process cake with cream filling, turned to a second keyboard and began navigating through files. After a moment, he pulled up a video and clicked play. Smithers felt his skin crawl as the images unfolded before him.

The quality was low, probably something like an older cell phone camera from a few years back, before the damn companies tried making everything movie quality for those idiot online influencers who had to film themselves eating massive amounts of cinnamon or doing shots of laundry detergent. But rather than a bunch of dumb teenagers, the video showed a dark, wooded area. Bright light flashed across the middle of the screen and a person appeared. They staggered for a step before swarms of people out of a science fiction movie bared down on them, pinning them down and restraining them before hauling the still form off to a van. In under ten seconds the video was over, but the chills of his memories of a similar such scene stayed with Smithers long after.

"When was that from?" Smithers asked, and he could tell his voice was shaking despite the effort he was putting in to stop it from doing so.

Simon and Damian gave each other a look that seemed to express some kind of worry, but Simon shrugged and turned to Smithers.

"It surfaced on the internet about four years ago," Simon explained, and Smithers breathed a little easier knowing that it was not the same scene he'd witnessed, despite the similarities. "It was promptly taken down, but someone had the good sense to archive it before that happened. Store it on an external server."

"Was that someone you?" Lee asked, though Smithers doubted with a couple days of reading that the strange priest knew what Simon had just described. Smithers watched the birth of that technology happen and didn't fully understand what was just said himself.

"I wish I could take credit for it," Simon said, grinning. "But I was only a teenager at the time. Had neither the skill nor the set up to go against the government."

"Your government is responsible for this?" Luis asked, indignation in his voice.

"At least part of it," Damian explained. "See, we're supposed to have this thing called 'checks and balances' where the government is broken up so that no one part of it becomes too powerful."

"Yeah," Smithers scoffed. "How's that working out?"

"About as well as any man made system, to be fair," Simon commented. "But the government can make groups or organizations that are dedicated to different tasks. I doubt the job DIARD is tasked with is specifically 'kidnap people from other worlds,' but it is the U.S. government, so who could really tell."

"Especially with this administration," Smithers said, coldly.

"I feel people here know things that we do not," Lee said, looking between Smithers and the brothers.

"If it's important we'll tell you," Simon said, shrugging slightly without taking his eyes off his screens. "Otherwise we're griping about failed leadership."

"Ah," Lee nodded, understanding. "Then I must ask, why are you two interested in the actions of DIARD and their ilk?"

"I'm confused by the question," Damian said, cocking an eyebrow at Lee.

"Why do you give a shit," Smithers translated.

"Oh," Damian looked over at Simon. "I mean, why wouldn't we? People are getting kidnapped, we know it's happening, and someone needs to do something."

Smithers eyed them both. Damian was pretty much a straight shooter, and the old man didn't think that he was much of a manipulator. Simon's expression, however, darkened slightly.

"We can do something about it, yeah," Simon said. "But also, I need the practice."

"Using a government organization for practice," Smithers said. "What's so dangerous that they're just practice."

"That's personal," Simon said with a tone that told Smithers not to push. "But that's years off. For now, trust that our focus is stopping DIARD from doing to others what they've done to people like you, especially with what you're capable of."

"You mean magic?" Morgan asked.

"Yeah," Damian nodded, and Smithers noted that Morgan again turn a deeper shade of pink. The boy hadn't seemed to notice, as he was distracted, and the old man couldn't help but smirk as he listened. "Though magic is only part of it. We think they have bigger plans behind the curtain."

"Weaponizing it?" Smithers asked, though really it wasn't that much of a question.

"What else do governments do?" Simon responded.

Oh, Smithers thought. *He and I are going to get along just fine.*

"The real question is," Simon continued. "How they're getting you folk here."

"Portal, obviously," Luis said, pointing at the screen.

"Yes, I can see that," Simon said, struggling to keep patience in his voice. "But how are the portals being created?"

"In our world, we have wizards who are able to open such pathways between the worlds," Luis explained.

Simon turned to Damian. "Hear that? 'Worlds.' plural. Multiverse theory is real."

"Focus," Damian said, in a stern voice that reflected a long and tiring argument he did not want to begin again.

"Right," Simon said, turning back to Luis. "We don't have wizards here. Or at least, none that I could find evidence of. There are plenty who claim the title, but they're all charlatans. So unless DIARD has captured every wizard off the face of the earth, then there's no way they're using what you would call 'conventional means' of opening those portals."

"How do you know there aren't any wizards?" Lee asked.

"Man's got a point," Smithers said. "Not like they advertise in the phone book."

"I mean, nowadays who does?" Simon asked.

"Point," Smithers said, conceding to the logic. "But still."

"We hunt the rumors down," Simon explained. "I dredge the web, Damian goes out and looks for the evidence."

Damian shook his head. "Once or twice we found something close to legitimate, but it was usually someone like you guys, or someone who got their hands on toys from your side of the fence."

"So there are magic items in this world as well," Luis said, and Smithers caught an edge of excitement to his voice.

"There are," Damian nodded. "However they're rare, and not native to our world. At least, not that we can tell."

"That can prove problematic," Luis nodded, scratching at his jaw.

"Not as problematic as that van of yours," Damian said, pushing off the wall he was leaning against and starting for the catwalk stairs. "And it's not going to fix itself. So I'd better get to work on it unless you guys are planning to stay the night."

Smithers smirked and did his best to keep any snide comments to himself. He looked over at Simon's set up and, while impressive, the entire thing just started to give him a headache. Shaking his head to clear away the oncoming irritation, he made his way over to the boy.

"Mind me picking your brain for a while?" Smithers asked, taking a seat next to him.

"Go for it," Simon said, sipping at a colorful can that was doubtlessly filled with liquid caffeine. "Seems we're going to have some time."

"That's what I hope," Smithers said. "Though it's never a given."

"No," Simon said, his voice far older than it should have sounded. "No it's not."

And so Smithers set to work, trying desperately to piece the puzzle, and his memories, together.

~ 12 ~

MORGAN

Morgan couldn't understand why her face felt so warm or why her heart was beating so quickly. Every time Damian spoke, she was reminded of the time she'd eaten those bad mushrooms and her stomach was in knots for a week. Even as he walked away down the stairs to look over their van, she could not tear her eyes away from him. The machinations of tinkerers had never interested her before, but she watched in quiet fascination as he gathered tools and, barely looking at what his hands were doing, seamlessly began to disassemble their vehicle with smooth and gentle ease.

She didn't know exactly how long she watched Damian work from the catwalk. Smithers and Simon spoke for a long while about how he monitors activities in the city that may involve DIARD using cameras and mainframes and other words that Morgan had no frame of reference for. From what she heard of Smithers' responses, he knew enough to follow the conversation, if not overly contribute it.

"I'm just impressed you were able to pick us up with your doohickies there," Smithers was saying. "I can't imagine DIARD doing much with the college there."

"Well considering I used to go there, I keep an eye on things. Mostly because I still have friends there," Simon responded. "That was the second time I saw you guys going to speak with Professor Arbuckle, so I figured it would be worth keeping an eye on you."

"You know Arbuckle?" Smithers asked.

"I took a few of his classes," Simon explained. "Considering what we were getting involved in, learning about legends, lore, and cryptids felt like a good investment of Uncle Sam's dollars."

"Nice of your uncle to pay for school," Morgan said, offhandedly, turning to face them. Simon was giving her a quizzical look.

"Uh, yeah," Simon said. "Sure."

"You get used to that," Smithers said.

"Have you?" Simon asked.

"Let me rephrase that," Smithers said. "I *assume* you get used to that."

"Right."

Morgan had no idea what they were going on about, but decided if it was important, they would explain it to her. She still felt a bit tense, but did her best to focus her mind on more pressing matters. She looked up at the images flying across the monitors. She saw their morning's battles replaying in front of her from a multitude of different angles. Every once in a while, a green bar at the bottom would finally reach the end of the grey bar and the words 'content deleted' would appear at the bottom of the clip before it vanished.

"Where are you deleting those from?" Morgan asked.

"From everywhere," Simon said. "Going right to its source and deleting it from the hardware that shot it in the first place, and then sending a virus to eat it up wherever it got sent or shared to."

Morgan's eyes went wide. "I thought you said there were no wizards in this world."

Simon laughed. "There aren't. I just took the tools given to me and got really good at them. To paraphrase Clarke, 'any technology advanced enough is indistinguishable from magic.'"

Morgan furrowed her brow at him. "What do you mean?"

"Hmm," Simon pondered for a moment. "You know what an abacus is?"

"That's the slidey thing with beads that counts stuff, right?" Morgan asked, remembering some of the wanderers who'd passed through their forest when she was a girl. They had said it was used for counting money, but had let her play with it as a toy.

"That's... a definition for it, yes," Simon said. He gestured to the machines behind him. "Think of this as a really big abacus, but one that can do a whole lot more than that. This lets me monitor traffic, give Damian a heads up on what's going on where he is, take over security cameras, and even erase some footage that makes its way to the wrong places."

Simon turned around and pressed a few keys on his keyboard, pulling up a repeating image of Morgan as she fell from one tree branch to the next, until finally landing on her back on the ground. Once the images stopped, they restarted from the beginning again, as though in an infinite loop.

"Graceful, by the way," Simon said, smirking.

"Yeah," Morgan sighed, suppressing a shudder. "I kind of got used to having eight legs there for a bit."

"Wait... what?" Simon blinked, and for the first time he seemed to be taken off guard.

"Anyway," Smithers cut in, stopping Morgan from having to relive the spider thing for yet another person. "You're the man behind the curtain, running the show while your brother pounds the pavement. And just the two of you have been taking on DIARD this whole time?"

"'*Taking on*' is a strong way of phrasing it," Simon explained, raising his hands and wiggling the first two fingers on each hand as he spoke. "Think of us more like horseflies and them as a clydesdale. Sure we can annoy them from time to time, but we really don't have the capabilities to cause more than a few tail flicks. Basically, we wait and watch."

"The whole city?" Morgan asked, a thought forming in her mind.

"And then some," Simon turned to look at her. "Looking for something?"

"Maybe something, maybe nothing," she said, fidgeting with her hair a bit. "But you haven't happened to see a ghostly elk wandering around on any of your... screens?"

Simon nodded that she'd used the correct word, then turned around, fingers flying, pulling up lists and pictures and moving images.

"Not seeing anything about a ghostly elk," Simon said, his eyes darting from one screen to the next. "Though we've got quite an influx of reports of dead animals in Paul Revere Park. Animal control reports a thirty percent increase in calls to the area in the past couple weeks. And there have been a few reports of an eerie green glow at night. Could be your ghost if that's what you're actually looking at."

"Think it's something else?" Smithers asked.

"I don't think anything," Simon shrugged. "I collect the data. I leave it to more adventurous types to follow the leads and make the findings make sense. The last thing I need is to get attacked by a bunch of irate pigeons in a park."

"Zombie pigeons?" Smithers asked, teasingly.

"Don't joke," Simon said. "I've seen that video of the kid getting swarmed by pigeons at the park. It would have been less hysterically funny to watch him getting chased in circles if the birds had been undead."

"Wait," Morgan interjected. "That happened?"

Simon shrugged. "I mean, not the undead part. But those pigeons did go all Hitchcock on that kid."

"Movie reference," Smithers said before Morgan could ask.

"Did go after that kid," Simon amended.

"You saw it?" Morgan asked, surprised at the fact that such tame animals would suddenly get so aggressive at a small child.

"I mean, I watched the video on the internet," Simon said.

"Please don't tell them about the internet," Smithers implored Simon. Then he turned to look at Morgan. "Wanna take tonight to check this park out?"

Morgan pursed her lips. "With all that's happened today, will it be safe to try?"

"The gunmen were probably just following the van, rather than you specifically," Simon stated. "And I've scrubbed enough footage off line that the cops will have a hard time pinning anything that happened today on any of you. So long as you keep your heads down and don't overtly try to cause trouble, I don't see a problem."

Morgan considered this for a moment. They had been in extreme danger today, and had even managed to drag Father Mitchell into it. The priest was shaken, and not just physically. Their very existence seemed to shake the foundation of his faith. Morgan felt they could hardly be blamed for the fact that his religion couldn't account for a new, outside force, but still didn't want to take it away from him. Putting him in more danger by hunting something that may follow them home to him would be entirely unfair.

However, that didn't remove the possibility that the creature was hunting them. When she had seen the horrid beast, she did not get the sense of a passive being, of a prey animal or peaceful herbivore. This was a vicious, callous beast. Unnatural in every way, and would gladly buck the expectations of the natural world in order to get what it wanted. Green and glowing, the beast's rotting flesh fell off it as though simply giving up on the existence the creature clung to.

No, this thing could not exist in this world. Should not exist. If left to its own wicked designs Morgan knew that it would bring more ruin on this city than if they were to step in. It was possible the beast would follow them. However, with the friends she had at her back now, Morgan doubted that it could flee, and knew that it could not fight against them. She turned her attention back to Smithers.

"It needs to be stopped," Morgan said, firmly. "Whatever this thing is, if it's in Paul Revere Park, we need to be sure that it never gets the opportunity to leave that place and harm anything else."

"Very Old Testament," Simon nodded. "I approve."

The young man turned and began typing at his computer again, completely unaware of how his choice of words had sent a shiver down Morgan's spine. The comparison between her zeal and that of those that belonged to the Brotherhood of Thorns was discomforting, but at least she sought to bring balance instead of doing harm.

"If you need anything, give us a call," Simon waved without looking back at them. "Damian's got our card if you need it, or text that number that called you today on your burner."

Morgan nodded, pushing back her uncomfortable thoughts, and looked at Smithers. "Ever hunt an elk before?"

"Been a while since I've had a rifle," Smithers grinned widely. "But they don't call it buck shot for nothing."

Morgan didn't fully understand what Smithers was saying, but she smiled. She knew the old man was in. Tonight that ghost would cease haunting her nightmares for good.

~ 13 ~

LUIS

As Smithers and Simon chattered, Luis' interest in the details behind their technology began to wane. While pulling details of his past life was nigh impossible, he did remember long, boring hours spent listening to wizards babble on and on about the details of their castings. At least then he could follow some of the examples and watered down explanations they despondently gave, but this was worse.

In hopes of learning something practical, or at the very least escaping the overly mundane, Luis walked down the metal stairs and found himself standing not far off from Lee, who had evidently followed Damian closely down to the lower level. The priest was staring with interest as Damian used different tools to take out and set aside an assortment of intricate metal parts. The vehicle had been stripped of most of its outer coverings and looked like a bare metal skeleton of some horrific beast.

"This sort of thing interest you?" Luis asked Lee, curious.

"All things interest me," Lee responded, plainly. "Though the opportunity to see how such a fabrication is forged would be quite fortuitous as well."

Luis liked Lee, though he liked the man less when he used words like 'fortuitous.' Another faceless and irritating wizard entered his memory spouting overly complicated words for no other reason than he finally got the opportunity to use them.

"Fortuitous indeed," Luis muttered darkly under his breath.

He looked around and saw Father Mitchell sitting in a rolling chair off to one side. This world's priest was staring at the van as Damian ripped it apart under the watchful eye of his world's priest. Luis could not tell if the man was actually seeing what his eyes were fixed upon, but the knight worried that if there had been an inkling of power in the man that his stare may well burn some new holes in the metal frame.

Luis took a step towards Father Mitchell as Lee placed a hand on his shoulder.

"I think it may be best if we wait for Morgan," Lee said, his tone cautious. "She seems to be best at helping him manage the world as he sees it now."

"I am more than capable of checking on our allies," Luis answered, sharply.

"I do not doubt that," Lee answered. His words were slow, and Luis realized that he was choosing them very carefully. "However, I feel that this task requires a more delicate instrument."

"Are you insinuating that I'm too blunt to speak to the man?" Luis asked, feeling irritated.

"I'm saying you may be more blade than is required for this fight," Lee replied diplomatically.

Luis was sure that the words were meant to be the kind of reply that Lee assumed he would find to make him feel both complemented and dissuaded, leaving the knight utterly convinced he did not need to step into this role because of all the good qualities he had as a man. That is not, however, how Luis took the words. He felt manipulated and insulted. As though he were being spoken to like a child. With a twist of his arm, he knocked Lee's free from his shoulder.

"How dare you?" Luis asked, his voice harsh, yet low. "Save your head games for the others. I know you hold secrets, and I care naught about them, but so help me, if you try to use your double-speak to manipulate me again, I will take it as an affront and act upon it appropriately."

With that, Luis stormed off, leaving Lee to justify his words in whatever way he felt necessary to only the empty air that was left to listen. Perhaps he had come at the priest too hard, and perhaps it was merely the piling on of difficulties that made him so irate, but Luis still loathed being handled by others.

He had not chosen to come to this world, and now he was being told that this DIARD was toying with them to create... what? A weapon? Maybe? They still had no answers there. Then the Brotherhood of Thorns made two attempts on a child's life because he had used the power of a different God from their own to save her? The pettiness filled his chest with rage, which quelled a moment later under the guilt of drawing their blades to her throat.

Had he not performed a 'miracle' on her, then this Brotherhood would never have come for her or her family. She would have died, yes, but her mother would have been safe. Luis thought of his own mother, the image of her face blurred slightly and name beyond his grasp, but even then, and even as a child, he knew he'd have given his life in defense of hers. But that would have been his choice to make, and should never be the choice of a child.

He looked again at Father Mitchell as he sat and stared vacantly at the van being disassembled and repaired. Much like the man himself, Luis mused, his own beliefs and understanding of the world were being deconstructed before his very eyes, and there was nothing that could be done about that. One couldn't ignore that much damage or that many bullet holes.

Luis sat down beside the Catholic Priest. They sat silently for a few minutes, watching Damian diligently work. The Black Rider, as Luis had once dubbed him, worked with a mechanical efficiency of one who was both competent in their position, and confident in their skill. To watch the simplicity of good work being done was second only to being the one performing it.

So it was time for Luis to get to work.

"How are you doing?" Luis asked, not looking away from Damian as he brushed away shattered glass.

"So much," Father Mitchell said, his voice dull and flat with a weariness that was deeper than physical exhaustion. "So much has happened. I can't even focus on it all. I think I finally hit my wall."

Luis sat quietly and reflected on all that had happened in the past two days. He was shocked, really, that it had only been that amount of time. So much had happened in that time, and Father Mitchell had only been privy to a small degree of it. The battles, the bloodshed, and the lives saved that would not have been possible without him came rushing into Luis' mind.

"In the past forty-eight hours..." Father Mitchell started to say, but Luis cut him off.

"You rose to the occasion," he said plainly.

Father Mitchell turned to look at Luis. He knew this because he could see the priest out of the corner of his eye, but he did not turn to meet the gaze. Instead, he watched as Damian slid under the van and the whirring sound of machinery filled the air.

"You rose to the occasion," Luis stated again. "You saved lives, some of those mine on more than one occasion. That is a lot to do in two days. It earns a man a lot of faith, and even more forgiveness."

"People got hurt," Father Mitchell replied. "That's not what I'm supposed to do. I don't hurt people."

"There would have been fewer hurt without your involvement, yes," Luis said bluntly. "Mostly because it would have been us who had been killed or captured. We wouldn't have charged into battle, killing all those men to save three women. We wouldn't have had to put those members of the Brotherhood to the blade because Patrice never would have drawn their attention from being cured, nor would she have continued to draw breath for much longer. Fewer lives would have been lost, this is true."

Father Mitchell was quiet for a moment. Luis let him sit in it and reflect. That was the part of battle that the songs and stories never spoke of. The quiet reflection of character that came after one knew that the spark of life in another had been snuffed out, either directly or indirectly, by their actions.

"Your book says an eye for an eye," Luis continued after a moment. "As if those eyes hold equal value. The value of a human is negligible. The value of our lives on a cosmic scale is nothing. But the value of our lives when we fight for a true victory, that's different. The value of a child's life is valued more than that of a brigand. The value of a loved one's life is valued more than the one trying to take it from them. People can preach that all our lives should be valued equally to one another, but in the end, when I face off with an opponent in battle, to me, my life is of higher value to me than his."

Father Mitchell sat in a silence so deep that Luis could feel the weight of it bearing down on his shoulders. That was good. Death was solemn. The act of taking life should never be easy, however, just as his master had taught him, it should not be a noose around your own neck.

"We'll try to get this mess out of your life," Luis said, standing up to leave the priest with his thoughts. "But remember, the number of lives lost is different from the value of lives saved. A thousand dead soldiers is a terrible loss. A thousand dead citizens is a travesty."

Luis returned to where Lee had been watching Damian and found that Smithers and Morgan had regrouped with him as well. Damian was talking and pointed to different parts of the van. Lee's eyes followed the explanation, though Luis was not sure if he actually understood what was being said. Morgan seemed captivated as well, but did not follow the instructions as closely as the words. Smithers, on the other hand, seemed quite competent at understanding the brothers. Well enough, at least, that they could be of some use in translating one another to the rest of the group.

"Basically, she's not totally slagged," Damian said. "Probably take me two hours to patch the rough damage the bullets caused, then eight hours for the body work, not including needing to go pick up some replacement parts from my... source."

Luis sensed there was some illicit meaning behind the way he said 'source,' but was beginning to find that in this world, sometimes the path to victory could not be measured by the honorable actions of others, but by accepting those actions as inevitable and acting as honorably as one could on one's own. He simply nodded along and waited for Smithers to give the order.

"Sounds good to me," Smithers said. "We'll be fine walking for a bit. What about you padre? Good for a walk?"

Father Mitchell looked up to where Smithers was calling to him. The priest stared for a moment, as though trying to understand what was just said, then simply shook his head.

"I'll be fine here for a while," he called back. "I don't think I'm good to go walking around the city right now."

"Suit yourself," Smithers called, then turned back to the group. "Now I talked to Simon and he's agreed to make some fake IDs for us all. Basically, he's going to give you some kind of legitimacy in this city."

"Through a *fake* ID?" Luis asked.

"A *sense* of legitimacy then," Smithers said, rolling his eyes. "Whatever, we'll come back in a few days for them, then maybe start making some long term plans. Before that, we need to pick Sleeping Dumbass up from the church, rest up a bit ourselves, then we can go check out Morgan's boogy-deer. Any questions?"

They all shook their heads.

"I cannot believe that you heard the same word-salad I did and have no questions." Damian said, reaching into his pocket. "If you think of any that involve the vehicles or our shared goals, give us a call at this number. Should be the most recent."

He held out a small paper rectangle with a number scrawled on it to the group. Morgan, being the closest, looked at it and then promptly turned red and lowered her eyes. Lee stepped forward and took the card almost immediately. Luis noted that Lee had stepped purposefully between Morgan and Damian, though it did not seem that Damian had noticed the maneuver. Luis pondered on this for a moment before dropping the matter. It was none of his business, and besides that, he didn't really care.

It seemed there would be another battle tonight.

As they walked through the door and out into the brisk Boston air, Luis could not stop himself from grinning. Despite all the cruelty and confusion this world seemed to have at its disposal, it didn't lack for challenges to his mettle. If he was going to have to endure the gauntlet of its sins, at the very least he could take solace in his ability to act against them.

~ 14 ~

TIMM

Timm woke up to discover that the others were gone. Looking at the clock that hung from one of the walls in the basement, he saw that it was well past noon and, if they had gotten Latoya and Patrice to the train, then they left a long while ago. With a yawn and a few stretches, Timm got up and went in search of some food. Recovering from his injuries was hungry work.

As he padded quietly over to the stairs, he saw Jess stir in her cot a bit. Her pale, drawn lips muttered wordlessly in her sleep, and Timm was sure that she was not dreaming sweet dreams. Her normally dark, tawny complexion was sallow and sweat dampened her forehead. Behind closed lids, her grey, almond eyes darted wildly in her panicked dream.

Timm hesitated for a moment, fearing any interaction he had with her would simply make the poor girl feel worse. Finally, he relented and walked over to the side of her bed. Picking up a clean cloth Lee had left by her bedside, Timm dabbed lightly at her forehead. The young woman whimpered slightly, and Timm had not noticed the song leaving his lips until he saw Jess starting to calm.

"Luí go socair, luí go ciúin. Codladh sámh, a ghrághil," Timm sang, the words of his native tongue flowing from him calmly. The words came easily as though they were something he'd heard every day of his life.

"Fan id' shuan, a thaiscidh buan," he continued, stroking back the damp curls from Jess' face. *"Go n-éirí tú ar maidin."*

He repeated the song a few more times until he saw Jess recess into a deep, and thankfully peaceful, slumber. Quietly he stood and made his way towards the stairs. When he reached the bottom step, he looked back at the sleeping woman. She was free of the man who terrorized her in reality, but his actions persisted into her dreams where even sleep was not a peaceful retreat from the world. Timm felt the anger in his chest starting to rise, but fought it down. It would do her no good to be angry now.

Timm made his way up the stairs and found that the church seemed quite quiet and empty for such a large building. He walked to the canteen seeing and hearing no sign of any other person. A pang of guilt shot through his chest as he thought of the others off on the mission without him. He appreciated them allowing him to rest and recover, but he couldn't help but feel he was letting them down in a sense.

Trying to shake the thought from his mind, Timm set to work making himself breakfast. He found the cereal and milk easily enough and shoveled away at least half the box. While it was quite filling and the cartoon cat on the box was correct in his assertion of their greatness, Timm had a difficult time feeling satisfied by the food in this world. Even back on the mountain with his master the food had been better. Hearty grains and stout vegetables mixed with cubes of meat from animals they had hunted. Timm smiled and repeated his master's words to himself: "The rewards of what's earned are always superior to what's taken."

"It's a shame I can only remember your words," Timm said mournfully to himself, the smile he wore slipping. "But not your name. What is it with this world?"

He leaned back in his chair a bit, balancing on the back two legs. Father Mitchell had warned him not to do that due to it being dangerous, but having spent the past couple days being shot and stabbed, Timm felt tipping a chair was the least of his worries.

His mind continued to wander to the strangeness of the world he found himself in and of the enemies they had faced.

Seemed that no matter what world he was in, enemies were always lingering in the shadows. *When there are dangers in the darkness around you*, his master's words echoed again, *shine a light*.

Timm pondered on that. He knew neither the name of his enemy nor their purpose. Only that they had come into the hospital that night to kill the little girl. If they were desperate or cruel enough for such an act, exposing them would be the best solution. Create more enemies for them to face. But how to convince the world that they were as terrible as what Timm had seen?

His eyes fell on a book someone had left on the table. He reached over and picked it up. It was what Father Mitchell called "the Bible." He had flipped through the one Father Mitchell had given him a while back, though dozed off not long after starting. From how people spoke about it, he knew that it held substantial value to the people of its faith, but Timm had been unable to see that value from what he read.

"Shine a light," Timm thought aloud.

Perhaps his master hadn't meant exposing the enemy to the world. Perhaps he had meant something else entirely. These men followed a god who was supposed to be the burning light of the world, a cleansing light as Father Mitchell had once said. A beacon of hope in the darkness.

And then it clicked. The light wasn't the awareness of others, but rather the enlightenment he would gain from learning about his enemy. Timm needed to peel back the shadows that hid them and see them for what they really were. And to do that, Timm would need to learn all he could about them, their faith, and the purpose they thought they held in the world.

With a new-found fervor, Timm opened the Bible and began reading, hoping it could shine a light to direct his path.

*　*　*

"Hey," a voice called out to Timm from the darkness. It sounded familiar, but so far away. Part of him wanted to respond, but an overwhelming feeling told him to put it out of his mind.

"Hey!" the voice called again, and Timm felt the back legs of the chair shudder as though struck. He began to tip back slightly and the sensation of falling kicked his brain into overdrive.

Rolling with the momentum of the chair, Timm took the inertia of the fall and put his shoulder between his head and the ground. Tucking his knees in close to his chest, he waited until he felt the balls of his feet make contact with the ground and then released the tension held in his legs to bound forward and get behind whoever had assaulted him. His arms shot out, one snaking around the assailant's neck while the other hooked around his own wrist to lock the choke in place.

He stood in the canteen, his arms wrapped tightly around Lee's throat.

They stood still for just a moment before Timm realized the others were all standing around him and his grip around Lee's neck had not loosened. Lee made a short choking sound, instantly snapping Timm back into reality. Timm dropped his arms and stepped back, allowing Lee to gasp in air.

"Sorry about that," Timm said, sheepishly. "You just... uh... startled me."

"Woke you up is more like," Luis said, pointing at the tipped over chair. "You were leaning back in the chair with a book on your face, snoring."

"Oh," Timm said, again sheepishly. "I was trying to do some reading on what those guys who attacked Patrice in the hospital believed in."

"The Brotherhood of Thorns," Morgan offered.

Timm turned to her, startled. "How did you learn that?"

"Have a seat," Smithers said, walking over to the coffee pot and setting it up to brew. "This is going to take a while."

Over the next hour or so, Morgan and the others filled Timm in on what he'd missed that morning. It was only barely after three in the afternoon and Timm felt that he had missed so much. Battling the Brotherhood, gathering information from Arbuckle, an attack from DIARD, and finally...

"We also made new allies," Morgan said, cheerfully. "Remember the guy who saved Lee?"

"He wasn't there for that," Smithers piped up, then turned towards Timm. "Remember that guy on the bike when we were coming out of the police station?"

"The one who led us away from the warehouse after we saved Carl's family?" Timm asked, thinking back to the previous night. "The one Luis called 'the Black Rider'?"

The knight grunted his affirmation and nodded, but said no more. Morgan provided far more information.

"His name is Damian," she said, and Timm felt a twinge in his stomach at the broad smile that she got when she said his name. "He and his brother Simon are fighting against DIARD, and they said they'd help us!"

"They said they annoy DIARD," Smithers corrected. "They're gnats in a horse's face, but sometimes that's all you need to slow em' down. Until we know more, we're going to proceed with caution. Simon's working on some IDs for you lot. Far less explaining to do if we have to talk to the police again. Or get to a hospital again. Plus, Damian's fixing up Father Mitchell's van."

"Where is Father Mitchell?" Timm asked.

Smithers shrugged. "With the van. Damn thing got all shot up and the man didn't feel ready to start wandering the city streets after getting shot at. To be honest with ya, I don't blame him."

Timm agreed. With the amount of time he was spending recovering from getting shot, he could only imagine how long it would take someone who didn't have his master's training to come to terms with the ordeal. His master had been many things. Lax, however, was not one of them.

"So what's our plan?" Timm asked.

"Simon found out about Morgan's ghost deer," Smithers said.

"Elk," Morgan corrected. "And we don't know if that's it. But we're going to go after it tonight. Do you think you'll be up for it?"

Timm's heart skipped a beat when she asked, and he did not have the time to start questioning that reaction. He pushed the sensation down and smiled at her.

"I'll be good to go," he nodded.

"Great! Then we should all rest up in preparation," Morgan said, determination clear on her face. She stood to go downstairs, but paused, looking at the canteen door.

Timm turned to see Jess standing in the doorway, looking tired and still slightly pale, but smirking at them.

"Save me, save Carl's family," she said, her voice stronger than Timm would have expected. "Don't you guys ever take a night off?"

Morgan stepped forward and helped Jess get to a seat while laughing.

"It seems we don't," Morgan said, steadying Jess as she eased into a seat. "Can I get you something to eat?"

"A lot of something, if you can," Jess said. "Feels like I haven't eaten for days."

"You haven't," Lee said, and Timm noticed for the first time since they'd woken him that the priest was standing at the furthest corner of the room from him. Another pang of guilt hit him.

"We did what we could for your wounds," Lee continued, keeping his focus on Jess. "However, your body needed to perform a great deal of healing on its own. That process takes quite a bit of energy, so I'm not surprised you're at the end of yours."

"Guess it's high time to fill the tank," Jess said, with a slight laugh. She winced and gingerly touched her ribs as she did.

Lee cocked his eyebrow at her, perplexed. Then a moment later he nodded.

"I see," he said. "Comparing your body to a vehicle like a car or van which requires a tank of gasoline as fuel. I understand your metaphor. Now, if no one needs me, I'm going to see to my wounds, mild as they are, in preparation for this evening."

Without a further word, Lee slipped out of the room.

Luis stood. "I have my own preparations to make. Summon me when we are prepared to leave."

He followed Lee out of the room, but Timm noted that he turned away from where the basement stairs were and headed off in the opposite direction.

"Tough crowd," Jess said. "Do I need a shower or something?"

"Probably yes," Morgan nodded. "You've been in bed for two days. However I doubt that had any effect on their decision to leave."

"Wow," Jess said, looking at Morgan. "You guys all have the same issue with humor, don't you."

"Welcome to my hell," Smithers said, taking a long pull from his coffee before pouring himself another cup. "It's all day with this."

"Heh," Jess laughed, lighter this time, before turning her attention to Timm. "By the way, I wanted to thank you."

"Me?" Timm asked. "Lee and Morgan have been the ones tending to your wounds. Believe me, you don't want me doing that. My hands aren't exactly for healing."

"No," Jess said, shaking her head. "Not for the healing. For the beating, though I suppose that makes me sound like a terrible person. I don't mean the beating you dished out on Colin, which was well deserved, let me tell you. But I'm not thanking you for the pain you were willing to inflict on others. That's a thing that this world needs a hell of a lot less of."

Timm shuffled uncomfortably in his seat. "That's really all I'm good at, so I'm not sure where this 'thank you' is going to go…"

"Thank you for the beating you took," Jess blurted out. "Thank you for being willing to shield me… shield us… from having to bear that. No one has done that for me before, stepped in front of the hurt and the pain of the world. Taken that load off my shoulders… or wherever else they're aiming. So, thank you, not for the pain you inflicted, but the pain you deflected away."

She seemed tired after saying it and deflated a little, but Timm could still feel the gratitude washing off of her. He smiled to himself and considered her words. He'd always thought of himself as someone who could fight for those in need, and thus it meant he should strike down evil wherever it is so no one else gets hurt. He had never considered that the hurt dealt to him was simply hurt that would have otherwise found itself inflicted on someone else.

Timm smiled at the way she framed his place in a world he felt held none for him.

"You're welcome," he said, standing up and bowing to her the way he and his master would bow after training. "I will be that shield, not just for you, but for others. You have my word."

"People like you in this messed up world," Jess said. "You're the reason I won't be scared to bring this baby into it."

The rage against Colin that had been burning in his chest softened and turned into a comfortable warmth. That warmth spread and for a moment Timm felt as though his whole body was encased in the radiance of sunlight.

Shine a light, his master's words returned to him.

No, Timm thought. *It is better to be the light.*

~ 15 ~

LUIS

Luis turned out of the canteen and made his way down the hall leading towards Donovan's workshop. Along the way, he stopped by the Cathedral's main altar. Wooden pews lined the vast space all pointing towards a slab of marble the size of a coffin and twice as tall. Upon it sat several objects that Luis recognized, but felt odd in this context: a goblet, a book, and an unlit brazier seemingly for incense. Father Mitchell had explained their representations and the metaphor that they held, but he still could not wrap his head around the oddities of this religion compared to his own. The knight knew these played important roles in the worship of this christian god, but none of it was like how the temple back home was.

He remembered faces only in blurred imaginings of people, and not a single name could be brought to mind, but Luis spent a moment reflecting on what it was to pray back where the world made sense. Worship were tests of strength, hymns were sung as they charged into battle, and people did not pray for answers, but for the strength to achieve Victory on their own. Nike did not bless her worshipers with miracles as these Christians seemed to love and fear, but with boons of inner strength to aid them on their journey.

And Luis felt a strong need for such a boon.

Leaving the quiet, empty halls of the cathedral behind, the knight followed the sound of the warbling radio Donovan kept in his shop. The discordant music blared about a highway leading to the hells, which Luis found quite amusing as he stepped into the cluttered, but organized space.

Donovan kept his workshop in a very particular way, as Luis had seen many artisans of his ilk do before. A stranger would see a mess, but the worker knew where each item and tool was placed. The term "organized chaos" came to mind. There was a workbench to Luis' left as he stepped through the door where tools were laid out in a line as though waiting in a queue for their turn to be used. The walls were adorned with assorted hooks and pegs from which ladders, yard tools, and oddly enough even a saddle was hung from one. The large door which took up the entire wall to Luis' right was open, letting in the cold air of winter, and Donovan stood ankle deep in snow with a shovel in hand, trying to clear away the fresh powder that had fallen.

"You gonna gawk or you gonna dig?" Donovan asked, calling over his shoulder.

Without a word, Luis walked over to the man, grabbing a spare shovel on his way, and the two spent the better part of a quarter of an hour digging a path from the workshop to the parking lot. They worked in silence, and it seemed to suit them both just fine. When they were finished, Donovan took the shovels, hung them from their respected pegs, and hit a button on the wall.

As he did, the large door to the outside whirred to life with grinding mechanical noises that grated against Luis' ears, but he watched in amazement as a series of gears and chains moved, pulling the door snugly into place. Donovan walked over to a box on the worktable and pressed a button. It sprang to life, glowing with red light and Luis started to feel the chill of winter abate in its presence.

"So, Sir Knight," Donovan said, pulling off his gloves to warm his hands by the strange box. "What can I do for you today?"

"You have working knowledge of this world's religions, correct?" Luis asked, with no preamble.

"I've got a working knowledge of one in particular," Donovan responded. "And a vague inkling of how the rest function."

"Do you know where any temples to Nike may be located?" Luis asked him, urgently.

"Temples to Nike?" Donovan asked, confused. "I mean there's a Buddhist Temple in Cambridge I think, but why would there be a temple to Nike? Don't they just make shoes and whatnot?"

"What?" Luis asked in confusion. "No, not some shoe company. Nike! The Goddess of Victory."

"Huh, hold on a second," Donovan said, pulling out a phone from his pocket. He flipped it open and started typing at the keys. He talked as he typed, "Damn thing is ancient, but does what I need it to. Rarely ever need to go on the internet with it, but when I do it takes forever."

After a few minutes, Donovan seemed to find what he was looking for. "A-ha! Here we go. Nike, ancient Greek goddess. Well that explains it."

"Explains what?" Luis asked, concerned.

"Well, for one, explains what you were talking about. Apparently she was worshiped thousands of years ago, and she's got a couple temples in Greece that are now tourist spots," Donovan explained.

"Tourist spots!" Luis cried, incredulously. "Her holy sites are being defaced for tourism?"

"Well, to be fair, son, she hasn't been worshiped in a while," Donovan said. "Tourism is probably the only reason they haven't knocked down the temples and replaced them with a burger hut by now."

Luis felt anger welling up in his chest. He thought of the careless, creedless, people who trekked through the sacred halls of his goddess and defiled them by treating the excursion as a day trip. The hallowed ground was to be kept sacred, but this wretched world let Her great name fall to ruin!

"Course I got confused considering the Nike store," Donovan continued.

Luis paused. "Nike store?"

"Well yeah," Donovan shrugged. "Guess I never made the connection. There's a sporting goods company called Nike too. Here look."

Donovan turned the phone around and showed Luis a picture of a pair of black shoes, much like the ones he currently wore, but these had a simplistic sigil of Nike along their heels.

"The winged boots of Nike!" Luis cried out in excitement, feeling a surge of vindication that, though this world may not recognize her as a goddess anymore, at least her name lived on through something that represented the pursuit of victory. Her core purpose was still seen and respected.

"Funny," Donovan said, taking back the phone. "I always thought they were a check mark or something. Never figured them for wings. Always figured that was more Hermes' deal."

"Who?" Luis asked in confusion.

"I guess you're not as big a mythology buff as I thought," Donovan said, only deepening Luis' confusion. "But if you're interested in getting a pair, or a hat, or something like that, I think the big mall... can't tell you the name of it at the moment, but if you ask about the big one people can tell you. Anyway, I think they've got a Nike store opening up in there. You should check it out."

"I will do just that," Luis said, his joy now biting back at the anger.

Luis made his way back to the group with a newfound charge running through his body. The worship of his Goddess was not dead. Though Her hallowed halls may be ruins of an ancient time for this world, Her name burned on representing glory and victory even to this day. Luis walked swiftly back to where the others were resting, feeling already as though he had wings on his feet. He would go to this mall, and he would get these shoes as a holy pilgrimage to his Goddess.

"No you ain't," Smithers said, bluntly.

Luis felt the blood in his face run hot as he tried to temper his anger. Upon learning what he had from Donovan, Luis thought the others would see the significance of this revelation. Morgan and Lee seemed supportive, and even Timm perked up with interest, but Smithers flat out denied hearing more.

"I am her knight!" Luis argued back, his voice sharp and loud enough to stir the family sitting in the back corner of the room. Carl winced and Norah pulled her girls closer to her. Shamed, but not deterred, Luis lowered his voice and continued.

"It is my duty to serve her," he said. "And to serve her best I must display her sigil with pride, as a conduit for her power."

"You got yer necklace," Smithers said, dismissively. "Ain't that enough?"

"It functions, yes," Luis said, crossing his arms. "However this 'store' is the closest thing to a temple to my lady this world has remaining. I must perform a pilgrimage and make an offering."

"God would the capitalists love a billion more of you," Smithers said, turning his eyes up to the sky. Luis didn't quite understand what he meant by this, but felt the heat rise again.

"As well they should!" Luis' voice grew loud again, and he bit down on his tongue to keep from screaming at the man. He respected Smithers and his knowledge of this world, but it was not this world that concerned Luis at the moment. Smithers just wasn't able to see that.

"Do you know how much a pair of Nikes cost?" Smithers asked, sharply. "Even cheap ones go for a hell of a lot more than we've got right now. I ain't spending our eatin' money on a pair of damned shoes."

Luis felt a snarl escape his throat and turned away from Smithers. He understood the man's logic, but that didn't mean he had to like it. Luis felt someone slide up beside him and had half a mind to snap at them as well, until he turned to see Morgan standing beside him.

"Maybe we can go after we've gotten ourselves more established?" Morgan suggested. "We've been trying to catch our balance for so long, once we figure out where we're staying, how to get money, and who's coming after us we'll be able to go and give Nike the offering she deserves."

Luis breathed out a sigh and worked to unclench his jaw. The latter was not overly successful, so he did his best to smile at Morgan and gave her a nod. She was speaking sense, of course, and in a much more diplomatic way than Smithers managed. While the old man's blunt mannerisms had amused Luis whilst directed at others, being the target of them was off-putting and irritating.

Luis conceded to wisdom. He would wait on the store, for now at least.

"Very well," Luis said, turning his burning eyes towards Smithers. "I will wait, but I will not stand for blasphemy of Her name."

"Boy, if you really understood what that place was you wouldn't be so hot and bothered to get there, but fine," Smithers said before turning and muttering darkly to himself.

Luis nodded at his turned back before addressing Morgan.

"Thank you for stepping in," Luis said.

Morgan shrugged. "No big deal, we're all pretty tense. It's been non-stop since we got here, so I guess we're all just a bit agitated."

"Indeed," Luis agreed, thinking of the past two days again and the lamentations of Father Mitchell. Life had often been like this for him when on patrol, and it had never bothered him then. However, the feeling of being a fish out of water most definitely added a tension to the situation that he'd never felt before. "Hopefully after we aid you in your hunt tonight, we'll be able to take a few days rest before continuing in our explorations of this world."

She smiled and set herself to organizing and preparing herself for the evening's excursions. There was not one moment that Luis believed that anything would be slowing down for them. Not with the Brotherhood hunting them. Not with DIARD lurking in the shadows. And most certainly not with the hornet's nest he was sure they were about to kick.

But at least, in this moment, they could pretend.

The reward for work well done... Luis thought bitterly.

~ 16 ~

MORGAN

Morgan had been bouncing around the church for hours, seemingly filled with nervous energy until Lee finally had enough.

"Would you like to go down to the park early?" he asked her.

"But the spirit probably won't be there yet," Morgan said mournfully. "Besides, not everyone is ready."

"This is true," Lee said, attempting to be diplomatic about the issue. He didn't want to deflate her more by telling her that her nervous energy was permeating the rest of them. "However perhaps those of us with more gifted eyes and a closer attunement to the land will find some clues to help us later this evening."

"Okay!" Morgan said, excitedly. She quickly scampered off to collect what she needed as Smithers approached Lee.

"What are you hoping to find?" the old man asked.

"A little peace," Lee responded. "Her excitement is making everyone tense, even the non-believer."

He gave Smithers a pointed look, which the old man answered with little more than a grin.

"Calling my faith into question?" Smithers asked.

"You've made your lack of it abundantly clear," Lee stated. "I'm more concerned for your eyes. With the truth staring you in the face you prefer the safety of your ignorance over the dangers of the truth."

"A man shot at us today," Smithers answered. The bluntness of the statement rocked Lee back a step. Chills swept over him and a cold sweat threatened to break across his brow. These guns, these horrific weapons, were having a terrible effect on him. Smithers seemed to know that as well as he pushed the point.

"More than one man," Smithers whispered. "Death was looking us in the face and you all, with whatever craziness has been placed on your shoulders, managed to hold it at bay. I can keep my faith in your abilities, though I'll be honest, I couldn't tell you if I think you're all bonkers or not."

"Bonkers?" Lee asked, finding his voice in the absurdity of the word.

"Bonkers, loony, psycho," Smithers supplied. "Or my favorite, 'bat-shit crazy.' Point is, Lee, I'm not sure I'm ready to face the truth of it head on. So I'll keep the craziness at arm's length for now. Or better yet, down the barrel of Sebastian at twenty paces."

Lee looked down and saw Smithers pat the butt of his shotgun, which sat barely visible in the holster under his open shirt.

"What happens when Sebastian isn't enough?" Lee asked.

"Well then," Smithers said. "Maybe then I'll have my 'great awakening.' But for now, I'm taking this one step at a time."

"Perhaps," Lee said, turning to see Morgan talking excitedly with Timm and the two hurried over to him. "That is the best way to approach these problems."

And so, one step at a time the trio made their way to Paul Revere Park. While Morgan's were springing and excited, both Lee and Timm found their own feet dragging. Lee was busy looking over his shoulder for the third or fourth time that block when Timm reached out and tapped him on the arm.

It took all of Lee's will not to jump out of his skin at the sudden contact.

"Bah! Ah," Lee breathed out a sigh. "Timm, yes, how can I help you?"

"I just wanted," Timm said, awkwardly rubbing his left hand against his other arm's triceps. "To say sorry. For, you know, what happened earlier?"

Lee cocked his eyebrow at Timm. "What are you talking about?"

"Back at the church," Timm explained, though Lee could sense confusion in his voice. "When I put you in that choke hold..."

"Oh, that," Lee said, finally understanding. He waved dismissively at Timm and turned back to watching their tail. "It's nothing. Don't worry about it."

"But I could have hurt you," Timm started to go on.

"And you did not," Lee interjected. "Your skills added to this group are ones that are dependent upon, but not limited to, your reflexive reactions against something that presents a physical danger. There have been several instances where my life, or those of others, has and in the future will depend on such reactions. I will approach future interactions with you with greater caution."

Lee felt he explained himself quite clearly, though the look on Timm's face refuted such a belief. With a heavy sigh, Lee tried again.

"It was a reflex," Lee said, slowing his speech down. "An important one. It was my fault for sneaking up on you. I'll be careful."

"Oh," Timm said, smiling and nodding. "Then I'll be careful too. Try to get better at thinking before I react to things."

"Right," Lee said. He was unsure of how well that would go for the young man, but far be it from him to dash Timm's hopes of self-improvement.

Paul Revere Park was not all that impressive to Lee. It was a small space of greenery in the middle of a metropolitan area that served more to accentuate the lack of nature around the citizens of the city rather than give them an escape to it. It did not take them long to circle the entire area, from the grassy field buried in the snow in the park center to the suspension bridge that loomed in the background. There were a few people who walked around the outer perimeter with dogs tethered on leashes, though the fresh shell of snow lay untouched and unbroken in the afternoon's golden light. They spent the better part of an hour searching with very little to show for it.

Lee slumped down on a bench made from a patchwork of stacked stones and wooden planks. It reminded him of the old country cobblestone walls that he would pass on pilgrimages between cities back... back in... he shook his head, rattling the memories loose and watched them tumble away. He began to feel the frustration and aggravation of the memory loss begin to build in him, but pushed it back in hopes of keeping his composure. It would not do for him to lose his temper now, especially not publicly.

"Hey," Morgan's voice cut through Lee's inner contemplation. "Who's that?"

Lee looked up to see who Morgan was talking about. A man, probably just south of forty winters leaned heavily on a wheeled cart he pushed across the icy ground. He wore a puffy jacket, thick with what Lee assumed to be down or another form of insulation, and a woolen cap with flaps on the side to keep his ears warm. Long strings dangled from the flaps, ending in puffs of yarn whose purpose Lee could not perceive. A patchy beard of black and silver covered the lower half of his dark face that wore an expression of quiet determination, but Lee sensed more to him. There was something present in his eyes that made this man more than just a vagabond.

"Maybe he knows something," Timm said, as he bounded toward the man.

"Timm!" Lee hissed after him. "Dammit."

Lee got up and followed the rash young man as he walked up to the vagabond and greeted him warmly.

"Hello! I'm Thola Igerk Mue Moonflayer," Timm said, offering the man his hand.

"Nice ta mee'cha, Moony," the man said, grinning broadly and revealing to Lee a missing tooth. "My name's Walter."

"Good afternoon, Walter," Lee said, bowing politely. "I apologize for our interrupting your day."

"We just wanted to ask you a few questions," Timm interjected. Lee looked sharply at him, seriously disagreeing with his use of the word 'we.'

"Oh now," Walter said. "What can I do ya for?"

"We were curious if you've seen anything suspicious in the park," Morgan said, approaching from behind Lee. "Specifically at night."

"Well now, that's something I can actually attest to," Walter said, scratching at his beard. "You see, I sleep under that bridge over yonder, and the past few weeks there've been lots of strange happenings around here."

"Really?" Timm asked, excitedly.

"Yeah, there've been some pretty strange glowings happening, late at night. And not just that ambient snow stuff neither, but a sickly green glow," Walter told them. "The kind you see in them haunted movies, but I betcha it's more like those government movies, with the secret organization what kidnaps people and experiments on them!"

"Like DIARD!" Timm practically shouted, and Lee jammed his elbow into the man's ribs to keep him quiet. Timm rubbed at them mournfully. "Ow..."

"Keep your voice down," Lee glowered at him.

"Yeah, don't want folks like that hearing you know about them," Walter said, lowering his own voice.

"You know about them?" Morgan asked, her voice barely a whisper.

"Know about them?" Walter responded. "Of course I do, I know about all sorts of secret organizations, even a member of a few, but

I can't tell you which ones. All I can tell you is that some of them out there really don't like me."

"Highly improbable due to your friendly nature," Lee caught himself saying. It was not like him to use sarcasm, but perhaps he was spending too much time around Smithers than was good for him.

"I know, right?" Walter said, apparently missing the sarcasm, or choosing to ignore it. Either way, Lee decided to move the conversation forward.

"Well, perhaps it would be best if you slept somewhere other than your bridge this evening," he said to Walter. "We were planning on investigating the glow and usually when we investigate such things, collateral damage happens."

"I wouldn't want to be collateral damage, now," Walter nodded in agreement. "Just be sure to keep an ear to the ground so the werewolves in the park don't get'cha."

Lee felt his left eyelid twitch slightly. Had he not thought this kook's information bad before, he was starting to get the feeling it was even worse than he'd anticipated. That didn't stop Morgan and Timm's eyes from becoming as wide as saucers, however.

"There are werewolves in the park too?" Morgan asked, excitedly.

"I hear the howls now and again," Walter nodded. "Too big to be dogs and no natural wolves live in the city."

Timm turned to Morgan and whispered excitedly, "We get to fight *werewolves!*"

"Let's not get ahead of ourselves," Lee warned, stepping in. "Walter, we will look into the issues of the park, and again I must stress that it would be best for you to not sleep here this evening. Timm, Morgan, we're going to return to the tavern to meet with Smithers and Luis to report our findings. From there we will make a plan."

"We didn't find much in the way of clues, though," Morgan said, mournfully. "No offense Walter, but there's not much planning we can make around a green glow and possible werewolves."

"No offense taken," Walter shook his head. "I wouldn't want to fight against government werewolves without a plan either. But, what kind of clues are you looking for?"

"Well," Morgan said, pensively. "I suppose anything that might indicate something unnatural. A way that the world is out of balance."

"Sweets," Walter said, cocking his eyebrow at Morgan. "You just described the entire human condition."

Lee narrowed his eyes at Walter. Something was odd about the man's behavior. One moment, he believed the man to be mad, but the next he appeared to be insightful and versed in philosophical thinking. He was unsure about this Walter character, but was convinced that he was just that: a character.

"Anything more specifically related to this park, then?" Lee asked, trying to keep his tone neutral so as to not let on to his thinking.

"Maybe," Walter said, scratching at the tangled mess that was his beard. "Lotta animals have been dying off lately."

"Getting killed by the werewolves?" Timm asked.

"Nah, werewolves hunt people, not tiny woodland critters," Walter waved off the comment dismissively. "Plus they'd be torn to pieces. This is different."

"Different how?" Morgan asked.

"Well, probably best if you see it for yourself," Walter said. "Check down by the water over there and you'll see what I mean."

Lee followed where Walter was pointing and saw he was guiding them toward a bridge in the distance. It was near the park, though much of the greenery had given way to broken stone and mud, as though the people felt that beyond the park itself, nature should fend for itself against the onset of the city. As he looked around, Lee couldn't help but feel the city was winning.

They thanked Walter and went their separate ways, the squeaking of the wheel on his cart mixed with him whistling some jaunty tune seemed to quickly get caught in Timm's head and promptly had him humming along with it as well. They walked down towards the water and Lee couldn't help but recoil slightly at the brackish brown muck that passed for river water in this world as it clashed horribly with the upbeat song coming from Timm.

Back home, wherever that may be, the rivers were clear and safe to drink from at the bank. Here he wouldn't feel comfortable using it to wash his clothes without first using his magic to purify it. The stench of dead fish and other unpleasantries filled the air, forcing Lee to choke back a gag. It smelled like rot, but then, something even more than rot. Not even the stench of the undead was not as horrific as this.

"Lee! Timm!" Lee heard Morgan cry out. He turned to see her down by the bank, oblivious to the putrid water washing over her bare feet. Lee felt himself gag a little and swallowed vomit that was attempting to break free. Then he noticed it, the small form curled up at Morgan's feet, just barely beyond the water.

He walked over to it, examining the still shape of the dead animal. Black fur, though perhaps at one time it had been brown, clung to the body in odd patches. Anywhere there wasn't fur Lee spied pink skin with angry red rashes. Except for the patterning, the priest would have determined them burn marks, but if that were true then he would have seen scorched fur or at least where the fire would have melted the skin. This creature looked as though its skin itself had been the source of the heat that burned it.

Morgan reached out her hand, but Lee's own shot out and caught her wrist. He met her eyes, shaking his head. Looking around, he spied a stick long and strong enough to flip the body over. Lee wished he hadn't. As the small body of the creature, perhaps a fox or house cat, rolled to one side a swarm of flies escaped the corpse in a cloud of rotten fumes.

"Gah!" Lee cried out, falling back unceremoniously, waving the stick wildly to keep the vermin at bay. His heart was pounding in his chest, and both the sight and smell in front of him set him to war against his own stomach, forcing it to keep from evacuating right then and there.

"That would explain the lack of bloating," Morgan said calmly as she knelt down to examine the corpse.

Lee tried to recover himself as best he could, aided by Timm who swatted away at any lingering flies, and marveled at Morgan's apparent detachment from the situation in front of her. Often he had witnessed her emotions taking over, causing her to second guess herself. Seeing her like this was both impressive and somewhat disconcerting.

"Anything interesting?" Timm asked as he clapped at Lee's clothing with a hand, shaking off any stragglers that remained. Lee felt his skin crawl, but donned his mask of indifference again, turning to hear Morgan's reply. It wouldn't do for him to be the one who lost his head in this situation.

"A few things," Morgan said, her eyes fixed on the creature. "The side of this creature is just missing."

"Eaten away," Lee said, choking back the bile and trying to focus on the logistics of the; situation. "Some other animal, perhaps."

"No, there's no rending in the flesh," Morgan said, shaking her head. "The only consumption done was by the flies. Usually a bigger animal would take the majority of the meat and sustain itself on that. The flies and other insects would come to break down what remained. No other animal has touched this, almost as though they knew it was poisoned."

"A poison did this?" Timm asked, his voice carrying more indignation than shock.

Morgan shook her head. Lee could sense her frustration, as though she had no words for what she was seeing, no way of communicating what she knew.

"Try, Morgan," Lee said, realizing what his true role in this moment was. He kept his voice steady and not demanding, encouraging Morgan to share as best she could so he could understand as best he could. "Work through it, you see something, and it's strange, what is it?"

"I..." Morgan started, shook her head, and took a deep breath. "I can't think of any other way to say this. It... it just rotted to death."

Timm cocked an eyebrow at her. "It what?"

"There's no other way to explain it," Morgan said, somewhat exasperated, throwing her hands up. "There's no wound, no poison, no nothing. It's as though the body just started decomposing while it was still alive and finally the body gave out and it died."

"That would have ruined the meat on it," Lee said. "Any other creature would know not to eat something sick and dying like that. But what kind of illness decomposes a living body?"

"There are some flesh eating diseases," Morgan said. "But then we'd still see damage to the flesh."

"There's a giant hole in it," Timm pointed out.

Morgan shook her head. "That came after death. You can tell by the edges of the skin. It was eaten from the inside out."

"Lovely," Lee said, taking a few steps back. "So, we have our clues."

"Information from Walter," Timm nodded.

"And this poor fox," Morgan said, solemnly.

"So our next step should be to reconvene with the others," Lee said, making his way back to the park and away from the carcass of the rotted animal as quickly as he could. "We'll report what we've found and come to a decision on how to handle this."

"Find whatever is doing it, and beat it down," Timm said, driving his fist into his opposite hand. Lee stared at the man for a moment, reflecting on the complexity of Morgan's character and the perpetual simplicity of his.

"Somehow I knew that would be the first suggestion," Lee sighed, knowing better than to either voice his opinions or reflect on them too long, for his own sanity's sake. "How often I'm regrettably right."

~ 17 ~

SMITHERS

Smithers sat and listened to the tale that the three were weaving in front of him and felt himself reliving his younger days of parenthood when three toddlers came before him and regaled him with tales so monumentally impossible and moronic that it was endearing. They told him about their search of the park. They told him about their conversation with the homeless kook named Walter. They told him about the rotted animal that apparently died to death. It was at that point he looked away from them, swirling the whiskey in his glass around the half melted cubes of ice and looked at the other patrons of O'Malley's Pub.

A few were giving them looks of disgust, apparently not endeared to them. Probably didn't help much that Morgan had walked in from the freezing cold with muddy feet and her sandals in her hands. Once they'd gotten to the part of the tale with the rotting animals, Delilah, one of the regulars here at the bar who dressed twenty years too young and a few sizes too small, had given Morgan a look that read of pure, unadulterated revulsion.

"You know," Smithers said, watching Delilah awkwardly get up and shuffle away, moving as quickly as she dared not to split a seam while she made her escape. "Some people come to bars to have a good time, and not to talk about rotting animal carcasses they found in the park. Some may call that a 'mood killer.'"

"But it's a clue!" Timm said, excitedly.

"Timm, sit down and have a drink," Smithers said, pointing at a stool. "Something non-alcoholic and non-caffeinated."

"So water?" Tom asked from behind the bar.

"Got one of those lemon-lime sodas?" Smithers asked him.

"Off brand," Tom responded.

"Good enough," Smithers said, turning to Morgan. "And you, go clean up. Women's bathroom."

Morgan began combing through her hair with her fingers. "Did something get on me?"

"Your feet girl!" Smithers said, pointing down, remembering parenthood yet again. "First of all, I don't know how you didn't lose them in the cold. Secondly, you're tracking mud and Tom probably doesn't want to clean that up."

"Oh!" Morgan squeaked, turning to Tom. "I'm so sorry, I'll clean it up."

"Feet first," Tom said, pointing at the bathroom. "Then the mop is in the back. You know how to use one, right?"

"Kind of," Morgan said, shrugging. She then hurried off to the bathroom and disappeared from sight, leaving nothing behind but a thin trail of muddy footprints.

"Gah..." Tom sighed. "Millennials."

"Do they even count?" Smithers asked. "We don't know what year their calendar is on."

Tom shook his head and pulled out a glass. He shoveled ice in and picked up the soda nozzle. Selecting the right button, he poured Timm's drink and slid it in front of the boy. It was crystal clear and filled with bubbles.

"What is this?" Timm asked.

"Remember that stuff that gave you the sugar high you were on?" Smithers asked.

Timm's expression at the drink soured and he leaned back.

"It's like that but without as much sugar and none of the caffeine," Smithers explained. "Honestly, it's the caffeine that gets ya."

Timm looked at Smithers skeptically and then back at the drink. Tentatively, he reached out and picked up the glass. He probably spent the better part of a minute examining it from every angle, and even sniffing it like a dog. Smithers calmly told himself that at least the boy was occupied and not to rush him. Finally, Timm took a sip.

"Wow!" He exclaimed. "That's really good!"

"Now, remember, it still has sugar," Tom warned him. "So go easy on the number you have, but without the caffeine you shouldn't have the same issue as last time."

"Got it," Timm nodded and sipped more enthusiastically.

"Well, that's one problem solved," Smithers said, turning to Luis who had come down to the pub with him about an hour ago. His drink still sat untouched on the bar, ice having vanished long ago. "Any thoughts on what they told us?"

Luis had watched as the others spoke. Smithers had come to trust the knight's judgement, if not his temperament. He had listened intently, not interrupting, and seemingly ignoring the other patrons the whole time. Smithers had spent the better part of story time making sure no one suspicious was trying to overhear them, though it wouldn't have taken an international super-spy to have listened in when Timm and Morgan started talking. Lee at least had the good sense to keep his voice down.

"My experience tells me it can be one of two things," Luis said, leaning back in his barstool, arms crossed. "Either it is some kind of demon, which seems unlikely given that the animals dying are small, people haven't gone missing, and the damage done to the bodies was from the inside out."

"Okay, so that leaves Option B," Smithers said, rolling his hand at the wrist trying to encourage more out of Luis. "Which would be?"

"When it comes to unnatural deaths, you're usually dealing with some kind of undead," Luis said, plainly.

"Right," Smithers nodded. He was trying very hard not to swig the rest of his whiskey down in one go.

This is what his life had become. Fighting terrorists on trains and having legitimate conversations about horror movie monsters. Maybe if he started carrying one of those night vision cameras around he could get a show on the science fiction channel like those guys that go into ancient castles and try to piss off ghosts. If there were any justice in this world, those assholes would have found these monsters instead of Smithers. Now that would be must-see-tv.

"So how useful will a bullet be against that?" Smithers asked, thinking about Sebastian pressing up against his leg. Carrying the shotgun in public wasn't exactly what you would call 'legal,' but with what his day had been like, Smithers would rather run the risk of being arrested over the risk of being given his Uncle Sam Funeral with a dollar store flag on his casket.

"Depends," Luis shrugged, swirling his drink absentmindedly as he strategized. "If it's non-corporal like the ghost we fought a couple days ago, not much. If it has a body, like a ghoul or zombie or something, it should work just fine."

"Wonderful," Smithers said, wondering when the thought 'hope whatever is waiting for us in the dark has a body' became a staple in his life. "What about you and Lee? You two seemed to be able to handle that ghost pretty well."

Lee, having quietly sat down at the bar when Timm and Morgan began their epic retelling of their adventure, looked over at Smithers before looking at Luis. These two were the weirdest of the bunch to Smithers, and that was saying something. While they could easily pass for normal members of society so long as they didn't open their mouths much, it was the silent communications they had that creeped Smithers out more than Morgan's morbid knowledge of the world and annoyed him more than Timm's self-sacrificing heroics. It made Smithers feel like a child again, when he would watch his parents communicate something right in front of him, but leaving him none the wiser.

"Could you at least talk out loud," Smithers finally asked, reaching for his glass again. "Share with the class, don't do that creepy telepathy thing you two have."

"We're not telepathic," Lee stated plainly.

"I know," Smithers said, and prayed he was right. "But you have this habit of having whole conversations with your eyes. It's like you're married or something."

"Could you and your wife have such conversations?" Luis asked.

Smithers felt his blood run cold and anger begin to swell in his chest. He fought with everything he had not to draw on the knight, or throw his drink in his face and start pounding on him. He counted backwards from ten, then tried again from a hundred. The damn therapists had given him so many different ways to cope that he couldn't focus on just one.

"That's the end of that conversation," Smithers said, suddenly aware of just how tightly his jaw had been clenched.

"Fair enough," Luis said, dropping the subject. "Then let us fill you in on our silent conversation."

Smithers was surprised. Usually when people brought up his wife or anything to that effect, they hounded him for answers, pressured him to reveal a clue or something to indicate what had happened. He had punched a few of those people, and stopped talking to family members entirely over such interactions, but no one had ever just dropped the matter when asked like that before. He looked at the knight and realized the question hadn't meant to pry, but was in reality, asked out of a legitimate interest in him as a person.

"Undead come in many forms," Luis was explaining, not missing a beat between subject changes. "As do the gods of our worlds. Though Lee and I worship different gods, both fall under the part of the pantheon that value inherently 'good' acts."

"How does one define 'good,'" Smithers asked. "I mean, to some people, killing infidels and forcing women into subjection is 'good' according to their god."

"Good is subjective only to certain degrees," Lee supplied. "As people, we know it is wrong to hurt others, and have to make excuses to justify it to ourselves later. Objectively, 'good' is something you don't need to excuse."

"Killing, for example, is not a good act," Luis supplied. "Killing to save someone is forgivable because the act of saving someone's life is good. The act of killing someone is not. If another way is available, it should be taken, however death is death."

"What does that have to do with our little problem tonight?" Smithers asked.

"The undead are abominations," Lee supplied, sipping at his water. "They are not truly alive, and thus are a mockery of the gift the gods have given us."

"So it's good to kill them?" Smithers asked.

"It is good to destroy them," Luis stated. "It was an evil act to bring them into the world in the first place. Their lives, their time, had run its course. Naturally or due to acts of fate, their lives were extinguished. To take the body of someone who had completed their cycle and use it as a puppet, that is a grave sin."

"So you're saying someone made these things?" Smithers asked, scowling. It didn't sit well with him that someone was out there digging up bodies and making them dance. It sat worse with him that that person was now his problem.

"Probably not in this case," Lee supplied. "Undead can form spontaneously on their own due to conditions around their deaths, but that is usually limited to specters and ghosts."

"Something physical is usually the work of necromancers," Luis picked up. "Evil wizards who plan to use them for their own gain."

"But there are no wizards here," Smithers said, swirling the whisky around the remnants of ice in his glass. "And if there are no wizards here, odds are we're not dealing with something physical."

"I honestly couldn't tell you what we're dealing with," Luis sighed, pushing his untouched drink away from him. "All I can tell you is that whatever we're facing will grow in power if it is not put down. Animal-killings will become people-killings soon enough. It always happens that way. That's why it is best that we put the beast down before it gets to that point, whether it be man-made or not."

The knight got up and walked over to where Timm had retreated. Morgan had come out of the bathroom at some point and was standing with the other two. They were talking excitedly, probably formulating a plan, or talking about similar experiences they'd had dealing with such monstrosities back home. A chill ran up the old man's spine.

Smithers thought about what the two had said. These things can create themselves in the world. Even though those tv shows were fake, Smithers was now facing his second undead threat in the week, proving that it could be possible that others exist around the world. He had assumed that it was due to his proximity to these people straight out of the bargain bin fantasy rack, but now he was starting to have doubts on that. People disappeared every year by the thousands without an explanation. Now he was faced with the possibility that there was an explanation after all, and it was staring him dead in the face.

"Out of curiosity," Smithers asked Lee, his voice low and soft. "Do you think that these things existed in this world before you all got here? Could I have been living in a world with them before meeting you all?"

"Of course," Lee said, his tone matter-of-fact. Smithers turned to stare at the priest as he stood up. "There is still magic in your world, or none of us would be able to draw on it. Just because your people have done all they can to choke it down does not mean that it does not yet live. Hiding away from it does not make it go away. You were just unlucky enough to stumble across the truth and lucky enough that you are the kind of man who can do something about it."

"How could you call living like this lucky?" Smithers asked, feeling that anger and frustration beginning to overtake him again.

Lee shrugged. "Simple. You could be dying like this instead. I've seen it. It's not a clean death."

With that, the priest walked over to the others and joined in the planning. Smithers sat, holding his empty glass and looking at the four of them. They buzzed with excitement and smiles, while he sat in terror of what was to come. Lee's words haunted him, but they did make some sense. How many times over the past couple days could he have been torn apart by some otherworldly horror? And how often had he been wrenched away from the jaws of death?

And how often had it been thanks to these nut jobs?

Smithers shook his head.

"One more," he said, standing up and placing his empty glass on the bar. "One more and I'm done."

"This from the man who reenlisted three times?" Smithers heard Tom say and turned to see the bartender smirking at him.

Despite himself, Smithers smirked back.

"You've got a point," Smithers nodded. "You've got a point."

He started walking over to the group, shaking his head.

"Sarge was right about me after all. The only way I retire is in a box," Smithers laughed to himself. "With a dollar store flag."

~ 18 ~

MORGAN

The air was still, making the frigid night feel less bone chilling. Morgan stood in the middle of the park with the others watching the lights of the city drown out the winking stars above until only the void of night wrapped around the city reflecting its own glow back down.

"Barely seems like night out here," Morgan said. "The glowing snow, the sky more grey than black, it's... sad."

"Light pollution," Smithers said, absently. "Happens a lot in cities. So much light that you can't see the stars. There's noise pollution too. Similar effect."

Morgan felt a sour taste in her mouth. There were so many things in this world she could not help but find distasteful. She had dissected a rotting animal carcass not hours ago in this very park, but what she saw now was even more revolting. The disregard was staggering, and the separation was sickening. Even the cities back home knew to respect the life of the world, but here...

There was a rustling in a bush not far off. Every muscle in Morgan's body tensed as she turned to face it. Having turned into so many predators recently, she started feeling their influence begin to take over parts of her own instinct.

"What is it?" Luis asked, his voice barely above a whisper.

Morgan held up her hand, indicating for them to stand down. Silently she slipped towards the bushes, barely disturbing the snow underfoot. The knight's heavy steps would no doubt reveal their presence, and Morgan wanted to take their quarry unaware.

She shook her head and cleared the thoughts of the hunters away. They were on the hunt, yes, but she had to remember the creature they were going after was no prey animal. Undead were tricky, if Lee and Luis' guess was correct. They felt no fear and would not react like a typical animal.

Morgan slipped forward and gently forced her hand through the leaves and bramble that had shaken loose most of the layers of snow built up on it. Once she'd gotten a firm grip in the inner branches, Morgan tore it aside creating a gap wide enough to reveal...

To reveal a pair of teenage kids in what Morgan could only describe as an uncomfortable position. The girl was clutching a tree, her clothing vastly misaligned and shivering slightly from either the cold or excitement, though potentially both. The boy, whose pants were fully down around his ankles, turned to face Morgan, though thankfully only turned from the waist up. The expression of naked fear on his face mirrored the nakedness of his fully exposed rump.

There was an awkward pause as the three stared at one another in shock at the situation they'd found themselves in. Morgan was suddenly aware of the four others who were standing not twenty feet behind her as she heard the sound of approaching footsteps.

"Hey, what did you find?" Timm asked, coming to stand beside her, breaking the spell.

The girl was the first to react. She screamed and made an attempt to cover herself that only served to expose more than they'd already seen. Timm turned to the source of the scream, saw the nearly naked girl and screamed himself, staggering back a step blindly as he threw his hands up over his eyes.

Caught in the surprise, the boy tried to step back out of his lady-friend's way, but seemingly forgot the placement of his pants and ended up tripping himself, falling backwards and missing another bramble bush by mere inches before landing in a mound of snow. He shrieked as the cold enveloped his... tender areas... and Morgan felt her face burst into flames from the heat of her embarrassment.

The entire ordeal lasted no more than a few seconds, and before any more words could be exchanged, the two young lovers were darting down the pathway leading out of the park, still struggling to fix their clothing as they ran.

Morgan had buried her face in her hands, trying hard not to think about the awkward situation she'd just found herself in. She could hear nothing but the blood rushing in her ears and wheezing laughter. Looking over at the others, Morgan saw Smithers clasping Luis' shoulder for support as he laughed so hard he was practically choking.

"Oh my god," the old man finally wheezed out. "It was like a goddamned movie! How does this shit happen to you people?"

Luis looked less amused than Smithers, but Morgan saw the hint of a smirk at the corners of his mouth. Lee was looking curiously down the path the lovers had run down, though his thoughts were alien to her. Timm was pulling himself off the ground and dusting snow off his clothing. He kept his eyes down and tried to hide his face, but Morgan could tell that it was as red as hers.

"I do not believe that they were our ghostly apparition," Lee stated. "Perhaps it will not reveal itself until closer to the witching hour."

"It's like six p.m. and pitch black out," Smithers said, though Morgan disagreed with his assertion of the lighting. "How long do we have to wait?"

"The witching hour is closer to midnight or later," Lee explained. "So we could well be here for hours yet."

"Hours," Smithers said, nonplussed. "Why the hell are we here with *hours* to go? This is the train station all over again! Can't you people understand how a damned clock works?"

"There's no guarantee that the creature will wait that long," Luis chimed in. "Better to wait longer and be prepared than to show up late to a collection of corpses."

Smithers relented after that. They took up their positions around the park, keeping an eye out for any strange activity. Luis patrolled over the next few hours, hitting each one of their points of interest in order to keep everyone in contact. Every now and then, Morgan saw a police car roll by, but thanks to Luis' warnings, everyone managed to hide before they could be spotted. Smithers had informed them that parks were usually closed to visitors at night to avoid things like what Morgan had found those teenagers doing from happening.

As she thought about the event again, Morgan could feel her face burning. Almost out of instinct, she turned her face away from the others in spite of the fact that there was no way they could see her. She found her gaze leading over towards the water. For a moment, she thought it was a trick of the heinous city lights, but as she continued to look, the hazy light became more evident, and a sickly green glow rippled off the waves.

Morgan felt fear grip her chest. She tried to form the warning bird call with her lips, but could not force the air from her lungs. Something was coming, and it was something beyond what she was prepared to face.

As the fog rolled in, she heard a cry from behind her. Startled, she turned to see Luis, his blade gleaming in the ambient snowlight. He called out to her, but his words were muddled as though he were shouting through water. She shook her head, trying to tell him she didn't understand. He shouted to her again and began violently pointing behind her at the water.

Morgan turned back to see what Luis was shouting about. What she saw made her blood run cold.

As the mist crawled across the waters the air crackled with the sound of ice forming and breaking and reforming like snapping bones. The scent of rotten fish became overwhelming as it mixed with the overwhelming aroma of decay. A shadow appeared in the midst of the fog, approaching as though walking across the freezing water, its gait that of a four legged creature, but by its shadow it stood nearly twelve feet tall.

The antlers broke the fog first, piercing through wide and wicked, like gnarled branches from a spindly, dying tree in the heart of winter. They were black and cracked with age and rot. The elk's face came next, or at least what was left of it. Half of its face was covered with matted, black fur, as though pasted down with gore. Sections of skin hung loosely, little more than chunks of meat peeling off from slashes and wounds that had torn its face apart. The other side of its face was pure bone, gleaming a pallid pale green in the miasma that surrounded it. In each of its empty eye sockets sat a pinprick of red light that seemed to focus on them each in turn, burning with hate.

With a guttural roar, the beast opened its mouth and sound flooded towards them. Morgan clasped her hands to her ears, waiting for the attack to hit, but as suddenly as it started, the sound stopped. Slowly she looked up at Luis and the others who had rushed forward to join him. They were all staring at the monster on the river.

"What the hell was that?" Smithers asked, shaking slightly, though the gun in his hand was steadily pointed at the creature.

"I think it was speaking to us," Lee said. "Though what language it was, I could not tell you."

"The beast wishes to talk?" Luis snarled, before shouting at the creature. "Then let it say its final words!"

The creature tilted its head at Luis as though in confusion before opening its mouth again. Morgan's hands rushed to the sides of her head, but this time the language came out softer, though still harsh, as though spoken through a dessicated husk rather than a living throat.

"Satadhhab. 'Atruk ardy litataeifan watukhrib," the creature stated, stepping forward.

As it did, Morgan saw that the rest of its body looked very much like its face. Matted fur and rotting flesh hung from a cracked and hideous skeleton. As it set a hoof down on the surface of the river, Morgan watched as the water seemed to shudder and turn black, icing over and solidifying under the beast, somehow supporting its weight.

Morgan felt her stomach roll as it did. Whatever this being was, it was an enemy of nature, twisting it into the image of this creature's sickening machinations. Its very touch was poison to the earth.

"Lee," Morgan heard Luis say. "Do you recognize this language?"

Lee shook his head. "I feel it is native to this world, and thus our languages do not translate."

"Very well," Luis said, turning back to the creature. "Speak clear, beast! What is it you want, so we can deny you and send you back to the realm of the dead where you belong!"

"Ah..." the beast gave in answer. Morgan suddenly knew that it could understand, and her fear redoubled. Whatever this was, it was not something Luis should be egging on. "So you are not a knight of the white god. That would have made this easier."

"It speaks English," Smithers spat in a harsh whisper. "Zombie deer speaks English!"

"Among other things," Lee said quietly. "Now hush."

"Elk," Morgan corrected, her mind latching on to the one thing she could focus on as fear made her innards turn to icy liquid in her gut.

"What?" Smithers asked, his voice getting higher and shriller.

"It's a zombie elk, not deer," Morgan said, getting shakily to her feet. "But it's not even that. It's something else entirely."

"Can we revisit the hush?" Lee asked.

"I shall speak my decree once again. Thrice I have said it, so shall it be," the rasping voice of the elk continued, the force of its words cutting through their conversation and driving them to silence. Morgan felt the air around her shift with a power that was tied to nature, but not in any way she recognized. It was wrong, everything about it was wrong.

"You will go," the Elk commanded. "Leave my land to rot and ruin."

Morgan suddenly felt very agreeable with this plan. This world they had found themselves in was already ruined and rotting. What more could this horrific creature do that was not already being done? Perhaps it was one of the spirits of nature in this world, twisted and deformed by the mistreatment of the humans who lived here. Maybe it was a figure of divine retribution. Maybe they should walk away and come at this again when they knew what they were dealing with.

All the predators in her mind screamed that fighting something like this could only lead to harm and death, there would be no victory. Predators are not vicious killers as the farm hands and goat herders would tell. They're smart, tactical, and will go for weakened prey as a means of guaranteeing food and that they will walk away from the fight to enjoy the meal. Morgan learned long ago that when a predator feels fear, whatever caused it had earned that respect.

Only the brave or foolhardy would stand against this thing.

"No." Luis' voice came booming out from beside her, strong and clear as the peal of a bell. The knight stepped forward, his sword grasped tightly in one hand as his jacket whipped around him, the picture of righteous defiance.

Morgan looked about but saw no source of wind. Confused, she looked back and saw twinges and sparks of white energy rippling up and down Luis' body. The energy blew his loose clothing wildly around him, but she could see the steady glow of his holy symbol beneath his shirt.

Nike stood with her champion.

"I have decreed it..." the elk bellowed, but was cut off by Lee's voice.

"Your decrees fall on deaf ears, beast." Lee stepped forward to stand next to Luis. Morgan could sense the subtle magics of his god flowing through him as well, in opposition to the elk, though not as wildly as Luis'.

"We have come to put you down," Lee continued. "And we shall do just that."

"Your insults have sealed your fate, O servants of forsaken gods," the elk bellowed, rearing back onto its hind legs.

The sound of cracking ice and bellowing rage filled the air as the elk lowered its massive antlers and surged towards them.

~ 19 ~

LUIS

Luis stood shoulder to shoulder with Lee facing off against the terrible creature. As the beast bellowed, lowering its antlers to gore them both, Luis calculated every possible way to counter the blow and retaliate with one of his own. A creature of this size would be incredibly powerful in its own right, but adding in what was undoubtedly impressive metaphysical prowess on top of that meant that taking such a fell creature head-on would be a fool's errand.

Which is why he shouted out in a mixture of both horror and frustration as Timm swiftly flew past them, feet barely touching the ground as he ran out on the ice, to confront the elk while screaming a battle cry like a man possessed.

The rippling water of the river had frozen beneath the elk's feet mid-crest of what passed for waves in the sludgy flow, making it so the surface of the ice was less than smooth. Timm's feet found purchase and rebounded before he even had a chance to slip. With an angry yell, he launched a series of attacks against the creature in a flurry of kicks and punches.

A terrible noise, like the haunting call of a warbling bugle, filled the air as Timm's fists made contact with the wretched creature. Timm screamed, and at first Luis thought it was a continuation of his defiance of the creature, but was stunned to see Timm recoil in pain, pulling back his smoking fists. The aura around the beast pulsed with a sickly green energy that sent shock waves over the frozen surface of the water, sending up puffs of snow and ice. Luis could see angry red sores erupt across Timm's exposed skin with each wave of sickly energy. The young man's scream continued, his voice nearly breaking with agony. The beast swung its rack with crushing force, and the scream died in Timm's throat and the knight watched his compatriot be thrown unceremoniously across the ice, landing with a sickening crack.

Luis felt the air go still as the beast charged, rearing back to raise its hooves over Timm, threatening to crush the man and send his body into the depths of the river in a single attack. The sudden violence had shocked the knight. He knew he was honor bound to fight this creature, to save Timm, but his limbs were frozen in place as he witnessed the spectacle of awesome power the creature exhibited. The creature had barely even struck Timm, but tore through his defenses with little more than its very presence. A haunting thought crawled from the back of his mind, a blasphemous thought, but it was hard not to doubt: how could they attain victory against something that outclassed them so badly?

Lee, it would seem, had not come to the same conclusion Luis had. The priest stepped forward, waving his left hand as though striking with a hammer and his right in a downward slicing motion. Almost simultaneously, a beam of holy light came down from the heavens, striking the beast while a spectral war hammer appeared behind it, sweeping the creature's hind legs. Unable to defend against the onslaught of attacks, the elk staggered, forgoing its attack against Timm and rather splayed out its narrow legs in a desperate attempt to keep itself from falling. Its front hooves came dangerously close to trampling Timm, but without the original murderous intent to drive them down, they passed his crumpled body harmlessly.

"Not a specter," Lee called out, more to his comrades than to the beast, though it never left his gaze. "As it does have a physical form."

Luis saw the coldness in the priest's eyes. They were calculating, determined, and most importantly, unafraid. Then, from behind, he heard the clacking sound as the slide of a pistol chambering a round as Smithers stepped forward. The knight gawked in awe as he saw the old man leveling his gun, grinning like a madman.

"That was all I needed to hear," the gunslinger said, taking aim at the creature. There was a sound of thunder when the bullet erupted from the weapon. Smithers' aim was true, and Luis watched as a chunk of decaying flesh was ripped away from the creature's haunches, scattering across the ice with a wet slap and spray of gore. Despite the sickening sight, the creature barely seemed to notice the blow, its flaming red eyes fixated on Lee.

"You dare attack me, priest?" The words ran like fetid water through Luis' mind, and his stomach rolled as a chill ran through him.

"Well, now I just feel insulted," Smithers said, the barrel of his gun dipping down. "What am I? Chopped liver?"

"If you were, it may want to assimilate you," Lee responded, his eyes still burning into the creature.

"Tear the body apart and the spirit won't be able to hold," Luis told him, feeling strength returning to his arms, fear dissipating, replaced by shame. To think, he let such a creature shake his faith not only in his goddess' will, but also in his own capacity to claim victory. He needed to atone for such weakness, and Nike only accepted one sort of absolution. Bringing his sword to bare, Luis grit his teeth and prepared to face his foe, his fate, and even his death.

"What?" Smithers asked, cocking an eyebrow at Luis, clearly not grasping the nuances of the creature's power or what held it to this world.

Before the knight had a chance to clarify, the beast charged forward, completely ignoring Timm's limp form and bearing down on Lee. It swept its antlers at the priest, who braced himself for the impact, but the force of the blow was too much. A spray of blood arched over the ice and Lee cried out in pain as he was thrown sideways from the force. Even from this distance, Luis could see the edges of the gash on Lee's arm turn black from the terror's touch.

Luis snarled in frustration and began to charge forward to impose himself between the monster and Lee. He only had enough time to yell the most basic explanation over his shoulder at Smithers, who could hopefully understand the simplest of directions.

"Just keep hitting it until it dies!"

"Oh," Smithers responded, perking up and grinning as he aimed his pistol again. "That I can do."

Luis ran forward, his sword raised, hoping that Smithers actually understood but not bothering to confirm. Instead, he moved in to take the creature's left flank and draw any further attacks away from Lee while keeping Timm out of its sights. He was forced to skid to a halt as his position was overtaken by a blur of snowy white fur that came barreling past him snarling in rage.

Morgan had taken the form of a massive shaggy cat, as tall at the shoulder as Luis' head, fur white as the driven snow speckled with flecks of grey so that should she be sitting still it would be nigh impossible to tell the difference between her and a snowy rock. She was most definitely not sitting still now. Luis watched her lithe body dart in and swipe out with a paw as large as his torso, sending meat and gore spraying across the ice in what felt to the knight to be an act of retribution for its attack on Lee.

It was a mighty hit, and Luis nearly cried out a cheer before joining his friends in combat, when something caught his eye that twisted his guts. Tufts of thick white fur begin to fall from Morgan's cat form. The freshly exposed skin bubbled, blistering from the very proximity of the horrific beast, turning an angry red and noxious green before beginning to blacken around the edges.

Luis realized that simple brute force would not be enough for victory. His allies were in peril, and another rash attack would do less to save them than proper planning. Nike wasn't ashamed of him for staying his blade, she had been forcing him to wait, to study, and to react properly. To ignore her subtle warnings and barrel in head first would be what brought him true shame in her eyes. Reaching up, he clutched his holy symbol rather than his sword, and began to whisper a prayer.

"Luis! Don't just stand there with your sword up your ass!" Smithers called out from behind him between the barking of his pistol. "Do something!"

"I am!" the knight snarled back, doing his best to focus on his faith rather than his irritation. Finishing his prayer, Luis released the power he had called for and been blessed with. A flickering radiant light flew from his outstretched hand, curling out in trails of sparks like three separate swarms of fireflies flying out enveloping Lee, Morgan, and Smithers in their flickering light.

"The fuck!" Smithers cried out, swatting at the motes of light, at least seeming to have the good sense for once to not shoot at them.

"A blessing from Nike," Luis said to Smithers, grinning at the old man's obvious discomfort. "I am a conduit of her power, and now, so are you. For the time being."

Smithers looked back at Luis for a moment, clearly not really understanding what was being said to him, but then just shrugged and returned the knight's grin.

"Works for me," he said, leveling his pistol at the creature again and letting off another round into the creature's side, sending bits of gore and bone out the other side of its body in a spray of ichor and shrapnel. "I'll just assume y'all know what ch'er doing and stick to 'hit it til it dies'."

The beast bellowed and turned to face off against the large cat that had carved away enough meat to expose more cracked bone beneath, swinging its rack again in an attempt to rend her flesh from her bones. Morgan narrowly dodged out of the way as Lee mimed the swinging of a hammer to drive his spectral weapon down at the creature, though the bulk and narrow legs were misleading. The creature managed to dodge out of the way of the spectral blow, then wailed out a throaty bugle call of challenge and Luis felt a ripple of nausea pass through his body as its aura extended out. Lee dropped to his knees and wretched, his long white hair cascading in front of his face to veil the sight of him losing whatever was left of their earlier meal.

Luis was forced to drive his sword into the muck of the riverbank in order to keep his balance, but managed to fight back the urge to void his own stomach. There was a sickening splashing sound from behind him as Smithers followed in Lee's suit, vomiting across the ice. The large cat made a sound that reminded Luis of when his old barn cat would get a hairball, but on a much grander, and more nauseating, scale.

Morgan shook out her coat angrily, looking larger as all of her fur stood on end. She turned her yellow eyes against the elk, letting out a yowl that sounded more like a human scream than anything that should come from a cat. Fueled by rage and defiance, Morgan lunged forward, sailing through the air in a devastating pounce, and drove her fangs into the creature's side.

It was at that moment that Morgan's constitution broke. She pulled back, gagging and staggering in a fruitless attempt to keep on her four feet. Luis could see red sores sprouting across her tongue and chops. Bile fell from her mouth in thick strands and pooled around her paws as she fought to regain her footing.

Realizing that the fight was not going their way in the slightest, even with Nike's blessing aiding them, Luis ran forward to lend his sword and not just his magic. He could feel his skin blister and burn as he came within an arm's length of the creature. Roaring in both pain and defiance, Luis raised his sword high, and forced his body to ignore the pain. He drove the blade down, carving deep through flesh and bone. The blade stuck fast in the creature's side as it turned to look at the knight.

"I'm not impressed with your feeble demonstrations, knight," the beast said, eyes mocking him.

"Prepare to be," Luis said, his voice coming out a quiet calm. Then, with a scream of defiance he channeled the power of his goddess through his blade, sending forth a pulse of white hot holy flame deep into the creature's body.

While the blade itself did not garner much of a reaction from the elk, the touch of the divine drove it mad with fury. It bucked, forcing Luis to reach out with his left hand to grip the blade and draw it free before the massive beast could rip it away from him. The searing wound bubbled with blisters and white fire where Luis had struck it, much like how Luis' own skin was blistering from the creature's aura. In the back of his mind, Luis wondered what terrible power this creature had that could affect mortals the same way the divine could affect the undead, but he pushed the thought back and vowed to consider it further after they had survived this initial encounter.

The beast turned its full attention to Luis, poised to attack, but as it reared back to strike, another beam of white light streaked down from the sky and enveloped it in holy flame. As it screamed, the spectral hammer drove down at its head, cracking one of its massive antlers with a sound that reminded Luis of lightning striking a tree, sending the shattered appendage scattering across the ice, still wreathed in white flame.

"Your power is impressive, abomination," Lee said, getting to his feet and wiping the back of his hand across his mouth, drawing a smear of blackened blood across his chin as more dribbled from between his lips. "But it is nothing compared to ours."

Luis grinned at the priest's persistence. Turning to face the creature again, he knew that with the power of both Priest of

Goibniu and Knight of Nike working in tandem, this abomination wouldn't stand a chance. With a new vigor pulsing through his veins, Luis lifted his sword into a defensive stance and began to circle the creature, trying to position himself so that they were flanking it, leaving no hope of escape.

As it turned out, he needn't have bothered, as the final blow was not destined to be his or Lee's to claim. The sound of heavy boots grinding ice and snow under their uneven treads reached Luis' ear moments before Smither's voice did.

"I'm sorry," Smithers said as he stepped into the knight's peripheral vision, one shaky hand raising his pistol level with the elk's head. "We didn't even get your name. How rude of me not to ask. So, would you kindly tell me..."

Smithers' face twisted into a furious expression that looked nothing like the usual curmudgeon he normally was. It took a moment for Luis to realize the difference. This time, he realized, the expression was twisted with hate.

"Who the fuck do you think you are?" The old man snarled as he pulled the trigger, the barrel of his weapon suddenly stabilizing to a perfect stillness, precision sharpened along with his focus.

Sparks of radiant energy flickered around the barrel of the gun as Nike's blessing enveloped the weapon and the warrior that held it. A deafening crack split the air as the bullet careened from the gun, a tail of brilliant white light emanating off of it like a comet. The corona lit up the night with the radiance of a small sun, until that sun suddenly set, winking out of existence as it penetrated the bone directly between the creature's flaming eyes.

The creature did not buck or roar this time. It stood very still, and for a long moment, Luis feared that Smithers' attack had done nothing. Slowly, however, the creature's flesh began to slough off of its bones, falling with wet, meaty slaps against the ice below. Ichor ran like small rivers from its body and bone began to crumble to dust. A back leg gave out, crumbling the form. The eyes, however, never left Smithers.

"You ask my name, mortal?" The voice came calm and steady, without fear or anger this time. "I am Nergal, though merely an aspect of him in this mortal flesh. You have not killed me, mortal. Know this, and know that you have earned my ire. This land is mine, and I shall reclaim it."

With those words, the skull crumbled to dust and the green glow vanished, leaving them in the silent, fae light of the early winter morning. Luis stared at the spot where the aspect claiming to be something called Nergal had stood, and mulled over the possibilities. He was unsure of what they were facing, but there were few such creatures who held power on this scale. He turned to ask Lee his opinion when he felt the ice shift and crack under his feet.

"Move!" the knight cried out, turning to dart for the shoreline. "Without the creature there's nothing sustaining the ice!"

As Luis ran, he looked over his shoulder and was glad to see Lee hot on his tail, but then a horrible thought nearly stopped his retreat as he turned to where Timm's limp form lay sprawled on the ice. He started to turn back, but before he could, Lee reached out and shoved him forward as the ice beneath them gave out. They landed on the muddy shoreline in a tumbled heap.

Scrambling to his feet, Luis prepared to dive into the water to grab Timm, but was once again thwarted as Lee grabbed his arm and pointed.

"Look!"

Luis did, and saw Morgan, her cat form gracefully leaping from ice floe to ice floe, her delicate paws leaving little impact on the ice in spite of her massive size. With the precision of a mother cat collecting her young, she snapped the back of Timm's coat with her powerful jaws, and gingerly lifted him. A moment later, she was depositing him in the mud next to the rest of them.

"So, did we win?" Smithers asked, his gun lowered but not holstered just yet. "Because it doesn't really feel like we won."

"This Aspect of Nergal was little more than a meat puppet," Lee stated, getting to his feet. "Literally. I can assure you that we have not seen the last of this Nergal."

"Who is Nergal?" Luis asked, cleaning his blade as best he could before sheathing it. There was nothing he currently had on him that was free of muck or blood, so he would have to do a better job when they returned to the church tonight.

"Doesn't sound familiar to me," Lee said, shaking his head.

"Sounds like something out of a cartoon my kids used to watch," Smithers said, scratching at the stubble on the side of his face. "Though they're probably not the same guy."

"Guys, we can research it tomorrow," Morgan said. Luis looked over and saw her kneeling beside Timm, no longer in her massive cat form. "Timm is hurt. I'm going to heal him, then we should probably get back to the church. We made a lot of noise."

"Shit," Smithers said, looking around and quickly holstering his gun. "Gonna be hard to hide this."

"Not really," Lee stated, pointing at the river.

Luis looked up and saw the ice floes breaking down and floating down the river. Along with them went the blood, ichor, and bits of rotted animal meat that were any evidence that a battle had taken place at all.

"Seems like we're in the clear," Luis said, smiling.

"I'm going to police my brass anyway," Smithers said, walking away and looking very hard at the ground. Luis was going to ask the old man what that meant, but his attention was drawn away as a flash of white light flickered in the corner of his eye.

He turned to see Morgan removing her hands from Timm's chest as the young man took a deep breath in. Suddenly, his eyes flashed open and he swung upward with a fist, narrowly missing Morgan's jaw as she threw herself back and out of the way. Timm looked around wildly, as though seeking an enemy, then turned and finally recognized Morgan. What he had just done dawned on him, and before any of them could say a word, the man leapt to his feet and darted off into the night.

They all stood in silence for a moment, watching Timm vanish into the trees. The quiet hung in the air for a moment longer before Smithers broke it.

"Again, I ask: did we win?"

When they returned to the church, Luis noted that the van was sitting in the parking lot. It did not look exactly good as new, but the bullet holes were gone and apparently it ran well enough that it could be transported here. Taking a leap in logic, Luis assumed that Father Mitchell would have returned as well, but as the rosy fingers of dawn were beginning to stretch across the sky, he felt it was best to allow the priest time to sleep and come to terms with the past few days rather than pile more onto his already overladen plate.

Upon heading downstairs to their bunks, they all quietly noticed that Timm's was still empty. They looked at each other for a moment before Smithers let out a sigh and began to bed down for some sleep. Luis pursed his lips, unsure of how he felt about leaving one of their own to fend for themselves, but they were tired, injured, and Timm had left of his own accord. Luis decided it was best to clean up and rest, and allow Timm the time he needed to sort out his own personal demons. Those were the only ones that even a knight of Nike could not fight for others.

Slipping into the men's bathroom, Luis entered probably his favorite thing about this new world he found himself in. While submerging oneself into a tub of near boiling water did wonders to soothe the ache and stiffness of overworked muscles, the ability to shower oneself with water at a temperature you control with the turn of a dial was far more convenient. For a short while, he simply allowed the hot water to pound down on his neck and back, loosening the muscles that had become so tense over the past few years.

After a few minutes of that, he took the soap and began to lather up, removing all remnants of the river muck and undead ichor that clung to him. As the black and brown washed away from his skin, he saw the violent red markings that covered his body. It seemed neither armor nor clothing had done anything to protect him from exposure to the assault.

"Very well," he sighed to himself, wincing as he placed his fingers on the rash on his arm. "I suppose I'll need to take care of this if I wish to have anything resembling restful sleep tonight."

With a flash of holy light, Luis reached for Nike's blessing to remove this ailment from his flesh. The pain of it vanished, and smiling, Luis opened his eyes to examine his healed flesh.

Except it wasn't healed.

The hateful red rash had dulled in some ways, but was by no means gone. Panicked, Luis began to examine the rest of his body. The blisters were for the most part tamed, but still present, and the red markings were still prevalent over most of his body. Any pain he had been feeling due to them was gone, but Luis felt worry creep into his mind. If the power of his goddess could not remove the ill effects of Nergal's presence...

"What was he?" Luis asked the running water quietly.

~ 20 ~

TIMM

Timm sat in the chapel of the Cathedral of the Holy Cross staring up at the altar. It was currently bare as no one would be using it anytime soon. Father Mitchell said he would be having services in the main church later that day and the next, and that the chapel was reserved for smaller gatherings. He would be able to be alone with his thoughts here for a while yet.

Most of his thoughts were currently angry. Some of it was directed at that being from last night, but most of them were pointed squarely at himself. He had been useless. Worse than useless. A liability. He'd contributed nothing to the fight last night, and hadn't even been there for the one earlier the previous morning. On top of that, he'd allowed himself to be baited close and taken down before the fight had even begun. The others were forced to protect his unconscious body rather than handle the threat.

He slammed his fist down on the pew in front of him and fought against the stinging tears that threatened to cloud his eyes.

It is a weak man who allows his emotions to control him rather than the other way around, his master's words echoed in his head. Timm took a deep breath and began to meditate on his lessons, on his master's teachings, and on the techniques his master had taught him to push past pain, both emotional and physical until he could fight unhindered by the handicaps of his limitations.

"Timm?" Morgan's voice called out softly into the chapel.

Timm nearly choked as he felt the barriers being built between his mind and his emotions crumble instantly. Hurriedly, he tried to force them back up before she realized he'd noticed her.

"Timm, oh good, there you are," he heard her say as her footsteps approached him.

As quickly as he could, Timm settled the mental blocks up and turned to face her, trying to put on a smile.

"Oh, hi Morgan," he said, voice cracking slightly. He cleared his throat and tried to play it off. "Are you feeling alright?"

"Better now that I know you're not dead in a ditch somewhere," Morgan said, smiling at him, though there was a slight edge to her voice that he couldn't recognize. Also, he could tell that there was something more in her expression beyond the relief she was claiming. Was it pity? Fear? Timm couldn't tell, but he knew he didn't like it, and his mind was working overtime trying to fill in the blanks.

"We were worried," she continued, either not noticing his discomfort or disregarding it. "Last night you were really hurt, and then for you to just run off like that, we were scared that you were confused or something. That you might run into trouble and we wouldn't be able to help you."

Timm felt a wave of guilt wash over him. He wasn't confused last night, he was ashamed. When she had pulled him from the darkness that surrounded him, Timm had panicked, still thinking he was in battle, and allowed his emotions to drive him. It was out of fear that he lashed out and had almost struck her. Morgan. The woman he...

Timm's eyes flashed up to meet hers.

"I was..." Timm started to say, unsure of where the sentence was going. He clawed at his mind, trying to think of something, anything he could tell her that would explain what had happened without having to tell her the truth. The word came out of his mouth before he even had a chance to consider the lie. "Meditating!"

Well, it was only a half lie, he supposed. He had spent the morning meditating on his failures after wandering the night hating himself for them. It was a form of progress, though one he was not particularly proud of.

"Okay," Morgan said, nodding. "That's good at least. Did you come across any good insights?"

"That I'm an idiot," Timm said, gloomily, before the good sense to avoid self depreciation took hold of him again.

Morgan rolled her eyes and punched him lightly in the shoulder.

"You're not an idiot, idiot," she said, smiling at him, but he couldn't bring himself to match it.

"I didn't wake up in time this morning, leaving you guys alone against the Brotherhood," Timm countered her argument, listing off his most recent failures. "And against that elk thing? I didn't even get to fight. It took me down immediately."

"Nergal," Morgan said.

"What?" Timm asked.

"The elk thing? Its name was Nergal," Morgan explained. "Well actually, it was only an aspect of Nergal, so think a puppet he could experience the world through, so probably not that strong compared to the real thing."

"Great," Timm said, mournfully, dropping his hands heavily into his lap. "That makes me feel so much better."

"You're missing the point," Morgan said, sitting down next to him. Timm felt his heartbeat skyrocket as she got closer. "Did you know we were going to get attacked by the Brotherhood?"

"No," Timm said, turning his face away so she couldn't see how red he was getting.

"No," she echoed, her voice soft and soothing. "Just like we had no idea they were going to attack you in the hospital. How do you think we felt about you being there without us, forced to stand against them on your own? You fought off two by yourself, all while protecting a child. Luis and I took on two together, and so did Smithers and Lee. You did better than all of us."

Timm contemplated that for a moment. It was true, he had been so worried about not pulling his weight in that fight that he'd forgotten that he'd had his own encounter with the Brotherhood on his own as well. He shook his head.

"That doesn't excuse not being there..." he started to say.

"But it does show that it can happen," Morgan said, her voice still soft, but more forceful now. She placed her hand reassuringly on his arm sending shocks of electric energy through his skin, causing him to tense up.

"As for the fight last night," she continued, seeming not to notice his reaction. "You dove in bravely, it wasn't your fault he was more powerful than we expected. At least you didn't freeze up in fear like I did."

Timm looked up at her and saw his own shame mirrored back at him. She wouldn't meet his gaze, but became extremely interested in her shoes, staring down at them as her face burned red with embarrassment.

"If Luis hadn't shouted out, that thing may have attacked me before I even knew what was happening," Morgan said, still not looking at him. "It could have gored me down because I froze. At least you tried. At least you went down swinging. If you hadn't, I would have gone down as a coward."

"You're not a coward," Timm said before his brain had a chance to stop his mouth. He bit back his words for a moment, then realized it would be worse not to continue. "You saved me, brought me back. You fought it, and you guys won."

"Well, the others did most of the heavy lifting on that one," Morgan said with a wry grin.

"You contributed," Timm said, refusing her deflection. "Without you it may have gotten more of us before they did put it down."

"You're right," Morgan said, contemplating his words. "Without us it may have taken more down before it got put down."

Timm realized what she had done mere seconds after she said it. He couldn't help but laugh a little. In making him defend her contributions, she forced him to admit the value of his own. He looked at her, smiling sweetly at him, green eyes sparkling as she watched him put the pieces together.

"Clever," he said to her, unable to keep from grinning. "Very clever."

"I'm smart in my own way," Morgan said, as she stood up. "If you're quite done meditating, we're going to go talk to Father Mitchell."

"About what?" Timm asked, as he shimmied sideways out of the pew. He didn't understand why they were packed so tightly together. It seemed almost as if this religion was designed to make people as physically uncomfortable as possible.

"Well, those of us that got close to Nergal last night wound up with a pretty bad rash," Morgan explained. "Luis and Lee tried everything in their arsenal to remove it magically, and while magical healing did wonders to remove the pain, the rash didn't seem affected at all."

Timm paused and looked down at the back of his hands. They had been a bit raw and itchy all morning, but as he was forcing the physical pain away, they'd dulled and became background noise in his mind. Slowly, he began lowering one barrier after the next until he could feel them itching and burning under the sleeves of his coat.

"Uh-oh," Timm said, as he reached down and rolled back his sleeves slightly. There on his arm was a red rash covered in blisters as though his skin had been cooked from the inside out.

"Damn!" Morgan swore and she turned and saw what he was looking at. Timm attempted to cover up his arms, but Morgan was on him in a flash. "Let me see, move your hand!"

Knowing better than to fight with her, Timm drew back his hand and removed his coat so Morgan could get a better look at the wounds. She worked gingerly, examining his arms and hands, muttering something to herself in a language that Timm did not understand, but sounded to him more like animal noises than actual words. At one point, Timm was actually grateful that he had the rash, because as she lifted his shirt Timm flushed so deeply that it was the only thing keeping her from recognizing his reaction.

"Okay, I'm going to give you some healing magic," Morgan said, closing her eyes and drawing in on the power of nature.

"That's not necessary," Timm said, fixing his shirt. "I can handle it. I don't even feel it."

"Wounds don't need to be felt to do harm," Morgan said as she stepped forward and slid her glowing hands up the front of Timm's shirt, pressing them against his bare skin.

The flow of healing magic rushed through him, and Timm watched in amazement as the blisters on his arms began to shrink, and the angry red sores died down to a mild rash. The pain ebbed away as well, though even through the barriers Timm was hastily trying to rebuild, he could feel the remnants of pain the rash brought with it.

He looked down to thank Morgan and suddenly realized just how close she was. How her body was pressed against his. His heart began to race wildly as she looked up at him, her gaze meeting his for a moment. Like a magnetic pull, Timm felt himself being drawn down to her.

She stepped back and the pull was broken.

"There," she said, dusting her hands off. "How do you feel?"

"Um..." Timm looked at her then down at himself. "Better? I think?"

"Good," Morgan smiled at him. "Then we're meeting upstairs in the canteen. Come on!"

Timm watched her bound through the door and swallowed hard. His throat felt tight and his heart refused to slow. He had never felt anything like what was currently flooding his senses, but it was warm, and wonderful, and terrifying.

It is a weak man who allows his emotions to control him rather than the other way around.

"Oh shut up," Timm muttered, grabbing his coat and throwing it on as he made his way to the chapel door.

~ 21 ~

LEE

"The magic didn't work?" Father Mitchell asked, sounding both shocked and, if Lee didn't know any better, a bit relieved.

"It did not," Lee responded, showing the red sores on his arm to the priest across from him. "The pain has been reduced, as has the swelling and blisters, but the rash remains, as well as a few sores, though nothing as bad as before."

"You'll excuse me if I'm a bit shocked," Father Mitchell said, examining the wounds on Lee's arm. "It's just, after you cured cancer with a touch I'm surprised at anything that you're incapable of fixing with magic."

"Magic is a tool," Luis said from where he was leaning against the counter. In spite of the warmth of the room, he wore his jacket. Lee assumed he was hiding his own sores. "Like a blade or a gun, I suppose. It has its purpose, but it is not designed to fix all your problems."

"I see," Father Mitchell said, pursing his lips. Lee could tell that he was attempting to make sense of what they were telling him and try to fit it into his world view as they went.

Lee needed to remind himself that Father Mitchell was thrown into this world without his consent, and finding its limits should both be comforting and terrifying to him. He was simultaneously watching people with what he deemed to be 'god-like' powers fixing problems he was powerless to stop, and watching them run

173

into problems he could never conceive of that they are incapable of dealing with. It made sense that he would feel relief watching all of them be humbled by something of his world.

"So what do you recommend?" Lee asked the priest.

"Well, I'd tell you what I'd tell any of my flock who came in here with a medical condition they didn't understand," Father Mitchell responded. "You need to go to the right professional. I'm a priest, not a doctor."

"Dammit, Jim!" Smithers exclaimed from behind his coffee cup.

Lee cocked his eyebrow at Smithers before turning to Father Mitchell. "I thought your first name was Franklin?"

"It is," Father Mitchell glowered at Smithers. "Could you refrain from making pop culture references in front of them? Especially if you haven't had the decency of showing them *Star Trek* yet."

"Nope," Smithers responded smugly.

Father Mitchell sighed. "Anyway, there are a few free clinics I can recommend, though you may have a hell of a wait on Saturday."

"Then we won't go on Saturday," Luis responded.

"Uh... today is Saturday," Father Mitchell replied. "And you probably don't want to put this off."

"Put what off?" Morgan asked as she and Timm entered the room.

"Oh, Timm, good," Father Mitchell said, seeming to be happy for the change in subject. "We were worried about you. I'm glad to see you're doing alright."

"Thanks," Timm said, nodding. Lee could tell there was something off about the boy, but nothing that appeared to be more life threatening than their current predicament, so he made a mental note to look into more later.

"We were discussing options," Lee said, bringing the conversation back on point. "Taking care of this rash should be paramount, but beyond that we need answers."

"Like, who is Nergal?" Timm practically growled.

"I'd like to know as well," Luis nodded. He turned to face Father Mitchell. "Have you heard of this being before?"

Father Mitchell shook his head. "I don't believe he appears in any holy or history texts from my studies. What do you know about him?"

"He's an asshole," Smithers chimed in from across the room.

"Helpful information, Smithers," Father Mitchell called back. "Limit yourself to providing *helpful* information."

"We don't know much," Lee interjected. "He is a powerful being, probably very old from the way he had to try three different languages to find one we had in common."

"That is disconcerting," Father Mitchell nodded. "Did you recognize any of the ones he spoke to you?"

Lee shook his head. "They weren't from our world, so that means that it must be a language from yours."

"Which makes him a being from ours as well," Father Mitchell nodded. "Or at least shared, like in the case of your goddess."

Father Mitchell gestured to Luis who nodded.

"Does that mean this being could be a god?" Luis asked

Father Mitchell laughed quietly. "There was a time I'd have answered your question by saying 'there's only one true God,' however it seems I've been proven wrong in that facet."

"How are you doing with that?" Lee asked as delicately as he could, knowing full well the weight of his question and the crisis of faith he was sure Father Mitchell was struggling with. .

"I'm... processing," Father Mitchell said, smiling. "It's a lot to take in, though I suppose there's a necessary level of respect and acceptance that must come along with worlds colliding as they are."

"This is true," Lee agreed, glad to see that, at least on the surface, Father Mitchell was coping.

"If worlds are colliding, then maybe we should go talk to Arbuckle!" Morgan suggested, excitedly as the idea struck her. Lee watched Father Mitchell tense up at the sound of the professor's name.

"Last time we did that, we got shot at," Luis noted.

"Oh," Morgan said, slightly deflated. "Right."

"Plus, he wouldn't be there today," Smithers said. "For the second time, it's Saturday."

"What does that have to do with anything?" Luis asked.

"For one thing, no school on Saturday," Smithers said. "For another, it's a day off for a lot of people. Not all, but a lot of people."

"So when will we be able to talk to him, do you think?" Timm asked.

Smithers pondered the question for a moment. "Oh, if he's like a normal teacher, couple days."

"A couple days?" Luis practically spat.

"Yeah, and that's if he teaches a class on Monday," Smithers nodded. "Some professors only have certain days on and off, so could be longer."

"We don't have that kind of time," Luis snarled. "Nergal could be coming for us now for all we know."

"I doubt he'd be able to reform that quickly. Most creatures from other planes of existence require several days to weeks to reform a usable body on the material plane," Lee refuted the idea, but then decided that diplomacy was the best course of action for now, as Luis still seemed eager for battle and the priest wanted it to be with the enemy rather than with himself. "However, I do agree with you, Luis. The quicker we get information we need, the better off we'll be. Is there another option that we can explore to gain the information we seek?"

"I mean, I could still give Arbuckle a call," Smithers said. "But there's no guarantee that he'll get back to us any time soon. All I have is his office number... wait..."

Morgan cocked her head to the side and looked at Smithers questioningly. Lee was strongly reminded of the hounds they trained at the temple.

"What is it, Smithers?" she asked.

"That kid, the one with the wheels. What was his name?"

"Damian?" Morgan answered quickly. Lee saw her face flush slightly but brushed it off.

"No, the other one," Smithers said. "The brother... Simon! That was his name. Maybe he'd know something."

"Why would he know anything?" Luis asked.

"Because he studied under Arbuckle," Lee said, remembering the conversation they had. "Good memory, Smithers."

"At my age, that's not a compliment you hear often," Smithers grinned, and nodded his thanks.

"So we have two options laid out before us," Lee explained. "We need to find out more about this ailment that plagues us. The clinic would be our best source for information for that. However, we also need to learn more about Nergal and his intentions. Simon may be able to give us a lead there. Where should we begin?"

"Two birds, one stone?" Smithers asked, shrugging. "A couple of you with the rash go to the clinic while the rest of us go see Simon? He told us that a large crowd at his front door would be an issue anyway."

"I do not feel comfortable moving separately in this city," Luis said, bluntly. "We were looking for trouble last night, this is true. But now trouble is hunting us."

"And we're weakened," Morgan added. "Injured. A predator would know which group to try and pick off first."

Smithers looked displeased by the consensus, but nodded.

"Fine, all for one and one for all instead of divide and conquer," the old man nodded. "But we're going to have to move smart. Can't have all five of us bunched up on the sidewalk. We'll look like a freaking parade."

"I'll get my things," Luis said. He left the room and Lee could hear him clomping down the stairs as he went.

"I should clean up a bit too," Timm said, rushing after him.

"Well then," Father Mitchell said, standing up. "It seems you have a plan of action. I need to prepare for services tomorrow. I'll see you all there, correct?"

"Uh, well Father, ya see..." Smithers started to say.

"Of course, Father Mitchell," Morgan said, cutting him off. "After all you've done for us, it's only fair we're there for you."

Father Mitchell smiled at her. "Thank you, Morgan. I look forward to seeing all of your faces out in the church at eight a.m. sharp. Oh, and be sure to wear something appropriate. Particularly Timm. Can't have him sitting there in a torn and bloodied shirt, can we?"

With that, Father Mitchell left the room. Lee could feel the air cooling as Smithers glowered at the girl.

"Really, girl?" Smithers muttered darkly. "Not enough you take my sleep during the week, but now you're dragging me to church."

"You're already in the church," Lee pointed out.

Smithers stood up, refilled his coffee, and started walking towards the door.

"I don't need to take this..." he continued muttering as he walked out. "I'm a *recovering* catholic..."

Morgan and Lee watched him leave, and it was all the priest could do to keep from laughing. Morgan, however, turned and Lee could see that her expression was confused and a little hurt.

"Did I say something wrong?" she asked, her voice heavy with worry.

Lee smiled at her. "Not at all. Now, let's go prepare to see Simon and Damian."

He watched in amusement as the worry melted away from her expression. As she ran off to get ready, Lee reflected on how it seemed that just the mere mention of the boy's name would make her face light up and her worries disappear.

"Ah," Lee mused. "At least there are still some simple pleasures in this world. Perhaps those will be the things that save us in the end."

~ 22 ~

MORGAN

Morgan was humming happily to herself as she moved along down the street. She and Timm were walking together about fifteen feet or so behind Smithers and Luis. Lee was hanging back behind the rest of them on his own, keeping an eye on their tail as he put it. As they made their way towards the old warehouse where Simon and Damian set up their garage, Morgan could feel her heart racing quicker and quicker. She wasn't quite sure what was causing this reaction in her, but she knew that it was both scary and wonderful.

For the third time in their walk, Timm drifted so close to her that she accidentally bumped him. His eyes were glazed over as he stared at a point in the distance, but never seemed to focus on anything in particular. As they collided briefly, Morgan saw him shake his head slightly, as if suddenly realizing where he was for the first time.

"Ooh, sorry about that," Morgan said, gently side stepping and giving him more room on the sidewalk. "Again. That seems to keep happening. You seem to be zoning out a bit today, are you okay?"

"Huh?" Timm asked, and Morgan gave him a moment to process her words. "Oh, yeah. Just have a lot on my mind."

"I suppose we all do," Morgan said, shrugging. "The Brotherhood, DIARD, now that thing in the park. The way Smithers was talking when we first got here, you'd think there was nothing magical about this world. Just normal people living normal lives."

"My normal life was training on a mountain," Timm offered, shrugging. "Normal is subjective."

Morgan thought about that for a moment. "Huh, I suppose you make a fair point. Mine was picking mushrooms in a forest to make dinner for my niece and nephew."

"Sounds pretty peaceful," Timm said, almost wistfully.

"You never went to my forest," Morgan grinned, enjoying the look of concern her comment drew from Timm. She continued humming as they slipped through the gate leading to the warehouse, acting nonplussed as she reminisced on what she could from what little she remembered of her home.

As she got closer to the door, it felt like butterflies had taken up residence in her stomach. The giddiness was practically overwhelming, but she held herself back as Smithers walked up to the door and rapped his knuckles against it five times in the same rhythm Damian had the previous day.

"Wow, Smithers," she said, impressed by his skill. "How did you remember the code so easily?"

"Well," Smithers said, scratching the back of his head uncomfortably. "The word 'code' may be a bit strong there."

A metal box next to the door that Morgan had not noticed a moment ago crackled with life suddenly, and Simon's voice came out of it, though he sounded distorted.

"Two bits," he said calmly, as if in response to the rhythm of the tapping. "What are you guys doing back so soon?"

"Simon?" Morgan called out, somewhat alarmed. "Simon, are you okay? Did someone trap you in that box?"

"What?" Came Simon's confused voice in reply.

"She... she thinks you're trapped in the intercom," Smithers said with a sigh.

"Wha... okay, never mind," Simon's voice came again, this time sounding exasperated. "No point leaving you all on the doorstep. Buzzing you in."

Simon's voice cut away and was replaced with a loud buzzing noise. Smithers quickly pulled on the door, swinging it open to reveal the inside of the warehouse. Not much had changed since the previous day. The same tool boxes were strewn around, the same lights were set up, though they were currently powered off on the lower floor, and even the same cars that had been in pieces were there, with the obvious exception of Father Mitchell's van and the motorcycle Damian had been riding.

Morgan felt her heart sink slightly as she noticed its absence. She pursed her lips and followed Smithers up the catwalk stairs to where Simon was sitting, tapping away at the keyboard, his eyes flicking from one monitor to the next. It seemed like he was tracking something in particular, but Morgan couldn't make heads or tails of what it could be.

"Second verse, same as the first," Simon said, not looking away from the screens. "Why are you guys back so soon?"

"Had a couple questions that we needed answered," Smithers said, swinging his leg over a folding chair and facing Simon.

"And I was your number one choice for explanations?" Simon asked, an edge of smugness to his voice.

"Actually, you were number two," Morgan said, hoping that he understood that they weren't trying to bother him, and really made an effort to find the information elsewhere first.

"Oh," he responded, his voice sounding as though it were deflating slightly, and his expression fell as well.

"All the tact of a flaming bag of..." Smithers muttered, shaking his head at her. "You take Norman Arbuckle's paranormal studies class?"

"Oh!" Simon said, his voice perking up a bit as if that explained everything. "Can't get the prof on the phone? Yeah, he likes his weekends to himself. Private guy... or paranoid, one of the two. But yeah, I took a couple of them. One twice for the sheer hell of it."

"Twice?" Smithers asked, surprised.

"Oh yeah, not like I'm paying for it," Simon shrugged. "And he's a funny guy. Lots of really weird theories about the world. Though to be fair, the more I learn about what's going on out there, the more I'm starting to think they may not be all that weird after all."

"Right," Smithers nodded, then gestured to Morgan. "Show him your arm."

Morgan stepped forward and pulled back the sleeve on her sweatshirt, revealing the red, still slightly blistered skin. Simon looked it over and grimaced.

"Coconut oil won't fix that," he muttered and let out a low whistle. "Don't know what you think I can tell you about it. I work with computers for a few very important reasons. One of which is biologicals creep me out. You should really see a doctor about this."

"We're less concerned with what it is," Smithers explained. "And more concerned about how she got it."

"Wear a rubber next time?" Simon suggested, shaking his head and shrugging.

"Not helping," Smithers said, eyeing Simon strangely.

"Still not sure how you expect me to," Simon shot back.

Morgan wasn't sure what the back and forth was about, but she could tell in spite of the look Smithers was giving Simon, he was enjoying the conversation. It then dawned on her that Smithers had been spending all of his time recently with them. And before that, locked in a hospital. He hadn't really had an opportunity to sit and talk with someone who shared a worldly experience with him, and though Simon was far younger than he was, at least the two shared a world.

"It was caused by a being calling itself the Aspect of Nergal," Luis said, stepping forward and revealing the burns on his own arm. "Those of us that got close to it left the battle with these injuries on our skin, regardless of protection."

"It was like it was surrounded with some kind of hideous aura," Lee added. "Timm took the brunt of it and nearly died just from getting too close."

"Yikes," Simon said, looking around at them, finally pointing at Timm. "I'm guessing dude I've never met that you brought into my safe house without my permission is Timm?"

"Yep," Smithers nodded. "That's the one. Sorry about that."

"No problem," Simon shrugged, turning to Timm. "I suppose if you're fighting alongside these guys you can't be too bad, am I right?"

"I... uh... suppose not?" Timm said, seemingly confused by the question. "Should I not be here?"

"You're fine," Simon said, waving his hand. "I just like to know when new people are coming. Helps us keep a step ahead of DIARD. Now, let's see what we can find about this Nergal individual."

Morgan leaned in, excited. "Do you have some kind of scrying magic that will help you hunt him down? Or learn legends about him?"

"Eh, close enough," Simon said. "I figured I'd just Google it."

"What?" Morgan asked.

With a few quick keystrokes, Simon began reading off information he'd found about Nergal from a source he referred to as 'Wikipedia.' After the first few lines he paused, shook his head, and sighed.

"Hang on, that was Wahapedia," Simon said, rolling his eyes and sending his fingers flying across the keyboard. "Seems there's a game or two out there that like to use this guy's name. Let me pull up the real one... and... there it is. Okay, Nergal is an old Messopotamian god. And by 'old,' I mean ancient. Like thousands of years before Christianity was even a twinkle in a theologist's eye."

"So he's from a place that doesn't even exist anymore," Smithers said. "Amazing that he's still kicking."

"In our world, gods gain strength and influence from worship," Lee explained. "The more followers a god has, the more power they will gain. If the same holds true in your world it would not matter that the place of his worship is gone so long as his followers remained true to his teachings."

"Which bares the question, what are his teachings?" Luis asked.

"Hopefully not the ones from Wahapedia... Oh shit," Simon said, the joke he was making with himself died on his lips as his eyes fixed to the screen. "You all best hope he doesn't have followers who are remaining true to a damn thing he teaches, real world or the forty whatever-th millenium."

"That bad?" Smithers asked, his voice sounding tighter than usual.

"Worse," Simon nodded. "Says here, he's a god of war, fire, death, plague, and destruction. Looks like the games were historically and mythologically accurate... for once. He's been around thousands of years, and was worshiped through several cultures, not just Mesopotamian. He also shows up in Babylonian, Sumarian, and there are even references to him written in Latin, meaning people still followed him after the Romans came to power."

"What does that mean?" Luis asked.

"It means it's not like some whackos dug up some temple or something and released him," Smithers said, bitterly. "It means he's never stopped being worshiped."

"So the number of worshippers may have changed, but he's been a constant presence in this world, going completely unnoticed until now," Morgan said, following their chain of thought.

"Who says he's gone unnoticed?" Simon asked, spinning his wheelchair around to face the group. "People may have noticed in the past, but how many people do you think could stand up to him the way you guys did?"

"From the way the people of your world fight, I would not expect many," Luis said, nodding.

"Aw shit," Smithers groaned. "Did we just paint a target on our backs?"

"I think you did," Simon said, smiling at him wryly. "Though if it makes you feel any better, you're probably not the first people in history to stumble upon a cult that worships this guy. You're probably just in better shape to survive the run in. Sorry I couldn't do anything more to help."

"But you did," Morgan said, earnestly. "You helped us learn what we were going up against."

"An ancient god that time forgot is hunting you down and there is little to nothing you can do about it," Simon said, his voice somehow both amused and flat at the same time. "I don't see how knowing that something you can't stop from coming after you is coming after you could be the least bit helpful."

"It is a step in the right direction," Lee said, nodding. "It does not matter how large the step is, so long as progress is being made.".

"You always that zen about stuff?" Simon asked, looking over at Lee, his expression somewhat puzzled.

"It is better to approach a problem with a clear mind rather than one filled with woeful frustrations," Lee responded.

"Damn, it's like talking to a fortune cookie," Simon said, clearly impressed. "I wish I could approach life like that. Usually when people piss me off I just drain their bank accounts or send a hundred pizzas to their house."

Smithers turned to look at Simon, his face showing far more concern than Morgan was used to coming from him.

"Wait, what was that about bank accounts?" he asked, voice tight.

Simon shrugged. "I don't do that to everyday people, just the really wealthy ones. Specifically those who have scorned me. CEO's, hedge fund assholes, you know the kind."

"So, you and your brother, you're criminals?" Smithers asked, his tone cautious, though there was a hint of his usual humor returning.

"Hey there, pot, my name is kettle," Simon said, sarcastically. "And on that note, there's something I needed for those fake IDs you wanted me to make for you."

"Good point," Smithers said. "How can we help?"

Simon tossed a small black box to Smithers, who reached out and caught it in surprise.

"Line them up against the wall and don't touch my settings," he said, turning to the computer again. "You guys needed fake IDs, well the hard part is mostly done, but I need pictures in order to make the driver's licenses."

"So we'll be able to drive like Smithers and Father Mitchell?" Luis asked as Smithers directed him to the wall.

Simon paused for a moment, turning to study Luis.

"I need pictures in order to make the state issued IDs that in no way allow you access to a motor vehicle," Simon said without changing his tone.

"Hey!" Luis responded, incredulously.

"No," Lee said, patting him on the arm. "That's fair."

"Is there a reason we're not allowed to drive?" Morgan asked Simon as Smithers lined up the little black box in his hand. Suddenly a bright flash of light went off, startling all but the locals.

"Nah," Simon said as an image of Luis appeared on his screen. Morgan looked between the image and the real thing a few times in amazement. "It's not that you're not allowed and more you don't know how. Flying around at sixty plus miles per hour in half a ton of metal could get you killed. Or worse."

He turned to face her and waggled his eyebrows grinning. "End up in a fancy chair like mine."

"Is that what..." Morgan began to ask.

"Next!" Smithers called out, cutting her off.

Timm stepped up, looking a bit apprehensive. His eyes lingered on the image of Luis that was now on the screen as the image of Lee took its place next to that of the knight. His steps faltered and Morgan could see him eyeing the door.

"Come on, boy," Smithers said, giving Timm a small shove to get him moving again. "Back to the wall, look at me, and don't bother smiling. No one at the RMV smiles."

"Wait, what?" Timm asked, as the flash of light went off in his face. Slowly, his image appeared between Luis and Lee's.

"Jumpy aren't you?" Simon asked, moving the images around the screen. "You one of those people who thinks these things steal your soul or something?"

"They do what!" Timm shouted, a look of panic overtaking his face.

Smithers flicked his ear and Timm immediately stopped shouting.

"They don't do that. It's just an old, stupid, superstition," Smithers said, pointing at a chair. "Go sit down so I can get Morgan's picture."

Timm grumbled as he walked over to the chair Smithers had pointed at, slumping down and glowering at the screen. Morgan stepped up to the wall and noticed for the first time that the box Smithers was holding had a little glass eye in the front of it.

"Now hold still," Smithers said, and Morgan braced herself for the flash of light.

Blinking away red and purple dots that now floated in her vision, Morgan walked over to Simon's screen and saw an image of herself appear. She pursed her lips and frowned slightly, looking at her frozen reflection. The girl looking back seemed so much different than the one she remembered seeing in the surfaces of lakes and ponds. She looked older, more tired, and somehow a little sad.

"Now that's an RMV photo," Smithers said, laughing.

"Who's going to take yours, Smithers?" Morgan asked, concerned about what horrors the RMV held that would make this expression perfect for it.

"I can just take your latest one from their records," Simon said.

"Aren't those sealed?" Smithers asked.

"What's your point?" Simon asked, as an image of Smithers, albeit a younger version of him, appeared in the collection on Simon's screen.

"Fair enough," Smithers said with a shrug.

"I'll probably work on this until Damian gets back with dinner," Simon said, beginning to work feverishly on his keyboard. Morgan could even see that he was beginning to forget they were even there with the fervor he took to.

"Uh... it's only mid morning," Morgan mentioned to him. "Won't you get hungry?"

"Damian always sees to it that I get my needed one square meal a day," Simon said, pulling a yellow bag out from under his desk. "The rest are round."

"What are..." Morgan asked, as Simon pulled open the top of the bag, filling the air with the scent of salt and onion. He took out a single golden ring and offered it to her.

"Is it a chip? Is it an onion ring? Who knows!" Simon said, grabbing a handful for himself. "That's the fun of it."

Morgan watched as he shoveled the handful into his mouth, wiped the crumbs on his pants, and got back to work at his computer. She looked down at the thing he had handed her. Tentatively, she brought it up to her mouth and bit down. The flavor was overwhelming, like that time she had wondered what the salt lick her uncle hung in the forest for the deer tasted like. Coughing, she held the ring at arm's length to observe it again.

"Yeah, junk food's like that," Smithers said, taking a couple out of the bag before munching on them himself. "It's an acquired taste. Empty calories though, no real nutrition."

"Who needs nutrition when you taste this good?" Simon asked, his voice practically sing-song with what was clearly mock enthusiasm.

Morgan stepped up to the desk and rolled her wrist, muttering a few words in the language of the trees. What was nothing but air a moment before, solidified in her hand as ten perfectly round, smooth, purple berries.

"Here, try these," Morgan said, offering Simon a berry.

Simon looked at them. "I never really found fruit to be all that... filling."

She smiled at him. "You'd be surprised by them. And I feel you'll be far more productive at your work if you at least eat one."

Simon sighed. "Okay, one it is."

He took the berry and popped it in his mouth. Simon chewed for a moment, swallowed, then looked at Morgan.

"Okay, oddly enough I'm not feeling overly hungry anymore," he said.

"And you won't for the rest of the day," Morgan said, popping a berry in her own mouth. "All your needed nutrition for a whole day in one berry."

"Wow," Simon said, eyeing the second berry she'd placed on the desk. "That seems really useful."

"Yeah," Smithers said from behind her, and Morgan could sense annoyance in his voice. "Would have been *really* useful when we were living off the dollar menu."

"To be fair," Lee said, before Morgan could respond. "You didn't believe we were magic back then. So telling you would have been a moot point anyway."

Smithers opened his mouth as if to respond, then closed it again, turning towards the stairs and grumbling to himself as he descended. Morgan caught Lee's eyes and the two shared a quiet laugh.

"Thank you for your help, Simon," Luis said, giving Simon a nod before following after Smithers.

"Any time, guys," Simon answered. "Except not any time, because too much foot traffic around here may arouse suspicion. Last thing I want to do is burn this place."

"As in lose this safehouse?" Lee asked.

Simon gave him a long look before answering.

"Yes," he said flatly. "That is exactly what I mean."

Before Lee could inquire further, Simon turned back to Morgan.

"I'll save this last berry for Damian," he said, nodding his thanks to her again. "I'm sure he'd love to try it."

Morgan felt the butterflies swarming once again in her stomach.

"Oh," she said, smiling. "Thank you! I hope he likes them."

Morgan followed the others down the stairs, feeling lighter than she had in a long time. She wondered quietly to herself, if Smithers had taken her picture now, would the reflection still look as worn and tired as the one she had just seen?

~ 23 ~

LUIS

Luis stood in front of the non-descript, stone building and looked up at the bland sign that simply read: *Walk In Clinic.* The wounds on his skin were somewhat healed, but the tenderness remained, reminding him of the fear he'd felt realizing that no power they possessed could completely heal them. He grit his jaw and looked over at Lee, who stood equally as hesitant beside him.

"Why did we volunteer for this again?" Luis asked.

"Because the alternative was sending Morgan in with Smithers," Lee reminded the knight. "The sarcastic curmudgeon and the anxious woman who has, on more than one occasion, set things on fire in a panicked state."

Luis huffed out a breath, accepting the better alternative, and pulled open the door to the clinic and stepped inside. As he passed through the door, a flash of memory set every nerve in his body alight. The pristine white walls, the hum of the lights overhead, and that rancid smell of sterilizing cleaning products that stripped the air of any sense of life. Instinctively, Luis reached for his sword, but he remembered as his hand gripped empty air that Smithers had forced him to leave it with the others. He still had his friction lock in his pocket, but by then Lee had come to his side.

"It is not the same place," Lee said, quietly. "Much like the hospital, this is a place of healing. Where we started was a mockery of places like this, not an extension."

Luis nodded and slowed his breathing. He still did not like where he found himself, but he had to admit that Lee's words were true. The people of this clinic had done him no wrong and, more than likely, meant him no harm. He would need to conduct himself with more decorum in the future.

"E... excuse me?" A woman's voice nervously called from behind a counter. She was wearing an outfit similar to that of Nurse Corbit from St. Augustine's, however rather than being covered with strange cartoon monkeys, her clothing was a deep, royal maroon color. "Can I help you?"

Luis cleared his throat as he approached the desk. Despite his discomfort, he put on his winningest smile and greeted her as politely as he could.

"Good morning, ma'am. I apologize for my reaction upon entering, without boring you with details I simply have a poor history with medical institutions, I'm sure you understand how it is," Luis said, taking great care to maintain polite eye contact without being overly relaxed. He dropped his soldier's stance, and even leaned slightly against the desk.

The change in the woman's demeanor was almost instantaneous. A tension that she was carrying upon their entry dropped, and she mirrored his smile. Luis even noticed a slight ruddiness to her features as she brushed a lock of auburn hair from her face, tucking it behind one ear.

"Oh, of course," she said, a slight stammer to her voice. "A lot of people have difficulties with... medical facilities. I know they're not the most welcoming, but we try our best here."

"And your efforts are appreciated," Luis said, nodding along with her words and pushing his smile further into his eyes, causing her already ruddy face to blush a shade deeper. "Would it be possible for my friend and I to see a doctor today?"

"Right!" the woman said, probably louder than she intended, suddenly sitting bolt upright and fumbling to collect different pieces of paper and clip them to wooden squares. "Please just fill out these forms and return them to me. Then we'll have you in right away. It's pretty slow this time of day, but it will pick up soon. You guys chose a great time to come in."

"Thank you," Luis said, accepting the forms. He handed one to Lee, then followed the priest to a line of chairs against the far wall where they sat to begin filling out the forms.

The forms were pretty straight forward at first: simple name, date, location of birth, things like that. However, when it asked for something called a social security number, Luis had no idea what to put.

"I used the ID number from the DIARD tag we were given," Lee said.

"There aren't enough digits!" Luis hissed in irritation.

"Then make up a few," Lee responded calmly. "Besides, by the time your new friend realizes they're fake, we'll have seen the doctor and left."

"My new what?" Luis looked up at him to see the priest eye him, then look over at the woman behind the desk. As Luis looked over at her, he saw she was staring in his direction. When their eyes met, she jumped and seemed to busy herself with work. "Oh, you mean her."

"Yes, quite impressive," Lee said. "She was so enamored with you I doubt she'd remember much else about this visit."

"I don't see what's so impressive about it," Luis shrugged, trying to determine what an 'Insurance Provider' was, inevitably determining that it was more than likely as useless as the other items on the list, and simply put 'none.' "We were taught at the academy that words were like blades, you cannot take any wound you make with them back. Precision is always key. Do no harm, unless you intend to. Then be devastating."

"Sound advice," Lee responded, but Luis got the feeling there were further thoughts behind the casual words. He narrowed his eyes at the priest, who continued to work on his forms behind a mask of indifference.

While Lee had proven himself to be the reliable sort, Luis had always had a difficult time reading the man. He was always bundled up tight, even when he slept, never exposing skin above the wrist or below the neck. He kept his appearance prim and proper, but never ostentatious. His words were just as guarded as his appearance. Luis had spent days with the man, fought side by side with him in multiple battles, and still knew nothing about him. It was unnerving.

When they had finished the forms, they silently approached the woman behind the desk and handed them to her. She informed them the wait would not be much longer, and after a quarter of an hour or so, both were called in to speak with separate doctors.

Luis was directed to a small room decorated with a desk, stool, and bed draped in a thin layer of paper. He felt his nerves beginning to edge towards the surface again, but took deep breaths in order to calm himself. The nurse, another woman wearing maroon colored garb, directed him to sit on the edge of the paper and wait for the doctor to arrive. Another quarter of an hour passed before a short man with a balding pate entered, adjusting his glasses and reading from a folder in front of him.

"Mr. Le-hop-it-al?" he asked, with a nasally voice, and Luis' frayed nerves grew close to snapping.

"L'hopital," Luis corrected.

"Oh! It's a French name. My apologies, I took Latin in school," the little man chattered. "Thought it would be helpful becoming a doctor or lawyer, whatever it was I was going to be. People always said it wouldn't be that useful in daily life, though."

"You'd be surprised," Luis responded, evenly.

"The world is full of them," the little man piped up cheerfully. "Well, Mr. L'hopital, my name is Dr. Costanza. What brings you in here today?"

Luis rolled up his sleeves and showed the burns to the doctor. "Last night I received these burns. I applied my own medical knowledge to the wounds and garnered limited results. It was my hope that your more specific training may aid me in determining exactly what I am dealing with here."

Dr. Costanza leaned in and adjusted his glasses. He stared at the wound for a moment before rushing over to the counter and pulling a pair of gloves from a small box affixed to the wall. They were stretchy and blue, and before Luis could pull back, he was gently pulling and stretching at the skin, turning the arm he grabbed in different directions to gain a better view.

"You said you got and treated these wounds last night?" Dr. Costanza asked, his voice strained as though in disbelief.

"I did," Luis confirmed. "On both accounts."

"They look like they've been healing for weeks," the doctor looked up at Luis. The knight couldn't help but grin.

"I am *very* good at what I do," Luis said, amused by the small man's amazement.

"So it would seem," the doctor said, releasing Luis' arm. "However I'm surprised you even managed to get such a wound. Do you work for the military, Mr. L'hopital?"

"I do not," Luis responded, feeling the tension in his shoulders begin to grow. In as relaxed a manner as he could, Luis rested his hand on the pocket concealing his friction lock.

"Then I'm at a loss for how you could have contracted radiation burns like those," Dr. Costanza said, scratching the back of his head. "Looks like really bad sun poisoning, though that seems unlikely this time of year. Other than that, I'd figure a military mishap. I'm going to have to report this one in. Please sit tight, Mr. L'hopital."

"I shall do that," Luis nodded at Dr. Costanza as the small man left the room. The knight gave it a ten count before getting to his feet and opening the door.

Outside the hallway was clear. Luis stepped out into the hall and saw Dr. Costanza's small frame sitting at a desk furiously punching buttons on a device connected by a curling wire to something he held pressed to his head. It reminded Luis of the cell phone that Smithers carried, only larger and less convenient, but thankfully just as distracting. He walked down the hallway towards the exit, when another door opened, taking him by surprise.

The friction lock was in his hand and extended before the person within had a chance to step out. Luis drove the baton in a lunge but pulled back at the last second as Lee parried the blow with a low chop. The two men stared at each other for a moment.

"Radiation poisoning?" Lee asked Luis, straightening his sleeve, pulling it down before Luis could catch any details of the tattoos hidden beneath it..

"My doctor called it a radiation burn," Luis responded, easing back into a more relaxed stance, concealing the friction lock but not putting it away..

"She went off to make a call about it," Lee said. "I'm assuming yours as well?"

"Indeed," Luis nodded. "Shall we make our escape?"

"We learned all we need to here," Lee nodded, then gestured at the baton in Luis' hand. "Put that away. Your friend at the front doesn't need to see *that* baton of yours."

"Right," Luis nodded and collapsed the weapon, following Lee to the door. A thought struck him a moment later. "Wait, are you implying something? What do you mean by *this* baton? What other baton is there?"

Lee did not answer as he held the door open for Luis. The knight glowered at him for a moment and stepped through, smiling at the woman behind the desk, who returned his smile. She was unable to say anything as she was dealing with another individual who was holding his arm. Luis caught the sight of blood soaking through the man's sleeve. She had been right about things getting busier.

They stepped out onto the street and swiftly made their way back to where the others were waiting.

"What's our next move?" Luis asked.

"The library, I believe," Lee answered. "They should have information on what this 'radiation' business is all about. And perhaps further detailed accounts on Nergal and his lore. I feel we have made ourselves a much more powerful enemy than we initially intended."

"DIARD, the Brotherhood of Thorns," Luis listed off each of their newfound antagonists on his fingers. "And now Nergal. How is it that we've only been here a few days and we've managed to amass this many enemies?"

Lee smiled at him. "Couldn't be you, with that glowing personality of yours."

The priest picked up his pace, leaving Luis staring curiously at him as he walked away. The knight shook his head.

"I just *cannot* get a read on that guy," he muttered to himself before hurrying to catch up.

~ 24 ~

TIMM

As they walked into the library at Boston University, Timm stuck close to Morgan. For some reason, he was feeling more and more drawn to be by her side, and was feeling this overwhelming need to keep her safe. They followed Smithers over to the directory and watched as he perused the listings.

"Okay, so it looks like we've got a few options," he read aloud. "Now I've got a basic understanding about how radiation works, though I'll admit it may be a little clouded by the works of Mr. Stan Lee."

"Mr. Stanley who?" Morgan asked, curiously.

"You are too precious for this world," Smithers responded, smiling. "But I feel we should probably divide and conquer here. Some of us probably want to go to the science section to look up what we may need to know about radiation..."

"I will do that," Luis said, gritting his teeth angrily. Timm could see that Luis was a man with a score to settle, and he clearly wanted to know how.

"I will go with you," Lee stepped up. "A clear head will probably aid you in your research."

Smithers nodded. "Two heads are usually better than one, unless they're both dumbasses, then you just get an internet-series-turned-TV-show of guys hitting each other in the danglies."

"I..." Luis stared at Smithers for a moment. "I don't know how to respond to that."

"Then instead, let's go research radiation," Lee said, referencing the directory then walking off. After a beat, Luis followed after him, not seeming entirely sure of what just happened.

"You two want to take Nergal?" Smithers asked.

Timm felt his fists clench in anger as he remembered how easily the Aspect of the hideous god had felled him. His chest felt as though it were going to burst, and a tingle of heat dripped down his arms, pooling in his hands.

"More than anything," Timm practically snarled.

He looked up and realized both Morgan and Smithers were staring at him strangely. They broke away, trading a glance with each other before looking back at him.

"Um, Timm?" Morgan asked, quietly. "I think he meant for us to take on the task of researching Nergal. Not taking him in a fight."

"Oh," Timm said, sheepishly, feeling the anger and heat melt away at her words.

"To be fair," Smithers interjected. "It's kind of my hope that one will lead to the other. Knowledge is power, after all."

"I thought power was power," Timm asked, confused.

"Easy there, Cerci," Smithers said, and Timm only grew more confused. "Anyway, world mythologies and legends are over that way."

Smithers pointed and Timm followed Morgan as they walked into a quiet and somewhat disused area. Looking behind him, Timm saw that Smithers had not followed. He assumed the old man probably had something he was going to focus on for his own research and made a mental note to ask him about that later.

After asking the reference desk for help, he carried a pile of books back to a table in the far corner of the room. Timm noticed the woman at the reference desk keeping a close eye on him and Morgan, and instantly grew suspicious she may be part of one of the groups looking for them. However, he started to notice a pattern: any time he or Morgan moved closer to each other, whether to share a finding or ask a question of the other, the woman's glower deepened. Timm felt himself blush and buried his face in the nearest reference book he could find.

Timm soon found himself reading a story called The Epic of Gilgamesh. It apparently was originally written on stone tablets, and in spite of having a difficult time understanding what he was reading, Timm managed to get the gist of the story. He was enjoying the tales of adventure and friendship between Gilgamesh and Enkidu, though felt a pang of remorse when he read of Enkidu's death and Gilgamesh's pain. He thought of his own master, gone from the world, regardless of which one Timm found himself in, and even began rooting for Gilgamesh to succeed in finding the secret to eternal life, until one name stood out to him.

"Nergal..." he muttered.

"What was that?" Morgan asked him.

"Nergal!" Timm said, more excitedly. "I found him in here, he's not just the god of war and fire, he's the god of the underworld!"

"We knew he was the god of death from Simon," Morgan began to say, but Timm's eyes were moving too quickly over the page to notice.

"He's more than that," Timm said, his voice getting quicker. "He's the king of the underworld. He took an army of demons into the Underworld, threatened to cut off the queen's head, and only spared her life when she was willing to become his wife, making him king. That didn't stop him though it seems he..."

Timm trailed off, his mind finally processing the next part of what his mouth was about to say. A shudder ran through him.

"What is it, Timm?" Morgan asked, looking up at him strangely.

"It's... uh..." Timm stuttered, feeling queasy and uncomfortable looking into her sparkling green eyes.

"Come on," she said, placing her hand on his forearm. Timm felt himself beginning to sweat. "If it is important, we need to know it so we know what we'll be facing when we run into him again."

Timm realized she made a good point. He looked back down at the page, at the crimes that Nergal not only committed, but enjoyed to his core. Timm felt his mouth go dry and his hands quake slightly.

"Nergal is a beast," Timm said, his voice raspy for reasons he did not truly understand. "He doesn't just kill people, he loves tormenting them. And being the god of death, he can do that for eternity. He has a habit of... well... it says here of 'claiming those who have been claimed by another,' and not caring about consent."

Morgan furrowed her brow at Timm, looking confused. "What does that mean, exactly?"

Timm awkwardly grasped at words, some way to lessen the effect of what he was trying to say, but there was nothing. His face burned hot and his heart beat quicker in his chest.

"He's a rapist," Timm finally said, blurting out what he needed to tell her, but desperately did not want to. "He rapes, kills, and king of the Underworld means..."

"Even in death," Morgan finished for him, putting the pieces together. "His victims cannot escape him."

Timm looked at Morgan's face, her expression a mix between primal fury and disgust. He was amazed that she seemed completely unaffected by the fear that gripped his own heart. To deal with a creature such as this one, wouldn't she be afraid that Nergal would try to... to...

He shook his head, unable or unwilling to complete the thought.

"To do this to someone," Morgan said, through clenched teeth that started to look a little sharper than Timm remembered them being. "He's a monster, and we're going to take him down."

Morgan got up, grabbing her coat and looked at Timm, a spark of pure fury in her eyes. "Come on, grab what you need, we're going to talk to the others."

*　*　*

Not wanting to discuss such private matters in the library, Smithers had suggested that they all retire to O'Malley's Pub in order to share information. The drive over and the drink Timm had thrown back almost immediately after stepping through the door did a lot to calm his nerves. As Morgan explained what they had found, Timm only found it necessary to add a snippet of information here or there. Otherwise, he was free to enjoy his second drink... or perhaps it was his third.

"To be fair," Luis pointed out. "We already knew he was a murderous monster. My intention was to drive him down and away from this world anyway. This information merely adds fuel to the fire."

"This is true," Lee added. "However it does give us more information to be on the lookout for."

"Not sure it will help much," Smithers said, sipping at his whiskey. "If we went through all the rape reports we'd probably be wasting time and coming up empty. Besides, so few get reported as it is, I doubt anyone is stepping forward to report that thing being the culprit."

"Why would such a crime not be reported?" Luis asked, swirling the wine delicately in its glass.

"Long answer is too complicated," Smithers said, waving his hand dismissively. "Short answer is gender politics suck, a lot of the people doing the investigating have a history of doing the crime, and women need to be treated better."

Luis nodded in agreement. "Women must always be treated well. I have fought alongside many and can speak from experience, there is no power on this earth that deserves more respect."

"Here here!" Timm said, gleefully cheering and lifting his glass.

The table grew quiet as they looked at him.

"Maybe you should slow down, boy," Smithers said gently, trying to take the glass out of Timm's hand, though Timm locked his grip on it.

"I'm fine," Timm said, prying Smithers' fingers off the glass. "I'm good. Back to the meeting."

"Er... yeah," Smithers said, turning away from Timm. "What about the radiation research?"

"From what I can gather, it comes from particles smaller than the cells in your body being launched with a great deal of energy and force from radioactive materials. They pass through your body and rip it up, altering the fabric of what makes you who you are and leaving behind nothing but damage and decay," Lee said, explaining the concept, or at least attempting to.

Timm looked at him, realizing that he had stopped understanding the words that Lee had been saying after 'particle' and had just been nodding along with the sounds he'd been making. Turning to look at the others, he saw Morgan also looked a bit confused, though Smithers seemed to understand perfectly.

Luis sighed, "Imagine a wave of energy coming from a rock that rips you apart on such a small scale you either don't notice or get burns like ours for getting too close. The damage could take years to see, or make you ill after short term exposure."

"So that's why our healing magic didn't work," Morgan said, thoughtfully. "Our wounds were healed, but there was much deeper damage that we couldn't see."

Lee nodded. "We needed more healing than we realized due to the scale of the damage."

At this point, Timm realized that he had nothing more to contribute to the conversation and more importantly his drink was empty. Just as they were discussing something called a 'radiation suit,' Timm wandered off to where Tom was standing.

"Hey," Timm said, falling onto a stool. "Got another for me?"

Tom looked up at him in surprise, then slowly began to speak in carefully measured words.

"Sorry if I am out of practice," Tom said, slowly. "It has been a while."

"What do you mean?" Timm asked. "You just poured me one. You're a professional!"

Tom laughed, pouring Timm another drink.

"I meant with the language," Tom said, passing Timm the glass. "I do not have much cause to speak Irish very often."

"Irish?" Timm asked, taking a sip. The liquor didn't bite as much now, and Timm wasn't sure if that was because he was getting used to it or if Tom was watering it down... nah, he would have noticed that. "What's Irish?"

Tom looked at him in surprise.

"The... uh... Language we're currently speaking," Tom said.

Timm felt shocked. "Did we start speaking another language?"

"You did," Tom said, confused. "When you came over here."

Timm noticed Tom look down at the drink he'd just poured. Slowly, Timm pulled it a little closer in a not so subtle way of letting Tom know he was not going to surrender it lightly. He has had too many people treating him like a child as it was lately, and he sure as hell didn't need another giving him the same shit.

"Guess I didn't notice," Timm said, pointedly taking another sip. He closed his eyes and took a deep breath.

They snapped open again as soon as the cold air hit his face.

"Wait, what?" Timm asked, looking around wildly at the dark streets in front of him.

"You, uh, fell asleep?" Morgan said, and Timm looked down to find his arm draped over her shoulder as she supported his weight. Looking around, he realized they were walking away from the bar.

"Blacked out was more like it," Smithers said, shuffling past them. "Started singing some old Irish ditty at the top of your lungs and we figured it was time to get your drunk ass out of there."

"To be fair," Lee stated. "I suggested fresh air would help. We did not quite phrase it that way."

"I did," Smithers said.

"Yeah," Timm said, using his free hand to rub his eyes. "Maybe some fresh air would do me some good. Do you guys mind taking a detour through the park? It's not exactly on the way, but it might help me clear my head a bit."

Smithers looked like he was about to complain, but Lee interjected before he got the chance.

"I wouldn't mind seeing the aftermath of yesterday's exploits," Lee said, glancing at Smithers with a look that told the old man to keep his mouth shut. "Perhaps this is a way to accomplish two tasks in a single action."

"We call that killing two birds with one stone," Smithers said, grumpily.

Lee looked shocked. "What is the point of that?"

"Saves rocks?" Timm suggested. Lee dropped the matter after that.

They were walking towards the park and Timm felt Morgan's pace slow slightly, pulling them back from the rest of the group.

"Am I too heavy?" Timm asked, worried that he was too much of a burden. "I can try to walk on my own now, I should be able to."

"No," Morgan shook her head. "That's not it at all. It's just..."

"Just what?" Timm asked, feeling his face heating up again in the cold air and began worrying his skin would start to steam.

"Just... " Morgan said, choosing her words carefully. "Just don't run away from us this time?"

Timm felt a mix of hurt and of shame. After his reaction to passing out and being healed, he'd worried that he would have driven her away. It was pure instinct to strike out at what was overhead when he woke up hurt in the dark, but he was worried the others wouldn't understand that. Wouldn't understand that this is the kind of weapon he had been honed into being.

Looking down at Morgan he shook his head.

"I won't," Timm promised. "I'll stick with you."

~ 25 ~

LEE

Lee glanced back at Timm who, with Morgan's help, was stumbling far less than he had been moments before. The crisp winter air seemed to be clearing much of the fog from that poison he kept drinking from his mind. He looked over at Luis who was walking beside him with the same purpose that always set his cadence.

"Could you lift the poison from his blood?" Lee asked the knight.

"As well as you," Luis responded. "But by attempting to pass the duty on to me you seem to be saying you fear what we may find in this park."

"It has me a bit concerned, yes," Lee admitted. "Timm seems to have gone off the deep end. I doubt he's ever dealt with a threat of this caliber before."

"Have you?" Luis asked.

"As often as you," Lee answered.

The knight smiled. "Well played."

"I do not favor the game, though it seems to, at times, favor me," Lee said, accepting the compliment. "Back to the matter at hand, however. We have run into trouble quite a bit out here in this world, and we two seem to be the only ones who are well equipped enough to handle it."

"I am not so sure about that," Luis remarked, nodding slightly at Smithers. "While Timm is inexperienced and Morgan is somewhat naive, I get the feeling the old man is something of a soldier. Or at least was at some point."

"A soldier with the perspective of one who is only just realizing the dangers he faces," Lee pointed out. "It would be like sending fresh recruits into a manticore's den. Even with a decent squad leader, it would be dangerous and deadly to assume they could manage it with such a handicap."

"I doubt we'll run into any trouble," Luis attempted to appease Lee's worries. "And if we do, Timm will snap out of it. He's flaky, and may run from his problems, but have you ever seen him run from a fight?"

Lee realized it was pointless to argue with Luis on this matter any further. He doubted that informing the knight that one doesn't just 'snap out of' poisonings would do any good, and if they were to get in a fight, Lee currently had not been prepared to remove poison from anyone that day. Luis was currently the only one with that particular skill available to him. Lee felt that Morgan probably would have already administered that particular healing to Timm rather than carry his weight were it available to her.

Unless the girl did not realize the significance of her current support for him...

Lee shook his head. It was not time to start speculating on the inner worlds in which his comrades lived. While during their down time it was exceptionally entertaining to watch them flounder about in their social ineptitude, they were returning to the site of their battle with a god. Though his power was greatly diminished in the form they fought, he was no less a god. Beyond that, the fight had not been easily won, which made Lee worry even more about the power that lurked behind that cervidae mask he wore.

Fresh snow had fallen on the park during the day and Lee saw how the blanket of white had all but erased the evidence of their battle. Their feet, having churned the mud under the snow, had stained it brown and red with river water and blood. The sickly odor that had permeated the air was still crisp and clean, or at least as clean as it could be within the boundaries of the city where they burned the fuel found deeper in the earth than he thought dwarves would be willing to dig.

People milled about the park, though with the sun having recently set, they were few in number, and he had little doubt that they would soon have the park once again all to themselves for the second time in as many days. He looked over at the edge of the river that flowed under the massive concrete and steel bridge and felt his sickness renew, but steeled himself and walked forward.

The squelching of mud under boots matched his own gait as he wandered towards the pristine battleground. Luis stepped in stride next to him, his keen eyes sweeping the ground in search of any evidence that may not have been wiped clean.

"Where did it come from?" Luis asked himself under his breath, though Lee managed to overhear him.

"What do you mean?" Lee asked.

"The aspect," Luis said, not clarifying much. "How did it get here?"

"Aspects can be sent," Lee answered, rattling off his knowledge on the subject as he flicked through the files in his mind. "Usually a being the god uses to represent themselves or by putting a piece of themselves into them."

"No," Luis shook his head. "That's an avatar, very different."

Lee pursed his lips and thought on the matter. Had he been confusing the two? That would be quite the embarrassment.

"An aspect *is* the god," Luis continued, earnestly. "Brought into the world by their followers."

"Are you saying there were followers here last night?" Lee asked. "I would have thought that upon seeing their deity struck down they would have stepped in to aid him, or at least avenge him. Cultists are funny that way."

"They are," Luis nodded. "Which leads me to believe they weren't here at all. Which means the aspect needed to be produced somehow. Some kind of altar or portal created for the sole purpose of giving him access to this world."

"Something his followers could set up ahead of time," Lee caught on to Luis' line of thinking. "Something they could, perhaps, activate remotely?"

"That could do it," Luis nodded in agreement.

"Then you're looking in the wrong place," Lee said, making his way across the field of snow into a small patch of spindly trees. "No god of fire would have his altar in the dirt. Fire chokes and dies in the dirt. He needs air, and kindling."

Lee stepped up to an array of thin trees, their leaves having fallen off long ago, they looked like little more than twigs jammed upright in the dirt by a petulant child. Each one dry to Lee's touch, and he was confident that the strike of a single match would set them ablaze. Running his hand over the smooth bark, about chest height he found what he was looking for. Hidden behind windswept snow, the bark of the tree grew rough, as though scored by something. Lee brushed away the snow, revealing a stone embedded in the tree's trunk, carved with a strange sigil made up of stark, harsh lines gouged into the stone.

"What is it?" Luis asked, peering at the symbol. "That's no language I know."

"Nor do I," Lee answered. "But perhaps Morgan will. I may not know the language, but it looks to me like the language of the trees."

"The kind of language a druid would speak," Luis nodded. "I'll go fetch her."

Luis returned with Morgan and the others a few minutes later. This time, Smithers was supporting Timm as they walked, though the young man did not seem to need much in the way of support beyond a guiding hand in the dark. Touching the symbol that hung from his neck, Lee whispered a word, and a soft white glow began to emanate from his holy symbol.

"Ah, thank you," Morgan said as she approached the symbol.

"Yeh know, we've got flash lights that do that too," Smithers said, but Lee just ignored him.

"Can you read it, Morgan?" Lee asked.

Morgan looked the symbol over, brushing more snow away from it.

"Yes," Morgan replied, though her voice was tight. "It is the druidic symbol for 'wrath.'""

"That seems strange to have carved into a tree like that," Luis said, looking at the sigil. "One would think you'd need more than that to summon the aspect of a god."

"You do," Morgan said, making her way to another tree a few paces to the right of the first. Brushing aside more snow, she revealed another stone sigil embedded in the tree. "Rage."

She stepped again to another tree, slowly circling the group as she read the symbols aloud for them all to hear.

"Flame."

"Death."

"Return."

Morgan paused upon completing the circle and looked at each of them.

"Separately these symbols have individual meanings," she explained. "But together they read out a phrase."

"What does it read as, Morgan?" Lee asked, his fear of this creature slowly being pushed back by his curiosity. Knowledge was always the greatest weapon against fear, and Lee felt like they were about to become quite effectively armed.

"It says, *Cleanse the land in his fire. The burning lord returns*," Morgan read aloud, her voice thick as though the very words were venom on her tongue.

Lee's shoulders sank. That had not been the enticing clue he had expected it to be. They knew already that Nergal was returning to this world, and that he planned to remake it in fire. Or at least, that was the conclusion that Lee had come to himself. Perhaps this was just a dead end. Perhaps they would just need to wait until Nergal attacked again. It was not ideal, but if his followers were using cryptic clues and remote portals, there was not much they could do.

"It's really dark," Timm said, staring up at the sky.

"Yes, it is Timm," Lee said, dismissing the man's musings for his own.

"Like, you can't even see the stars," Timm said, leaning back against a tree and looking up.

"Yeah," Smithers said, rolling his eyes. "Light pollution, buddy. We've gone over this."

"You can't even see the buildings from in here," Timm continued, as though no one had spoken to him. "It's like being in a forest back home."

"Just like home," Morgan mused, her head dropping slightly. Lee was getting a bit irate with Timm's antics at this point. Morgan did not need further reminders of being so far from home, especially while they were sitting in the middle of a summoning circle...

That didn't actually have a summoning incantation on it.

"Morgan," Lee said, cautiously. "You said that's written in Druidic?"

She looked over at him, perplexed.

"Yes," Morgan nodded. "The language the trees and flowers use to communicate with us."

"And Timm just pointed out that we're in the middle of what passes for woods around here, looking at sigils that spelled out a message rather than the summoning we expected, out of the eye-line of any possible witnesses?" Lee continued, feeling a new tension beginning to grow between his shoulderblades.

"Yes..." Morgan said, the same realization slowly dawning on her. She and Luis snapped around, facing outside the circle of trees. Lee followed suit, but Timm continued leaning against the tree as Smithers jumped to attention looking at all of them.

"What!" Smithers asked, drawing his gun when he saw Luis' sword appear in his hand. "What's going on?"

"We're not in a summoning circle," Lee said.

"We're in a trap," Morgan finished, her eyes tracking movement in the treeline that Lee could not follow.

"This isn't a trap," Luis snarled, gripping his sword with two hands in a defensive position. "This is an ambush."

It was then that Lee saw them emerge from the trees around them. Four wolves emerged from darkness as though materializing from nothing. They were at least nine feet in length and stood at least five feet tall at the shoulder. The only wolf Lee had ever seen match them in size was when Morgan took the field of battle in their skin, though she probably would never wish to wear this kind of skin.

These wolves were not packed with the lean, whipcord muscle that Morgan's form would take. They were gaunt, harrowed, and looked emaciated, as though starved. Their fur was matted where it hadn't already fallen out. Angry red rashes and blisters appeared on their visible skin. A deep, guttural snarl rumbled from the narrow chests of these beasts, and Lee could see the cracked yellow fangs that lined their blackened jawline under milky white eyes.

"What kind of beasts are these?" Luis asked, an edge of horror to his voice. That alone scared Lee more than any wicked creature.

"Sick," Morgan answered. "They're diseased. Poisoned by radiation."

One snarled in answer, as though refuting Morgan. Sick though it may be, it was not weakened by its sickness. Possibly, it could have been empowered by it.

There was a pregnant moment of silence where they all looked at one another. Lee could sense the tension just as it was about to burst, and threw up his arm to protect himself just as the howls pierced the still night air.

Lee watched in horror as the salivating monster bounded towards him, covering the distance in less time than it took him to suck in a breath. The beast dropped down, rebounding like a spring as it leapt, fangs gleaming as it launched itself at Lee. The priest knew he couldn't meet the force of the beast and win. Ducking down, Lee dropped into a roll feeling the beast's belly scrape against him as it sailed clean over, skidding back from Lee, putting about ten feet of distance between them by the time it came snarling to a halt.

Looking up, Lee saw that Smithers had decided to take the opposite approach to dealing with his assailant. Bringing up his shotgun, but unable to level a shot, the old man held it sideways and caught the slavering jaws of the wolf on him. He staggered back a step, but with a surprising amount of strength for an older man, he twisted the gun, throwing the wolf to one side. A loud cracking noise filled the air as he chambered his shot. Thunder and rotted flesh filled the air as the birdshot tore through the writhing form of the wolf who spat and snarled, twisting its deformed body on the ground as it clawed its way to its feet.

"Oh, come on!" Smithers spat in frustration.

"They're not normal wolves!" Morgan cried out a warning. "They are just like…"

Morgan's voice cut out and was replaced by a high pitched scream as one of the massive rotting forms slammed into her back, fangs driven deep into her shoulder. It drove her to the ground, shaking its head violently, sending up a spray of blood.

Lee couldn't see Morgan through the mound of fur and flesh that pinned her down.

"Morgan!" Timm cried out, running toward her.

In his haste, he didn't notice the wolf emerging from the trees behind him. With a hideous snarl, the beast's fangs snapped closed on his leg, staggering him. Timm cried out in pain, eyes gleaming in anger. Matching the wolf's snarl, Timm swung his upper body around, sending a backwards hammerfist into the jaw of the wolf. Lee heard a sickening crack. Timm's leg came suddenly free and he launched forward, throwing wild punches at the wolf's head. The wolf, ready for Timm's onslaught this time, ducked and weaved as it retreated. Timm followed it as though he had it on the ropes, but Lee saw what it was doing. The wolf wasn't retreating from the attack, but rather drawing Timm away from his allies.

"Divide and conquer," Lee said, looking at the wolf before him. It may have been a trick of the moonlight, but the priest could have sworn he saw it grin at him. Morgan's words filled his mind: They're just like...

"You're just like her," Lee addressed the wolf. Raising his voice he called out, "They're druids! Morgan! Get up!"

Stretching out a hand at the girl's mauled form, a ripple of white hot sparks like those from the hammer striking molten metal flew from his fingertips and hissed against Morgan's torn flesh. The blood vanished and skin knitted closed, eliciting a gasp from the downed girl.

"And you!" Lee snarled at the wolf on her. "Back off!"

He slashed his hand in the air, summoning a streak of brilliant white light from the sky that struck down with the force of a hammer's blow. The wolf yowled in pain, staggering back from Morgan as it shook its head violently against the holy onslaught. Lee, satisfied with his work, turned back to face the wolf who had attacked him.

"Fight fire with fire, as they say," Lee smirked at the beast.

The wolf cocked its head in confusion, as though trying to make sense of Lee's words. A deep bellow filled the air and without turning around, Lee knew that Morgan had put her game face on. The wolf's ears dropped back in fear and anger as it turned to look at Lee. The priest couldn't help but smile as he looked over his shoulder at the hulking form of Morgan as she stood nearly ten feet tall on her hind legs, swiping her massive bear paw at the wolf that had attacked her.

With preternatural speed, the wolf ducked out of the way of Morgan's strike, forcing her to fall to all four paws to keep from toppling over under the weight of her own bulk. What the wolf had not expected was Luis coming from the darkness, sweeping his short blade up at its flank. An explosion of holy light illuminated the woods, sending cascades of blinding radiance and deep shadow flickering around them as the blade sent an arc of blood and ichor through the air, painting the white bark of a birch tree red.

Lee felt a surge of confidence now that the Knight of Victory was weighing in and turning the tide of the battle, though he instantly regretted the thought as he heard the rapid patter of paws charging through the snow and dirt directly at him. Barely getting his arm up in time, Lee felt fangs sink through his thick coat and the heat of his blood running across his skin. His stomach rolled with nausea that reminded him of the sickening aura that surrounded the Aspect of Nergal as the fangs pierced his flesh.

Screams filled the night alongside another sound of thunder as Smithers and Timm fought off their own assailants. Lee looked over and saw Timm, blood pouring down his face and arms as he swung wildly at the beast, his form getting sloppier as the blood drained from his body. Lee whispered a word and sent another set of sparks flying towards Timm, closing his wounds as well. Timm's form tightened up, and he caught the wolf across the jaw with what Lee thought was called a cross, followed by a knee to the throat. The wolf staggered and stepped back.

Looking over at Luis, Lee summoned down another beam of holy light from the sky, hoping to free the knight up to aid others, but the fangs in his arm tightened and Lee's shot went wide. He cried out in pain and looked down at the wolf in front of him. Its piercing eyes seeming to say: *You're fighting* me *and don't you forget it.*

The roar of the bear forced Lee's eyes to snap over to where Luis and Morgan were double teaming the other wolf. Morgan swiped with her paw, catching the wolf in its wounded flank and sending it sprawling. Moving in on the dazed target, Luis drove his sword down, pinning the wolf to the earth, though no howl of pain came from the beast. Instead, the scream of a woman pierced the night air, as the wolf was no more. A woman, skin tight and gaunt against her bone, brittle brown hair like straw in a tangled nest, and dressed in ragged, torn clothing lay screaming on the ground, Luis' sword piercing through her shoulder.

The wolves paused, seeing their packmate fall. The one in front of Smithers threw back its head, howling mournfully and darted off into the trees.

"Oh no you don't!" Smithers snarled, pulling a pistol from under his coat. He let off two shots into the darkness where the wolf disappeared, but if he hit the wolf gave no indication.

Lee felt the fangs in his arm begin to loosen, but the anger and frustration Smithers had just exhibited must have been contagious as Lee clamped his hand down on the wolf's muzzle, pinning its fangs in place.

"Don't start what you can't finish," Lee hissed, a maliciousness he did not recognize in his voice.

Lee dug his fingernails into the muzzle of the beast and summoned all the negative emotions that had been boiling under the surface of his mind, not just since getting to this strange world, but since he'd lost them... lost all of them... but mostly since he lost her...

He roared incoherently, sending a ripple of all his negative emotions through his fingers and into the wolf's body. The fangs broke loose as the wolf screamed, its already diseased flesh split and bled with Lee's will. The priest pushed all he had into the spell, tearing the wolf asunder, but could not hold it in place. The wolf pulled back and fled, yelping, into the darkness.

Lee fell to his knees, panting, as he felt the blood seeping down his own arm. He was tempted to close the wound, but needed to be sure that the others were not in need of his touch. Breathing deeply in an attempt to regain his composure.

His head snapped up as he heard the woman who was once a wolf cry out in pain. Morgan was pressing her paw against the woman's chest, not hard enough to crush her, but certainly making a point to hold her in place. Luis pulled his sword from her shoulder and cleaned the blade before sheathing it.

"You're not going anywhere," Luis said, his voice steady and cold. "You have questions to answer. You're a druid, yes?"

"I am blessed by Nergal, the power he grants me is far more than that of your simple beast!" the woman snarled, turning to face Morgan and spitting in the bear's face. Morgan winced and Lee felt more than heard the rumbling growl she unleashed.

To her credit, the woman did not flinch. Lee was unsure if they would get anything from her, but anything they could get out of her would be impossible to interpret without Morgan's help. Unbuckling his belt, Lee walked over to Luis.

"Here," he said, handing the knight his belt. "Bind her hands, Morgan will be of more use to us with the ability to speak."

Luis nodded, kneeling down and binding the woman's hands together, not taking any particular care with her wounded arm. She sucked in a breath, but besides that did little to express that she was in any pain. Once he was sure she was held, Luis pulled the woman over to a tree, propped her up, and nodded at Morgan who dropped the form of the bear.

"What Circle are you from?" Morgan asked, the harshness of the bear not yet gone from her voice.

"What does it matter to you, Moondancer?" the woman laughed, coughing up blood as she did. "Your ilk have such little power in this world, what could you hope to accomplish against us?"

"My ilk?" Morgan asked. "So there are more druids in my Circle here."

"Circle?" Smithers asked, stumbling over while reloading his shotgun. "What does that mean?"

"Druids gather in groups called Circles," Morgan explained. "Something like a larger tribe, where we share beliefs if not a home. My Circle reveres the cycles of the moon, the power of the beasts who rove the land, and we bind ourselves to the might of fur and fang. We focus our power on our bond with the beast."

"And there are other circles?" Luis asked.

"Several," Morgan nodded. "Some who bind themselves to the land, to the cycle of seasons, to the bond between the wilds and civilization, and even a few I've met who focus on the decay that allows life to flourish."

"Is she one of those?" Lee asked, regarding the decaying woman. "She looks the part."

"I would not have you call me such filth!" the woman spat. "I am no Spore Eater! I am of the Circle of the Wastes! We revere the God Nergal and his cleansing fire that will purge the world of the weak, wipe the plague of humanity from the land, and reshape the planet in his image!"

"You realize you're part of humanity," Smithers pointed out. "Right?"

The woman grinned, revealing cracked, yellow teeth that matched the wolfish fangs she had worn earlier. Flakes of skin cracked and fell away from the corners of her bloodstained mouth as she did, making Lee's skin crawl.

"We are no more," the woman said, her voice smug and condescending. "Humanity has fallen, and we shall replace it in the forms of those superior creatures."

Morgan rushed forward with blinding speed, her hands reaching out for the woman's throat, but it was too late. Her hand grasped empty air as the woman's form shrunk and vanished from sight. Lee's sharp eyes caught sight of a small, black insect crawling over the snow, before it opened its carapace, revealing a pair of black, membranous wings and flew off, vanishing in the dark.

"Damn it!" Morgan snarled. "You bound her with leather! It needs to be metal!"

"I'm sorry," Luis said, mournfully, clearly just as upset with himself for letting her go as Morgan was. Morgan shook her head and sighed.

"No, no need to be sorry," she said, her voice becoming hers again. "She just... made my skin crawl. And now she's out there..."

"Watching us," Timm said from where he sat, slumped against a tree.

"There were gunshots," Smithers said. "We should move."

"Agreed," Lee said. "We'll find a safer spot, I'll tend to our wounds, then we should head back to the church. I'm unsure of how safe we'll be there, but it will be a great deal safer than here."

Morgan turned to look at him with true fear in her eyes since the first time he'd met her.

"I don't think we'll find any place safe in this world," she said, her voice haunting. She walked over to one of the trees and dug the stone out of its trunk before walking up the path back to the park proper.

Lee tried not to think too much on what she may have meant. If anyone knew the danger this Circle of the Wastes posed, it was her. A chill ran up Lee's spine that had nothing to do with the cold as he gathered himself and followed her up the path.

~ 26 ~

MORGAN

Morgan stormed away from the battlefield still shaking from the experience. In her hand she held the stone carved so blasphemously with the druidic sigil for "fire." She gripped it tightly, partially from anger, but mostly to keep herself from trembling too visibly for the others. She did not want them to realize just how horrified she was with what she had just seen.

Her whole life, she'd been taught of the power of nature. Its cycles and constancy. It seemed like a paradox as a child. How could something be constant if it was constantly in a state of change? But as she grew older, it began to make more sense because the change itself could be predicted. She learned to watch the stars and note how long before the changing of the season. She learned to pay attention to the behaviors of animals and to feel the subtle difference in the scent and pressure of the air to predict storms long before they formed. She learned of the flora: where it could be found, what ailments it could heal, and what poisons could be derived from its roots.

Whatever she needed, whatever she could want for, nature would provide.

But this woman, this Circle of the Wastes, they were not part of the cycle. They were something else, something tainted. What they tapped into was no true power of nature. Her skin itched and burned where the wolf had bitten her, and she knew the noxious power of Nergal was flowing through the beast form the tainted druid had taken.

Morgan crested the small hill that had led them down into the wooded area and found her feet moving far more comfortably across the ice laden concrete than they ever had before. Normally, she'd have hated the feel of the manmade material under foot as opposed to the natural soil, but those druids had tainted even that with their very presence. Morgan wondered if she would ever feel right in a world that would allow such a heinous creation to exist.

Her thoughts were broken by the sound of a squealing wheel and rattle of metal. She looked up to see a familiar figure walking towards her, bundled up against the cold and pushing a metal wagon Smithers referred to as a 'shopping cart.' The figure was hunched over, attempting to keep the biting wind from sinking its icy fangs into his face, but all the same, Morgan recognized him.

"Walter!" she cried out, happily.

The figure looked up, and Morgan saw his wide smile through the tangled nest of his beard. Pulling back his hood, she could see his grey woolen cap pulled down over his long, messily braided hair, his bright eyes glimmered in the ambient light of the snow. Walter turned the cart towards her and walked over, not changing his pace, but walking with far more purpose.

"Well hey there, Sweets," Walter said as he approached her. "Been a minute. How are you and your possy doing?"

"Possy?" Morgan asked, quizzically cocking her head to one side.

"He means us," Smithers said, pulling himself up onto the concrete, breathing a little heavier than Morgan thought was healthy. "And I take it you're that Walter fella they've been going on about?"

Walter nodded at Smithers, though seemed to shoot him a look that Morgan couldn't quite peg down. It was something between amusement and contempt, but was gone too soon for Morgan to really identify. He turned back to face her as Lee stepped up to him as well.

"I heard them werewolves getting frisky again out here, so I figured I'd take a look," Walter said, no longer acknowledging anyone other than those he'd already spoken to. "Seemed like they were a bit more active than usual, especially since that glow hasn't appeared tonight."

"That's because we've taken care of the glow," Lee said plainly. "For now at the very least. Though I'm curious, why are you investigating the werewolves? I thought you said that was too dangerous for you."

"Oh it is," Walter said, nodding. "But I've got Stuffers with me, so I should be alright."

Morgan looked at the filthy, patchwork teddy bear that sat in the top rack of the shopping cart. Its little legs were each sticking out of a hole made by the bars that created a seat the perfect size to fit him, though Morgan was sure this Stuffers appreciated not being a living thing, as there was nothing that looked comfortable about the seating arrangement.

"Well the werewolves are not that," Morgan said, still eyeing Stuffers the bear nervously. Something about it made her skin crawl. "They're actually something a lot worse than that. They're druids."

"Them people that worship the planets and stars?" Walter asked.

Morgan knitted her eyebrows in confusion. "Uh... maybe? But usually druids revere nature and can turn into animals."

"Ah, so not werewolves, wolf men!" Walter said, as though he were making perfect sense. "Does Moony know about this?"

"He knows," Luis' voice came from the trees behind them. Morgan turned to see the knight half supporting, half carrying Timm as he pulled him out of the brush and bramble.

"Oh no! Moony!" Walter cried out. "Are you okay, buddy?"

"He's fine, just drunk," Luis said, irritation clear in his voice. Pressing his hand against Timm, there was a flash of light, and suddenly the glassy expression in Timm's eyes vanished. "And now he's not."

"Wouldn't it have been better to do that before dragging him up the hill?" Lee asked.

The knight opened his mouth to answer, stopped, then grit his teeth angrily and walked over to the nearest park bench. He sat down heavily and began muttering darkly to himself.

"Wow, that's a lot better!" Timm said, stretching himself out and testing his newfound mobility. "Thanks Luis!"

"Whatever," the knight responded curtly.

Not seeming to notice Luis' newfound foul mood, Timm turned to Walter.

"Hey, Walter!" he exclaimed. "How are you doing tonight?"

"As well as could be expected with druid werewolves on the loose," Walter replied.

"Still not werewolves," Lee said, though he may as well have been talking to himself for all the notice Walter took of it.

"Well if you don't feel safe staying here, you can always come with us," Timm offered. "We're staying down at the Cathedral of the Holy Cross. I'm sure Father Mitchell has a bed for you there."

Walter was shaking his head almost as soon as Timm had uttered the name of the church.

"Oh no," Walter said, pulling in on himself a bit. "Mitchell is a good man, no doubt there, but that Father Pearson..."

Walter shuddered.

"There's something wrong with that man," Walter said quietly. "And besides, he doesn't really like Stuffers all that much. Can't leave my good buddy behind like that. Even if Pearson calls him a 'false idol,' you don't leave your friends out in the cold."

"A false idol?" Smithers asked, eyeing the bear curiously. "You worship that thing?"

"Careful how you speak about him," Walter warned. "But no, I don't worship Stuffers. We're friends who have a working relationship."

"Uh-huh," Smithers said, nodding slowly. "And how does that relationship work, exactly?"

"It's complicated," Walter said, dismissively.

"I'm sure it is," Smithers responded. Turning to the rest of the group, he said, "Okay folks, I think that's enough crazy and excitement for one night, don't you? Let's head back to the church, regroup, and pass out for a while."

Morgan nodded. "I am pretty tired."

She turned to Walter. "You know where you can find us if you need us. Just be sure to stay safe out here."

"Oh not to worry, Sweets," Walter said, smiling at her. "This is my home. You've never got nothing to fear at home."

Morgan smiled, knowing that he was quite wrong on that point, but would prefer that he continued feeling secure in his home. She worried that the druids may cause him problems, but if he'd been able to fend them off this long, then maybe there was more to this Walter than she was aware of.

Exiting the park, Morgan pulled her hood up against the cold wind walking between Timm and Lee as Luis went ahead with Smithers. The two men flanked her on either side, creating a nice buffer from the cold, but nothing could stop it from finding the creases and crevices of her strange new clothes. The 'hoodie' she was given was nowhere near as thick and warm as furs were, though it was much easier to move around in. She was debating the trade off between the two as Timm broke the silence.

"I like him," Timm said, staring straight ahead.

Morgan looked where Timm's eyes were pointed, then back at Timm.

"Who? Luis?"

"No," Timm answered. "Well, yes, but he wasn't who I meant."

"Oh," Morgan said. "Who then?"

"Walter," Timm said, smiling. "He's a little kooky, and a lot mysterious, but I like him a lot. He kind of reminds me of my master."

"Your master?" Morgan asked. "How does he remind you of your master?"

Timm smiled, but didn't answer. When they finally got to the church, he excused himself and went down to the chapel. Morgan wanted to ask him more questions, or perhaps go with him to learn more, but Lee put his hand on her shoulder.

"It is not the time," Lee stated plainly. "He needs his time for prayer, as we all need our time to reflect. Best to tend to your garden before infringing on his."

Morgan didn't feel like she was infringing on anything by reaching out a helping hand, but she had learned that Lee's wisdom was best heeded. With a sigh of resignation, Morgan made her way down to the cots, tossed herself into one, and stared at the ceiling thinking about the horrific Circle until bitter sleep finally found her.

~ 27 ~

SMITHERS

Smithers was having a wonderful dream. It was a dream where no supernatural freaks from another dimension were forcing him to do battle with monsters and zealots. No doctors telling him he was crazy or in need of being put in an 'assisted living facility.' And best of all, no disingenuous brats telling him what to do with his life, money, or property. All this bliss came crashing down around him as blaring white light flashed against his eyeballs, painting the whole world red.

Grumpily he sat up out of bed, swinging his feet over the edge of the cot and looking up at his offender.

Father Mitchell stood at the foot of the stairs, his hand still on the switch that had activated the heinous light. He was wearing the white robes of his station over the black shirt and collar. A green stole was slung over his neck and fell down past the ropes tied around his waist in lieu of a belt.

"Ah, good, you're awake," Father Mitchell said to them all as they were roused from bed. "Service begins in about ten minutes. Please be ready and in the church by then. I wouldn't want you to miss today's Gospel."

Before Smithers' sleep-addled mind could come up with anything resembling a witty retort, Father Mitchell had already retreated up the stairs.

"Wouldn't miss it for the world," Smithers muttered, listening to his joints pop and protest as he pulled himself out of the stiff cot. "Apparently."

He looked up to see Morgan shuffling sleepily out of bed, her hair twisted and tangled around her like a rat's nest. Poor girl looked like she got next to no sleep, and though Smithers felt for her, he had to stifle a laugh when he looked at the ridiculous bed-head she was sporting. It took him more will power than he was willing to admit to stop himself from asking her where the twigs and leaves were. Thankfully, she wandered off into the bathroom to prepare herself as the others set about their morning tasks on their own.

Lee, seemingly Morgan's morning-routine nemesis, looked pristine and proper, which was exceptionally impressive as he had slept in his clothes as usual. His long, platinum blonde hair was pin-straight and smooth, his clothing somehow didn't look rumpled at all, and having gotten no more sleep than the rest of them, he still looked refreshed and ready for the day. Smithers watched the priest as he pulled on his shoes and made his way towards the stairs without a single groan of protest or stifled yawn.

"I'll have coffee ready for you all in a minute," he said, as he ascended the stairs. "We won't have long to drink it, but something is better than nothing with how exhausted we are."

Smithers didn't have the energy to argue or even make a snarky comment, which probably said something about how right the man was. Luis simply nodded, tucking his weapons away where they wouldn't be obvious. His sword went under his pillow while the friction lock baton got slipped into his pant's pocket. At least the so-called-knight had learned where and when to have his weapons on him.

The only one not particularly moving was Timm. While Smithers would usually be surprised by this, considering the boundless energy the boy seemed to run on, he wasn't all that shocked today. While Luis had done his magical-whosie-whatsit hand thing to get rid of the drunkenness, and by extension the hangover that would be otherwise unavoidable, Timm had been the last to go to bed the previous night because he'd stayed up to 'meditate' in the chapel. Smithers had half a mind to take mercy on the boy and let him sleep, but in the end, the old man decided that if he was going to have to suffer the service, there was no way Timm was getting out of it.

"Come on, lazy-bones," Smithers said, tugging on the bottom of Timm's blanket to avoid the knee jerk reaction that had put Lee in a chokehold the day before and nearly knocked Morgan's block off at the river. "The padre wants us up and at 'em for the service this morning."

Timm groaned as the light fell across his eyes and made an attempt to pull the blanket over his head again. Luis came from the other side and firmly planted his foot on the blanket's edge, stopping him.

"Come now," Luis said, his voice stern, but not unkind. "The father has done us a great kindness, we owe him far greater repayment than a request as small as this."

Timm opened one eye blearily and looked up at Luis. For a moment, Smithers thought the young man was about to argue with him, but finally Timm nodded his head weakly and began to drag himself out of bed. He shuffled over to the men's bathroom and disappeared inside.

"Think he'll make it?" Smithers asked Luis.

"So long as he doesn't fall asleep in the shower," Luis grinned. "He may end up drowning himself."

"Heh, better the shower than the toilet," Smithers laughed, walking back over to his cot, flopping down and pulling on his boots. "What do you think is with him, anyway?"

"What do you mean?" Luis asked, checking his jacket before pulling it on. Smithers assumed for rips or scuffs on the leather, but double checking for blood probably wasn't a bad idea either.

"Well, and I say this with all due affection and respect, but for as weird as you guys are, he's been acting *really* weird lately," Smithers said, trying to keep his tone light so as to not offend the knight this early in the morning.

Luis pondered Smithers' words for a moment. "He did run from us after the battle against Nergal. Though he had taken a panicked swing at an ally upon waking. I've seen many a young soldier do just that in the heat of battle. He may be grappling with the shame of his action, but a warrior's reflex is nothing to be ashamed of. Especially when no harm was caused."

"Yeah, I guess," Smithers said, scratching at his beard thoughtfully. "But he was acting weird last night too. Something was off, but I just couldn't put my finger on it."

"He was intoxicated," Luis shrugged, dismissively. "Considering that, I feel he fought quite effectively in his state."

"But him getting drunk in the first place was weird," Smithers said, pushing the subject harder despite the knight's flippant appraisal of Timm's performance. "I mean, he's had a drink before, but how drunk he got last night? That was intentional."

Luis shrugged again, and Smithers felt his annoyance with the knight growing even more potent.

"He is young, impulsive. And on top of that, he fell to an opponent before getting to land a single blow. Something like that hurts a man's pride, especially a young man. Last night's failings were faults only of his own making. He probably recognized that and needed to reflect upon it," Luis explained, and as he talked Smithers found his anger subsiding, much like it would when Lee would take time to parse through his own thoughts on a troubling matter. "Spending time in a chapel, even if it is not with your god, or to commune with any god for that matter, is a good way to look back and determine your future course of action. Mistakes are necessary for growth, so long as they only happen one time."

Smithers pursed his lips and thought about what the knight was saying. Timm had made mistakes, that's true, but Smithers knew he'd made more than his fair share when he'd been the boy's age. And he'd learned himself, there's no point trying to teach a boy a lesson with a story or a word. That boy was going to have to learn it himself, and most likely learn it the hard way.

"You know something, Luis?" Smithers said, looking up at the knight and smiling.

"What's that?" Luis asked as he finished lacing up his boot.

"You've got a lot more wisdom knocking around your old noggin than you let on," Smithers said with a grin.

Luis answered with his own. "It is best to let others underestimate you. People look at those like Father Mitchell and Lee and determine that they are wise and knowledgeable, though meek and defenseless."

He gestured to himself, and Smithers noticed for the first time that the lean, toned muscle that he carried was perfectly by design. No wasted bulk, no flashy presentation. Luis had shaped his body in the same way he shared his thoughts, with intention and precision.

"They see layers of muscle and they assume you're powerful, but slow of body and wit," Luis continued. "But Victory can be achieved through many paths. It is in our best interest to be sure of what paths are open to us, and to carve our own when none are available to us. I make no attempt to deceive others, but I owe no obligation to correct their misconceptions of me."

"Makes sense," Smithers nodded, impressed with the deliberateness of the man's stoic nature. "You're quiet because you're listening. Not a bad way to be. Best to let the talkers talk."

"You learn more and give away less that way," Luis nodded in agreement. "Now, I think it is best if we collect that coffee before we lose the time to drink it."

"Yeah," Smithers nodded. "And if Timm's not up there in five minutes, one of us will have to come back and check that he didn't drown."

"One of us will," Luis said, ascending the stairs with a wicked grin that told Smithers the job had been settled on his shoulders.

"Aw, hell," Smithers muttered, following the knight up the stairs to the most blessed elixir knowing full well who was going to be saddled with the job of toddler-wrangling.

~ 28 ~

TIMM

Timm sat in the pew next to Morgan, taking his cues from her the entire morning. He stood when she stood, sat when she sat, and knelt when she knelt. All in all it was a pretty zen experience, much like when his master would work Timm to near exhaustion before forcing him to meditate on the day's lessons. Timm reflected on those much like how he reflected on the lessons of the readings being preached at him right now, with feigned attention and no comprehension.

Sleep called to Timm like a wayward siren in the candlelit halls. The heavy scent of incense drifted through the air, clouding his mind and making his eyes heavy. It was a wonder anyone managed to stay awake during these services. Every now and then Morgan would squeeze his hand and the jolt would snap him back to focus for a moment before the atmosphere had him wavering again.

"Now it happened that he was standing one day by the Lake of Gennesaret, with the crowd pressing round him listening to the word of God, when he caught sight of two boats at the water's edge. The fishermen had got out of them and were washing their nets," Father Mitchell's voice began to say. Timm attempted to pull his attention together for the story, but found himself beginning to drift again until Morgan squeezed his hand.

"He got into one of the boats -- it was Simon's -- and asked him to put out a little from the shore. Then he sat down and taught the crowds from the boat," Father Mitchell continued. "When he had finished speaking he said to Simon, 'Put out into deep water and pay out your nets for a catch.' Simon replied, 'Master, we worked hard all night long and caught nothing, but if you say so, I will pay out the nets.'"

"Gotta get those nets out," Timm muttered under his breath, eliciting another, harder squeeze from Morgan, pulling him briefly from the groggy half-sleep he was entering, though he soon felt himself sliding back into the warm comfort of dreamless dozing.

"And when they had done this they netted such a huge number of fish that their nets began to tear, so they signalled to their companions in the other boat to come and help them; when these came, they filled both boats to sinking point," Father Mitchell went on, paying no mind to Timm's reaction. "When Simon Peter saw this he fell at the knees of Jesus saying, 'Leave me, Lord; I am a sinful man.' For he and all his companions were completely awestruck at the catch they had made; so also were James and John, sons of Zebedee, who were Simon's partners. But Jesus said to Simon, 'Do not be afraid; from now on it is people you will be catching.' Then, bringing their boats back to land they left everything and followed him."

"What kind of sorcerer was this Jesus person anyway?" Luis whispered to Smithers, who sighed and rolled his eyes.

"He wasn't a sorcerer," Smithers said. "According to the Catholic religion he was the son of god who could work miracles."

"So more of a cleric," Lee noted.

Smithers opened his mouth, then closed it thoughtfully. "Yeah, I suppose that's probably the best way to explain it to you. Now hush, the padre's got his preaching to do."

Timm, who had been half listening to their conversation, forced his eyes open and looked up at the pulpit where Father Mitchell was standing. He had his hands on either side of it, seeming to need it for support, and he looked tired. He looked more tired than Timm currently felt. The realization struck Timm funny, and suddenly it was easier for him to hold his eyes open.

"Every day the world seems harder to live in, doesn't it?" Mitchell asked the crowd. Timm felt himself nod in agreement, and noticed quite a few others were nodding along with his words. "And it feels less and less often we get to see a sign from God that He's there, listening to you, watching out for you. Sometimes you feel like you need an enormous flare from the sky just to feel comfort in knowing that He's there. Or maybe, a massive amount of fish."

Laughter rolled throughout the church, and Timm felt himself swept up in it along with the regulars.

"And sometimes, you're given signs, but they are not there to give you comfort. They are there to test your faith," Father Mitchell continued. Timm felt his heart sink as he looked over at Morgan. All the color had drained from her face. She met his eyes and nodded. He was talking about them.

"Then, you'll be overwhelmed by signs! You won't know which way to go, or what He is telling you to do, so what can you do?" Father Mitchell asked the crowd, who sat silently, hoping desperately that they wouldn't have to give an answer. Timm knew that he was desperately hoping for the same thing.

"You feel overwhelmed, that you're unworthy of your faith. In spite of all the good you may have done in your life, God has made a mistake in sending these signs to you. Of putting this burden on your shoulders. It's too much! And you feel you're at your breaking point," he continued, his tired voice growing with conviction and a subtle desperation that struck Timm as if it were his own. "And much like Simon-Peter, you only feel unworthy because of the sins you have committed. We know that in our faith we are worthy of having our sins forgiven. But sometimes those sins feel so wretched that we only feel worthy of the hate."

Timm squirmed uncomfortably in his seat, stopping only when Smithers gave him a dirty look. He saw the grimace on the old man's face that mirrored his own discomfort. Clearly, he could also clearly make out the subtext of Father Mitchell's sermon: they were reaching the end of his hospitality.

"There is no time in any of our lives when we aren't tempted to give into that despair, that we deserve some of what we're getting. The suffering being sent us, for it could very well be a punishment from on high! A punishment that we feel we deserve. But if you're not careful, that kind of thinking can drag you down." Father Mitchell said, his voice softening. "You need to let those thoughts go, focus on others instead of yourself. Be as Simon-Peter, and become a fisher of men. Taking on too much will only tear you apart, and much like the fishermen, you need to ask for help. You need to ask for aid just as you must go out and offer it to others. God has told you plainly what to do. Go, be a fisher of men, help them, but don't let your interpretation of the signs misdirect you away from his true Word. Amen."

The congregation around them repeated the amen and the service continued, though Timm still could not give it his full attention. This time it was not because of sleep deprivation, but because of the weight of Father Mitchell's words. There was a lot being said there that Timm could not perfectly follow. He recognized the displeasure in his subtext, but Mitchell didn't seem to be revoking his offer of help to them. Or at the very least, he seemed to still want to help them help others. Timm grit his teeth, waiting impatiently for the service to be over so he could talk to the others about what was just said. As Mitchell said, trying to interpret things was a waste of time. He just wanted clear, direct communication.

He felt frustrated, he felt angry, but most of all he felt guilty. It was their actions that had put the father at risk, and their ignorance of the world that had drawn so many enemies down on them at once. It was inevitable that someone helping them so closely would end up in the crossfire, and it was stupid of them not to realize that.

Morgan squeezed his hand, harder than she had before. He looked over at her to see panic in her eyes.

"What?" Timm whispered.

"Your hands!" Morgan hissed back.

"What?" Timm asked, alarmed.

"They're glowing!" Morgan said, pushing his hand away, trying desperately to hide it without being noticed by the crowd around them.

"What!" Timm said, louder than he meant to, drawing the eye of those around him. As quickly as he could, Timm stuffed his hands into his pockets and tried to grin casually to the people around them. Smithers looked at him intensely, as though trying to scream at Timm with his eyes. Timm could only answer with a shrug, and stuffed his hands deeper in his pockets.

It was a long, grueling end to the service, and Timm's mind was now ablaze with questions and theories of what was going on. He couldn't manage to peg a single coherent thought down and just sat, bouncing his leg impatiently, until he got the opportunity to talk to someone, anyone, about what was going on.

After what felt like an eternity passed, Father Mitchell said his final blessing and dismissed the crowd, who took their sweet time leaving. As soon as they were far enough away, Timm leaned over to Lee.

"Did you see?" Timm asked in a hushed voice.

"I did," Lee nodded at the pulpit where Father Mitchell was still set about cleaning up after the service. "It seems Father Mitchell no longer wishes to risk his life to help us, though seems to be willing to help us in ways that will not endanger his life. I feel that was good of him, to set boundaries like that."

"All it took was a bullet in the shoulder," Smithers said, gravely.

"This is true," Lee nodded. "He probably isn't willing to do *that* again for us."

"Not that!" Timm said, his voice rising. "This!"

He pulled one of his still glowing hands from his pocket, presenting it to the group. Lee's eyes opened in amazement as both Luis and Smithers forced Timm's hand down and away from the view of others.

"What is the matter with you?" Smithers hissed at him.

Timm shook his head and pulled out his other hand, but kept it low in order to avoid them completely dog piling on top of him.

"I have no idea!" Timm said, bringing his voice back down to a harsh whisper. "I was just thinking about what was going on with the sermon, feeling a bit guilty, and suddenly my hands started to glow."

"Has this happened before?" Lee asked Timm, and the calmness of the priest's voice wafted out and washed over him like a warm breeze. Timm immediately felt more relaxed.

"Well, last night after the fight, I'd been feeling kind of guilty about not being able to contribute as well because I'd made the decision to get drunk," Timm explained. As he did, he noted a knowing look between Luis and Smithers, but chose to ignore it. "I went back to the chapel to try and commune with my god a little, like my master had told me, and my holy symbol glowed. Though, now that I think about it, it's possible that my hands were glowing under the symbol..."

Timm trailed off in that thought, trying to remember if there was ever a time he'd seen his master's symbol glow, but as he tried to reach through the mists of his memories, a sharp pain pierced his mind and the memory was lost.

"Ah... dammit," Timm shook his head, clearing away the pain. "Nothing, sorry."

"I didn't know you were a holy man," Luis said, stepping forward. "Who do you pray to? Maybe that can help us get some answers."

"Oh, here," Timm said, fishing the holy symbol out of his pocket and showing it to the group.

The gold was a little dirty, but still shone in the midmorning sun that peeked through the stained glass windows of the church. Though the tines of the edges were sharp, the smooth circular sun that lay in his hand only felt warm. Criss-crossing knot patterns adorned the center, carved as one continuous line to represent the infinite cycle of the sun's path across the sky, or so his master had taught him. To look at it openly filled him with greater warmth and his hands began to glow more brightly.

"That may well prove there is a connection," Lee nodded at Timm's now brightly glowing hands.

"Could someone throw some mittens on him?" Smithers asked, irritated.

Timm buried his hands back in his pockets along with the symbol.

"I do not recognize that god," Luis nodded at the symbol, now out of sight. "Who does it represent?"

"Oh, I'm not surprised," Timm said, shrugging. "It belongs to Belenus, god of the sun. It's really uncommon for anyone to worship him where I'm from. Really, just me and my master did, though I guess that means just me now..."

Timm's voice trailed off as the thought crossed his mind. To be the last worshipper of a god may carry some heavy consequences and responsibilities with it. What could he possibly have to offer?

"Take your hands out," Luis said with such authority that Timm didn't realize he'd already removed his hands by the time the knight started speaking again. "Now, focus your energy, I believe you call it Ki?"

"Yes," Timm nodded. "That's what we call it."

"Then you already know how to channel and focus it, that makes my life easier," Luis nodded. "Focus it on your hands and will them to stop glowing."

Closing his eyes, Timm tried to focus on his master's teaching on how best to control the energy that flowed through and around him. His emotions seemed to be making his hands glow, and the more powerfully he felt them, the brighter they grew. *It is not healthy to not feel at all,* his master had said, *but to channel your feelings productively. To feel too strongly is to invite devastation.*

Slowing his breathing, and with it his heart, Timm ordered his thoughts and tethered down his emotions. Guilt was still there, but he pulled it back into a manageable place. While he was haunted by past failings, there was nothing he could do about them now, only changing his behavior in the future could affect guilt. Frustration was present, but unproductive, so he boxed it away to be dealt with later. Shame, which had weighed heavily on him, had no use outside of stunting his learning, so that emotion he took in and focused his attention in an attempt to let go. It was easier said than done, but a moment later he opened his eyes to see Luis' approving grin.

"Well done," the knight said, and Timm looked down at his hands, now free from any illumination. "It took me much longer to learn to control my abilities when Nike chose to bless me with them."

"Wait," Timm asked, apprehension growing in his chest, though he quickly tethered that too. "Are you saying I'm a knight like you?"

Luis shrugged. "I cannot say for certain, but I can say that your god has blessed you with a gift. What that means is for you to determine."

"Honestly, I was beginning to think that perhaps he wasn't real," Timm said, breathing deeply. He was surprised that he was willing to admit such blasphemy to others, but realized that his doubts held no shame for him. "I'm surprised he would choose me as one to bless. Though he isn't exactly spoiled for choice."

Luis looked as though he was going to respond to that, but was interrupted when Father Mitchell walked over to join them.

"I'm glad to see you all made it," Father Mitchell said. "What did you think of the service?"

"It was a wonderful service," Lee answered, voice steady and calm. "And your sermon was inspired. I'm sure that all of us will take your words to heart as we progress forward with our lives here."

"That is good to hear," Father Mitchell said, relief evident in his voice. "I was hoping that it would do something to help mitigate some of the collateral effects."

Lee smiled. "Quite."

Timm sensed the awkwardness that hung in the air as the two men talked. Heat began to tingle in the palms of his hands and he had to refocus his Ki and put up walls between his body and his emotions. This would require a great deal of effort and training on his part, but Luis' deduction about its source filled him with a great deal of excitement.

Father Mitchell cleared his throat.

"Well, I'm glad that you all enjoyed it," he nodded. "I think I'll go get out of these heavy robes and back into..."

A loud crash broke the tension in the air. Timm turned, hands flaring to life with the sudden surge of adrenaline. Rather than being met with an attack, Timm saw the staggering form of Walter leaning against the pillar that sat in the back of the church with a dish of holy water in it. The ground around his feet was wet and the pan was turned upside down on the ground. Walter was clutching his side, and it was then that Timm noticed there was more than just water dripping onto the floor.

"They came!" Walter cried out, falling to his knees. "They came!"

Walter fell face down into the pool of holy water and blood gathering at his feet.

$$\sim 29 \sim$$

LUIS

Before his mind had fully processed what was happening, Luis had vaulted over the pew and taken off at a run down the aisle. He reached Walter's fallen form with Morgan hot on his heels. Pressing his hand against Walter's chest, Luis called for the power of Nike to spare the man from death. He could feel the slickness of the blood under the palm of his hand and the ripple of Walter's flesh as the wound closed.

Something round and cold pushed its way out from the wound, and when Luis pulled his hand away, he looked at the small, mis-shapened, metal ball that rolled in his bloody palm.

"You pulled it out?" Walter asked, looking up at Luis. "Oh... thank god."

Walter's eyes rolled back into his head and the man lost consciousness. Luis quickly checked his vitals and noted that his heartbeat was steady if not strong. He looked up and met Morgan's worried expression.

"He's fine, just passed out," Luis said with a nod. He turned his attention to Timm. "Help me carry him downstairs. The wound is closed, but he's lost a lot of blood."

"All over the floor here, it seems," Father Mitchell said, concern in his voice. Luis felt hot words flare up on the tip of his tongue, but they were quelled as Father Mitchell looked up with worry in his eyes. "If people are after him, this is a direct trail. We need to hide him well."

Luis felt a smile tug at the sides of his mouth. Help the people indeed, he thought.

Morgan hopped up from where she was squatting in the blood and water. "I'll clean it up, Lee, go with them and see what you can do. Father Mitchell, show me where the supplies are."

"Yes, right," Father Mitchell nodded, following Morgan as she darted off down one of the side doors that led out into the office areas of the church.

With Timm's help, Luis managed to get Walter down the stairs with little struggle. With every bump and jostle, he moaned or gasped with pain, and Luis felt a twinge of guilt that he couldn't do more to aid the man when he was wounded. Lee would have to see to him to make sure that the job was properly done.

When they placed Walter on the cot, Lee came over and examined him. Luis could feel the tension rise in his body as the minutes ticked by and Lee continued to test parts of the man's body before muttering to himself and moving on.

"Well?" Luis finally asked, exasperated.

"Well, there's nothing more to be done," Lee said with a shrug. "You tended to his wound admirably, but the damage here is mental strain. Nothing any of us can provide appeasement for while he is unconscious. We are just going to have to wait for him to recover."

Luis grit his teeth, but nodded and walked over to his cot, sitting down to watch over Walter as he rested.

"Go help Morgan and Father Mitchell," Lee told him.

"But what if..." Luis started.

"I will fetch you if he wakes," Lee said calmly. "But you are radiating nervous energy and need to be doing something. If you sit here too long you will wind up driving yourself insane."

Luis thought about Lee's words and resigned with a sigh. He reached under his pillow, pulling the sword from its hiding place and fastened it to his belt, hiding it under the coat. After securing it, he stood and marched up the stairs without a further word on the matter. With the help of Father Mitchell, Morgan, and Timm, they cleaned the blood from both the church and the hall leading into it. Father Mitchel even had Donovan come out with a specialized hose he called a 'pressure washer' and Luis watched in amazement as it spewed forth water so mightily that not only the blood on the sidewalk vanished in its torrent, but it also left patches a different color.

"You know, people won't be happy if this ices over," Donovan said.

"Throw some salt down, Don," Father Mitchell said, worriedly looking around. "We don't want anyone getting hurt, but that also means that..."

Donovan held up a hand. "Don't wanna know, if I know, then my life becomes as complicated as yours. Salt it is, then I'm going on lunch."

And so, Luis passed the four hours it took for Walter to wake up. They were made aware of the change in his status, not by Smithers or Lee coming to tell them, but from the bloodcurdling scream that echoed through the church, as though a demon were being driven from his body.

Luis flew down the stairs, skipping quite a few of them to get to the bottom. Walter was sitting shock upright in bed, his hands clenched against the place his wound should have been, breathing heavily.

"I'm dead," the man said, eyes wide in panic. "I should be dead. There's nothing else. Not with the wound I had."

"Your wound has been taken care of," Lee said in a gentle voice. "Luis over there saw to that."

Walter looked up at Luis. "Is that true? Wait... Yes! I remember you! I remember your face! You were standing over me, in the church!"

"That was me," Luis nodded, keeping his voice as steady as he could as he pushed back on the adrenaline rush that had spurred him forward to nothing more than a startled awakening. "I am glad you are feeling better. Do you know who did this to you?"

"Maybe we shouldn't start in with the questions so quickly?" Father Mitchell suggested. "The poor man has only just woken up. He needs time to rest, recuperate."

Walter shook his head. "I'm fine to talk, father. It was the suits. The ones in the black vans. Never trust a man in a suit driving in a black van..."

"Men in suits?" Luis pondered.

"DIARD," Lee said, his voice certain.

"They didn't have that on their vans, but probably them," Walter nodded in agreement. "DIARD had been snooping around my park, and you don't get more government issue than black vans and suits. It's an easy uniform to afford on a government salary."

Luis wasn't quite sure what Walter meant by that, but that would make the second person they had gotten help from ending up at the end of one of DIARD's guns. Thankfully they had gotten to him in time, or rather, he'd gotten to them, but the next time the victim of these government animals may not be so lucky. Luis clenched his fist tightly.

"Why did they attack you?" Luis asked, trying to keep his temper under control.

"Because I tried to stop them," Walter said, as though it was obvious. "You see, I was heading back to my bridge, when out of nowhere these guys appeared holding guns. They demanded Stuffers, and I refused to give him to them. So they shot me and took him."

"They shot you over a teddy bear?" Smithers asked, flabbergasted.

"He's not just a teddy bear," Walter said, shaking his head. "But they shot me, and I fell into the river. Next thing I know, I'm dragging my sorry carcass out of the river, freezing as I go, and Stuffers is long gone, no doubt in the clutches of DIARD. So I pulled myself together and got here as quickly as I could. I knew if anyone could get Stuffers back, it would be you all."

"So you're asking us to hunt down a group of government lackeys," Smithers said. "Storm their compound, and risk almost certain death... for your teddy bear."

"I told you, he's no teddy bear!" Walter said, clearly getting upset.

Luis stood up and stepped between the two men, holding his hands out peaceably.

"Listen, Smithers," Luis said. "DIARD was willing to shoot a man in order to get their hands on Stuffers. Regardless of what he is, he's valuable to DIARD, which means we probably don't want them to have him. Besides, the worst outcome is that Stuffers is nothing more than a teddy bear..."

"Which he's not," Walter interjected.

"Which he's not," Luis repeated placatingly. "But we still get the opportunity to learn more about DIARD."

Smithers thought about that for a moment. "You make a pretty reasoned argument there, you know?"

"Someone once told me that I'm wiser than I look," Luis said, smiling at Smithers.

The old man just shook his head. "Okay, say we go along with this crazy plan. We don't even know where they are, or where their compound is."

"I can show you," Walter offered.

"You know where they went?" Smithers asked.

"No," Walter said. "But I can find them, or at least, I can find Stuffers. When he wants me to."

The room was silent for a moment.

"Yeah," Smithters said, breaking the spell and starting up the stairs to the canteen. "That's not unnerving at all. Alright, kids, get your school bags ready, we're hopping aboard the bus to loony-ville and fighting the government for control of a teddy bear. Because that might as well be my life…"

Timm clenched his fists tightly as he addressed Walter.

"Don't worry," he said, as Luis noticed a faint glow beginning to appear in the man's balled up fist. "We'll get Stuffers, and we'll pay these guys back for shooting you."

"Morgan," Luis barked so suddenly that Timm turned to face him as well. "Please assist Timm with his hand. I'll head by the thrift shop upstairs and pick him up a pair of gloves. Wouldn't want that issue of his suffering from *exposure*."

Luis let that last word hang in the air as he locked eyes with Timm. Embarrassment flooded Timm's expression, but Luis did not let him go. He wanted to be sure that Timm understood what his eyes were screaming at him.

Keep that hidden, was what Luis tried to convey. *Otherwise you can give us away.*

Luis was unsure if Timm had understood the message, but Morgan nodded furiously at him and pulled Timm away to talk to him on the other side of the room. They spoke in harsh whispers, but Luis did not want to waste his energy trying to overhear the conversation. Instead, he turned his attention to Walter.

"When we leave, we'll help you upstairs," Luis said. "Until then, I need you to rest so that you'll be able to help us when the time comes."

"You can count on me," Walter said, leaning back in the cot and settling in. "I'll be good… to go…"

Soon Walter was snoring. Luis smiled for a moment, glad that the man had found peace among the chaos. But he had work to do, and could not seek out his own. So Luis dove head first into the brimming chaos to find a pair of gloves.

~ 30 ~

MORGAN

Morgan pulled Timm away from where Luis and Walter were talking, whispering quietly to him in an attempt to get him to calm down. They had linked that his glowing hands were somehow connected to his emotions, and shone brighter when he felt more deeply. Morgan had grown to admire how deeply Timm felt things, from his passion for justice and protecting others to his joy and excitement at life. Even in battle, when he would lose himself in the rhythm of combat, he would throw himself in with everything he had. Morgan didn't think he could function any other way.

But now, to keep their existence secret, or at least as secret as they could muster, he was going to have to start tempering those emotions. Feel them just a little less. She was worried, not if he would be able to do so, but what would happen to a man like him that felt so deeply to just... not anymore.

"Are you okay?" Morgan asked him as the glow began to fade.

"Yeah," Timm said, nodding. "Yeah, I think I've got it now."

"You have to be careful," Morgan said quietly. "You get so excited so quickly."

"I know," Timm said, though she could sense the irritation in his voice. It didn't seem to be directed at her, but she knew that she was not helping matters by drawing his attention to his shortcomings. She tried a different approach.

"So are you becoming a knight, like Luis?" she asked, allowing a bit of her own excitement to shine through. She didn't even have to fake it, if Timm was becoming a holy knight like Luis, it would mean that his god recognized him as a great warrior and wanted to bestow a blessing on him. It would be an amazing honor.

Apparently, Timm thought so as well. He couldn't stop a smile from creeping across his face. Or, for that matter, a light glow to appear in the center of his palms. He took a breath and both the smile and glow faded.

"I don't know," Timm said, shaking his head. "It's so new, and my master never told me about anything like this. He had said that he saw the Light of Belenus within me, but I never thought he meant anything as literal as this."

"Whatever it is, just know we are here to help you figure it out," Morgan said, putting her hand on his shoulder. "You won't have to face it alone. And with Lee and Luis, and maybe even Father Mitchell, you've got a holy arsenal at your back."

"Don't your powers come from the divine as well?" Timm asked, curiously.

Morgan shrugged. "I guess you could say that, for lack of a better term. There are gods of nature, but my people don't necessarily need to revere them. There's a power in nature all its own, apart from the gods. Though it is a divine power."

"Gods get their power from the number of people who worship them," Timm said, thinking out loud about what they'd learned about divinity in their search for Nergal. "If you consider the number of creatures who rely on nature for survival as worshipers..."

"Then we would probably be the largest religion in the world," Morgan said, smiling.

"That's pretty wild," Timm said, grinning.

"Was that a pun?" Morgan asked.

"What's a pun?"

"Nevermind," Morgan shook her head. "I can make some magical healing berries. They don't restore a lot, but they can get you moving again, and they last all day. I'll go conjure some and then I think my preparation will be done."

"That's a good idea," Timm said. "Can I bounce one off you too?"

"Uh, sure," Morgan nodded as she crossed her legs on the floor, trying to get comfortable.

She pulled a sprig of mistletoe out of her bag and began twirling it lightly in one hand, the scent of evergreens filling the air around her as warmth pulsed through her leather bracelet. Rich, red berries grew from the sprig and swelled to the size of cherries until one by one they fell off and landed softly on the carpeted floor in front of her.

"Wow," Timm said. "That's cool."

"Thanks," Morgan said, smiling. "Now what was your idea?"

"Oh, right!" Timm said excitedly, his hands pulsing with light as he did. "We should call Damian in for help. He knows a lot about these people, right?"

Morgan was suddenly very happy that her hands did not glow as her emotions rose, otherwise she felt she would be a bright enough beacon to lead ships into port. Her heart slammed into her chest as it beat furiously at the idea of seeing Damian again.

"Uh..." Morgan said, clearing her throat and trying to calm her nerves. "Yeah, I suppose that is a good idea. He and Simon should know what we'd be walking into at the very least."

"Perfect," Timm said, grinning. "We can visit them on the way."

"Visit who?" Smithers asked, coming over to where they were currently sitting. He began unpacking his bag and repacking it so things fit better inside.

"Damian and Simon," Timm said. "They know more about DI-ARD than anyone else we've spoken to, right? So it would be a good idea to visit them."

"I mean, we could just call them," Smithers said, plainly.

"I don't think I know magic powerful enough to just call out to them," Morgan said. "Perhaps Lee might?"

Smithers rolled his eyes. "Always with the magic, you people."

Smithers dug through his bag and pulled out a black rectangle about three inches long, two inches wide, and about half an inch thick. He held it up and pointed at it.

"Phones, people," Smithers said. "You keep forgetting we have phones."

"Oh!" Morgan said. "That's right, you used that to contact the church the other day."

"Yeah, the other day after we were attacked by a bunch of 'Deus Vult' psychopaths," Smithers nodded in agreement, his smile sardonic at best. "Damian gave you a card? Right?"

"Uh, yeah," Morgan said, instinctively pressing her hand against her pocket where she kept the card close to her.

"Good, gimme," Smithers said, holding his hand out.

Morgan reluctantly passed the card to Smithers who looked at it for a moment, then began fiddling with the phone in his hand. He passed the card back to Morgan, who quickly slipped it into her pocket where it would be safe. He put the phone to his ear and waited.

"Hey, Simon?" Smithers said, and paused. Morgan assumed Simon was talking back, but was unable to hear him from the distance she stood. "Yeah, the dumbass wants to talk to you about something."

Smithers passed the phone to Timm.

"Can you hear me, wizard?" Timm shouted at the phone in Smithers' hand.

The old man sighed and rubbed his temples. "No, you put it to your head and talk."

Timm took the phone from Smithers and placed it on top of his head, carefully balancing it where he stood. Smithers looked at him for a beat, and Morgan could tell that the old man was trying to determine if Timm was being serious or sarcastic, but inevitably decided that he did not care enough about the answer. Smithers stepped up, took the phone off of Timm's head, and passed it to Morgan.

Taking the phone, she held it up to her ear and heard Simon's voice. "Guys, I have work to do, if this is a crank call, can you pull it on someone else? I'm busy."

"Simon?" Morgan asked. "Sorry, we were having..."

She looked at Smithers who was glowering angrily at Timm.

"Difficulties," Morgan finished.

"Okay then, hi Morgan," Simon said, some of the edge in his voice gone, but not all of it. "What can I do to help you help me get off this call faster?"

"Well, you see," Morgan said, awkwardly talking to Simon's disembodied voice. "We're taking a trip up to a DIARD facility and wanted to know if you..."

"*And* look who's using words on an unsecured line and shouldn't be!" Simon said, cutting her off. "Do me a favor, put Smithers back on the phone."

Morgan sheepishly handed the phone to Smithers. "He, uh... wants to talk to you."

Smithers rolled his eyes, flipped the phone over, and pressed a button.

"You're on speaker and they promise to keep their mouths shut," Smithers said, glaring at both her and Timm. They nodded.

"Alright, so it sounds to me like you're off to visit some of our *mutual friends*," Simon said, emphasizing certain words.

"We are making a day trip of it soon," Smithers answered. "We were wondering if you wanted to send a tagalong?"

"Sorry," Simon said. "But he's off visiting a different friend today. But do send our love, won't you?"

"Sure thing, want us to pass anything along?" Smithers asked.

"Nothing in particular," Simon answered. "But if you could get grandma's address from them, we'd be obliged. Though if you can't, I understand. I'm sure it will be really crowded."

"Think we should choose a different day to visit?" Smithers asked. "So we can beat the traffic?"

"Nah, you should be fine if you park down the road a bit," Simon said.

"Thanks for the heads up," Smithers responded. "I'll let you know if we hit a snag on the trip. Goodbye."

Smithers hung up the phone and sighed.

"Seriously, you guys?" He said, exasperated. "You've been here for weeks and you say the name of the damn government agency looking for us on the phone? I'm going to have to burn this thing now, and I *just* got it!"

"Why?" Timm asked. "It's not like you said anything impor-tant."

Smithers looked coldly at Timm before taking a deep breath.

"First, I asked if Damian wanted to join us, but Simon said he's currently on another mission," Smithers explained, holding up a finger for every point he made. "Secondly, I asked if Simon needed us to do anything at the facility while we were there, he said no but wanted to know if we could find the location of another facil-ity that might be higher up the chain, hence calling it 'grandma.' Thirdly, he told us that he was familiar with the facility in ques-tion, and that it would be full of guards."

"Wait," Morgan interjected. "How did he know where it was? We don't know where it is."

"Day trip," Smithers explained. "Walter said it wasn't too far away, figure it will take a couple hours of driving. I asked Simon if we should hold off, wait for a changing of the guard or something, but Simon said we'd be fine if we approached cautiously on foot. Finally, I told him to await word from us, so he knows if we don't contact him, that we ran into trouble, and maybe he or Damian can do something to help us out."

"You said all of that," Timm asked, stunned. "Through an inane conversation?"

"Called speaking in code," Smithers said, pulling something out of the back of the phone and tossing it in the trash. "And now we're stopping for a new burner phone on the way."

Smithers got up and walked across the room. "Luis! Lee! Ready for a crusade against the evils of armed bureaucracy?"

"That is probably the most exciting way you could have described that for me, Smithers," Luis said, grinning as he double checked the belts keeping his short sword latched to his leg.

"I do what I can," Smithers said, heading up the stairs. "I'm gonna grab the keys from the padre. Meet me at the van."

Morgan stood and began passing out berries to people, being sure to hold on to a couple to give to Smithers. The others understood their properties well enough, but she felt she would need to spend more time explaining it to Smithers, and even more time trying to get him to accept how they work.

As she was talking to Lee, she overheard Luis handing the gloves to Timm. She looked over her shoulder and saw him excitedly putting them on, stifling the glow of his hands beneath the soft leather.

"There," Luis was saying. "I had to get leather because the light would have shone through the stitching of cloth ones. Try to be careful with them."

"They feel pretty good," Timm said, throwing a few punches at the air, hopping on the balls of his feet and bobbing back and forth. "Alright! I'm ready!"

He whooped with excitement, but no glow escaped the gloves around his hands. Morgan couldn't help it, she laughed with relief. Timm turned to her and smiled, throwing a few more shadow punches, and finished off the combo with flourish.

A beam of brilliant, radiant light shot from his balled up fist, bypassing the glove entirely, and slammed into Morgan's chest with the force of a full grown man tackling her.

Blinded by the brilliance of the light and tumbling backwards from the force, she lost all sense of up and down as she slammed into the wall and crumpled to the ground in a heap.

It took a moment for her to orient herself since her vision was a bit blurry and there was a strange ringing in her ears that made it hard to hear, but when she cleared her vision she was finally able to see Lee standing over her. His mouth was moving, but she couldn't make out what he was saying. Slowly sound began to leak through the piercing wailing that was so persistent in her head.

"Morgan!" Lee's voice cried urgently, but seemed to be so far away. "Morgan, are you okay?"

Morgan groaned as she tried to stand up, Lee tried to push her back down, but she waved him off, as she glanced up and saw at the mess of cots that were now toppled on their sides, probably from her flying through them. Tracing her path back to where she'd been standing, she saw Luis restraining Timm, who was wailing in anguish. Sound was rushing back to her quicker now, and she could hear Timm crying over and over.

"I'm sorry!" he practically screamed. "I'm sorry! I don't know what that was! I'm sorry!"

Luis held Timm back, keeping his arms pinned behind his back in a way that Morgan was sure had to be painful, as he looked at Lee, his expression grim. Morgan looked up in time to see the priest shake his head at Luis, before looking back at Morgan.

"It's okay," Morgan said softly to Lee, holding her hand up. Lee nodded, took her hand, and helped her to her feet. Slowly, making sure she wasn't more hurt than she thought, Morgan crossed the room to the distraught Timm.

He was wordless now, bawling uncontrollably, face ruddy and voice strained. Luis seemed to be having a difficult time holding him up, if not back, and the man sunk to his knees, weeping.

Morgan knelt down next to him, then looked up at Luis, giving him a slow, gentle nod that told him to let Timm go.

"Are you sure?" Luis asked.

"It's okay," she said to the knight, nodding her head. Luis nodded back and gently let go of Timm's arms. The man slumped forward, arms hanging limply by his side.

Morgan placed her hands on his shoulders, and held fast as Timm tried to flinch away.

"Hey," she said softly, as if speaking to a wounded animal. "Hey, it's okay."

Timm's bloodshot eyes met hers and she smiled her best smile at him, doing everything she could to ignore the pain and discomfort she was in.

"I'm okay," she smiled, meeting his mistake with gentleness. His power was wild, beyond his understanding, and tied to his emotional state. Getting angry or making him experience more, stronger emotions was only going to put them all in the path of greater harm.

A sob wracked his body again, and gently, Morgan pulled Timm in and held him, letting him cry. They stayed like that for a few moments, all the while Morgan whispering to him that everything would be okay. It was important that he felt these emotions now, because Morgan feared what could happen if he waited.

~ 31 ~

SMITHERS

"Seriously," Father Mitchell asked, staring at Smithers unblinkingly. "Did you even listen to the sermon this morning?"

"I did," Smithers nodded. "And it was lovely. Can we borrow the van?"

"It literally *just* got the bullet holes fixed," Father Mitchell replied.

"Which means it's good to go," Smithers responded. "Can we borrow the van?"

"I feel like you're not listening to my concerns here," Father Mitchell said, his voice somehow sounding even more tired than earlier.

"You don't want us to involve you in any more shenanigans that can get you hurt. I'm not asking you to come with us. You don't want knowledge of things that could potentially get you in trouble, so I'm not telling you where we are taking the van. You *do* want us to continue to help people who are in trouble. We are literally trying to protect the interests of the man resting up downstairs from a bullet wound," Smithers listed off.

Father Mitchell paused and thought over what Smithers had said to him.

"Huh, it seems you were listening after all," he said, shaking his head.

"Selectively," Smithers nodded.

260

"Fine," Father Mitchell said, pulling a ring of keys out from his desk. "Just bring it back with a full tank."

"Got it," Smithers nodded, taking the keys and heading for the door.

"Full of *gas!*" Father Mitchell cried after him as he exited. "Not bullets!"

"*I got it!*" Smithers shouted back over his shoulder as he walked down the hallway towards the parking lot, his weapons bag thrown over his shoulder.

There was a little part of Smithers that wanted desperately to admit he was enjoying this. In spite of the monsters, magic, and crazy yahoos he'd fallen in with, it was starting to feel a bit like the good old days of his youth. Walking down a hallway, just a bag over one shoulder as he made his way to the transport to take down an enemy facility. Butterflies filled his belly again just like the first time he'd strapped on that camo and went into the field.

"Heh," Smithers laughed to himself. "Those were the days."

And part of him truly thought they were, so long as he kept the dark thoughts at bay. The nightmares that came from watching those die around him, both by his hand and not. Friend and foe, didn't matter out there, blood was blood. It was always red and always flowed freely.

He shook the thoughts away and steeled himself. Couldn't afford to show weakness like that anymore. Not in front of the new kids, and not in front of the monsters he was facing now. Now, blood wasn't always red. Hell, blood wasn't always *there.* He'd fought a goddamned ghost, mobsters, and a pack of irradiated wolves that were really people transformed. All within the past week.

If that didn't skew your world view, Smithers couldn't tell you what would.

But now wasn't the time to let his cage get rattled. The kids didn't understand where they had ended up, and they were more likely to get themselves or each other killed than take out an enemy the caliber of DIARD without someone who was level headed and knowledgeable enough to guide them.

And in lieu of that, Smithers would have to do.

He got outside and saw Luis helping Walter into the passenger seat of the van. Apparently Father Mitchell had elected to keep it unlocked, which Smithers disapproved of strongly under normal circumstances, but considering it sped their process along considerably he chose to refrain from complaining about it. Seemed old dogs could learn new tricks after all.

Approaching the van, Smithers could tell that something was wrong. The air was tense and Timm was standing a bit too far away from the group. He walked over and looked at Lee, who silently shook his head.

If it's important they'll fill me in later, Smithers reasoned as he clambered into the driver's seat.

"Alright folks," he called out the open window, beckoning them inside. "Let's get this show on the road."

He turned to Walter and asked. "You know where you're going?"

"Yeah," the man nodded, eyes slightly distant. "He's not far, maybe two hours away?"

"Two hours?" Smithers asked. "We'll be there and back by dinner.

Four hours later, Smithers had taken to gripping the wheel as tightly as he could to keep himself from wrapping his hands around Walter's throat. The man's directions were manic, having Smithers exit the highway, travel in a direction for ten minutes, only to turn around after 'they'd lost the trail.'

"Who?" Smithers asked, angrily after the third or fourth time he'd done it. "Who is on our trail? Who could possibly know we're coming?"

"They know, man," was Walter's answer. "They always know."

Smithers decided it was safer for everyone if he'd just stopped engaging Walter from now on, and let 'Sweets' take care of it. Morgan seemed to have a much easier time interacting with Walter than others. Lee was sitting beside her in the second row, directly behind where he and Walter were.

Timm had gone to sit in the third row, but Lee had given him a look that could curdle milk, and Timm elected to sit in the back row. Instead, Luis took the third, sprawled out across it, and went to sleep.

Smithers was quite jealous of this, considering the early rising they had been forced to do in exchange for hospitality, and made a mental note that one of these idiots should be taught to drive despite Simon's warning. The risk of a ten car pileup wouldn't be any worse than what came from normal New England drivers, and as a bonus he wouldn't always be the designated driver.

"We're here!" Walter said, causing Smithers to slam on the brakes and look around wildly, hoping to god they weren't sitting ducks for a sniper's nest.

"Where?" Smithers asked, looking for the facility, but seeing only bare limbed trees, snow, and rocks. A few sparse evergreens dotted the landscape, but he didn't see anything that resembled a structure.

"It's about a mile that way," Walter pointed deeper into the woods off the road.

The urge to strangle came flying back to Smithers, but years of training and a few mandated anger management classes had taught him that it is very bad to strangle an injured man. Especially one you were trying to help.

"Pull off here, and we'll hide the van as best we can," Morgan suggested. "And we should probably leave Walter here, this way he won't slow us down or freeze to death out there. He has lost a lot of blood."

"Yes," Smithers jumped to agree, probably quicker than he should have. "Yes, I love this plan. Let's do this plan."

It didn't take long to hide the van, mostly because they didn't do a very good job. Smithers felt it would probably look less conspicuous as an abandoned van than with the sparse sticks and pine needles they'd managed to coat it with. And shoveling snow over it to camouflage would just make it harder to get into as an escape vehicle.

Walter sat in the driver's seat, rubbing his hands together in front of the heater. Smithers decided it would be best to keep the van running as a getaway vehicle. The trail of smog coming from the tailpipe wasn't going to draw any more attention than the shoddily disguised van sitting in the middle of the trees, so it would be minimal risk at best. Besides, they were going to be where all the shooting was anyway.

He looked over and saw Lee, hands slightly outstretched in prayer. A dim light pulsed in his hands as he reached out to touch both Luis and Timm on the shoulder. It may have been Smithers' imagination, but he thought he saw new light spark to life in their eyes. He'd seen too much to dismiss it outright, but to start giving them credit for magic without knowing what was going on would only serve to make them more terrifying in his mind. Best to keep the benefit of the doubt from them and his sanity along with it.

Silently, they began making their way through the forest. Snow crunched lightly underfoot, but the blanket of pine needles that lay beneath helped to soften their footfalls. The cold air did not do anything for Smithers' breathing, and soon his throat felt raw and his lungs ached. They had probably only hiked about half a mile when Morgan called for them to stop.

"Really?" wheezed Smithers. "I'm an old man and I'm not ready to stop just yet."

"Is that because you're feeling well enough to continue," Luis asked, grinning. "Or because you're a stubborn old goat who won't request to stop first?"

"I can be two things," Smithers panted heavily, leaning against a tree desperately trying to catch his breath.

"I'm not too tired to keep going," Morgan said, rolling her eyes. "We're just getting close. I wanted to make sure no one spotted us coming."

"Yeah, five random people armed to the teeth wandering through the woods at sunset," Smithers muttered. "Oh no, sir with the large assault rifle, we're just on a romantic stroll. Just four millennials and a geezer. Perfectly normal."

Luis looked at him. "Half of what you just said made sense to any of us. Who do you complain for?"

"Myself, mostly," Smithers answered. "Keeps me full of piss and vinegar."

"I have my doubts about one of those two things," Luis said, cocking his eyebrow and turning back to Morgan.

The girl was kneeling in an area mostly devoid of snow. She brushed it aside and pressed her fingers to the earth. Reaching into her pocket, she began to mutter something in a language Smithers did not understand, but felt a familiar presence behind. It sounded like every language ever used by a witch doctor in any movie that chose voodoo as the villain's weapon of choice. Just as he was about to ask what Morgan was doing, the girl pulled her hand from her pocket, snarling a final hushed word and blew on her hand.

A cloud of ash filled the air, blotting out the sun and dimming the reflection of the snow around them. Wispy images of the others moved around Smithers, their ghostly forms ashen grey, eyes bare glints of orange amid the darkness.

"What in the hell..." Smithers said, but his own voice seemed dull and distant, as though he was hearing himself from far away.

"It's a spell," Morgan said from far off, though Smithers looked up to see an outline that resembled her reaching a wispy hand out to take his. "Makes it harder to detect us. Bends the shadows, stifles sound. You could walk past a bloodhound and they'd never know you're there."

"That is..." Smithers looked at his own shadowy form as Morgan helped him to his feet. "Really hard to deny. Imagine if you'd done this in O'Malley's that one time. I wouldn't have been able to doubt you then."

"I couldn't have done this back then," Morgan said, and Smithers thought he caught the barest hint of a smile in the apparition of her face. "But I've gotten a lot more powerful since then."

Morgan took point and Smithers focused all his energy on following her, because otherwise he would have a hard time keeping track of where she passed. He would also have to unpack what she said about how quickly her power was growing. It had only been a few days, maybe a week, and she'd gone from party tricks to turning five people into walking shadows. What more could this girl be capable of...

Shut up, Smithers! He thought to himself. *Fear for your life now, assess the breakdown of your reality later!*

They moved slightly slower as they approached the facility, needing to take the extra time to be sure they didn't lose each other in the snow. There were no footprints to follow, and calling out was just as useless as trying to track them with your eyes. Eventually, they settled on a daisy chain, linking hands and following Morgan's lead, trusting in her to find the way.

The sun had dipped below the edges of the trees by the time they had settled outside the edges of the bright spotlight that bathed a snow covered parking lot in white light. The spotlight was fixed to a nondescript looking building that would have passed for a doctor's office in a suburban town. The only difference was the tall wire fence that winged off from either side and encircled a large outdoor area behind it blocked off with slats of grey plastic woven through the chain link.

"What's the plan?" Timm asked, nervously. Smithers noticed the boy was hanging a bit back from the group, and between the dark and the misty visage Morgan's magic had given him, it was hard to really make out what he was doing back there.

"The plan is to make a plan," Smithers answered. "And Morgan, how long does this last? I can barely hear any of you."

Morgan waved her hand and the world came rushing back into clarity around Smithers. He had to blink his eyes several times to try and adjust to just how colorful the world became the moment the spell was gone. It was really true what they said, you don't know what you've been missing until it's gone.

"Thank you, that's better," Smithers said, turning to observe the building itself. Not much had changed with it as the world snapped back to how Smithers remembered. Drab color, snow covered roof, and cookie-cutter fence screamed government run. But something bothered Smithers as he observed. Something was missing.

"Cameras," Smithers muttered.

"You see them?" Lee asked.

"No," Smithers said thoughtfully.

"That's a good thing, right?" asked Timm. "If there are no cameras then we can just walk right up to the front door and head inside."

"We could," Smithers nodded in agreement. "But we don't know what's inside there. And the lack of cameras actually makes me nervous about doing just that."

"Why?" Luis asked.

"Well, far as I can reckon, there's only two real reasons a government facility wouldn't have cameras attached to it. Either they don't want footage of what goes on in there leaking out, or whatever's in there doesn't need cameras to protect it," Smithers explained. "And I've got to say, I don't like the idea of tangling with either prospect."

"We need more to go off of," Luis nodded in agreement.

"Then I'll get it," Morgan said, stepping forward towards the light.

Smithers reached up to grab her by the arm and pull her back, but his hand closed on empty air. Where Morgan had been standing just a moment before was now occupied by a large cat with bright white fur. Not quite as large as the one she'd transformed into when they fought the Nergal Elk from hell, but a pretty large domestic that reminded Smithers of a Maine Coon. She shook herself out and turned her green, feline eyes towards Smithers, and he wasn't sure if it was her or the basic nature of cats, but he couldn't help but feel like she was mocking him. With a quiet mew, she bounded off into the snow, barely visible except for shadows of movement.

"Well," Smithers said, staring after her. "That is one way of going about it."

"Her kind are quite useful to have around," Luis agreed. "Druids are the best infiltrators in the world. Or rather, in any world."

"Ain't many places that can keep nature out," Smithers nodded, trying not to focus too much on the implications of his own words in regards to that Circle of the Wastes group. Seemed every advantage they had was something the enemy could have too. And enemies were piling up around them.

Quite borrowing trouble from tomorrow, he chastised himself. *Focus on the gun pointed at you, not the ones marching down the road miles away.*

They sat in silence for a long while. Long enough that even Smithers was starting to get nervous. While Timm became antsy almost immediately, Smithers had been repeating to himself that while cats were fast, they also had shorter legs. She could be slowed down by the snow, or avoiding wild animals, or any other number of perfectly reasonable reasons to be held up. But as night took its final hold of the world and thirty minutes officially passed, he was beginning to feel his level of anxiety rise to meet Timm's own.

Smithers was about to suggest that they go look for her, he felt something bump against his leg. Hand going for the pistol on his hip, Smithers looked down to see the white cat slip past him and brush past Luis, Lee, and Timm as well.

"Oh good, you're back," Smithers said, breathing out a sigh of relief. "What did you find?"

Morgan meowed at him.

"Please... don't pull this trope," Smithers said, pinching the bridge of his nose with two fingers.

Morgan meowed again before turning to the snow and pawing at it. Smithers had half a mind to shoo this cat as there was no way it could be Morgan with the way it was frustrating him, only to be proven wrong. He looked down to see that Cat-Morgan was carving out a crude map of the fence and surrounding structures.

The facility didn't look that big, but it also seemed to have limited avenues of approach. The front door was still a possibility, but on the other side it looked as though there was a break in the fence. And in the corner she had drawn something that looked like an attempt at a circle.

"Okay, the map is great and all," Smithers said to the cat. "But unless the plan is to have you meow at the front door to lure someone out, can you change back and explain it to us?"

The cat gave him a flat look, which did not change as she grew back into full Morgan form.

"Thank you," Smithers said.

Morgan ignored him and started to explain. "The fence goes around the entire back side of the facility, but there's a gate in the back. One large enough to fit our van through. There was also a really tall tower right there."

Morgan pointed at the attempted circular shape.

"Was there someone in it?" Smithers asked.

"I think so," Morgan nodded. "It was hard to see though, there was no light up there."

"Sniper nest," Smithers said. "He'll see us coming a mile away and put a bullet in our skulls from half that distance."

"So we give up?" Luis asked, irritation in his voice.

Smithers shook his head. "Nope, but the back would be the worst way to go in."

"That leaves the front door," Lee said.

"That it does," Smithers said, turning to Timm. "Looks like we're going with your plan."

"My plan?" Timm asked, sounding confused. "I didn't suggest a plan?"

"You never suggest it, you just do it," Smithers said, the cutting remark diluted by the grin he couldn't keep off his face. "Buckle up, this is going to be a bumpy ride."

~ 32 ~

LUIS

Luis listened to the rest bicker about a plan for the next five minutes while noting how steadily his patience waned. A plan was usually a surefire way to victory, he did need to admit, however he knew them to be useless if those concocting it could not agree on the parameters. There were half-baked schemes of subterfuge and rash plans of rushing the door. The knight sighed as he listened to them argue and finally decided that he would simply have to be the one to take a leap of faith.

He was probably about halfway between the treeline and the building before any of the others noticed that he was no longer with them. He could hear their harsh whispers beckoning him back and felt something brush against his boot in the snow. Looking down, Luis saw Morgan in her white cat form looking up at him, and if a cat's expression could show worry, Luis now knew what that looked like.

"Have faith," Luis whispered down to her. "Victory is assured."

The knight was sure that he imagined the look of doubt that crossed the cat's expression, because he was sure that was an emotion that cats were incapable of feeling. She walked with him to the door, and without breaking stride, Luis clutched the handle and threw it open.

Inside was a bleak, though functioning office space. The walls were a creamy white and the carpet was the reddish brown of dried blood. A bookcase was perched against one wall filled with blank, flat spined books of unsettling exactness. Two doors sat on adjacent walls, though one was behind a large wooden desk. At the desk sat a woman in her middle years, chestnut hair showing streaks of grey in it. She looked up at him behind round spectacles in surprise and opened her mouth as though to say something.

Luis did not give her a chance. He lifted his hand, palm up, and flicked two of his fingers at himself in a beckoning motion. Pushing the power of Nike and his own will through the motion, he sealed the spell with the verbal command.

"*Come.*"

The woman's expression went blank. She stood and stepped purposefully around the desk, stepping directly up to Luis. As she stood before him, her eyes cleared and she looked around confused as to how she got where she stood.

"Thank you," Luis said, smiling at her. Then again, before she could respond, Luis threw his elbow across her jaw. There was a slight cracking sound as her confused eyes rolled back in her head and she dropped to the floor unconscious.

Nodding in satisfaction, the knight turned around and made the beckoning motion to his allies in the trees. There was no need to imbue the action with any power, for he knew they would be joining him. He bent down and tucked his hands under the woman's arms and dragged her back into the room so the biting cold would not affect her.

Smithers was the first through the door.

"See, that's the kind of plan I expected from Timm. You just pulled a Timm. Congratulations. And also, what the hell was that?" the old man asked, voice shaking a bit. "Mind control?"

"When you speak with the voice of a goddess, people will obey," Luis said as he bound the woman's hands behind her back with her own belt. He looked up at Smithers and shrugged. "Sometimes at least."

"So that could have failed spectacularly," Smithers said, cocking his eyebrow at Luis.

Luis shrugged again. "So could anything in life. I had faith, and it worked."

"I like to go on a little more than faith," Smithers said, but then looked down at the unconscious woman. "Though I suppose the results speak for themselves. What does she have on her?"

Timm stepped over and helped Luis pat her down. They managed to find a set of keys, her ID badge, and a handgun. Luis originally had some reservations of striking at her so violently, but it seemed his intuition paid off. She was indeed an enemy combatant. Smithers had stepped behind the desk and was looking at her computer. It looked boxier than the one Simon worked on, and the screen was black with green letters on it rather than running videos and scrolling text.

"They're running software right out of the eighties," Smithers said, sounding exacerbated. "Every page is password protected. I can't get anything except for what she was looking at before we came in."

"What was that?" Lee asked. He was standing on the opposite side of the room watching one of the doors.

"Shipping manifests," Smithers answered. "Looks like they've got a delivery pick up tomorrow for what's called 'S Class' items. Like this is some kind of Japanese video game."

"What's a video game?" Luis asked.

"What's a Japanese?" Timm asked.

Smithers sighed.

"Neither of those things are important at this moment," Smithers answered. "But 'S Class' usually means really powerful stuff. Before meeting you guys I'd have said weapons or nukes, but I've got a feeling it might be that Stuffers thing, which I still think is just a teddy bear, but if Walter believes it's more, and you believe it's more, then who the fuck am I to day that DIARD doesn't think it's more?"

"They brought it here and are planning on shipping it out somewhere else," Lee nodded. "Probably to a more secure facility."

"If four schmucks and a cat made it this far, probably yeah," Smithers nodded. "So we keep looking for it. Which way should we go?"

Luis looked around at the set up of the room. He noted the door Lee was attending then looked at the one behind the desk he and Smithers were standing in front of.

"This way," Luis said, pointing at the door behind the desk.

"How can you be sure?" Lee asked. "This door is more accessible."

"That's how I'm sure," Luis nodded. "She wasn't a receptionist, she was a guard. That door probably leads to little or nothing, while the door behind her looks like a closet of sorts. However, if I were defending the facility, I'd be sure to put as many obstacles between an intruder and what I was protecting as possible."

"Well," Smithers said, taking the keys from Timm's hand. "Only one way to find out."

The old man started rummaging through the ring of keys, and after a few attempts finally found the one that fit the lock. With a click the door swung open to reveal a long hallway with several doors on either side.

"Huh," Lee said, looking down the hallway. "It appears you were correct in your assessment, Luis. Commendable."

Luis nodded and started to take a step, but Smithers put his hand out and shook his head.

"Best to let recon check it out first," Smithers said, nodding at the cat.

Silently, Morgan slipped past them and stepped into the hall. She slinked up to the first door on the left hand side and all but pressed her feline ear to it. Morgan sat there for a few seconds, listening, then tapped her back paw twice. Luis nodded and turned to the others.

"Two in that room," he whispered, stepping past Smithers into the hallway, pressing himself against the opposite wall. Moving past where Morgan sat, he came to another door and put his ear to it. There was no sound inside, so he turned to the others and shook his head before reaching down for the doorknob.

Surprisingly, the door was unlocked. Carefully, Luis opened the door and looked inside. Long tables took up a lot of space in this room, each covered in an assortment of glass containers made up of exceptionally strange shapes. Crates lined one wall, while a humanoid figure against the opposite wall made Luis jump and reach for his sword. It was only a moment later that he realized that it was a mannequin.

Stepping inside, he dismissed the other strange items in the room and looked towards the mannequin. The thing had seen better days, and as Luis examined the damage to its torso, he recognized what kind of weapon could produce such compact puncture marks because he had seen that exact same damage on his clothing after being shot. Surely enough, as Luis turned around, the table exactly opposite the mannequin displayed several different guns laid out in a row.

"Target practice?" Luis whispered quietly to himself. "To what purpose? At this range it's almost impossible to miss."

He turned to look at the mannequin again and noted that the wall behind it was covered with more holes than the dummy itself was. Luis knew that he was no crack shot like Smithers was, but even he couldn't miss an unmoving target at such a close range. There had to be something special about the...

A glint of metal caught Luis' eye. On the mannequin's finger there was a sparkle of a red gem on a silver band. It wasn't anything too ornate, but the ring had to be worth a decent amount. Suspicion itched at the back of Luis' mind and he reached out with his senses towards the ring. He was unable to identify its purpose, but the unmistakable tingle of arcane energy wafted from the ring.

"A magical item?" Luis said, slipping the ring off the mannequin's finger and rolling it in his fingers. "I haven't seen one of these in a long time."

Luis turned to see the others had filed into the room and were making their own investigations. Timm was holding a longbow in one hand, and a scimitar in the other, which he offered to cat-Morgan to sniff. Lee was examining the ornate glasses while Smithers was looking over the guns on the table closest to Luis.

"Guys," Luis said, his voice barely above a whisper. "Look what I found."

Luis held up the ring for them all to see.

"Aw, well I'm flattered," Smithers said. "And while you're a very handsome man, I just gotta say you are not my type."

Luis gave Smithers a flat look. "It's magical."

"Magical?" Lee asked, a mixture of curiosity and excitement in his voice. "I thought this world didn't have any tangible magic left?"

"What?" Smithers asked. "But you said there's still magic in the world or you guys wouldn't be able to draw on it."

"Life itself produces the energy that we call magic," Lee said, as he stepped forward to examine the ring. "Those wild energies create a woven pattern of ley lines and threads of magic we call the Arcane. Luis, myself, and even Morgan to an extent draw our power from the Divine. Faith creates power. Your Christian god..."

"He ain't my god," Smithers interrupted.

"...still creates that energy in the world because there are followers that have true faith in him." Lee finished explaining, ignoring the interruption. "But those sources of magic are not tangible. Magic items, artifacts that have been imbued with either arcane or divine purpose, those require a skilled crafter. Without those in your world, it would be impossible for your people to make new ones."

"Then where did this one come from?" Smithers asked.

"It could be very old," Luis shrugged. "The magic protects the item from the ravages of time and will keep it looking new regardless of age."

"Or DIARD stole it," Timm said darkly as he walked over, bow in hand, quiver of arrows on his hip. The scimitar hung opposite it, though Luis knew the man did not favor a sword, though remembered that it was the preferred weapon of druids.

"Stole it from where?" Smithers asked.

"Not where," Timm said. "Who. Remember how they took our stuff at the hospital? Who's to say this bow isn't mine? This scimitar isn't Morgan's?"

"Did you see a longsword?" Luis asked hopefully.

His heart sank as Timm shook his head.

"I would have grabbed it for you if I had," Timm said somberly.

Luis nodded. "Thank you, Timm."

"Well that's just dandy," Smithers said. "But that still doesn't get us the bear or out of here, so pocket the ring and let's keep moving."

Luis slipped the ring into his pocket and nodded, being sure to draw his sword and keep it in hand. Quietly, they made their way out of the room and checked the next couple doors. Lee hung back a bit to listen in on the room they knew people were in. One door led to another similar room as to the one they had just pilfered, though no further treasures could be found while the next was a simple bathroom. Timm ducked quickly into it and snatched the toilet paper. Luis and Morgan watched as he did, then exchanged an odd look with each other.

"What?" Timm asked.

Luis and Morgan elected to ignore the question and press on. Luis came up to the final door next to Smithers.

"Sounds like animals," Smithers whispered, his ear to the door.

"Do you think it leads outside?" Luis asked.

"We know there's a courtyard of sorts," Smithers nodded. "And a sniper's nest. Since we haven't found a door to the outside yet, I gotta say this is probably it."

"Do we want to go back?" Timm asked. "Take out those two in the other room so they don't come up behind us?"

Luis pondered that for a moment. He would hate to have someone come up behind them in their worst moment, but to seek out trouble may well bring more down on their heads. The knight shook his head.

"No," he said firmly. "If anything went wrong, that would pull every enemy here from their positions to ours. I feel the best path to victory is through cautious avoidance rather than brash confrontation."

Timm nodded and Smithers smiled at him.

"Good call," the old man said. "So, cautiously open the door and head out then?"

Luis nodded, sword in hand. Smithers quietly opened the door and they slipped outside.

The sound and thick musky scent of animals hit Luis immediately. They were standing in a muddy courtyard. A goat stood not far off in a small wooden pen separating it from a small vegetable garden that sat slightly wilted under large lamps that emitted more heat than light.

The courtyard was surrounded by a large fence that contained two other buildings and the tall tower that Smithers called a sniper's nest. In the middle of the yard sat a black van that looked similar to the one they had driven here in, though looked to be in much better shape.

"Spoiled for choice," Smithers said, quietly looking around. "What's the play?"

"Hug the buildings," Luis nodded. "Check each one. Stay quiet and out of sight."

"Alright," Smithers nodded. "Lead the way."

"To victory," Luis nodded, and started making his way to the next building, taking cautiously quiet steps through the squelching mud.

~ 33 ~

LEE

As the rest of the group slowly made its way through the court-yard of the compound, Lee hung back away from the others. They may say he was heading up the rear, or watching their backs, but in reality he constantly found his eyes being drawn up and over to the so-called sniper's nest.

Ever since the incident with the drive by shooting, as Damian had called it, Lee had been feeling exceptionally nervous around guns. The battle on the train had done nothing to soothe his nerves about the matter, and even through the intervention of his god, Goibniu, he still felt a chill every time he thought of one.

Smithers had used his own weapons to deadly efficiency, and Lee did his best to keep away from the old man on the battlefield. He did not doubt that Smithers could avoid harming him with the weapon, but any close proximity to his weapons was quite unnerving for Lee. He'd never brought it up, as his concerns would find little to no remedy through expression. The battles would continue, and the old man would fight as he had been trained, so it fell to Lee to manage his emotions rather than ask others to change themselves for his benefit. He knew from experience that such a request was impossible.

This gun, this sniper, was supposed to be even more dangerous than anything Smithers carried. The old man had said that he knew of snipers who could kill an opponent from almost a mile away if the conditions were right. If such a weapon carried with it a power that great, Lee was concerned with what it could do to a person who got too close.

They made their way, squelching through the mud of the compound. Snow fell here, but nothing stuck to the ground, it merely melted and joined in creating deeper patches of sludge underfoot. At one point, Luis lost his footing and fell face first into a thick pile of the stuff that had built up behind the wheels of the black van. Lee froze in fear, positive that the noise would draw the sniper's attention. However, after a dozen or so rapid heartbeats, it was clear that they were still unnoticed.

Timm and Morgan led the way to the first building on the edge of the sniper's nest and tested the handle. The door was unlocked, and the two shared an expression of resolve before twisting it and stepping inside. Lee steeled himself for the sounds of combat and the attention of the ever-present sniper, but nothing followed. Smithers nodded at him and Luis before stepping inside. Not wanting to be left outside in view of the angel of death hovering over him, Lee followed Luis inside.

Several bunk beds made of mundane steel and thin pads lined the room. In front of each were a pair of footlockers. The floors were tiled in a monochromatic color, and the walls were a drab grey. One window adorned the southern wall, but the light let in from the humming electrical lights outside only seemed to make the quarters less inviting. Lee remembered being in prison cells that were more cheerful than this.

"Anything good in those footlockers?" Smithers asked.

"We're going to steal from these people?" Lee asked in return.

"They've shot at us," Smithers responded, his tone flat and merciless. "After kidnapping us."

"He makes a fair point," Luis responded, walking over to one of the footlockers, and slipping his blade in between the latch and the lid, twisted it sharply, popping the top off with little effort.

Inside they found little of import. A few sets of athletic clothing, undergarments, and a box of ammunition, which Smithers excitedly added to his own collection after he checked its compatibility with his own weapon. The other footlockers were more of the same. Having gotten little more than a happier Smithers from this room, they decided to keep moving.

"We're going to have to swing around closer to where the sniper is," Smithers explained. "If we want to cross over to the other building we've got two options: either we hug the wall underneath him and hope he doesn't look down, or we go back the way we came and use the vans for cover."

"It would make most sense to put something between us and any rounds he may fire off our way, would it not?" Lee asked.

"Unless that van is armored it's not going to do a hell of a lot to stop a shot from a sniper rifle," Smithers said, shaking his head. "Not at that distance. We'd just be using it to block his view. He could probably put a bullet through one side of the van, out the other, into one of us, out the other side, and still risk shooting someone inside that building. Through the wall, not the window."

Lee felt himself blanch. "What is the point of that kind of firepower?"

"Overkill is just the right amount of kill," Smithers responded with a shrug. "Plus, it's not meant to take someone out from fifty feet away. It's meant to hit someone before they hear the explosion. At that distance, the bullet travels faster than the sound it makes."

Lee began to ponder the frightening effect of such weapons. It seemed that in a world where magic was beyond the grasp of the inhabitants, they reverted to barbarity and perfected the art. A new concern began to grow in the back of his mind: what if one of them got hit by this sniper's bullet? Would the healing magic he knew be able to patch the wounds it left behind? Would there be anything left to heal?

"The van," Luis said, with a firm nod.

"It won't stop the bullet, he said," Timm pointed out.

"I would much rather his vision be obscured as we pass than to pass under him unobstructed from view in any way," Luis continued, his voice resolute.

"If we want to obscure his vision as much as possible," Morgan said, reaching into her pocket and bringing out a handful of gritty ash. "I can help with that."

"Where do you keep getting that stuff?" Smithers asked, exasperated.

Morgan shrugged. "The church had a huge thing of ashes just sitting there."

"I know I don't really have a leg to stand on when it comes to blasphemy, but I cannot express in words how messed up that is," Smithers sighed.

Morgan ignored the comment, whispered a few words in a language Lee did not understand, and blew lightly onto the ash in her hand. The gritty material blew up and around them, turning the world dim and grey. Lee felt as though someone had stuffed cotton in his ears and in his mind. As he looked down at his now ashy-grey appearance, he reflected on how disconcerting the effect of such a spell was, but suddenly felt grateful to be encased in it.

"Let's go," Timm said, sounding miles away from the doorway less than ten feet away. "I'll lead the way."

Timm all but vanished from Lee's sight just by walking out the door. The others followed, and thankfully they had agreed on their next location without needing to follow each other, or they'd have all been lost in the haze that surrounded them. Lee trudged through the mounting mud and slop, forcing his way toward the van as his first waypoint. Upon reaching it, he thought for a moment that he saw Luis in front of him, but couldn't tell. While the world was crystal clear to him, his allies were but flickering shadows walking unheeded through it.

Lee slipped behind the van, placing it between himself and the sniper's nest. Suddenly he realized he had stopped breathing at some point. Taking a deep breath and steeling himself, Lee prepared to move forward, not wanting to move out of the range of Morgan's spell.

Moving as quickly as he dared, Lee darted out from behind the van and made for the door on the opposite side of the courtyard. He had made it about halfway there, when suddenly he felt his foot catch and get pulled out from under him. With a yelp, Lee fell ungracefully into the mud. The sour, foul smelling grit of wet earth filled his mouth as he hit the ground.

Coughing and sputtering, Lee turned to see what had tripped him up and noticed for the first time a tether nailed to the outside of the goat enclosure. The leash had fallen by the wayside and gotten tangled in the mud, acting as a perfectly hidden snare, which Lee had stumbled into like any animal running for its life.

Panic gripped his chest, and he froze in place. As quickly as he dared, Lee turned to face the sniper's nest, almost expecting his last mortal image of the world to be the muzzle of the sniper's rifle ending his life in a flash.

Instead, he looked up and saw a pair of gilded eyes looking back at him. They belonged to a small white chicken that sat in the mud next to Lee, just barely under the van where it must have taken shelter from the icy wind. It cocked its head to one side, clucked, then started to walk over to where Lee lay prone in the mud.

"No!" Lee whispered, hoarsely, feeling the grit of dirt scraping uncomfortably against his teeth. "Go away, bird!"

The chicken either could not hear or ignored him and continued forward. Clucking and bobbing its head. Lee attempted to get to his feet, but could not manage it before the chicken hopped up on his back and began to settle in.

"Get off," Lee snarled as quietly as he could, hunching so he wouldn't toss the creature and elicit a stream of squawks and clucking that would most definitely attract the attention of the sniper.

From far away, Lee heard a voice calling out to him.

"Lee! Stop playing with that chicken and get over here!" Smithers called out to him.

Panicking again, Lee looked up at Smithers who stood no more than thirty feet away, then back at the sniper's nest, fearing he may have heard the call. Looking back at his allies, he saw Smithers working the lock with the multitool he'd picked up from St. Augustine's. A moment later, the door sprung open and the others began to file inside. Lee felt strength surge into his limbs at the idea of being left outside in the dark alone with the sniper.

He rushed forward, sending the chicken sprawling and squawking in his wake. Not stopping to see if the sniper had noticed him, Lee barrelled into the room they had been attempting to reach and hugged the wall, desperately trying to catch his breath. He looked up and saw the others staring at him, the gritty grey spectrum that enveloped them dissolving away.

"Are you okay, Lee?" Morgan asked him quietly.

"I'm fine," Lee answered, more breathlessly than he would have liked.

"Good, because I think we found the place," Smithers said.

"How can you tell?" Lee asked, straightening his clothing in an attempt to regain his composure.

In answer, Smithers hooked his thumb at the door opposite the one they had just entered from. The room that surrounded it was bare, which only made the door stand out more. It was made of solid steel reinforced with multiple plates at the hinges and handle. The handle itself was as long as Lee's forearm and as thick as his fore and middle fingers put together. On the right hand side, by the handle was a small black box, very similar to the keycard readers from St. Augustine.

"Ah," Lee said. "I suppose we may have run into an issue here."

$$\sim 34 \sim$$

TIMM

"What about the woman's ID?" Luis asked.

"What, the one you knocked out?" Smithers responded. "She was the front door guard, who gives an access badge that opens your most secret room in a government facility to the person who guards the front door?"

"Do you have a better idea?" Luis asked, his voice hot.

"Maybe the sniper?" Smithers pondered. "We could sneak up there, try to take him out, get his card and see if it works."

"No," Lee said firmly. "I don't want to, as you say, tangle with him. We'd have better luck with those two we ignored in the first building having access."

Timm half listened to the argument the others were having about how to deal with the door he was currently analyzing in front of him. It was impressive, something he'd have only ever imagined be made by dwarvish hands. This wasn't beaten steel, but rather looked forged for this exact purpose, something even an amature like him would be able to recognize. There was no way they were breaking this door down.

"Funny that we get stuck by a door, isn't it?" Morgan asked him, leaning against the wall to the left of the door. It seemed she also wanted to keep herself out of the argument.

"This one at least," Timm said, looking at the panel next to the door. "Is doing a very good job of doing its job."

Morgan nodded. "I'm not really a fan of any of these ideas. I don't like the idea of hunting the people here down and killing them."

"They don't have much of a problem doing it to us," Timm responded, pressing his hand against the wall, pushing on it slightly.

"Doesn't mean we should be like them," Morgan said. "Don't you think it's weird? There's only four people here. It's a big complex."

"Could be they're all out," Timm said. "Looked like there was enough room for another van out there. Maybe two."

"True," Morgan admitted.

"Do you think it's locked?" Timm asked, looking at the door.

Morgan looked at him strangely. "We know it's locked, we checked it when we came in."

"Right, I know that," Timm said. "I meant from the other side."

"Oh," Morgan shrugged. "I feel like if you're on the other side you don't really need to worry about it being locked."

"That's what I thought," Timm said, nodding. He turned to look at Smithers. "Hey, Smithers! What are these walls made of?"

"Huh, what?" Smithers asked, stopping mid-sentence in his argument with Lee about taking on one man rather than two. "Oh, uh, building this old, I'd guess drywall or something. Doesn't look like concrete at least."

"Thank you!" Timm said, turning back to face the door.

"Why?" Smithers asked, and Timm could hear worry in his voice, but elected to ignore it.

He took his stance and tensed his body. Smithers started to cry out, but Timm elected to ignore that too as he sent his fist through the black plastic panel, the wall, and out the other side. With a smile, he reached over, found the handle on the other side, and gave it a push. The door popped open easily.

"There," Timm said, gripping the handle. "Door's open."

"Well I'll be damned," Timm heard Smithers say.

Grinning at the old man, Timm threw the door open wide. Standing just on the other side were two humanoid figures wearing bulky yellow garments that covered them from head to toe. Timm couldn't see their faces due to the strange, cylindrical helmets that topped off the ensemble, but he could clearly see the pair of pistols pointed at him and Morgan.

"Correction," Smithers said. "Well *we'll* be *fucked.*"

The pistols fired, knocking Timm out of his stupor. He jumped back out of the way of the shots only to realize the men had not been aiming for him. Morgan yelped in pain as a bullet tore through her arm, sending a spray of blood backward. Behind him, Timm heard Luis grunt in exertion, but looking up he saw the knight did not stagger a step.

Smithers whirled on the one who shot Morgan and grinned manically.

"Hello gentlemen or madam," he said, leveling his pistol. "Are you happy with your health insurance?"

The pistol barked in the small space, hitting the gunman square in the shoulder, spinning him into the wall. Faster than Timm would have expected him to move, Luis closed the distance, driving his sword point first through the man's chest in an explosion of white hot light. The gurgling scream that came from within the suit was shrill, but brief, and the man went limp on the end of Luis' sword. With a flick of the blade, the knight dropped the extra weight and turned to face his final opponent.

"Probably should have asked about *life* insurance," the knight said, his tone level and his eyes sharp and focused.

Morgan clutched her arm and screamed, partially in pain, but Timm could feel the rage emanating off of her. As he watched, her teeth sharpened and elongated, her green eyes yellowed and her pupils narrowed into slits. Snow white fur bristled from her now forming muzzle and rippled down her form as she fell silently on four massive paws. What horrified Timm more than anything about this transformation, was that as Morgan took the form of this massive cat, the scream did not change at all except to grow louder. It still sounded... *human.*

She charged forward, drawing Timm's attention away from the horrific implications of her feral scream, and swiped a massive paw at the man who'd shot at Luis originally, but Timm wasn't sure Morgan knew or cared which one of them he'd shot at. Her rage seemed to be indiscriminate to who offered the affront, making Timm wonder how much of her earlier words were her true feelings, and how much they were what she *wished* she believed. The gunman cried out in panic, dropping to one knee as the blow that was meant for his head took out a chunk of drywall behind him, sending a cloud of dust and debris down the hallway.

Timm reached into his backpack and pulled out one of the heavier items in it. The heft of the crowbar made it unbalanced compared to the weapons he had trained with under his master, but moving in to flank the man with Luis, it didn't really matter much. Timm just needed to make contact.

Unfortunately, this was one slippery fish, and just as Timm came in swinging, the man jumped back to avoid the blow, pressing himself against the wall Morgan had opened with her claws. Out of frustration, Timm threw an awkward left cross at the man's head. At the last moment, the man ducked again, and rather than breaking the man's teeth, Timm's fist found the wooden stud behind the drywall. It snapped with a satisfying crack, and for one brief moment Timm thought he could see the wide, horrified eyes hidden behind the glass helm the man wore.

Brilliant white fire cascaded down from the ceiling, engulfing the terrified man, who screamed in agony. Timm looked up to see Lee's eyes glowing white as he murmured a prayer, pointing at the object of his wrath.

Seeming to finally have had enough terror and seeing an opening, the man ducked out of Timm's grip and weaved around Luis' sword. Before anyone could stop him, he hit the main door and burst into the courtyard screaming. It was somehow muffled, but Timm was certain that the sniper must have heard him.

"Goddamnit!" Smithers snarled, squaring up his shot. The pistol barked once and dropped the man face first into the mud and filth. "Come on, we're going to be lousy with these guys soon. Get through the door and see if we can't hold ourselves up. A kill-box is still a better place to be than a shooting gallery."

The blaring sound of a siren began echoing through the compound and must have been audible from far beyond it as well. Morgan planted her feet firmly and snarled at the main door.

"Come on," Timm said to her. "There's no way we can fight them all."

Morgan looked at the door and then at herself.

"She's too big to get through the door," Luis said, translating her posture into words. "If we have any hope of fighting them off, we'll need her strength. Morgan, guard the door, call out to us if you need help, we'll come running."

Awkwardly, Morgan nodded her large feline head and stared steadily at the main door. Smithers grabbed the handle and slammed the door shut.

"No reason to give them too much of an advantage," he said, moving towards the metal door. "Now come on!"

He grabbed Timm's wrist and hauled him into the next room. Timm allowed himself to be dragged, but looked back mournfully at Morgan, feeling a tightness in his chest that threatened to stop his breath.

Inside this room Timm saw that DIARD seemed to keep to the 'sparse' aspect of decorating. As far as furniture, there were only two long tables topped with four clear cases. Only three of the cases seemed to have anything in them. In one there was a ratty old backpack, the case next to it had a twisted ball made of iron bands, and the last one on the opposite table had some kind of brass choker necklace. Another metal door, less impressive than the last, was framed on the same wall as the one they'd entered from and Timm was suddenly really glad he hadn't tried to punch through the wall on the left side or he may have broken his hand.

"What the hell is this crap?" Smithers asked. "And why is it so well guarded?"

Luis held up his hand, showing the ring he'd grabbed from the mannequin from the main building and pointed at the empty case.

"What if this belonged in here?" Luis asked, nodding at the empty case, and Timm saw a small, clear plinth that would have been perfect to rest a ring on for viewing.

"And what if I'd gone for Chinese instead of a walk in the woods that night?" Smithers asked.

"Must you be so hostile and sarcastic?" Lee asked.

"This is how I cope!" Smithers said his voice rough and hard. Timm was worried it was about to become another argument when suddenly he saw the old man's shoulders drooping. "Damnit... we're fucked."

"I see, well your coping mechanism are your business, but as 'fucked' as you believe us to be, there may be an answer here in front of us," Lee said, walking over to where Luis was standing. "To Luis' point, if the ring were normally stored here, and it itself is a magic item, then it would stand to reason that these items, also being stored here, are themselves magical in nature."

"This is just a storage room?" Timm asked, confused. "That's a lot of security for a storage room."

Lee shrugged. "But much more understandable for a *vault*."

"We're pulling a heist?" Smithers asked, his head falling into his non-gun hand. "We were just supposed to get a fucking teddy bear and now we're pulling a heist on the US Government... Getting paid in maybe-magic items? What *is* my life?"

"You're right, Smithers. A heist sounds a bit too fancy for us. Too much planning," Timm said, grinning like a madman as he stepped up to the case with the iron ball. "I prefer 'smash and grab.'"

Calming his mind he took his stance. Tensing his body he threw a palm strike forward, driving the heel of his hand into the smooth clear exterior. The glass was stronger than he expected, and though his blow cracked the shell, the case held fast.

"Or," Smithers said as Timm shook out his stinging hand. "You could try the latch."

"Oh," Timm said, awkwardly looking at the latch on the side of the case that opened one of the panes. "We can do that. Is it still considered a smash and grab? I thought that line was pretty cool."

"Very cool," Smithers said, though Timm thought he sounded tired in his response. "And technically, you've already smashed the wall, so yes. Still a smash and grab."

Timm, happy to know that his one-liner was still appropriate to the situation, unlatched the glass case and reached in to grab the ball. It was about the size of an orange and easily slipped into one of his pockets. As quickly as they could, the others collected the remaining items, securing them the best they could. Lee copied Timm and slipped the metal collar into his own pocket, patting it gently to, Timm assumed, reassure himself that it remained there. Smithers, who was not wearing a pack of his own since he left his weapon's bag in the van, opting instead to only take the weapons, was given the magical one to wear, which he begrudgingly took.

"This isn't gonna blow up on me or something, is it?" he asked, nervously looking over his shoulder at the bag.

"Probably not," Lee said, shrugging. "Though I am no mage and thus am ill equipped to tell you the nature of such items."

"Comforting," Smithers said, his voice so hollow that even the sarcasm felt numb.

"Guys," Timm interjected. "We still haven't found the bear."

"Why are we doing all this for a stuffed bear again?" Smithers asked, shifting his shoulders uncomfortably, still adjusting to the bag.

"Magical bear," Luis said, moving towards the last door. "Here, I see it. They're keeping it in a separate room."

"Huh," Timm said, peeking through the window. "Magic bear indeed."

As he looked through the window Luis pointed out, Timm could see another case like the ones that held the magic items. This one was slightly different however. Rather than a cube with a door and latch, this one was a perfect cylinder held aloft between two metal tubes that kept it at eye level. The creepy stuffed bear, which could be no other than Stuffers himself based on the strangely shiny material and heavy stitching, was floating suspended in some kind of liquid.

Timm looked at the door and saw the frame around this one was metal. There would be no way he could punch this one open.

"So how are we going to open this one?" he asked, looking back at the others.

"By taking a step back," Smithers said, pointing his pistol at the handle. Quickly, Timm jumped back as Smithers' pistol barked. Sparks flew as the handle jerked once before falling to the floor. The door swung lazily inward on its hinges.

"Yeah," Timm nodded. "That should do it."

They stepped inside and even through his coat, Timm could feel the chill as the temperature suddenly dropped by at least twenty degrees.

"Is there some kind of thing where cold makes magic less effective?" Smithers asked.

"Not to my knowledge," Lee responded, examining the cylinder that held Stuffers. "The question is, how do we..."

Timm grabbed Lee by the back of the coat and pulled him back as Smithers let off another shot into the top of the glass cylinder.

Glass and water showered backwards and Smithers stepped forwards, using the butt of his gun to break the remaining glass that stood between them and their prize.

"I really should have seen that coming," Lee said quietly to Timm.

"I'm sort of surprised you didn't," Timm said, smirking.

"Hey," Smithers called out to them.

Timm turned to look at Smithers who had the disturbing looking teddy bear aloft in his left hand. Liquid that seemed to be too thick to be water dripped from the leathery material the bear was made from. The presence of it made the haphazard stitching across its body even more grotesque than the last time Timm had seen it.

"We got it," Smithers said. "What do we do now?"

The head of the bear slowly turned and looked at Smithers. A dark, horrific voice came from the bear, but Timm didn't hear it aloud so much as it echoed horribly in his mind.

"You return me to my ward, mortal," Stuffers said. "I have work to do."

~ 35 ~

SMITHERS

Smithers yelped and nearly dropped the horrific little bear, but stopped himself just in time. If Annabelle and Chucky had taught him anything, it was that you do not draw the ire of an evil children's toy if you don't absolutely have to. And since he'd already drawn the ire of something else horrific this week, it was probably best to keep the bear aloft.

"Uh... okay then," Smithers said, not taking his eyes off the bear. "I think Walter was right and that this bear is actually very powerful and important after all."

"My ward was correct to inform you of such," the bear responded, creepily nodding its head. How it was managing to do so without any skeleton or muscles, Smithers did not know, but by the same token, he probably didn't want to know.

"So this is Stuffers?" Timm asked, slowly approaching and looking at the bear. "When we saw you before, I never would have guessed you were alive."

"Regardless you would have guessed wrong, mortal," Stuffers responded, his deep, horrific voice rattling Smithers to his core. "Now bring me to Walter."

Smithers looked nervously at the door.

"Well, ya see, we'd really like to..." Smithers said, trailing off.

"You dare refuse me?" Stuffers asked.

"No!" Smithers said, panic entering his voice. With an extraordinary amount of willpower, he swallowed hard and tried to get his heartbeat under control. When his voice worked again, it came out a little higher than he intended, but at the same time, it was at least calm enough that he wasn't crying or whimpering. "No, we're not refusing you. It's just there's a little snag in the exit strategy."

As if on cue to prove Smithers' point, the pounding of booted feet echoed through the air. Moments later, the door to the outside of the building crunched as if under a heavy blow. Smithers could practically feel the vibrations of Morgan's giant cat form as she growled in anticipation of the coming battle.

"Come out with your hands up!" Smithers heard a voice yell, and Morgan answered with an inhuman scream that sounded like it came straight out of the uncanny valley itself. For half a second, he flashed back to videos about the Appalachian mountains he'd used to watch to spook his grandkids, but shook the thought from his mind. He had enough creepy shit to deal with right now.

"We need to go help her," Luis said, sword clutched in his hand.

"We need to fall back and regroup," Smithers responded. "They're armed with military grade weaponry and you've got a sword!"

"I am very good with a sword," Luis replied.

"They're very good with military grade weaponry!" Smithers shot back, exasperated.

"Then what do you suggest we do?" Lee asked, and hopelessness washed over Smithers.

"I don't know," Smithers said, shaking his head as he felt his shoulders slump. "Timm, grab Morgan and bring her in here. Hold down the fort until we can figure something out?"

"That doesn't seem like much of a plan," Lee said, though he nodded at Luis. "Neither does a frontal assault to a glorious death. While a more honorable way to go than huddled like rats in a barrel waiting to be shot, it still doesn't lead to victory."

The sound of the door crunching under the blow from the guards sounded again. Smithers knew the outer door was not going to hold much longer, and the inner door had been broken open when Timm smashed the panel to make it possible for them to enter the room. There was no way they were going to be able to hold off a siege for longer than a few moments. Even with magical powers, it seemed like their situation was the textbook definition of FUBAR.

Another resounding crunch echoed against the door and Smithers felt his whole body tense. They were coming through and there wasn't a damn thing anyone could do or say to stop them. Maybe they'd be shot dead, or maybe they'd be captured and tortured for information. Worse yet, maybe they'd be dissected. Smithers screwed his eyes shut and waited for the inevitable.

"Release me, mortal," Stuffers said.

Smithers opened his eyes and turned to look at the grotesque little bear. Its eyes were a swirling mist of blackness, and the old man couldn't help but think of the void that Nietzsche spoke of so often. He turned away before it could gaze into him any longer than it had already gotten.

"Yeah," Smithers said, setting the bear down on the ground carefully. "Sure."

The old man had to stifle a laugh as he watched the stuffed bear get carefully to its feet. There were no elbows or knees stitched into the creature and Smithers was reminded of a toddler getting to its feet for the first time. He was considering actually making a comment about it, since they were so beyond fucked at this point that he didn't think insulting a being of such terrible power could possibly make the situation any worse than it already was, when he heard the sound of the door breaking down completely in the other room.

Explosive rounds echoed through the halls in time with the horrific shrieking of the beast form Morgan had taken. The sound of running feet was coming swiftly towards them and Smithers raised his gun to the door in preparation to go out in that blaze of glory Luis had been talking about. A figure appeared at the door and Smithers started to squeeze the trigger when Lee yelled out.

"Stop! It's Morgan!"

The priest was right. In the doorway, covered in blood of indeterminable sources, stood the young girl. She was panting and shaken, but she stumbled into the room where Timm rushed forward to support her.

"I held them off a bit," Morgan said breathlessly. "They're coming though. They're regrouping and they're coming."

"Not that this hasn't been fun, mortals," Stuffers said, waddling up to the door. "But I believe that I have gathered all the information I need from this facility. I assume that Walter had brokered your aid in my escape, unnecessarily so. All the same, you acted in good faith, and such faith should be rewarded."

Morgan looked at Timm, looked at Stuffers, and looked back at Timm.

"Did that teddy bear just talk?" she asked.

Before anyone could answer her, DIARD agents broke into the room beyond and swarmed the door, preparing to shoot them all dead. Smithers felt his hand twitch to bring the gun at his side up, but when he saw their numbers he realized he needn't bother. By the time he leveled the gun he'd be so full of holes they wouldn't need to tie rocks to his body to make it sink.

But the agents froze in place, not one gun pointed at Smithers or the others. All of them were staring at the bear. There was an eerie stillness that fell over the room, and Smithers wondered what it would look like to an outside observer. He had a funny little image pop into his head, a Norman Rockwell painting but instead of a snapshot of a warm, happy family preparing for Christmas dinner, it was a small, disturbing teddy bear standing between a group of bloodied and outnumbered misfits and armed, tactical military professionals like he was protecting a group of children from the monster under their bed.

"It's loose!" one agent shouted, his voice breaking the silent stillness of the moment, and as the spell broke, the DIARD agents began opening fire on Stuffers.

"It is," Stuffers said, ignoring every bullet that tore through his diminutive leathery body.

Seams that held the grotesque bear together split and a dark mist filled the room beyond. Shadowy appendages reached out from Stuffers, shooting out into the mist, which obscured their visage from sight, but Smithers thought for just a moment that he caught a glimpse of writhing black tentacles in the darkness beyond.

But it was not the *sight* that would haunt his nightmares for the rest of his life. In fact, he could barely see anything happening at all. In many ways, that was something of a comfort to him. Smithers had been in war before. He'd seen battle. Watched men die in some of the most horrific ways imaginable. There was little left in this world that could create worse night terrors than what he'd already seen and experienced in his tenure with the military.

Or so he'd thought.

He couldn't *see* the men being ripped apart, this is true, but the tearing sounds were unmistakable. Even over the sound of screams that sounded more animal than human and the futile bursts of gunfire, it was the popping and tearing of flesh that echoed most horrifically in his ears. Escape was impossible for these men, death was their inevitable fate, but even with this knowledge Smithers felt something cold settle in his stomach. He had no idea how long it took for Stuffers to kill all the men in the room. It probably only took him seconds, but it seemed like those seconds stretched into eternity. More than anything, Smithers knew one thing for sure: Stuffers had enjoyed doing it.

When the mist finally withdrew and Stuffers stood before them, seams bulging slightly more than they had before, and again all was quiet. Blood painted the walls of the room and the Plexiglas cases that had been see-through when they'd walked in were now completely opaque.

"Where are all the bodies?" Timm asked, nervously.

"Don't ask," Smithers said, trying very hard not to look at the bulging seams on the teddy bear's body. "That is not a question you want the answer to."

"But..." Timm started.

"I have taken care of the slaves of DIARD," Stuffers explained, and Smithers could feel the malevolent glare of the creature on him. There was amusement in its voice, as much as something like it could feel amusement, and Smithers did not want to show it just how disturbed he was.

"I think they're called agents," Lee stated, stoic in his mannerisms as always.

"Slaves. Agents," Stuffers said, tipping his hands back and forth, mimicking a scale. "It matters naught to me what titles you mortals choose to anoint yourselves with these days. Terminology doesn't, in any way, change what they were. When one is sold into bondage, either by force or by indoctrination, one is a slave."

"You saved us," Morgan said, getting to her feet. She gave the bear a little bow, as much of one as she would risk with her injuries. "Thank you."

The bear smiled and it was probably the creepiest thing Smithers had ever seen, and that included the hentai of death he'd just been witness to.

"You are polite," Stuffers said, looking up at Morgan approvingly. "I like that."

"So are you a good bear," Timm asked, gesturing to the group. He then gestured to the blood soaked room on the other side of the door. "Or a bad bear?"

"A bad bear," Luis said, gripping his sword so tightly that Smithers saw his hands tremble as his knuckles turned white. "A very, *very* bad bear."

"That's not true," Stuffers said, turning to face them both, and in ways Smithers couldn't describe, the smile grew worse as a new wickedness stretched across his leather face. "I'm not even a bear."

Smithers heard the sound of seams ripping and quickly averted his eyes. Timm and Luis' screams were horrific, though thankfully there was not the sound of rending flesh and blood spattering around the room that accompanied the deaths of the DIARD agents. When the screaming stopped, Smithers slowly turned to face the scene. Lee and Morgan stood, blanched and horrified, but on their feet.

Luis was on his knees, sword on the floor beside him, clutching himself in a hug while rocking back and forth. Timm seemed to have gotten the worst of it, curled up on the floor in the fetal position, facing the massacre of a room rather than the bear, and Smithers agreed that he too would have chosen that sight over whatever the bear had revealed to them.

"What..." Morgan started to say, but Smithers stepped forward and placed his hand on her arm.

"Don't ask, don't make him angry," Smithers said, quietly. "Or worse, bored."

Lee turned to look at Smithers.

"How are you so calm?" Lee asked, his normal composure shaken. Smithers was surprised to see how wide the priest's eyes had gotten, but even more shocked to see that his skin was capable of being paler than it normally was.

"I read a lot of cosmic horror in my day. H.P. and I go way back," Smithers said, and without looking over his shoulder at the bear, he managed to turn his head slightly and call back to the creature. "I'm guessing you're an Outsider, then. One of the Great Old Ones?"

"You are well versed for a mortal, it seems," Stuffers responded, the amusement in his tone confirmation enough.

"Right, but aren't your kind trying to kill us all?" Smithers asked, still without turning around. He didn't want to risk seeing something he didn't want to see. "Or drive us all mad?"

"Not my schtick," Stuffers said, shrugging his leathery shoulders in a way that made Smithers exceptionally uncomfortable. "I am here for fun, and fun alone. And though primitive, your world is rife with sources of entertainment for me. Now, enough inane chatter. I have aided you, thus in return you must aid me. Bring me to Walter."

"Right," Smithers said, grabbing Timm by the shoulder as Lee focused on helping Luis to his feet. "Morgan, grab the other side of him"

"Oh... okay," Morgan said, coming around to help support Timm as they made their way out of the building.

As they made their way into the cold and quiet courtyard, Smithers noted the arrival of two more black vans that must have been carrying the excess people that had just been slaughtered inside. Checking the sniper's nest, Smithers saw that he too was gone. They must have sent in everyone in hopes of containing the Outsider that they had thought to keep inside. He almost laughed out loud at how stupid and arrogant an idea that was, but considering this was the U.S. Government, after all, there was a good chance that they would learn absolutely nothing from this experience and would definitely try something similar again.

"This is as good a spot as any," Stuffers said, stepping out into the muddy courtyard.

"Good enough for what?" Smithers asked. "The van is still a fifteen minute walk away. Through pitch black woods, so make that a half hour."

"No need, mortal," Stuffers said, reaching out his stubby bear arms. "Now that I am no longer contained, I have full access to my abilities."

The swirling mists of black that made up the bear's eyes began to spin rapidly as a dark energy enveloped him. Smithers tried to look away, but became mesmerized by the vortex of darkness being summoned forth from the slurry beneath their feet. A bulbous, somewhat humanoid form began to grow from the mud. Smithers felt his hand reach for his gun on instinct, but knew better than to draw it. Whatever Stuffers was doing, if he meant them harm, they would come to harm.

The form stepped forward, out of the muck. More and more mud fell away from the body until finally the visage of Walter was all that remained. He looked around, seemingly startled to see where he found himself, then looked down at the little bear and smiled.

"Up," Stuffers said, holding his pudgy arms up like a toddler demanding to be held. Walter obliged him, bending over and scooping the bear up.

"Well then," Walter said, though in a voice Smithers barely recognized as his. It wasn't the voice of the bear or some other unworldly entity, but his cadence had shifted. He sounded far more educated and far more together than he had when Smithers had first met him. "It seems you all can be trusted with sensitive information as well as carry out the promises you make. That's fairly rare."

"Wait a minute," Smithers said, narrowing his eyes. "You played us."

Walter tutted slightly. "That is such an ugly way of saying it. I much prefer to say that you passed your audition with flying colors.

"So all of this was a set up?" Smithers asked, a note of anger entering his voice, pushing back the fear he felt for the cursed teddy bear. "Did they even attack you? Or was that a set up too?"

"Oh no, the bullet wound was real," Walter said, waving a hand at Smithers placatingly. "When we got jumped, Stuffers here told me to find you guys for help. He would take care of DIARD. Not that I don't trust him, but Stuffers can sometimes get a bit cocky. Figured since I was going to be seeing you anyway, and I'd already been thinking about recruiting you, that I may as well kill two birds with one stone.

"What is it with people killing birds with stones in this world?" Lee asked, and Smithers could hear the priest's composure breaking. In honesty, he couldn't blame the man, considering he was feeling his own coming undone.

"So what now?" Smithers asked Walter, his jaw set to keep him from screaming at the deceptive man.

"Now? Now you should probably get home and rest, there's a lot going on out there," Walter said, grinning at them all. "The Black Lotus will be calling upon you again in the future."

Smithers had a few choice words for Walter about where he could shove his Black Lotus, but before he could open his mouth the blackness enveloped Walter and Stuffers once more, and without ceremony, the two vanished.

"What just happened?" Morgan asked a moment later, breaking the silence.

"There's another player in the game," Smithers said bitterly. "Come on, let's go raid this place for supplies and get the hell out of here."

He stepped forward a few paces before stopping dead in his tracks and swearing violently.

"What's wrong, Smithers?" Lee asked.

"I bet you anything Walter didn't kill the ignition before getting beamed up," Smithers said sourly. "We're going to need to syphon these clunkers for gas..."

~ 36 ~

LEE

After the events with Stuffers, Lee did not think anything else they encountered that day would be able to set him more on edge, but soon found while wandering through the abandoned compound they had just been sneaking around proved him wrong. Every life, save the front desk clerk Luis had knocked out, had been extinguished by the bear. Smithers, seizing the opportunity to explore unabated, was sitting at one of the computers in the lab they had ransacked in an attempt to gather more information while the others milled about and, assumedly, came to terms with the horrors they had all witnessed.

Luis busied himself collecting gas from the vans through syphoning as Smithers had instructed, though a couple of the red plastic containers latched to the back of the vehicles were at least partially full. At one point, the knight paused, looked down in the mud, and smiled. Lee walked over to see what had improved his mood in such a horrific situation.

Beside the van there was a tactical bag that one of the DIARD agents must have dropped during their hasty exit. The knight was rummaging through it as Lee approached.

"Anything of use?" the priest asked. In answer, Luis simply pulled a long blade in a plain, black leather scabbard from within the dark canvas bag.

"A longsword," he said, his grin widening. "Finally, a proper weapon."

Morgan spent most of her time tending to the animals DIARD left behind. She expressed that she was unsure about whether it would be better to let them free into the wilderness out back of the compound or keep them within their pens. She did not, however, trust the woman they'd restrained to take the time to care for them properly.

As she debated, and possibly deliberated with the animals, Timm sat by the front door where they were to make their egress, curled up with his knees to his chest. After what Lee had seen Stuffers reveal, he did not blame the poor boy and assured Smithers to just let him be.

Lee roamed the hallways, but soon found he had little to do and less to learn from them and decided instead to check the room where the two agents they had ignored on the way in were originally. The room was empty now, and those agents were most likely torn to shreds, their blood painting the walls of their agency's secret lab. Lee shook his head and pushed the thought from his mind. He did not wish to entertain those thoughts too long as they were likely to lead him down a dark road.

Instead, he busied himself looking through the refrigerators and large boxes filled with food locked behind glass. Smithers had called these vending machines and informed them all that they would exchange food for money. Taking the crowbar he procured from the Irish mafia hideout, he broke the lock on the side of the machine and took what food he could for the journey home.

Under normal circumstances, Lee would probably debate the morality of stealing food the way he was. Were this a starve or die situation, he'd easily admit that the theft was justifiable, though currently he was just hoping to replenish their personal stocks for the future. Since no one remained in the compound to consume the food, it was senseless to let it go to waste. There would be people returning here that could benefit from it, but those people were their enemies, and it would be even more wasteful to allow one's enemies to retain their resources upon anything other than their final defeat. DIARD would be back to reclaim the facility, Lee knew this, so for now, he would use their means to support his goals.

Lee entered the room where Smithers was working and tossed a bag of chips next to him.

"It is best to refuel after a traumatic incident," Lee said, opening his own bag. "And our encounter with an Outsider most definitely qualifies as traumatic."

"You know," Smithers said as he opened the bag of chips and started crunching on them. "I'm not all that hungry."

"Anyone who was feeling hungry after witnessing such an encounter would no doubt be afflicted by a sickness so great and twisted that I don't feel any god from any world could heal in them what was broken," Lee responded with a nod. "We should untie the woman."

"When we leave," Smithers nodded. "Gives her less time to stab one of us in the back when we're not looking. Leave some food for her too. Just in case."

"Traumatic incident?" Lee asked.

"To be fair, she was mind-whammied by Luis. Not the most horrific person who could have done it, but I suppose any form of Mind Control would be seen as traumatic enough," Smithers said, his voice just short of sounding accusatory. "I didn't know you guys could do that."

"Speak with the authority of our gods?" Lee asked. "It is possible for us, yes. However I don't like to do that much. I know too well what it is to be forced to do something you don't want to do."

"Yeah," Smithers nodded. "I feel you on that one."

"What of the other vans?" Lee asked, changing the subject before this particular road could be traveled too far. "Luis has syphoned their gasoline, but they could still be useful for us."

"Probably have some kind of tracker in them that will lead DI-ARD right back to the church," Smithers sighed, standing up and going over to the tool bench. "Plus we came here in the padre's van and it wouldn't be right to leave that behind. And I don't trust any of you to drive the thing."

"A sensible decision," Lee nodded, turning over the bag of chips. As his eyes wandered over the ingredient list, his stomach turned not from what he saw, but from what he couldn't pronounce.

Smithers found the tool he was looking for, a screwdriver, and walked over to the computer. He disconnected the power and began opening the device with steady precision. Once the side panel was off, the old man reached inside and gently pulled out a small, silver rectangle.

"Hand me that plastic bag there, would ya?" Smithers asked, without looking up.

Lee did as he was bid, but asked, "What is that?"

"A hard drive," Smithers said. "Basically it's the computer's brain. I ain't smart enough to do anything with it, but I figure if we give it to Simon he may be able to pull something useful out of it."

"Then I assume our work here is complete?" Lee asked.

"Yeah," Smithers nodded. "You collect the others, I'll cut the woman loose, and we'll head down to the van."

It was well into the night when they arrived at the van. Just as Smithers suspected, it was still running, though on fumes as the old man bitterly said. He told them to get inside, which they all obliged heartily as it was comfortably warm within, while he killed the engine and topped off the tank.

The ride back was quiet and uncomfortable, though traffic flowed much more easily now that night had fallen. On top of that, they weren't doubling back constantly due to Walter's fevered instructions. Smithers explained how traffic worked, and that most people had work on Monday mornings, and thus were likely to be in their homes if not in bed at this point. Lee appreciated not being forced to follow such an asinine schedule, though felt a small pang of envy at the reliable structure their lives had. Thinking back to what all they'd been through in just the past two days, it made him ponder what their erratic lives would bring down upon them tomorrow.

They have, in less than one week, uncovered a rising god, a fanatic group of holy knights, and discovered a plot by a shadow agency that they could not possibly comprehend from the information they had. So much was happening around them however they had such little to go on. There was no way to plan a counter strike, there was nowhere to search for clues, and there was nothing that could be done. During the ride back, Lee continued to meditate on these problems and came to only one possible conclusion: they would need to wait for a sign before they could act. Lee found peace in this answer, and decided to rest rather than worry the entire journey back.

It was approximately two in the morning by the time they returned to the church. Smithers had stopped to top off the gas tank again, citing that he promised the father to be sure to bring it back with as full a tank as possible. They slipped inside the building as quietly as they could, hoping that the father would not question them about their activities. Or the blood. As per usual, they were not so lucky.

Father Mitchell was waiting for them in the basement, sitting on one of the cots they used for their nightly rest. He was still dressed in his dark denim jeans and black pastor's top, though both his collar and glasses were slightly askew. He stirred as they entered and sat up to greet them.

"There seems to be one of you missing," Father Mitchell noted as they entered.

"Aw shit," Smithers moaned. "Did we lose Timm again?"

"I'm right here," Timm said from next to him.

"Oh, sorry," Smithers said. "Habit."

"I meant Walter," Father Mitchell explained.

"We uh…" Smithers said awkwardly. "Dropped him off at a friend's place."

"You dropped off a man with a bullet wound after storming a government compound?" Father Mitchell asked, his tone skeptical.

"To be fair," Lee said. "We had healed him."

Father Mitchell looked Lee up and down and cocked an eyebrow at him.

"Be that as it may, you are not the type of person who would just willingly cast a person in need to the side of the road," Father Mitchell deduced. "You are, however, terrible liars. Something happened at the compound. Is Walter dead?"

"We'd have told you if he were dead," Luis said, walking past the group and beginning his nightly ritual of getting ready for bed, though now he took off both a short and longsword, which he leaned carefully by the bed.

"Yeah," Timm agreed. "It was just the crazy magic stuff."

Lee shot Timm a look that he was sure struck the man harder than any blow, and he saw Timm grimace slightly.

"Crazy magic stuff?" Father Mitchell asked, raising his eyebrow slightly as his face drained of color. He was clearly trying to keep his composure, but wasn't managing to do so very well.

"Yeah," Morgan said, sighing slightly. "It was Stuffers."

"The teddy bear?"

"That wasn't a bear," Lee said darkly, realizing that keeping Father Mitchell in the dark was no longer an option. "It was an Outsider, a being from beyond the gates of reality that somehow found its way into our plane of existence."

"Think tentacles and madness," Smithers said.

"Ah," Father Mitchell nodded, keeping his composure, but paling slightly. "It would seem that I should likely brush up on my Lovecraft."

The father got up and started to make his way towards the stairs. Lee stepped up and walked next to him for a moment.

"I must apologize," Lee said. "For lying to you."

"It was done in an attempt to protect me from things I'd rather not know," Father Mitchell said, smiling. "I asked you to keep me in the dark then prodded you until you shone a light on what I said I wished not to see. It is I who should be apologizing to you."

"You were worried for Walter," Lee said. "It is understandable."

"Perhaps," Father Mitchell said, scratching at the beginnings of a beard that was showing on his chin. "However, I should not be so hypocritical. Either I must truly desire to stay in the dark or I want to be a part of this. There is no middle ground."

"There is always a middle ground to be had," Lee said.

Father Mitchell smiled, but Lee could see the sadness that touched the edges of that smile. "In my experience the only things in the middle of the road are painted lines and indecisive squirrels. Good night, Lee. May it be peaceful and lead to a quiet morning."

"We can only hope," Lee said, reflecting on the Father's words.

It was a crude analogy, to be sure. One was either a painted line or roadkill, but as Lee followed the others' lead and began to settle into bed, adjusting his sleeves and settling in for the night, he began to toy with the metaphor a bit more. When one is indecisive, decisions will be made for them regardless. Those that couldn't decide what side they wanted to be on were often removed from the equation. As for the line, it can be a painted path, drawn by another, that one may be forced to follow, either at command or by conditioning.

There was a third option, however, that gave Lee a modicum of hope. Sometimes that line could be one that he drew himself. A line he would not cross, no matter the outcome or consequence. A boundary, a morality, a philosophy, whatever it would be called, it was something that also required decisive choice. There were many lines he'd drawn in his life that he never thought he'd cross, only to now recognize that those lines were so far behind them that he barely remembered they existed anymore.

As he drifted off to sleep, he wondered whether he was truly living his life decisively as he'd once thought, or if in reality he was just following the painted path set down by another. He was unsure, and worse than that, unsure if it was more comforting to have free will or to be set on a path that cannot be overcome, merely experienced.

~ 37 ~

TIMM

Timm woke up earlier than anyone else in hopes of getting a little time to himself. He dressed quickly and in complete silence, checking over his shoulders more than once in the gloom of the basement, but found no one awake or watching him this early in the morning. As he stood, confident that he was able to leave unmolested, and headed for the stairs, Smithers' voice croaked out to him, nearly causing him to trip on the first landing.

"Going somewhere, son?"

Timm winced slightly and turned to see Smithers not quite sitting up in bed, but clearly looking at him in the dark.

"I needed to meditate," Timm said, not feeling any need to lie to the old man. Getting caught doing that would just lead to an argument and it didn't seem like anyone else was awake yet to get involved. "To try to get a handle on this thing with my hands. I hurt Morgan yesterday, and I... I don't want to do that again."

"Alright," Smithers nodded. "Sounds fair. But don't go running off without telling people where yer going. Likely to get killed and never find your body that way."

"I can take care of myself," Timm said.

"Yeh sure can," Smithers said. "But what happens if you get jumped by DIARD and we don't know where yeh went? Or the Brotherhood pays yeh a visit? Or you find that undead elk bastard again?"

"Okay, I get your point," Timm sighed. "I'm going to the park. Figured being in a bit of nature may help me, and I can go back into the trees where no one will see me if my hands start glowing."

"See, now was that so hard?" Smithers asked, grinning. "You enjoy that, I'm going to spend my day picking up my stun gun from the cops, then seeing about where I can store all these guns we've been collecting. Can't keep hiding an arsenal under a cot in a church."

Timm shrugged. "Why not put it in that bag we grabbed yesterday?"

"The backpack?" Smithers asked, cocking his eyebrow at Timm. "I could fit a couple handguns in there, but it wouldn't be much better than an ammo bag. An inconvenient one at that."

Timm smiled at the old man and walked over to where the backpack sat. He flipped it open and set it on an empty cot. Then, looking Smithers dead in the eye, Timm picked up one of the rifles Smithers had collected from the warehouse fight against the Irish mafia and slowly lowered it into the bag. There was no way that the rifle should have been able to fit normally, and Timm had to hold back a laugh as Smithers watched in amazement while the rifle disappeared into the bag without even ruffling an edge.

"It'll all fit," Timm said, grinning at the old man's amazement. "Magic stuff."

"How... both how does it do that, and how did you know it did that?" Smithers asked.

"Magic stuff," Timm repeated, shrugging. "I don't really know *how* it's made, but I mean, if you're going to make a magic bag, what other purpose would you give it besides holding more stuff?"

"Huh," Smithers said, still marveling at the bag. "You know Timm, sometimes you're a lot smarter than you look."

"Thanks," Timm said, and he left Smithers with his new toy, only realizing what the comment the old man made meant when he was halfway to the park.

Shrugging the comment away, Timm found an area of the park that was not occupied by anyone else. As it was early in the morning, cold, and what the people of this world called a 'work day,' it was not hard to find a secluded spot. Timm cleared away a section of snow on the ground and nestled in, crossing his legs and setting his back against a tree.

Slowly, he breathed in, held, then released, just as his master had taught him to long ago. Controlling the breath was the first step to controlling the body. The first step to controlling the heart. The first step to mastering the mind. Control and mastery of the self meant that no outside force could possibly take control or mastery from you. However, Timm realized he was facing a much more difficult threat. There was no external force that was exerting its control over him, but a force that seemed to be coming from deep within.

When he got emotional, excited, his hands began to glow. First in the church, then in the basement, but not at the compound. There was a great deal of excitement there. Why hadn't he had to deal with the glow there?

He tried reflecting on what had been happening the first time the power began to reveal itself in the church. He tried to remember the story that Father Mitchell had been telling, but he'd been too sleepy to really focus. There was something about fish and nets, and the smell of lavender and the warmth in his hand as it began to glow...

Timm's eyes snapped open as he looked down. His hands were brightly glowing, reflecting off the snow and practically wrapping him in an aura of light. He felt the warmth of the glow, the feeling of power enveloping him, and... the scent of lavender.

"Morgan," Timm whispered to himself. The light in his hands pulsed powerfully. "Is it because of her that I can do this? But it hurt her, how can it be because of her?"

It is a weak man who allows his emotions to control him, his master's voice echoed in his mind.

"But the strong man who can control his emotions," Timm whispered the remainder of the mantra.

He stood up, facing away from where there may be people and looked at the thicket that lay before him. Calming his mind, Timm focused on one thought and one thought alone. The smell of lavender flooded his mind as the light welled up against the tips of his fingers. He controlled it as long as he could, until finally he released the energy built up. Light shot from his fingertips, searing through the brush and bramble, burning away the edges of vegetation in smokeless, radiant fire.

Timm whooped in victory and drew on the power again. Just as before he managed to build the force behind a wall of emotion, then release it when the wall was broken down. Again and again until finally he had cleared a path to the river with his focused beams or radiant light.

"Huh, and I thought I was the early bird," a voice behind Timm said, stopping him a moment before he began to draw on the energy again. He whirled around to face whomever had snuck up on him.

A tall woman with warm tan skin that contrasted the cold world around her stood at the edge of the bramble where Timm had been hiding. She was dressed in an assortment of skin tight clothing that showed an athletic frame. Long, dark brown hair was tied back in a sloppy bun. Slung over one of her shoulders was a long, tube shaped bag that had a metal bottle clipped to the side. She smiled a crooked half smile at Timm, blue eyes sparkling with an intelligence that Timm could recognize without needing to hear her speak further, though she did, her voice rasping out with a low, gravelly edge that was actually quite pleasant.

"What are you doing down there?" she asked, her voice warm and curious rather than accusatory. The smile that played on her lips seemed to make her eyes sparkle with genuine kindness that threw Timm off slightly. He'd grown to be suspicious of most people he ran into in this world, but there was something different about this woman. Something... normal?

"Uh," Timm said, trying to think quickly. "Stretches?"

"Trying to warm up before class?" the woman asked, grinning. "Well come on, if you're going to be stretching, might as well keep me company while I do the same."

Timm didn't know what class she was talking about, but not wanting to be rude or draw more attention to what he'd *actually* been doing down in the brambles, he clambered out and followed her to a cleared away section of the park. The grass was exposed here, not a single patch of snow to be seen, just several tall lamp posts with thick, heavy looking bases. As he stepped under one of them, he felt a warmth flood over him, sinking deep into his very core.

"Wow," Timm said, looking around. "It's so warm here, just like magic!"

The woman laughed. "Yeah, those heat lamps practically are. Without them, yoga in the park would be impossible this time of year. But too many of us just want to keep the class going, so we petitioned the city to put them up."

"Heat lamps?" Timm asked, looking closer at what he'd thought were just lamp posts. They were each set about six feet apart from one another and the domed tops hummed and glowed red with warmth rather than the brilliant white light Timm was used to. As Timm approached one, he felt the heat radiating off of the glowing coils under the dome.

"Summer in winter," the woman said, unrolling a thin purple mat and sitting down on it, crossing her legs and leaning to one side, rolling her neck in slow circles. Timm recognized what muscle groups she was stretching out, and so sat opposite her to do the same.

"Don't have a mat?" she asked.

"No, but that's okay, I prefer a connection with the earth," Timm said.

"Ah, you're one of those granola types. That's kind of surprising, you don't really look the part," she said, smiling, and Timm felt that if it had been Smithers who had called him a 'granola type,' he probably would have been offended, but when she said it, he could tell there was no malice in her words.

"I'm Celia, by the way," she said, holding out her hand. "It's nice to meet you..."

"Uh, Timm," Timm answered, wiping the dirt from his hand and focusing hard to ensure it didn't start glowing before shaking hers. He looked around at the large space under the lamps and suddenly felt very exposed. "So is it just you here or..."

"Oh no," Celia said, laughing. "The instructor comes at eight, but I like to come a half hour or so early. Lets me get the best spot and do a little warm up of my own. You're lucky you came early too, we're starting with beginner techniques before coming to the advanced stuff."

Timm scoffed. "I'm sure I can keep up with the advanced stuff."

"Oh really?" Celia smiled wickedly, eyes sparkling with that same dangerous wit that Timm had noticed before. Her tone was challenging, as if there was a deep seeded competitive nature buried under the warmth she projected. "Well then, I would sure like to see that."

Over the next half hour Timm was engrossed in conversation with Celia, barely noticing as others showed up to join the class. They too set up their thin yoga mats, as Celia had called them, and prepared for the instructor to arrive. When she did, the students and Timm all stood, bowed, and spoke a word of greeting. It reminded Timm a lot of how he and his master would start training sessions.

The first half hour of class was just as easy as Timm had expected. His master would have laughed at the simple stretches that a novice would have mastered quickly. Every now and then, he would turn to see Celia performing the stretch with ease and smirk, showing her just how simple it was for him to keep up. She would return his smirk with one of her own but in the form of a true student, not say a word.

The second half hour of class, Timm began to realize exactly what Celia had been talking about. While his balance and form were excellent for fighting, it seemed that his master had failed to teach him techniques that would have allowed him to stand up to the pressure the advanced techniques were putting on his body. He struggled to stay on his feet at some points, barely managing it, but refusing to topple while Celia was standing beside him, perfectly balanced like a leaf floating on water.

By the time class ended, Timm was sweating and working hard to control his breath. He refused to start panting like a dog, probably due to his own deep seeded competitive nature. Celia wiped her brow with a towel from her bag and smiled at him, her face ruddy and breath heavy, but a wide grin on her face.

"So, keep up alright?" she asked.

Timm laughed. "Okay, I admit, it was a lot harder than I thought it would be."

"A lot of people realize that," Celia said, rolling up her mat to put it in the bag. "They call yoga some hippie thing and dismiss it as not being a real form of exercise. They won't even give it a chance. But put them into a situation where they need to work their way through the poses, and half fall over like bowling pins. At least you had it in you to admit that it was harder than it looked."

"I will always admit to my failings," Timm nodded. "I've experienced enough to know that I'm far from perfect. But I'm working on it."

Celia laughed. "Well, if you want to keep working on it, we have class at the same time every Monday, Wednesday, and Friday. Will I see you next time?"

"I will do my very best to attend," Timm nodded, getting to his feet. "But for the moment, I need to be going."

"Same here, I need to get to work," Celia said. "Doesn't look good when the boss is late. I look forward to seeing you again, Timm."

"You too," Timm said, giving her a slight bow, which she returned with a laugh.

Afterwards, Timm headed back to the church feeling a lightness in his step that had felt so much heavier this morning. He'd found success with the glow, at least a step toward mastery and even learned of another physical challenge that could push him in new ways he'd never considered before. Today was, undeniably, starting off as a wonderful day.

~ 38 ~

LUIS

Luis waited until after Timm and Smithers had finished discussing the magical bag before getting up and dressed for his run. His eyes lingered over the magical ring that had been in the pocket of his jeans ever since the night before and decided to slip it on. As soon as he did, he felt a wave of energy slip over him, as though a protective barrier between him and the world was suddenly erected. It was not enough to stop bullets, if the mannequin was any indication, but any added defense was welcome.

He finished lacing up his running shoes and went over to Lee's bed. He shook the priest lightly, and Lee's eyes opened immediately.

"I am awake," Lee said, quietly.

"I figured," Luis answered. "Timm's gone for meditation and Smithers is playing with his new toys. Care to go for a run with me?"

"You could ask Morgan," Lee responded.

"I don't feel like getting out paced by a wolf," Luis answered.

"Fair enough," Lee said, pulling himself out of bed. "Allow me to get dressed for the occasion."

Fifteen minutes later, Luis felt the familiar rhythm of his feet pounding the ground beneath him, the burning of cold air against his face and lungs, and the exhilaration of his muscles singing against the strain. To his credit, Lee kept up well enough, his usual scholarly appearance apparently hid his athleticism well.

"There was another reason I wanted you to come with me on the run today," Luis said, regulating his breathing to be sure that he did not lose pace.

"Oh?" Lee asked, panting slightly. "What is that?"

"You are another holy man," Luis said. "And unlike Father Mitchell, you know the true nature of men like us?"

"True nature?" Lee asked.

"We are to reshape the world," Luis said. "Not just heal the wounds evil opens, but prevent them from occurring."

"A noble goal from a noble knight," Lee answered. "However, that is not my position within my church. Nor is it Mitchell's in his. Healers heal, knights avenge."

"It is not vengeance," Luis said. "It is eliminating the need for vengeance."

"Strike first?" Lee asked. "You're calling for a crusade."

"Exactly," Luis responded.

They turned the corner and Luis altered his pace, feeling the slickness of ice beneath his feet. This stretch of sidewalk sat in the shade and had not yet had the night's icy build up melted by the sun.

"A crusade against who?" Lee asked, slipping once or twice before catching his balance and adjusting his gait. "We have no shortage of enemies."

"The most dangerous one," Luis responded.

"That doesn't answer my question," Lee said.

"We can discuss that with the others," Luis said, his voice coming out sharper than he meant it to, though he didn't back down. "But I am getting sick and tired of sitting around and waiting to react."

"While this is true, you don't exactly have the right to call a crusade, do you?" Lee pointed out.

"And they have the right to kill children?" Luis barked, far louder than was appropriate in the early morning streets. While there weren't many passerbys on the streets, there were enough that turned to stare at him, but he paid them no mind. Instead, he slowed his pace until he stood in the middle of the icy sidewalk, steam rising off his heated skin. Lee stood next to him, catching his breath.

"You do not have the right to call a crusade," Lee repeated, firmly. "Your goddess will call you to action. Do not presume to know her will, for that belief among the so-called holy men of this world, that they knew better than their own gods, is what sent it spiraling into the darkness it now dwells in."

"So, what do I do?" Luis asked, eyes burning into the ground, and impotent rage burning unchecked in his chest, seeking any means of escape from within him.

Lee clapped him on the shoulder, forcing Luis to look up at the priest's smiling face.

"You follow your goddess's signs," Lee said, pointing at an on-coming runner. Luis recognized the man. He wore the same woolen cap with Nike's sigil on it, though the clothes he wore were different.

"Good morning!" the man called out.

"Good morning, again," Luis responded, grinning. "Glad to meet you like this rather than tumbling into a mound of ice and snow."

"Definitely preferable," the man smiled. "I don't think I got your name last time."

"Luis," Luis said, then gestured to Lee. "And this is my friend, Lee."

"Pleasure to meet you both," the man smiled. "I'm Eric. Well, not to be rude, but I've got another mile and need to keep my heart rate up."

"Of course," Luis said, but then a thought struck him. "But before you go, could you tell me where you got that hat?"

"This old thing?" Eric asked, patting his head. "I've had it since high school. Though if you want one like it, I think they've opened a new Nike store at the mall."

"A Nike store?" Luis asked, turning to Lee. "Is that like a temple?"

"A temple to capitalism, maybe," Eric said. "But if you want all things Nike, that's where you go. Anyway, have a great morning gentlemen."

"You too," Lee waved to him as he left.

"We must go," Luis said, feeling like the heat in his chest had reformed itself into a mighty flame that burned not with impotent rage, but with holy purpose.

"I suppose in order to do so, we need to return to the church first," Lee said, watching Eric as he continued his run, disappearing into the distance. "Figure out whatever this 'mall' thing is."

*　　*　　*

"It's an indoor town square," Smithers explained. "And it's complete hogwash."

Luis had quickly learned that Smithers was greatly opposed to the idea of them going to the mall. According to the old man, they were nothing more than 'tax shelters for assholes who are content to let the world fall into disrepair so long as you could get a pretzel.'

"I understand your position on the matter, Smithers," Luis said, trying to keep his words diplomatic but his position immovable. "However, I wish to see this temple to Nike."

"It ain't a temple," Smithers said, tiredly. "It's a store. And you're not going to like what you see in there."

"A store dedicated to selling a sigil of my goddess and promoting victory?" Luis asked. "How could that possibly be a bad thing?"

"Because what you ain't getting is, *that ain't what it is!*" Smithers practically yelled. "All the people who run that place care about is money. Something, might I remind you, that we don't have a lot of."

"We've collected a fair bit," Luis said. "Mostly from the wallets of those that attacked us, but still, there's enough to browse a bit."

"You grossly underestimate how expensive that store is," Smithers muttered as he finished reassembling one of the newly acquired pistols and dropped it unceremoniously into the magic bag.

"What's the harm in looking?" Morgan asked, putting her dulcimer away. She'd apparently been practicing while they'd all been out.

Currently, Timm and Lee were showering in the men's bath room, though with only two stalls, Luis had forgone one of his own for the time being. He had also been excited to ask Smithers about going to the mall, though his hopes on that matter were quickly getting dashed. Perhaps Morgan would be able to talk some sense into him.

"I'm pretty sure going to an extremely public place while multiple organizations of death are looking for you is a terrible idea," Smithers said.

"All the more reason to outfit your knight of Nike in her garb," Luis responded, his voice building more forcefully.

"Would you stop with that," Smithers snapped, sitting down heavily on his cot, burying his head in his hands. He muttered a few words that were inaudible, then finally lifted his head. "Fine, but you can't wear the longsword."

"I had no intention," Luis sniffed. "For close quarters like that, I planned to wear the short sword."

"No swords!" Smithers barked, then he sighed. "If you need to have your weapons, just throw them in my bag. I'll carry them, and we'll have them in case of an emergency. I just don't want you walking around armed like you're going to the round table. Cops will be on you in seconds."

"What's the round table?" Morgan asked.

"Irrelevant," Luis responded, not wanting Smithers to get distracted now that he was seeing sense. "That is a fair assessment and I agree to your terms."

"Huh, finally, one of you that will listen to reason and compromise," Smithers said, getting up. "Toss what you need in the bag and I'll go talk to the padre about borrowing the van again. I swear, we're going to triple that thing's mileage."

Within the hour, they were all cleaned up and ready to head out to the mall. Luis was excited to see what treasures awaited at the Nike store, but apparently there was something for just about everyone.

"So they have a pet store?" Morgan asked, excitedly.

"Yes, but we're not buying anything there," Smithers said, irritatedly. "You can play with the puppies or something, but we do not need another mouth to feed."

"What about books?" Lee asked.

"Tons of them," Smithers said. "I think they have two or three different book stores in the building."

"What about yoga stuff?" Timm asked.

Smithers paused at that one.

"Why on earth do you want to know about yoga?" he asked. "When did you even learn what yoga was?"

"This morning in the park," Timm answered, blunt and direct.

"I don't know what I was expecting," Smithers sighed. "But yeah, good chance that you'll find some hippie store that sells that stuff."

"Funny, that's exactly what Celia said people who knew nothing about it, called it," Timm mused.

Smithers grumbled the rest of the way to the mall under his breath, but even his sour mood couldn't deflate the air of excitement in the van. After a half hour of travel, and almost as much time looking for a place to park, they had arrived at the mall.

While in Boston, Luis had seen a number of exceptionally large buildings, most of them were built to be excessively tall. This one, however, looked much more like a coliseum than a town square. It was so massive that he was unsure if he could see both sides or if the building itself was blocking his view of even more of itself. There was a good view of the city skyline behind it, as the building itself was probably only four or five stories compared to the over twenty that most other buildings seemed to be, and even more space seemed to be taken up by a field of concrete filled with cars and trucks rows deep.

"This seems like an excessive waste of space," Luis commented as they began the long walk from their parking spot to the entrance of the mall. "Other buildings conserve space by building upwards, which you clearly have the technology to do. Why isn't your 'mall' built the same way?"

"Visibility," Smithers said, his tone sour. "People are more likely to buy something if they can see it. If I need to go thirty floors up to get to something, I sure as hell ain't climbing the stairs to do that. And with this many people, elevators would be slow and crowded. Most people probably wouldn't see more than the first couple floors, meaning the only way you're selling something is if you're on those floors. By making it flat, you got an even playing field."

"All this space is being wasted just to make money?" Lee asked, somewhat confused.

"Now you're getting it," Smithers said with mock enthusiasm. "Waste time, space, and resources so you can make money. It's the American way!"

Luis pondered over this revelation and Smithers' warning about what the Nike store would actually be like. A sliver of doubt began to pierce his mind and a coldness gripped at his heart, but he pushed both away, praying to Nike that her name and visage would be spared such garish commercialization.

"Alright, just remember we came in through Penny's," Smithers said as they approached a wall of four dozen glass doors.

"We can remember that," Morgan said. "But what does that mean?"

"Name of the store we're going in through," Smithers explained, pointing up at the letters illuminated on the side of the wall above them. Each was probably four or five times the length of the van. "It's easier than remembering or finding one of the damn entrances littered around the sides of the building. Just be wary of the perfume ladies."

"What do they do?" Luis asked, feeling suddenly very small as he looked up at the letters overhead.

"Try to sell you perfume," Smithers answered. "By spraying you with it."

Luis did not see the problem with that, as perfume was usually quite lovely, and having some applied to your wrists wasn't all that intrusive. He stepped boldly towards the JCPenny entrance of what was called the Prudential Center of Boston. Apparently, malls were given fancy names by those who owned them, but were unceremoniously addressed by their descriptor by the common people. Luis had to agree that the common vernacular made far more sense in this case. He was beginning to understand Smithers' distaste for such places.

As they stepped inside, a woman in her middle years approached Luis. She was wearing a professional looking suit of clothing and a name tag that said 'Doris' in bold, black letters.

"Can I interest you in our new Armani for men?" she asked Luis, holding up a bottle.

"Uh, sure," Luis said, not wanting to be rude.

Before he could react, she sprayed him with a fine mist of strong smelling, and foul tasting, liquid. Luis coughed and sputtered, pushing past the woman in a desperate attempt to find fresh air. He heard her apologizing behind him, but could not take the time to address anything beyond the horrific assault he'd just undergone.

Passing through an archway exiting the store, Luis finally found air clear enough to start passing the foul perfume from his system. It still burned his nose and throat, but at last he could breathe again. Smithers came up next to him and patted him on the shoulder.

"Told ya," he said. "Always say no to the perfume lady."

"I don't know," Morgan said as she came up next to them. "I think it smells rather nice."

"Try tasting it," Luis wheezed as he blinked his eyes rapidly in an attempt to stop them from watering.

"Come on," Smithers said. "Let's find the map and..."

Smithers looked up and his voice trailed off.

"Oh goddamn it," the old man muttered. "Where did Lee and Timm go?"

Luis looked around and saw that only he, Smithers, and Morgan remained. Lee had been looking for a bookstore, so there was a good chance they'd find him there. But as Smithers had said, there were quite a few of them to choose from, so determining which he went to would take time. As for Timm, there was no telling where he might have gone off to.

"We have a quest," Luis said. "The others will find us if necessary, or we can follow the shouts of trouble."

"You've got a point on that one," Smithers said, under his breath. "Okay, fine, we'll find the map, find your overpriced Nike store, then find the others. God I hate malls."

It didn't take long to find the Nike store, though cutting through the crowds and keeping Morgan's attention on the task at hand created a far more difficult path than even Luis could have anticipated. They traversed probably half of the mall when Luis caught his first glimpse.

The wings of his goddess unfurled before him, her name illuminated in brilliant white light that mimicked the light of her power through his blade. Fit, strong veterans of athletic affairs wandered through the massive space, milling about as new initiates, overwhelmed with intimidation, approached and took their first steps towards victory. Truly the temple of victory called all to her glory, and Luis felt his heart pound uproariously in his chest.

Forgetting himself, forgetting the others, with no other purpose driving him, Luis rushed forward filled with determination and purpose that had so long been denied to him here in this world. He dove wholeheartedly into the glimmering tribute to his goddess, a beacon of glory in this strange, faithless world.

~ 39 ~

SMITHERS

Smithers stood and watched Luis rush forward into the Nike store like a kid being set loose on a Toys R Us. Morgan slurped on a lemonade they'd picked up at the pretzel place along the way he'd begrudgingly stopped at because it was only after they arrived that they'd realized no one really stopped for breakfast that morning.

"You win again, Annie," Smithers muttered under his breath.

"What?" Morgan asked, looking up from another one of those giant maps dotted around the landscape.

"Nothing," Smithers said, waving her off. "What are you looking at anyway?"

"Trying to find someplace that would be interesting to check out," she said. "Ooh! How about this one? Magic Bean! Can we go to Magic Bean?"

Smithers looked around and saw them getting strange looks from passerbys and quickly tried to hush the girl.

"No!" Smithers whispered harshly. "Why on earth would you want to go there?"

"Because I make magic berries," Morgan said, her voice quiet and quavering a bit. "I thought maybe I could learn some more magic there."

Smithers sighed and shook his head.

"That's not what they do there," Smithers said. "Magic Bean is a store for baby supplies. I was just... look, I'm sorry I was harsh. It's just people were staring."

"It's okay," Morgan said, smiling at him. "You're stressed, we've all been. But we really appreciate you taking us here. Everything in this world has been danger and disaster. It's nice to have a day where we can just relax and see what it has to offer."

Smithers laughed a little. "Believe me, kid, this place is not the best this world has to offer. One day, you'll get to see the real good things we've got."

"I hope so," Morgan beamed. "Though you're probably right, I probably shouldn't be shouting that I want to go to a baby store with you, considering the age gap. Might send the wrong message.

She went back to her lemonade and Smithers couldn't help but laugh as he turned back to see what Luis was up to. Unfortunately he had lost sight of the knight somewhere in the store, though if there was anything he could trust in this world, it was that the Knight of Nike wouldn't wander too far from the Nike store.

"Though that brings up a question. Why would they call a baby store 'Magic Bean'?" Morgan asked, confused.

Smithers felt his face burn as she asked the question and was immediately grateful to hear Luis' voice bellowing out his name if it meant not needing to explain that question to Morgan.

"SMITHERS!" Luis' voice rang out through the mall, turning heads and drawing stares as a full grown man ran at full tilt towards him, screaming at the top of his lungs. "SMITHERS!"

"I hear you, I hear you," Smithers said, smiling embarrassedly at the fresh batch of people staring at them, trying to placate the situation. One woman looked shocked when Luis barreled up to Smithers, almost crashing into him. Smithers caught him by the shoulders and smiled at her. "It's fine, special needs."

"Oh," she nodded, seeming to understand and began to walk away.

"What's special needs?" Luis asked, confused.

"You are," Smithers hissed. "Now what do you need from me that's so special you needed to howl like an animal through the mall to get my attention rather than just walking out like a person to come get me?"

"Oh," Luis said, straightening up and composing himself properly. "Well I found a pair of shoes."

"Yeah, one tends to do that in an athletics store," Smithers said, nodding, waiting for anything more than just 'shoes'.

"But they have Nike's sigil on the heels," Luis said, his excitement growing. "Just like her winged sandals!"

"Yeah, that's pretty common too... wait, wasn't that Hermes?" Smithers asked.

"Who?" Luis asked with what looked like genuine confusion.

Smithers stared blankly at the knight for a moment, feeling as though his brain was going to short circuit. Either the knight was fucking with him, or their world was seriously messed up beyond all comprehension.

"Nevermind," Smithers said. "You still haven't explained why you needed to come flying out of there like a howler monkey."

"I just did," Luis said, looking confused. "I found the shoes. I just need currency to get them."

"Don't you have some... currency?" Smithers asked, choosing to speak with him on his level.

"I do, but not enough," Luis explained. "I need some to borrow from the party's funds."

"How much are we talking here?" Smithers asked, suspiciously.

"Two hundred of your dollars on top of what I already have," Luis said, matter-of-factly.

This time Smithers really did feel his brain short circuit.

"Are you *insane?*" Smithers hissed. "Two hundred dollars? Do you understand just how expensive that is?"

"The cost of victory is high," Luis said, unphased.

Smithers began counting backwards from one hundred until he realized that was half as much as Luis was asking to buy a *damn pair of shoes!* Breathing a deeply and trying to keep his cool, he just looked up at Luis and asked:

"Were those the cheapest pair you found?"

"I did not really look based on price," Luis answered. "I was focused on following the call of my goddess. She led me to those."

"Of course she did," Smithers sighed, accepting that there was no way he could shout Luis out of wanting these shoes. He would have to be more accommodating. "What if we find a nice pair, cheaper than that one? Do you think she'll be satisfied with that?"

Luis pondered the question for a moment.

"I would have to sense how she reacted to the pair you selected," Luis answered.

"Okay, because I don't think that Nike has fallen victim to the capitalism of her name here. Even one with nothing can be victorious, right?" Smithers asked, beginning to realize just how easy Luis was to work with when you chose the right words. All he had to do was gently nudge the knight how he wanted and they could both walk away happy and not completely flat broke.

"Of course," Luis answered. "Victory belongs to those with strong wills, not endless pockets."

"Well, since we don't have endless pockets," Smithers said, putting his arm around Luis' shoulder and leading him inside the store. "How about we find something a little more cost effective that you can still be satisfied with?"

By the time they had found a pair of shoes that both satisfied Smithers' frugal needs and Luis' goddess's standards, the old man was down to his last frayed nerve. They paid nearly a hundred dollars for a pair of plain black running shoes with a white check mark that Luis insisted be called a wing.

He waited by a bench while Luis finished putting on the new shoes and placing his old, hand-me-down versions in the magical backpack in case of an emergency. The knight sat for a solid five minutes just looking down at the shoes that probably cost three dollars for a child in some third world country to make and admired them the entire time. Smithers had half a mind to explain to Luis what child labor was, but thought better of it, deciding that sating the knight's zeal with the shoes would be undone if he knew what the company using his goddess's name was doing to boost their profits. Either he'd reject the shoes and they'd just be out the money, or worse, he'd start a war with capitalism and drag them all halfway around the world to fight a crusade against inequality. While Smithers wasn't against that, it was hardly feasible with their current situation.

Finally, he'd had enough.

"Come on," Smithers said, grouchily. "We need to find the others, and I'm actually getting hungry enough to stoop so low as to eat food court food."

"Ooh!" Morgan said, excitedly. "More pretzels?"

"I said food, kid," Smithers glowered. "Not oily dough."

They began walking through the endless crowds of braying people buying pointless things with money they didn't actually have and Smithers found himself growing more and more irritated with each step. He'd always hated malls, and not just because of the senseless consumerism. He'd hated them for the mockery of what they were.

Malls had started out as a good idea, something that Smithers would have probably gotten behind if greedy assholes hadn't gotten involved. They were supposed to be a way to revitalize communities, bring people together, create a new town square where people could interact and embrace their culture. Instead, consumerism found a way to cash in on them and turned them into a wasteland of wants rather than havens for the spiritual need for community. Smithers wasn't a godly man, but interaction with good people was necessary for the soul. This place did little more for a soul than crush it.

A vaguely Irish melody began to fill the air, carried by the sweeping strings of a violin. Morgan noticed it too, and started pulling away from the group. Smithers tried to grab her, but she slipped from his grasp. He and Luis pushed their way through the crowd until they came across what had drawn it to begin with.

Standing in the center of the crowd was Timm, eyes closed and body bending back and forth with the music. His violin case was open at his feet and people would toss a few bills in here and there, but the man did not seem to notice. The music had enraptured him completely, and the beauty of it was drawing people away from the shops and putting their feet into motion.

Morgan squealed with excitement, shoving the cup of ice that had once been lemonade into Smithers hands and she reached into the bag on his back, pulling out her dulcimer. The woman next to him saw the large instrument come from such a small bag and stared in wonder. Smithers just shrugged at her.

"Live long enough and you learn to pack your kids' stuff right," he said, smiling, both unsure and uncaring if she believed him.

He turned to see Morgan joining in on the music, adding another layer to the song, mixing cultures in a way that Smithers had not expected in the song, but was not at all unpleasant. The crowd reacted as well, some dancing, some clapping, and quite a few with their phones out recording. Smithers tensed at this, but decided to shrug it off. It wasn't likely that the bad guys were checking for them playing music in a mall. The kids should get to enjoy themselves.

And besides that, Smithers thought, smiling as he watched the people come to life as the two of them played. *This is what this place was supposed to be about.*

The old man wasn't sure how long he got to stand there and actually enjoy the strange little community that popped up around him, but whether it had been hours or minutes, the time was too short. It was broken by the same thing that had plagued him for over a week now, so it shouldn't have come as a surprise.

"Trouble," Luis whispered in Smithers' ear and suddenly the old man snapped to attention.

"Where?" he asked, his eyes moving away from Timm and Morgan, focusing on the crowd, scanning for danger like his training taught him to.

"There," Luis nodded, barely perceptible if you weren't looking for it. The man was a professional, Smithers had to give him that.

Smithers looked over in the direction Luis had indicated. A couple of men in mock-police uniforms were walking over, flashlights on their belts rather than guns. Each had a walkie-talkie clipped to their shoulders right above an iron-on patch that said 'Prudential Security.'

"That's nothing," Smithers whispered to Luis. "Just some security guards. Probably going to tell these two to knock it off or get kicked out. Or try to charge them for a permit to play music. Greedy bastards..."

Luis shook his head. "Not them. Further back."

Smithers craned his neck as much as he dared as to not let whomever Luis was looking at catch on to them. The crowd looked to be made up of the typical generic people, mothers with strollers, old folks using this as their exercise for the day, and teenage kids who were probably supposed to be in school but were skipping. Just as Smithers was about to give up the search, he noticed one person out of place.

A thin, frail looking person that Smithers could not discern as either a man or woman, stood still and slightly apart from the crowd. They wore a baggy hoodie that had seen better days. It was faded and filled with holes, and the hood was up, hiding any potential distinguishing facial features. All that stuck out from underneath the hood was stringy, straw-like hair, stiff and brittle looking.

"Can't really tell... but does that person look familiar?" Smithers asked, his eyes lingering on the strangely unhealthy hair when suddenly they shifted and his eyes were drawn down to what they were cradling in their arms.

They were wearing a relatively nondescript backpack, but the straps were worn specifically to make it hang from their chest rather than back. This wasn't anything particularly unusual in itself, except they were supporting it with great care, as if the slightest motion could...

Smithers eyes went wide.

There was a wire coming out of the bag. Four of them, to be precise. Each a different color, coiled together, and attached to something up the figure's baggy sleeve. It was subtle, but Smithers had seen these kinds of makeshift devices before, and it was enough to make his blood run cold.

"Bomb," he whispered suddenly.

"What?" Luis asked, alarmed.

"*Bomb!*" Smithers shouted, and the world devolved into chaos.

~ 40 ~

LEE

The past few days had been exceptionally stressful for Lee. He'd been shot at, bitten by men in the skins of wild animals, and attacked on a moving train. There was no chance that he was letting an opportunity like this slip by him, so once Luis inadvertently provided the distraction for him, he ventured forth alone into the Prudential Center in search of a quiet place where he could be alone with his thoughts and a few books.

Crowds pressed in on him from all sides as he traversed the mall, creating an uncomfortable sense of claustrophobia that he hadn't felt in a long time. Stepping through the archway that led into the tan and green bookstore of Barnes and Noble sent a wave of relief washing over him.

There were few people in the space, or perhaps not as few as he thought, but the rows and stacks controlled the flow of people as they moved and browsed the silent shop. While many voices chattered about in the main thoroughfares, here within the stacks the unwritten rule of silence among the tomes reigned supreme. There seemed to be a universal respect for books regardless of world, and Lee smiled at the comfort that thought brought to him.

While Simon had introduced them to the internet, and the library at Boston University was immense, there was something in the comfort of a bookshop that warmed the cockles of Lee's heart. He pursued the shelves, finding himself waffling between the sciences and history. Knowing the advancements of this world would definitely be beneficial, however knowing how they came to these advancements may be an even greater boon.

Unable to fully decide, Lee took a pile of books from both sections and found a comfortable area away from others where he could sit and read in peace. The next few hours passed peacefully as he learned the history of the world he now found himself in. He read of how technology advanced and advanced until an overly religious zeal in an era known as the Dark Ages kneecapped the world's progress. Lee considered this a shame for both scientific leaps and spiritual growth. To value one over the other created an imbalance that darkened history and made the time marred by it remembered as little more than a stain on mankind's development.

The time that followed, however, lifted Lee's spirits as he saw the majestic artworks that were born of a time called the Renaissance. Finally, Smithers' comments about them looking as though they belonged at a Renaissance Faire finally made sense. The clothing and artwork, the sense of adventure and poetry made Lee's heart ache a little for home. He spent more time looking at the images portraying the time period than reading about it, but did not feel he lost anything in the way of education. People moved about him, but they meant nothing. All that mattered was the art.

However, like everything else in the world, the art could not last. Mankind needed to spread, needed to expand, and needed to adapt. With the heel of the church off their throats, mankind developed faster and more dangerously than anyone could have possibly predicted. Monsters rose to power, and each of them wore the face of a man. There were times when Lee needed to put the books down to keep from weeping. Great technologies created in the wake of a war that left behind it a trail of bodies and blood so vast an army could drown in it.

He thought guns had been the worst of it, but it seemed the people of this world were not content with creating weapons capable of killing just a few people in a swath, but level cities. During their research on radiation, he'd come across mentions of Hiroshima and Nagasaki, two cities whose citizens were affected by devastating radiation, however at the time he had not understood their references to an atom bomb. Apparently, the cities were leveled by such devastating power simply to make a point and end a war.

"What a way to end a war," Lee shook his head sadly. "Senseless. Are all the people of this world so senseless?"

He looked up, away from the image of a so-called 'mushroom cloud,' and saw three figures wearing ratty sweaters with hoods. Their attire reminded him of Morgan's, though hers was in far better condition than what he saw before him. They were moving quickly, coming from the stacks behind him, walking towards the glass doors that lead to the outside rather than the archways that lead into the mall proper.

Lee narrowed his eyes as he watched them leave. Their gait suggested that they were fleeing. Perhaps they were thieves?

Lee stood up, concerned now. He placed the book down and began to follow them at a distance. He had no evidence that they had done anything, but a gnawing thought persisted in the back of his mind. Perhaps it was all he'd just read that made him think the worst of the people of this world, but something just did not seem right.

The group made their way through the glass doors, unhindered by any security, and continued walking until they reached the lot of parked cars. Lee stood in the doorway, watching them, trying to decide what to do. One looked back over their shoulder briefly, said something to the others, and then all three broke into a run.

Lee was tempted to follow, but a new thought nagged at him. They were not holding themselves to keep from dropping anything. They were not toting bags of any kind, so there was no way that they were hiding anything taken illicitly from the shop.

"What were they doing if not stealing?" Lee pondered, watching as they ran.

Wandering back over to where he was sitting, he saw a disgruntled looking employee collecting the books he had been reading and placing them on a cart. She looked up at him and Lee recognized irritation in her expression, but did not stop to apologize. Something about the situation was bothering him greatly.

He turned the corner down the aisle where the three had first entered his vision and saw, leaning against a support beam that was either inconveniently placed in the space or improperly planned around, a worn, tattered knapsack. The condition of the bag did match the condition of their clothing, and Lee found it odd that they would have purposefully left their bag behind, especially in such a rush.

Out of curiosity, he knelt down in front of the bag and undid the metal clasp holding the canvas flap down. Flipping the flap over, he looked inside and was met by the flashing red lights of a clock. Rather than keeping time, however, this clock seemed to be counting down from one and a half minutes accompanied by a soft beeping noise that kept the beat of its descent.

Lee's blood ran cold as he recognized what he was looking at. The atom bomb had been far larger and did not have a timer on it like this one. But the book he'd been reading talked about terrorist attacks and their use of explosives. And if that timer was accurate, he had little more than a minute to get himself, and others to safety.

He had no means of contacting his comrades, they would have to fare for themselves, but there were people that he could save. That was where he needed to secure his focus right now, on doing what was actionable rather than lamenting what wasn't.

Breaking from behind the shelves, he saw the employee finish stacking the books onto a cart. She began pushing it when Lee grabbed her by the arm and pulled hard.

"Hey! What are you doing?" she asked, but she was dragged along, unable to break Lee's grip.

"There's a bomb!" Lee shouted urgently. "We need to get out of here!"

The employee stopped resisting the pull, but still seemed staggered, as if unable to process what Lee had just told her.

"Wait... what?" she asked.

Lee recognized that the time for calm, level diplomacy was long past. He tugged her hard until she was between him and the door, and then shoved her forward, sending her sprawling on her feet towards the exit.

"Run!" Lee shouted.

The once quiet and peaceful atmosphere of the bookshop was broken as screams pierced the air. People flurried from the aisles and from behind counters, pushing past one another in blind panic. Lee tried to keep a count going in his head of where the timer would be, and how much time he had left to escape the blast, but his mind was racing too quickly to trust the numbers in his head.

Gritting his teeth, Lee forced himself to accept that he'd done all that he could do and made his own way to the door, scooping a downed man back onto his feet without breaking stride as he passed through the doorway.

He had thought the screams had been deafening, but they were nothing compared to the sound of the explosion that came from the building just moments after he'd set foot into the frigid air outside. It roared like thunder before Lee suddenly realized he couldn't hear anything at all anymore.

Something hit him from behind. It didn't pelt him in any particular place, but rather it felt as though the entirety of his being was suddenly struck at once by a force so powerful that it lifted him bodily off the ground and threw him twenty feet through the air before finally settling him in a pile of tangled limbs and snow with the man he'd been attempting to help.

Pain lanced through Lee's body as he was pelted by a hailstorm of sharpness. Orienting himself, Lee realized he was on his back in the snow, now dyed with soot and blood. He saw that his entire body was covered in shattered glass and broken stone. He tried to move his leg and winced as electric agony surged through him. He soon found the cause of the pain, a ribbed shard of rusty brown metal jutted from his calf, piercing his leg entirely.

Gingerly, Lee sat up, careful not to tug on the leg until he could see it properly. With slow, even motions, he gripped his leg in his hands and slid it off of the jutting spike of metal. The sheer pain of it would have made him pass out but for the mental conditioning he'd endured in his youth. The pain was debilitating, yes, but that was something he could worry about later.

Once freed from the spike, Lee pressed his hands to the wound and felt the power of his god surge through him. The agony ebbed away to a dull ache, and when Lee pulled his hands away, he saw the gaping hole reduced to an angry red sore.

Nodding in approval, Lee gently brought himself to his feet. He turned to the man he'd been helping to continue carrying him to safety, but found he had been impaled likewise on a similar metal spike. This one, however, had gone through his chest. The man's mouth moved wordlessly for a moment, and Lee watched his last breath escape into the frigid air.

Death was inevitable, and this was not the first Lee had witnessed, but watching one who had been in your care pass on was different than seeing an enemy or friend die. Lee had made him a silent promise of safety and failed to deliver on that promise. There was a tightness in his chest for a moment as he looked down at the man who had been alive and pursuing books just moments ago, now bloody and cold in the snow.

A scream from behind him shook Lee from the thought. There was no time to entertain thoughts of failure or lost potential now. Others needed his help. He thought of Morgan, Luis, Timm and Smithers, still somewhere in the mall. Looking up, Lee saw trails of smoke coming from all across the Prudential Center.

"There was more than one," Lee said, gritting his teeth. Part of him wanted to run in, find the others, help the people trapped inside, but another scream sealed his decision.

"I'm sorry," Lee whispered, glancing down at the corpse that had just moments before been a man and silently swore to himself that while he could not ensure this didn't happen to anyone else, he could ensure that he reduced the suffering by all he could. "But I have faith in your success. I am needed elsewhere."

Lee turned his back to the mall and made his way into the crowd, to help in any way he could.

~ 41 ~

MORGAN

"**B**omb!" Smithers screamed, pulling Morgan's attention away from the security guards who were harassing her and Timm about their playing.

She had already been slipping her bulky instrument into her bag in anticipation of a quick escape when the cry went up. The people around them reacted immediately, screaming and dispersing in a panic. The security guards appeared staggered for a moment, unsure what to do in the situation.

Morgan, also not entirely sure what was going on, looked over to where Smithers was standing. The old man had his hand under his coat, where she knew Sebastian the shotgun was hidden, but he did not draw it. He locked eyes with her, and she saw a mixture of fear and concern in his eyes.

"It's the Nargles!" he shouted, pointing. Morgan followed his direction and saw three people with tight, gaunt skin, brittle straw like hair, and yellowed grins standing calmly amongst the crowd.

A blur of motion shot past Morgan as Timm whipped past the security guards who had been addressing them and ran in on the closest member of the Circle of the Wastes. He drove his fist across the druid's jaw, sending yellow teeth scattering across the floor, but as Timm came up for a second blow, he dodged nimbly out of the way.

Luis stepped forward, releasing his friction lock as he did, his eyes flashing with silvery white light.

"I sense no otherworldly evils," the knight pronounced more than said. "They stand alone without their false god."

"Spectacular!" Smithers called out, somehow still managing to express sarcasm through the panic in his voice. "But they've still got a *bomb!*"

The figure in the middle holding the bag began laughing maniacally as she placed the satchel down, revealing the flashing red lights counting down.

"Oh," she said, the skin around her mouth cracking and flaking away as she smiled. "We have more than that."

The two men who had been flanking her lunged forward, their forms twisting and stretching as bristling fur sprouted from their skin. Angry patches of red sores sat raw and exposed on their swelling bodies. Yellow teeth elongated into fangs that dripped with long strands of brown saliva. The men were gone, replaced with the hideous forms of rotting wolves.

Morgan looked to the woman, expecting her to take a similar form, only to see her slight frame growing thicker and taller. Her clothing fell away, revealing bare naked skin so riddled with rashes that only sparse patches of spiky fur managed to grow. Her ears crawled to the top of her head, rounding out as her nose pushed forward into a muzzle. Her breathing was heavy and raw, as she towered over the others, her body now that of a mutilated bear, was thick with the scent of decay.

The druids were gone, replaced by the twisted mockeries of beasts. And all three surrounded a very surprised looking Timm.

"You want a bear?" Morgan growled, throwing her bag over her shoulder. She charged forward, pushing past the three now *very* surprised security guards, and shouted, "Let me show you what a real one looks like!"

Morgan knew that her slender frame was not enough to cause much damage being that she did not have all that much mass behind her, but the light patter of her feet against the tiled floor shifted to heavy poundings as her body swelled with the mass of a grizzly. Thick brown fur exploded across her form, rippling down in waves to cover her entire body. Her muscles doubled, then tripled, then quadrupled in size, and did not stop there. The scream that ripped from her throat echoed out in an earth rumbling roar as her face bulged out into a wide, snarling maw that snapped down on one of the rotting wolves.

Her teeth found purchase and sank deep into the vile creature's flank, eliciting a horrified yelp of pain. Almost immediately, the foul taste of bile filled Morgan's mouth causing her to release the wolf in an attempt to keep herself from vomiting. Trying to create some distance, she swung her clawed paw at the wolf, hoping that despite releasing the bite, she could keep pressing the attack.

The wolf waited until the last possible moment to dodge, and by that point it was too late for Morgan to stop the attack. In horror, she watched as her own claws rend through Timm's arm, sending a gout of blood arching through the air. The wolf, now at her flank, seemed to grin at her through broken fangs. Morgan glowered at the beast, then whimpered her apology to Timm.

"It's alright," Timm said, wincing slightly. "They're like you, not just dumb animals. They're smart and they're going to use that against us. We need to watch out for that."

Morgan nodded her heavy head. She could not allow her anger at the Wastes to drive her to make foolish decisions in battle. They were a mockery of nature, this was true, but she needed to keep a level head if she wanted to remove such a hideous spectacle from the world.

"Oh the humanity!" she heard Smithers yelling behind her, his voice strange, as though he were saying the words mockingly. "Someone should really help that man!"

Morgan turned her head in time to see him rush forward and drive his taser into the neck of the other wolf, sending sparks of energy surging through it. Morgan grinned as she recognized

Smithers' tactic. He feigned knowing nothing about the situation and gave himself a reason to get involved. The old man was a lot craftier than he let on.

The security guards watched as Smithers charged in, and looked at each other in horror. In the same moment, they turned tail and ran as fast as they could towards the nearest exit doors. Morgan could not blame them for not wanting to get involved with something out of their realm of understanding, but that didn't mean she wasn't annoyed at their cowardice. Their position as guards should have at least meant they would help in some way.

The wolf beside Morgan snarled, readying itself for an attack, but turned at the last moment as Luis' heavy boot falls drew its attention away from her. The knight slid past her bulky form easily, and with the precision that only a trained warrior could have, drove the tip of the friction lock baton in a sweeping backhanded strike that audibly shattered the wolf's ribs. A thunderous flash of holy light filled the air as the blow struck home, staggering the wolf back a few steps. Weakly, yet defiantly, it stood before them, slavering brown spittle.

"You know," Luis cried out, pressing his back to Morgan's flank. "This would be a lot easier with a *sword!*"

"Oh bitch, bitch, bitch!" Smithers yelled back sarcastically.

The smell of rotten flesh rolled across Morgan in a sickening wave, and it was all she could do to keep from vomiting. She turned to see the other bear looming over Timm, who was clutching his stomach, roiling in pain. Driving her claws down, the bear slammed Timm's form prone to the floor, and brought them back bloody. Mercilessly, she fell to all fours, clamping her jaws down. Timm managed to twist his body in such a way to avoid letting her fangs find his throat, but rather intercepting the blow with his arm. Timm screamed in agony as the crunch of bones filled the air.

Morgan turned, desperate to charge the bear and take its focus away from Timm, but found she could not move as piercing pain screamed through her back leg. Turning, Morgan saw one of the wolves had sunk its fangs into her haunch, jerking its head from side to side, ripping and tearing through her borrowed flesh.

Anger welled up inside Morgan again as she rounded on the wolf that dared to stand in her way. As a pack, wolves could easily down a bear. Morgan knew that. She also knew, however, that one lone wolf stood no chance of besting her. If she was going to save Timm, she was going to have to deal with this wolf and do so with extreme prejudice.

Twisting her massive bulk faster than a creature of her size had any business doing, Morgan swung her meaty paw into the side of the wolf's head. She didn't even bother with the claws, knowing full well that if she went for a precise strike the wolf was most likely going to dodge out of the way. Instead, she spread the force out with such a wide area that her strike was sure to connect.

Surely enough, the wolf released its hold on her, expecting to dodge out of the way. Instead, it caught her paw across the side of the head, staggering it for a moment. That moment was all Morgan needed. She moved in, bracing the wolf's body with her forepaw and drove her fangs viciously into its neck. Clamping down with full force, she shook the wolf violently feeling the vibrations of vertebrae snapping ripple through her jaw. Flicking her head back, she released the beast, sending it flying into the air.

What landed several feet away from her with a meaty thump was unequivocally human. Weakly, the man tried to get to his feet, but as he pulled himself to his elbows, he began shaking violently, unable to keep his balance. He looked up at Morgan, trying to speak, but as he opened his mouth, no sound came out, just a bubble of blood that poured out of him like a waterfall.

Morgan huffed at him, turning her attention to the other bear standing over Timm and released a bellowing roar of challenge.

The other bear paused its attack against Timm, not bothering to release his arm from its mouth. Timm cried out in pain as joints popped from being jerked carelessly at inhuman angles.

Morgan's eyes burned as they met the other druid's. There was something like amusement behind her eyes, and with a lazy loll of her head, she dropped Timm unceremoniously. She began to circle Morgan, giving Timm the opportunity to begin crawling out of the path of either bear.

With Timm out of the way, the dam holding back her rage burst, and Morgan charged forward to meet the bear head on, ready to oust these interlopers from her territory. Permanently.

~ 42 ~

LUIS

As Morgan turned her bulky form to beat on the wolf that had taken a bite out of her haunch, Luis saw the other wolf lunge forward from behind her. He realized at the last moment it must have been using her size for cover and managed to put his arm up in time to protect his throat, but the sudden mass of the beast sent him staggering backwards onto the ground.

Driven into a frenzy from having downed its prey, the wolf began to attack furiously, scratching with claws while clamping down harder with its jaws. It was all Luis could do to keep the monster from fully piercing the leather of the coat he wore. Brown globules of foaming saliva hung down in strands threatening at any moment to break and coat Luis' face with the rancid fluid. With the stench of the bear so close and the slavering beast on top of him, the knight feared he would be seeing that pretzel he ate again, and did not think it would taste any better the second time.

"Don't worry, Luis!" Smithers shouted. "I'm a-coming!"

Luis' eyes went wide, expecting the explosion that came with one of Smithers' guns. He was about to call off the old man, not wanting to be riddled with holes himself, but rather than bullets tearing through either the hide of the beast or himself, the creature went suddenly rigid, every muscle in its body tensing in an instant. Luis yelped in pain as its teeth dug deeper and he feared the tension would shatter his arm. The tension released and Luis felt the beast relax slightly.

Smithers looked over the wolf at Luis, taser in his hand.

"Oh, whoops," Smithers said, sheepishly. "Forgot about electricity and muscles."

"Just kill the damn thing!" Luis snarled in anger, trying to ignore the pain in his arm and the heat of his blood seeping down his sleeve.

"Okay! Okay!" Smithers said, charging up the taser again and driving it into the side of the wolf. A tingle of electricity danced through the fangs and numbed the tips of Luis' fingers.

The pressure on Luis' arm lessened as the massive bulk of the wolf shrank down to that of a mere emaciated man. Even in this form, he snarled like a senseless animal, shaking his head violently in an attempt to tear through the leather that protected the knight from his decaying teeth. Luis felt revulsion as he looked down at the disgusting excuse for a man.

"You slobbering bastard!" Luis snarled, bringing down the friction lock clean into the back of the druid's skull. There was a cracking noise as several of his yellow teeth broke, causing the twisted druid to release his hold and fall back on his hands and knees away from the knight. The druid was panting and coughing, spitting out blood and rotting teeth as he tried to catch his breath.

Before the knight could make another strike against the staggered man, the bellowing of bears shook the air around them and Luis turned to see Morgan in her full fury swiping at the wicked druid in her own bear form. Heavy sounds of impact rolled out from the battle and Luis watched in wonder at the ferocity of it.

"Timm!" Smithers shouted. "Get out of there, boy!"

Luis hadn't noticed before, but as the two massive bears circled each other again for a second pass at one another, he saw between their legs Timm's form crawling across the floor, cradling one arm in his hand.

The Waste druid staggered back from a particularly heavy blow, her clawed foot nearly slashing through Timm's midsection. He rolled out of the way in time to avoid the blow, but Luis saw him gasp in pain and clutch his wounded arm closer to his body as he rolled.

"Timm! Move!" Luis shouted, fear and frustration causing his voice to crack slightly. The knight couldn't understand why the man was still underfoot. Normally he'd be bounding away, ducking and weaving through space like chaos incarnate.

Rather than listen to reason, Timm scooted back on his butt and turned to face the beast. Luis recognized the look of anger and frustration on his face. That of a man who wished so badly to be useful but felt utterly useless. A man being pushed to his breaking point. The kind of man, Luis recognized, who would make any desperate attempt to vanquish a foe.

"Dammit!" Luis called out to him, knowing full well the words were wasted, but knew he had to try anyway. "Don't!"

Timm lifted his good arm, pointing it at the Waste druid. For a moment, Luis thought his eyes were playing tricks on him, but soon the image got clearer and clearer. The tips of Timm's fingers began to glow with a soft yellow glow, but grew brighter until his entire hand was engulfed in brilliant white light like that of a burning sun. With a roar, Timm released the energy in a radiant beam at the back of the Wastes druid.

More nimbly than Luis would have given such a large beast credit for, the bear pushed itself back and away from Morgan, using her bulk to help its rebound. The beam of light shot between the two bears and slammed into a support column, sending debris flying out in a spray of rock and concrete.

"What the *fuck* was that!" Smithers shouted.

"Some kind of radiant burst," Luis shouted back. "I've seen him do it before, but this is the first I know of him doing it on purpose."

"*That's* what he hit Morgan with?" Smithers asked, shocked. "Damn that girl's sturdy."

Luis looked back at the battle of the behemoths raging before them, the living walls of fur and flesh clashing into one another with heavy, meaty blows that shook the air around them more violently than any clash of steel he'd ever experienced.

"I would definitely call that an understatement," Luis said, agreeing.

Movement in the corner of Luis' eye pulled his attention away from the bear fight. The man who'd been the wolf attacking him was attempting to crawl away.

"Hey!" Luis yelled at him. The man turned to face him, and what Luis saw nearly made him scream.

The druid's eyes had turned glassy and black, bulging out of his head as the skin around them darkened and hardened like amber. He opened mouth as though to speak, but instead of sound, two long, narrow appendages unfolded from between his jaws. Serrated mandibles clacked as his inhuman throat could only hiss. A pair of antennae sprouted from his forehead as an extra pair of limbs exploded from his chest. All the while, his form was shrinking, though not quickly enough to allow Luis to avoid watching his transformation in grave detail.

Where the man had been a moment earlier now sat an oversized cockroach. Time stretched on for a moment before the druid made his last ditch effort to escape. The form darted off, but Luis' reflexes were faster. He rolled, bringing down the friction lock in his hand. With an explosion of holy light, the cockroach splattered and careened off towards a bench. It was the body of a man, however, that slammed into it with the full force of Luis' divine fury and slumped lifelessly to the ground.

"This time," Luis panted. "Stay down."

"I don't think you really gave him much of a choice," Smithers said, looking over at the corpse hanging off the bench.

A bellowing roar drew their attention back to the bear fight, where they saw Morgan with her jaws buried deep into the back of the Waste druid's neck. Blood was pouring down the wretched bear's neck, but still she struggled to get free.

Timm pulled himself to his feet, drawing more power to his finger tips and sent a series of more blasts directly into the sides of the bear. The first scorched her side. The second blasted her back out of Morgan's grip, sending a sheet of blood down the side of her neck. In anger, the Waste druid reared back onto her hind legs and bellowed out a challenge.

Which was met by Timm's final blast, square in her chest, cutting the bellow short by making it nothing more than a pathetic, gasping whimper.

"Well," Smithers said, dropping the magical bag from his shoulder and pulling a handgun out from within. "In for a penny I suppose."

He leveled the pistol at her and let a bullet fly, tearing in through the front of the bear's chest and ripping through until it exited the woman's back instead, her form shifting down from massive bear to slight woman doing nothing to protect her from Smithers' expert marksmanship. She staggered to one knee, no longer the imposing figure she had been.

"Quickly!" Luis shouted, getting to his feet and running over to Smithers. The knight reached into the magical bag and pulled out the longsword stowed within. "Kill her before she can transform again!"

"When the *fuck* did you put that in there?" Smithers asked, shocked as the blade, which was twice as long as the bag, came sliding out.

The decayed looking woman glanced over at the wounded man who had once been a wolf as he too shifted from man to insect. No one had been close enough to stop him at the moment and it did not take Luis long to lose sight of his escape in the bedlam of the moment.

"Oh, I don't think I'll be wasting my time with that form again," the woman said, her raspy voice sounding dry and cracked, perfectly reflecting the condition of her skin. "I feel I've already wasted enough of yours."

She looked away towards the bag she'd kicked aside at the beginning of the fight. Luis saw the timer flashing down from 30... 29... 28...

By the time he looked back, the woman was gone, and another cockroach form was flying off into the diminished crowd. He took a step after her, but was stopped by Smithers, who ran past him screaming.

"Forget her!" the old man screamed, grabbing the thick mane of fur around Morgan's neck and pulling himself up onto her broad back. "Run! Hi-ho, Shaggy! Away!"

Doing as she was prompted, Morgan turned to run. Luis caught Timm's eye from the other side of the wide passage and they nodded at each other. Luis turned to follow bear-Morgan, who was cutting an easy path through the remaining crowd. As he turned, his eyes caught the flashing numbers of the bomb they were now running from.

15... 14... 13...

Luis ran, falling behind the bear but still moving as quickly as he could manage.

12... 11... 10...

His lungs burned and his legs ached. He hadn't realized just how much of a beating he'd taken in that fight.

9... 8... 7...

He could see the doors, the bright sunlight that was pouring in. It was his passage to freedom.

6... 5... 4...

A thought dawned on him. He was struggling to escape, the battle with the Wastes having taken its toll on him. He turned to look behind him and saw Timm, staggering along at least a hundred feet behind him.

3...

There was no way Timm could catch up.

2...

There was no way he could go back for him.

1...

The world erupted into sound and light.

~ 43 ~

SMITHERS

There were few experiences in life Smithers didn't have some kind of frame of reference for. After a career in the military that had more sharpie ink in it than white space, a long and successful marriage that was nowhere near perfect despite how he felt about it, and raising several children as well as a couple grandchildren, he felt pretty confident about saying that he's lived a full life. In fact, looking back on it, he could probably be one of those old-timers who could say 'now I've seen everything' and legitimately mean it. He'd seen and done it all.

Or at least, that's what he *would* have thought up until the point where he found himself, on a Monday afternoon, riding a grizzly bear with the mind of an anxiety riddled girl bareback through a collapsing mall trying to outpace the explosion of a bomb planted by a terrorist organization made up entirely of shapeshifting meth heads on a mission from their fucked up god. A mission whose parameters seemed to have something to do with radiation.

To be fair, ever since meeting this rag-tag little group of whack-jobs, he was beginning to realize that there were many things left in the world for him to learn about and experience. However, this particular one wasn't exactly an experience he'd been hoping to have.

One thing he'd known before, but never really put much thought into, was that grizzly bears could *move*. While Morgan had a lot of bulk she had to force into motion, she could do so with amazing efficiency. Large creatures such as bears, moose, and even elephants had a tendency to be able to react or run at speeds that surprised people when they saw it in action for the first time. These creatures tended not to move at such speeds often, mostly because it took a lot of energy to get their larger bodies moving, a lot more energy to sustain that kind of pace, and trying to *stop* that much energy once it was in motion bordered on nigh impossible without causing a severe amount of damage to the creature exerting that energy. Normally, these creatures would avoid such movement unless the situation was exceptionally motivating.

And *this* situation seemed to motivate Morgan quite a bit. They soon out-paced both Luis and Timm. Smithers looked back over his shoulder to call to the two of them to hurry their asses up, when he saw something that made him pause. Luis staggered, which seemed odd to Smithers considering he was such an experienced runner, but then she saw the knight looking back the way they came as though stunned. The old man was about to call out to the idiot and tell him to keep going when he saw what the knight was looking at and a cold feeling flooded the pit of his stomach.

Timm was behind them. *Far* behind them. He must have injured his leg during the scrap with the Wastes because he was limping along at much too slow a pace to ever possibly catch up to them, let alone escape the explosion. Smithers watched in horror as the man slowly staggered forward, face tight with determination despite the blossom of red hot fire and shrapnel blooming up behind him.

The blast wasn't overly powerful, not by the standards Smithers held and not at the distance he and Morgan were currently at. He'd been close enough to one once that he'd thought his hearing would never return, though considering it had thrown him through a window, he was surprised he lived long enough to need to consider learning sign language. This particular explosion seemed strong enough to blow out the support beam it was sitting by and, to a much lesser extent, his eardrums, but didn't have a wide enough spread to pelt him full of shrapnel.

The concussive force, however, was another thing altogether. Smithers suddenly felt like he was standing in a wind tunnel and someone turned it on full blast with no need for a warm up time. Before he could get blown off the bear, Smithers twisted back around so he was facing forward and pressed his chest against Morgan's shaggy back. His fingers twisted into the thick fur in hopes of finding purchase and anchoring himself in place. The wall of force washed over him and nearly took him bodily from his mount, but either sheer luck or happenstance was looking out for him today, and he managed to hang on.

Luis, on the other hand, was not so lucky.

Smithers looked up as the knight flew overhead, caught up in the shockwave of the blast. If the situation hadn't been so dire, the image of it may have even been comical. The knight, sword in hand, was tossed ass over teakettle and landed with what Smithers would have called a heavy thump if he'd been able to hear it. Amazingly, the sword only clattered away after impact, and then slid just a few inches away.

"Damn good grip," Smithers said. He smacked Morgan on the side of her meaty neck to get her attention and pointed at the felled knight. The bear nodded, an action that Smithers still could not get used to coming from so many different animals, and lumbered over to Luis' still form.

Smithers feared the worst at first, but when they approached Luis, they found he was groaning while trying to get to his feet. Smithers slid off Morgan's back and got one of the knight's arms over his shoulder to help.

"Get the sword," Smithers said to Morgan. "Get it in my bag. We need to go."

The bear gave him a worried look. She stood on her hind legs and gestured to her body.

"Well hands might help!" Smithers snapped. "I think we've officially entered the part of the day where a damned *bear* isn't going to help solve our problems!"

He felt a little guilty for yelling at her, but as he looked around, he saw it was only by sheer luck or bad planning on the Wastes' part that the building hadn't completely caved in around them. That would not last for long, and these people didn't have a frame of reference for just how fucked they'd be if they stayed where they were. Smoke filled the air and Smithers could see the glow of orange fires in the distance. He started coughing, and hoped that there was no asbestos in these walls.

"Come on!" he urged Morgan, hoping that his tone was coming out more panicked now than aggressive.

If a bear could look apprehensive Morgan certainly did. She held the form for just a moment more before shifting back. As quickly as she could, the girl ran over and grabbed Luis' sword, returning back to Smithers and slipping it easily back into the magical space in the bag.

"Okay, good," Smithers said, giving her a quick nod and turning to where he believed the exit was, shifting Luis' weight as he pulled the knight's arm across his shoulders. "Let's go."

"But what about Timm?" Morgan said, desperation in her voice. "And Lee?"

"I don't know where Lee is," Smithers said, trying to keep calm and stick to his training. "And stumbling around with an injured man through ground zero is not going to help us find him. We need to get Luis to help."

"But Timm!" Morgan pleaded, and he could see just how young and out of her depth she was despite the immense power she controlled. "He was right behind us, he *has* to be close!"

Guilt gnawed at Smithers chest. He saw where Timm had been and knew for a fact where he was when the blast went off: right in its radius. The blast may not have been that powerful as far as ones he'd seen in his life, but there was no way, even with as sturdy as these folks were, that he could have survived an explosion from that distance..

"Morgan," Smithers said quietly, trying to keep his voice calm despite the groaning of the building around them and the thickness of dust and debris in the air making him nervous about what he could be breathing in. "I don't think there's anything we can do for Timm right now."

Realization slowly dawned over Morgan's face as she finally began to understand what he was trying to tell her. The horror in her eyes nearly made Smithers break, but despite the hurt and fear in her expression he held himself together and adjusted Luis' half limp form on his shoulder.

"We have to help the people that can be helped right now," Smithers said. "Come on, we need to go before this place comes down on us."

"No!" Morgan shouted, taking a step back from him. "No! We have to find him! We have to help him!"

"Morgan, stop," Smithers said, with the kind of tone one saves for a child, which he took a moment to remind himself, she practically was.

"No!" Morgan continued, emphatically, thrashing her arms violently as if she could swipe the very thoughts of Timm's fate away from her. "No! We have to do something! *I* have to do something!"

Before Smithers could stop her, Morgan turned on her heel and darted back into the choking dust and smoke, vanishing from sight. The old man cursed under his breath. For half a second he entertained the thought of going in after her. Luis groaned and coughed, drawing Smithers back into the moment, forcing him to remember his own words.

"We need to help the people that can be helped," Smithers muttered, supporting Luis as he turned and continued on towards the door. "And you just can't help some people. Especially if they don't want to be helped."

He pushed on, towards the bright light that he hoped was the sun and not, in fact, the end of a very long, tiring tunnel.

~ 44 ~

MORGAN

Morgan's heart raced as she pushed on through the choking smoke and dust that obscured her vision and painted the whole world around her in tones of ash and brown. It reminded her slightly of the spell she'd used to obscure them when they went after the DIARD facility. That thought made her panic even more as she recalled how difficult it was to keep track of each other then, let alone find Timm now while she was panicking and he was hurt.

Coughing and spitting, she tried in vain to call out Timm's name, but every time she opened her mouth she felt her tongue get coated with a thick layer of dust that stole her breath away as it turned the saliva in her mouth to paste. Desperate to do something to actually save him, she staggered forward undeterred and scanned what little she could see of the wreckage for any sign of her missing friend.

She did so completely alone. Anger swelled up in her chest at the thought of Smithers' disregard for Timm. She knew that Timm and Smithers had never really gotten along, but that was no excuse to let him *die* in here. *Alone* in here... abandoned by them. Of course Luis needed help as well, she couldn't argue with that fact, but Timm needed help just as much! Even if Timm wasn't... she paused, shaking that thought from her mind. Even if she couldn't find him, she still had to try. He deserved that much after all they'd been through together.

She considered taking on another animal form that could perhaps help her find Timm faster, or to be strong enough to dig him out of some rubble if it came to that. However, the more she thought about it, the less sense that plan made. Anything that could track him by his scent would be absolutely useless in this dust cloud, and worse she may end up choking to death trying to find the scent.

Was there anything she could become that wouldn't be affected by the dust? She went through the list of creatures from her forest and nothing came to mind. She started thinking about the creatures who lived in the so-called wilds around Boston, but all she'd seen had been small birds and squirrels for the most part.

Except of course, a tiny voice in the back of her mind muttered, *for the creatures the Wastes turned into.* They *might be able to survive this hell.*

Revulsion rolled over Morgan at the thought and it was all she could do to stay upright. Bile rose from her stomach, stopping her long enough so that she could vomit against a still standing pillar. Her body shook violently as she coughed and hacked at the air. The very thought of ever becoming one of those twisted creatures was worse than potentially dying while choking on this tainted air.

Never. She thought violently in retort to the intrusive idea, *I will never become one of those... things. Not for any reason. Not even for...*

She kept moving on her shaking legs, trying to keep her focus on finding Timm. Each step was agony, but one step further was still a step further. Once or twice she collapsed to her knees as the ground shook and the heavy cracking noise of collapsing concrete and the screech of tearing steel echoed above her head. She closed her eyes, blinded by the dust, and found they were burning mercilessly. She tried to shout, but found her throat equally dry, the air itself having stolen her voice from her.

Morgan suddenly realized that she was laying face down on the ground. She tried in vain to summon her strength, to pull her limbs underneath her and get up, but soon realized that she was unable to stand. If her body lacked the strength, then maybe something else could, something with four legs, thicker muscles, or even quicker feet. But she soon realized she was unable to focus on taking another form. Her thoughts were blurred and her head felt fuzzy. The burning in her lungs told her that she was suffocating and her own brain was dying.

And what form would be of any use? She thought, laying down her head and giving into the exhaustion that was overtaking her.. *I would just suffocate twice.*

Something cold rained down from above her and it took Morgan a moment to recognize there was somehow water cascading down from the broken ceiling above her. Weakly, she opened her mouth, trying to catch any droplets that could clear away the grime that suffocated her. It smelled rancid and tasted worse, but the moisture still revitalized her enough to look around. The dust in the air was being beaten down by the rain, but it hadn't been enough to completely smother the fires and smoke still hung in the air, obscuring her vision.

Movement flickered between the coils of black smoke, catching her eye. Morgan recognized beams of golden light cutting through the darkness, waving wildly in all directions, but it was nearly impossible for her eyes to focus on them for very long. Somewhere in the dull, heavy air and incessant ringing in her ears, Morgan thought she heard a voice call out.

Morgan's heart leapt with joy.

Timm! She thought. It had to be Timm. He was using those radiant rays to try and find her, to find their way out, to...

A dark thought flickered across her oxygen starved mind.

He didn't know she was there.

No one besides Smithers knew she was there, and by the time Timm made it outside to freedom, found Smithers and Luis to even be told where she was, it would be too late.

No one was coming for her.

Her eyes fluttered closed and a brilliant white light fell across her vision and the world disappeared.

*　*　*

Morgan choked violently at the air that forced its way into her lungs. Her eyes snapped open to see the sun burning through trails of smoke. Her first thought was to wonder how the rain had come and gone so quickly. She looked around wildly, trying to get her bearings, but found herself unable to move. Looking down at her body, she found herself strapped down to a cart with thick, leather restraints. She was lying on a bed of some kind being wheeled away from the burning Prudential Center.

Panic flooded her mind as images of DIARD flashed across her memory. The days spent in the hospital, tied down to a bed and unable to concentrate enough to feel that connection to nature had nearly driven her insane. She refused to ever be taken by them again. Reaching out to nature to find anything that could help, the bear, the wolf, any creature that could fight or flee, she attempted to shift her form.

Her arm burned with intensely hot pain. Morgan tried to scream, but found her mouth smothered by something that encompassed the bottom half of her face. She breathed deep, finding her breath at least was unobscured, but the air she pulled in tasted foul and left a chemical tingle at the tip of her tongue.

If she couldn't shift to escape, then she would try something, anything else. Call down lightning, burn the restraints away, anything else to keep her from becoming a prisoner again. Morgan reached for her magic, but the burning in her arm flared up hotter than before as she struggled and fought to escape her bindings.

"Whoa! Whoa! Hey!" said a voice. A man stood over her wearing a mask that obscured the bottom half of his face leaned into view. "Calm down there, miss! Calm down!"

Morgan fought on, trying desperately to somehow escape the bindings in spite of the pain rippling through her body.

"Goddamn it girl!" Smithers' voice came to her. "Would you simmer down and just let the EMTs do their job!"

Morgan paused. Looking over, she saw Smithers walking on the other side of the cart wheeling her away. He stood free, unrestrained, and without Luis by his side. Fear gripped Morgan's heart as a hundred questions flooded her mind. Had he betrayed them? Had he given her up to DIARD like he'd abandoned Timm? Or was this something else? And where was Luis?

"Thanks sir," the EMT said to Smithers, interrupting Morgan's panicked thoughts. "Your granddaughter has lost a lot of fluids, so the IV will need to stay in until we get her to the hospital."

Morgan looked down at her burning arm and saw the tube attached to an IV bag, similar to the one the doctors had given Patrice when they visited her in the hospital. It was attached to her arm by a single, metal needle which was pierced through her skin, preventing her from accessing her druidic magic. The harder she fought, the more pain she would put herself through.

"Thanks, doc," Smithers said. "Sorry for her reaction. She's not a fan of needles."

"I'm not a doctor, but you're welcome," the EMT said. "You said she ran back in there for someone?"

"Yeah, a friend of ours," Smithers said, nodding. "Tall fella, dark hair, covered in scars. He was caught in the blast, so I didn't think we'd be able to help him by ourselves, not with an injured man."

"Smart to get out of there and get help, " the EMT nodded. "Though it was very brave of your granddaughter to go back for her friend."

"There's a thin line between bravery and stupidity," Smithers said, giving Morgan a sharp look. She quailed a bit under it, though that may have been the exhaustion wearing her down.

"You didn't happen to see the lad in there when you found her, did you?" Smithers asked.

The EMT shook his head. "Mostly just found the dead in there, though no one that matched the description you gave. Once the firefighters get the blaze under control they'll go in and search for more survivors. There's still a chance that he's been or will be pulled out."

Morgan felt hope spring up in her chest, but as she looked to Smithers and saw the grimace on his face, that hope began to wilt. In its place, guilt began to grow. The old man had been trying to save her, get her to safety, and get Luis to safety. He'd seen Timm get caught in the blast and just wanted to save who he could. He'd said as much to her back in the mall, but she'd refused to listen.

On top of all that, Morgan had thought the absolute worst of him. In her mind she'd called him a traitor and thought that he'd been so quick at abandoning Timm that he cared nothing for any of them. But he'd carried Luis out of danger, sent help in after her, and trusted that the others would have been smart enough to handle themselves. He hadn't done anything wrong, in fact of any of them he probably understood best what was the right thing to do in this situation. He hadn't failed them, she had failed him. She'd let her fear and panic rule her head like a dumb animal and almost gotten herself killed over it.

Morgan looked at Smithers. He was dirty, covered in soot and sweat, and looked absolutely exhausted. She was surprised that the old man was still on his feet, though she thought she might have seen him waver slightly where he stood. He took a deep breath, before turning to face the smoking building.

"I'm going to go look for Lee," Smithers said. "You and Luis are going to the hospital."

Morgan tried to say something, but the pain in her throat caused the words to come out something more like a croak.

"You ain't in any position to fight me on this," Smithers said, turning to face her, and Morgan suddenly had the feeling of a small girl looking into the face of a furious father. "You're strapped down and have a piece of metal jammed in your arm, and from what I see, that's going to keep you right where you are. So you're going to go, you're going to recover, and I swear to any and all gods that are listening at this moment that if you go and get yourself dead out of some stupid idea of saving someone else, I will bring you back to life just to kill you myself. D'ya hear?"

Morgan felt herself shrink back from him, not in fear exactly, but by the sheer intimidating force that was radiating out of him. His lie to the EMT about being her grandfather was certainly believable from the look in his eye. The old man was far more complex than Morgan had given him credit for in the past.

But he was still only human. Morgan couldn't speak, but she whimpered, trying to indicate the building with her hand still strapped down to the bed that was being rolled through the parking lot. Smithers studied her for a moment, then looked back at the building.

"Ah," he said, suddenly understanding her. "Don't worry, I ain't going back in there. I'd get myself killed if I tried something as stupid as that."

The words stung Morgan a little, but she assumed that was the point of them. They were meant to hurt because sometimes pain was the best teacher. Besides that, it wasn't like he was wrong in his assessment either.

"I'm going to go around the outside," Smithers continued, not lingering on the matter. They both knew that the point had been driven home, and there was no sense in harping on it any longer. "If I know Lee, and for a man I met less than a week ago, I feel I know him pretty well all things considered, he's got the skills to get himself out of a collapsing building so long as he wasn't too close to one of those bombs when it went off. Probably able to get some other people out of there as well. Best chance of finding him is to go where a lot of survivors are gathered. Probably talking about weird shit having happened that got them out."

Smithers' words made sense, but Morgan realized he was also pointedly avoiding the obvious issue with the plan: Timm had been capable too, but the Wastes had attacked and now they didn't know if he was alive or dead. What if the Wastes had cornered Lee as well? They had trouble fighting the druids and they'd outnumbered them.

Lee had been all alone.

"I let the EMTs know that you and Luis are friends," Smithers said. "They'll keep you close. Oh, and sorry about this."

Morgan looked at Smithers, confused for a moment. Then she felt heat enter her arm. Looking up, she saw another EMT remove a needle from a tube connected to her IV bag. Her mind started growing fuzzy and her head was too heavy to lift.

"I told them to dose you," Smithers said, brushing the hair back from her eyes as they began to flutter closed. "You all are too pig headed for your own good, and you need rest or you're going to hurt yourself. Now rest. I'll take care of everything else."

Morgan felt hot words on the tip of her tongue that cooled and dissipated into steam as soon as she tried to give them form. Smithers' face blurred and mixed with the bright sun hanging in the sky behind his head. She blinked to make the sunspots across her vision go away.

Once.

Twice.

And then the darkness took her.

~ 45 ~

LEE

Exhaustion threatened to drive Lee to his knees, but instead he sat on the tailgate of an ambulance as several EMTs moved around him like bees set to work on a hive. He had done all he could to help the people who were injured, saving the energy needed for his most powerful healing spells for only those in critical condition, but there were so many of those at this point that he'd long run out of power. Now he worked with his hands, putting his knowledge of healing to the absolute test.

Several EMTs had told him to get back and allow the professionals to handle the situation, though not one of them had the medical training to rival his own, and after he'd stabilized half a dozen near death patients, the so-called professionals stopped giving him a hard time about helping. He'd avoided letting on that he was still using a minor spell that took very little energy to cast, but he was getting the impression that these EMTs wouldn't care if he was using magic or medicine at this point. Much like him, they too were weary of people becoming little more than bodies.

But he'd been at this for over an hour and his body was beginning to give out on him. Exhaustion was beginning to set in and at a certain point he realized that he couldn't even feel the cold anymore. Immediately recognizing that as a problem, he sat down and allowed someone to put a blanket on him. For the past quarter of an hour he sat there on the back of the ambulance, just staring at the smoldering remains of the Prudential Center and tried not to think of all the people he lacked the strength to help.

Trails of black smoke curled listlessly into the sky, only disturbed in the still air as flying machines kept aloft by whirling blades drew too near to their paths. He'd asked one of the EMTs what they were called, and received a confused look and the word 'helicopter' from the man. He'd asked Lee how someone so well trained in medicine didn't know what it was called, to which Lee simply answered:

"I've lived a sheltered life."

That seemed to satisfy the man, or at least was enough of an answer that he didn't care to pursue when there was so much more work to be done. At this point, the term 'work' had taken on new meaning. It was less about saving people now as much as it was just pulling more and more corpses from the wreckage. Lee had grown distraught at first by the sheer number that were being found dead, however by this point he was feeling too tired to feel anything else anymore. He had heard one of the police officers on the scene say something about how there was evidence of several dozen bombs being planted strategically to try and collapse the whole building, though there'd been some commotion that had disrupted the terrorists part way through.

Lee assumed that the word 'disruption' most likely referred to his companions and prayed that meant they were still okay. Without any means of checking further and not exposing them to the authorities, Lee had continued to do what he could to help the people. But now he sat, for there was little more he could do beyond that. Corpses did not need the help of a man who'd devoted himself to life.

A hand moved into Lee's field of vision, obscuring his view of the destruction with a plain white paper cup. Lee looked up to find the hand's owner, a man dressed as an EMT that looked equally as plain as the cup he held and equally as tired as Lee felt.

"Here," the man said, offering Lee the cup. The priest took it but stared up at the man. He was somewhat tall, had dark hair and pale skin, though nowhere near as pale as Lee's own. The man was in his early thirties from what Lee could tell, and his eyes were a nondescript brown. Everything about him seemed to scream mediocrity, but despite his generic appearance, Lee couldn't shake the feeling that he'd seen this man before.

"You look familiar," Lee said, reaching up to take the cup. It was hot in his hand, despite the foam cup's purpose of blocking the heat and containing it.

"Name's Emit," the EMT responded, shrugging. "Apparently I have one of those faces. I'd be surprised if you knew me. Usually pull the night shift, but this pretty much called for all hands on deck. Drink before we have to haul you in for hypothermia."

Lee took a sip of the dark brown liquid. It was a bit bitter to his liking, but smelled wonderful and left a trail of heat from his tongue to his stomach that blossomed out in a delightful wave, cutting back at the bitter coldness he'd grown so used to that he hadn't even noticed its bite.

"Thank you," Lee said, without looking up from the cup.

"Hell, it's the least any of us could do," Emit said, a slight laugh in his voice.

Lee looked up, confused at how a man like Emit could be laughing at the scene before him. But when the priest saw his face, he understood. Emit's eyes were swollen and red, either from smoke or from tears, though Lee suspected there may have been a healthy mix of both involved. There was a slight quiver in his form that had absolutely nothing to do with cold. Dirt and soot clung to just about every part of him, and blood had been spattered over any part that may have otherwise been clean.

"Are you alright?" Lee asked the man.

His words seemed to strike like a physical blow. Emit barked out another laugh and all but collapsed onto the tailgate next to Lee.

He clutched his own cup, the contents of which sloshed precariously in Emit's shaking grip.

"No," the EMT responded. "No I am not. None of this is alright. This is not the job."

"Helping people is not the job?" Lee asked.

"That's not what we're doing here anymore," Emit said, shaking his head. "At first we were. You were there with us, pulling people out, ripping them from the jaws of death… but now. Now we're just hauling corpses. And that's going to keep being the job for days. I don't know if I can handle that."

"Days?" Lee asked, startled.

"Yeah," Emit said, nodding. "We need to bring people in to clear the debris. Once it's moved, there are going to be more, the unlucky ones that didn't get out in time. People who were pinned, trapped, and died in there, unable to call for help. People who were too far away from exits to make their own way out or be found. People who weren't lucky enough to have someone like you there."

Lee was startled.

"Someone like me?" Lee asked.

"We heard what you did," Emit looked up at Lee, smiling. "Girl over there said how you saw the bomb and dragged her out, shouting your head off to get people to move. You probably saved a dozen people, maybe more."

"Not enough," Lee said, looking down at his bitter drink, feeling his tone of voice matched it perfectly.

Emit shook his head, but he didn't seem to be disagreeing with Lee.

"Never is," he said, his voice sad in spite of the small smile on his face. "No matter what we do, we'll always feel like we didn't save enough people."

The EMT laughed again, and Lee began to recognize it as the laugh of a man clinging to sanity and hope by whatever means necessary.

"But then, what did you do? Started dragging people out of harm's way, blew off every authority figure who told you to stop, and just kept on helping," he said, his grin widening. "I swear there were a few cops who wanted to slap the cuffs on you then and there, but to us you were a godsend. I think those cops were worried about the EMT riot that would happen if they took an ounce of help away from us."

Lee couldn't help but smile at the thought of that. An army of people who didn't know his name standing up to protect him from the authorities. It seemed far-fetched until he realized he'd been doing the exact same thing for them by helping. He started to understand why Emit was laughing. In the shadow of horrific tragedy, the absurdities that kept order in the world were revealed to be nothing more than laughable.

"There's even a news crew looking for you," Emit said. "They want to talk to you about your actions, you know, interview the hero. Though to be fair, the police want to interview you too, but we've been running interference for you on both accounts."

"I suppose I should thank you for that," Lee smiled. "I don't usually enjoy talking to the police."

"Man, I work with them and I don't enjoy talking to them," Emit laughed. "But the good ones aren't too bad, and the bad ones are pricks. Though you can say that for just about anyone these days."

"You are not incorrect," Lee said, assuming that agreeing with Emit here would be the best possible option considering he wasn't entirely sure if the EMT was correct or not. To avoid needing to delve deeper into the subject, he sipped on the rapidly cooling drink, deciding to indulge in as much warmth as he could draw from it. He drained the cup of its contents in one final swig, preparing himself with the courage he needed to ask Emit the question he'd been avoiding. "If I were looking for someone, where would I go for that?"

"You had friends inside?" Emit asked, a note of worry touching his voice.

"My companions were indeed inside," Lee nodded, sidestepping the use of the word 'friends' like he always did. "They would have been in the area of the Nike store. Luis is quite devoted."

"Strange to be devoted to a sporting goods company, but we all need something to make us happy these days," Emit said. He reached out and pointed across the parking lot. "Odds are they'd be over that way. Though to be fair, you may come across that news crew and a slew of police if you try to find them."

Lee followed the direction that Emit was pointing. He saw a white van with several words and decals on it, but the only one he cared about was the word 'news.' He may be able to use the crew as a cloak to pass the police unmolested and make his way to the EMTs on the other side who may be able to direct him to the others.

Plan firmly set, Lee nodded at Emit.

"Thank you for your help, Emit," Lee said, offering his hand. Emit took it and gave a hardy shake.

"Seriously," he said, shaking his head. "You're the one who needs to be thanked. People come together during tragedy, but you went above and beyond, man. Thank you."

Lee smiled. "We all need to do our part to help those in need."

"Amen," Emit said before getting up and heading back to where the others were working.

Lee watched as the man threw himself in with a renewed fervor and smiled. Though the work was grisly and weighed heavily on his mind, Emit was a good man who would see it through to the end. In spite of all the horrors Lee had seen this world be capable of, at least there were those like him who were willing to sacrifice for the good of others.

Taking a deep breath, Lee stood up and began putting his plan into action. Using the pandemonium of the scene as cover, he made his way, weaving through the parked cars people had abandoned in their haste to escape. No one seemed to even look in his direction as he made his way through to the next crowd of people who were standing around the news vehicle. A woman in a neatly pressed suit stood talking to a man holding a strange black box on one shoulder as Lee approached.

"Excuse me," Lee said as he approached.

The woman stopped mid sentence, and looked at Lee with mild annoyance.

"Sir, we're live right now, please get back behind the line," she said. "There is an emergency going on."

"I am aware," Lee responded, unsure why the woman felt the need to point out something as obvious as that, but decided it was better to focus on one matter at a time. "One of the EMTs on the other side of the building said you were looking to speak with me."

"We were?" The woman looked at him curiously, then her face lit up excitedly as she turned to the man with the box. "Ladies and gentlemen! I believe we've found him! The hero who helped pull dozens of people from the building before it collapsed! Excuse me, sir, what is your name?"

"Uh," Lee said, confused at why she was addressing one man as many, but decided that was irrelevant for the moment. "My name is Lee. Lee Errapel."

"Mr. Errapel," the woman continued, holding a strange wand up to Lee's face. "What was going through your mind when you learned of the danger?"

"Well, I was reading in the book store, trying to learn more about the history of your... well world history in general," Lee said, catching himself. "When I saw a few individuals dressed in tattered clothing moving quickly through the store to the exit. I followed them to see if they were going to cause trouble, but soon saw that they were in fact fleeing."

"What tipped you off to the bomb?" the woman asked, enthusiastically.

"I went back inside to the location they came from, hoping to find some sort of clue as to why they were there. They hadn't been carrying anything, so theft was unlikely," Lee said, explaining his thought process. "There I found the bag they'd left behind. Upon opening it, I saw the countdown timer and alerted others to flee as well."

"Your actions saved many lives today," she said, an air of seriousness taking over her voice. "Do you wish to say anything to the public at large?"

"I do," Lee said, nodding. "I recognized these individuals not by face, but by creed. They call themselves the Circle of the Wastes and I believe they are an organization who are bent on causing harm to the global environment. They seek to burn that which you've built up. They are ravaged by radiation and follow a dark, forgotten god. Their zeal could spell danger or death for many. The people must know this and must be prepared. Only by working together can we overcome them."

"You're saying that this is a terrorist organization?" the woman asked, fear in her voice.

"I assume such an organization uses fear and intimidation to get their way?" Lee asked, and the woman nodded at him. "Then they are not that. Fear is not a tool for them. They don't want people afraid, they want them dead. Fear is just a byproduct of recognizing that there are people out there in the world that have never met you, and still wish to take your life."

His words hung in the air, delivered in what he thought was a stern, yet calm manner, but the woman returned his look utterly stunned.

"You... you get all that, Harry?" she said to the man holding the box.

"Uh..." the man called Harry said. "Yeah, yeah I got that."

"Okay," the woman said, her voice shaking as she turned to the man. "Well, you heard it here first. This is Carrie Anderson, live from the Prudential Center."

The man lowered the box from his shoulder. He and Carrie turned to look at Lee in stunned silence.

"You know," Carrie said. "We probably should have focused more on the heroics. The doom and gloom stuff has been a bit heavy the past couple years, people probably can't take much more really bad crap."

"A shame that the world fosters so much then," Lee nodded. "I hope that you will be able to get the message of these fiends out quickly."

Carrie turned to look at Harry, confusion and concern clear on her face.

"Oh yeah," Carrie said, nodding. "It'll be out there before you know it."

"Very good," Lee nodded. "Now if you excuse me, I need to seek out my allies. They may be around here somewhere."

At that moment, Lee saw the wandering shape of an older man moving between cars and headed in the direction he'd just come from.

"Oh, there may be one of them now," Lee said, moving past the news crew to follow the man. "Excuse me."

They let him pass without comment, though Lee could feel their gazes follow him well beyond his leaving. He did not have time to care, however, as he moved with as much agility as he could through the rows of parked cars and panicked people. Eventually, he caught up to the man.

"Smithers!" Lee called out. "Is that you?"

The man turned, and for a moment Lee had thought he found the wrong man. He looked older than Smithers had, and was far dirtier. But upon seeing the priest, the old man's face lit up.

"Lee! Oh thank whatever god you people worship," Smithers said.

"Goibniu," Lee said, but was cut off as Smithers clapped his hands onto his shoulders.

"Have you seen Timm?" Smithers asked, fretfully.

Lee shook his head. "I thought he was with you? As well as Morgan and Luis?"

"Morgan and Luis are fine," Smithers said, looking around, as though scanning for Timm. "They're on their way to the hospital."

"The hospital? I thought you said they were okay," Lee said, surprised by the heat in his own voice.

"By comparison. Besides that, they're getting help and aren't dead," Smithers said, his voice tired. "Listen, Timm got caught in the blast, we were fighting a bunch of those radioactive freaks. We probably should have run, but we tried to stop them. We got one, but the two others fled right before the bomb went off. We ran, but Timm wasn't fast enough... he got hit. It was all I could do to get Morgan and Luis out okay and I'm... I'm..."

Lee saw the man beginning to break down in front of him despite putting every ounce of his remaining energy into holding himself together. He suddenly seemed so frail and helpless, like mere mortals always did when something they could not stop came barreling in to destroy their lives. All anyone could do would be to stand in the wreckage and pick up whatever pieces they could.

Emit's words came back to him, and Lee realized that Timm's may be one of those bodies they pull out in the coming days. Whether he be alive or dead when they do, that was for the gods to determine. At the current moment, there was nothing else that could be done from here. Lee reached out and put his hand on Smithers' shoulder.

"Come," he said gently. "We should return to the church."

"But," Smithers started, but Lee gently cut him off.

"There are teams of people searching for all survivors," Lee said, his voice steady and calm. "We are two exhausted men with little to no training in this aspect. Allow those who dedicate their lives to this cause to work and grant them the space they need to do that work in."

Smithers stood for a moment, the emotions on his face changing rapidly between defiance, anger, understanding, and finally resignation. His shoulders slumped, and that aged appearance returned to him.

"Okay," Smithers said, quietly nodding to Lee. "Okay, let's head back to the church. And who knows, Timm may have outrun that blast after all and just kept going until he hit the front doors."

Lee smiled and nodded, not able to bring himself to refute Smithers' utterly fantastical claim.

*   *   *

"I count two," Father Mitchell said, standing up quickly as they entered his office.

"It wasn't us this time," Smithers said, defensively.

"I count two," Father Mitchell repeated much more sternly and it was clear to Lee that the priest wasn't in a joking mood.

"Morgan and Luis are at the hospital," Lee supplied, hoping to avoid any further conflict today. "Smithers managed to get them out of harm's way, but Morgan reentered the area in search of Timm, whom Smithers saw engulfed by the explosion."

"The one set by the Circle of the Wastes?" Father Mitchell asked.

Lee was taken aback.

"How did you know about that?" Lee asked, not bothering to hide the surprise in his voice. "Did Carrie Anderson and Harry get the message out that quickly?"

"What are you talking about..." Father Mitchell asked, trailing off as realization seemed to dawn on him. "You have no idea what a camera is, do you?"

"Of course I do," Lee said. "They were those things mounted on the ceilings of St. Augustine."

Father Mitchell dropped his head into his hands and leaned back against his desk. The old wood creaked under the strain, though Lee felt that it could not compare to the strain Father Mitchell was under.

"Cameras come in a lot of shapes and sizes," Father Mitchell explained. "The thing is, the guy, I think you said his name was Harry? The thing he was holding was also a camera. Everything you said to Ms. Anderson was recorded and broadcast to the nation, probably the world at this point."

Lee felt confused. He looked over to Smithers who'd just gone pale as a ghost.

"What did he say?" Smithers asked, slowly turning to Lee. "What did you say?"

"It was an interview," Father Mitchell answered. "So basic interview questions. Name, his thoughts on the situation, any thoughts on who caused it."

"You didn't," Smithers said, his voice quavering. "Please tell me you didn't."

"Didn't what?" Lee asked.

"That's how I knew," Father Mitchell said, looking at Smithers. "Lee here just announced to the world who the Circle of the Wastes were and drew global attention down on them."

"Wouldn't the blast have done that as well?" Lee asked.

"It would," Smithers said. "Yes. And that's exactly what they wanted. But we still wrecked the majority of their plan. Dropped their kill count by a lot."

"Police suspect that if there hadn't been an intervention hundreds more lives could have been lost and the entire building could have come down," Father Mitchell explained. "And as you said, the Circle isn't in this for the fear, they're in it for the kill count."

"And you gave them your name," Smithers said, sighing deeply. "Yep, okay. I'm going to the bar to drown myself."

With that, Smithers tossed the keys to the van on Father Mitchell's desk and walked out of the room. Lee watched him walk down the hallway before turning to Father Mitchell.

"Did I do something wrong?" Lee asked.

"No," Father Mitchell sighed. "But there are times when we can do everything right and still lose. Lose the day, lose what matters to us, or lose hope. And it is on those days when we need faith most of all. But we also need to remember that there will be days when we do everything wrong and can still come out victorious, so no matter how lost our hope may seem, it is still there somewhere, waiting for us."

Lee nodded. "Wise words."

"Heh," Father Mitchell laughed. "Well, you're not the only priest in these parts."

"I suppose I'm not," Lee nodded. "He's going out to make mistakes, isn't he?"

Father Mitchell nodded. "I'm afraid he is."

"Very well then," Lee said, walking to the door. "I'm going to go with him."

"To make your own mistakes?" Father Mitchell asked.

"No," Lee said, shaking his head. "I've already done that today. Now I need to stand by someone else to prevent them from coming to harm as I wish someone had been doing for me. If it is my duty to be a shield for others, I will wear that honor proudly."

"Be careful with that pride," Father Mitchell said. "It cometh before the fall. And if a shield gets too battered, the fall will come sooner rather than later."

"So long as it is me who falls. Not someone else," Lee said, exiting the room to follow Smithers down the dark halls through which he walked.

~ 46 ~

LUIS

Luis sat in the room and watched the green line of Morgan's heartbeat rise and fall in steady rhythm. He had been tempted to heal her himself, but upon waking he was told that Father Mitchell had called the hospital and relayed directions from Lee that Morgan should be allowed to rest and heal naturally. His impatience battled against his better judgment, and judgment won out.

Though that did not stop him from healing his own wounds himself. It never failed to amuse the knight when doctors who saw him bleeding and broken not moments ago become flustered at the sight of him walking under his own power again. One had tried to stop him from getting to Morgan's room, citing the need for rest, but wilted under the stare he met as they passed.

He took what little joy he could from these interactions because Father Mitchell had also passed on the bad news about Timm's disappearance. In spite of what Smithers told the priest, Luis refused to refer to it by any other name: it was a disappearance. Until there was a body in front of them, Timm was missing, not dead.

And so, unable to affect change on anything of consequence, Luis stood sentinel over Morgan instead. The nurses had cleaned her up, apparently, washing away the soot and grime from the collapsing building off of her as the wounds she sustained were minor at best. Luis was not surprised by this, as she had been in bear form during the combat, through the detonation of the bombs, and most of the subsequent damage that happened to the world around them directly after. Despite her insistence on returning to rescue Timm, her human body had been kept safe from the very worst of the incident, though it seemed her mind was wrought with pain.

One of the nurses stepped into the room, and before he could open his mouth to ask, she shook her head at him.

"Sorry sir," she said, already knowing what he was going to ask. "We haven't gotten anyone in by the name Timm. Also, if he lost his ID he may be one of our John Doe's, but as far as I can tell from your description we don't have any who match who you're looking for."

Luis deflated slightly. "Thank you anyway."

"Take heart, dear," the nurse said, placing her hand on Luis' shoulder. "Not being one of the John Doe's also means he's not one of the dead. No news is good news in this case."

Luis smiled at her attempt to comfort him. He knew that no news could just as easily mean that Timm was buried under a mountain of rock and steel, but he appreciated her attempts regardless. He placed his hand on hers, patting it reassuringly, and then went back to his vigil over Morgan.

It was around three in the morning that Morgan finally woke up. Luis had been dozing in his chair, though was unable to fully fall asleep due to the lighting, discomfort, and hourly visits from the nurses.

"Where... what's going on?" Morgan's voice rasped, pulling Luis from the edges of sleep.

He stood and walked to her side, pouring a cup of water from the odd pink pitcher, dropping in a straw, and offered it to Morgan. She tried to ask again, but he staunchly held out the cup and refused to answer until she'd at least taken a sip. Knowing better than to test his stubbornness, Morgan accepted the cup and sipped at the straw.

"We're at the hospital," Luis responded, satisfied with her compliance to taking care of her damaged body and its needs. "Have been for about ten hours. I woke up approximately seven ago. You arrived after me, but they gave you some kind of drug to keep you knocked out."

"Why didn't you cure me of that?" Morgan asked, a flash of anger in her voice that was mirrored in her eyes with a kind of ferocity Luis had only seen in predatory creatures. The intensity of it may have frightened a lesser man, or one who hadn't seen her walk face first into a streetlamp because she saw a 'cute kitty,' but Luis was too tired and too well versed to find her intimidating at the moment.

"Lee told me not to," Luis shrugged, taking the cup from her and refilling it.

"And you always listen to Lee?" Morgan asked hotly, not reaching out to accept the cup a second time, so Luis placed it on the rolling tray beside her.

"Yes," Luis answered, without missing a beat. "That is how things work. I am a knight, he is a priest."

"Wait," Morgan said, the heat in her voice fading as she took on a more confused tone. "Is that part of the hierarchy? But you two are from different churches. You follow different gods"

"That doesn't matter," Luis said, pulling the chair up and sitting down next to Morgan. "The holy knight's job is to be the sword of our god. The priest's job is to be the word of our god. I am a warrior and that's all I've ever trained to be. Smithers saw that I allow others to think me more imprudent or rash than I truly am, but just because I carry my own wisdom does not mean I am arrogant enough to think my own counsel is superior to one whose very position within the realm of faith is to parse out wisdom. I will always respect the wishes and wisdom of a priest, because it is the priests who guide the path of our blades."

"So you don't listen to Lee because you always think he's right?" Morgan asked, seemingly more confused after his answer than before it. "You do it because of habit?"

"If I truly felt Lee was wrong about something, I would entirely disregard his words and act of my own accord," Luis answered. "But that would only occur if I believed that he was acting out of a place of personal grievance or fear rather than a place of wisdom and faith. It is my experience that the wisdom of a priest is gleaned from a vision that my own mind may be blind to. The battlefield narrows my focus and limits my ability to see the bigger picture. It is the duty of priests to broaden a warrior's perspective when they feel we need a guiding hand."

"And so you didn't remove the poison from me because?" Morgan asked, a tinge of annoyance still in her voice, but she'd lost the accusatory tone at the very least.

"Because it wasn't poison," Luis answered, keeping his voice calm and steady. "It was to help you rest, to allow your body and mind time to heal. Our magic can seal wounds and knit flesh back together. But the tortures of the mind are beyond our ability to touch and take away. Lee was telling me that you needed time for those wounds to heal, so I granted it to you."

Morgan sat quietly for a moment, sipping at the water in her cup. When it became clear that she had emptied it again Luis took it from her, filled it, and returned it. She nodded her thanks, continued to sip at it for a few more quiet moments before placing the cup down on the small table by her bed.

"I don't agree with Lee's decision," Morgan said, thoughtfully. "However, I understand yours. I'm sorry I took my anger and frustration out on you. I've been doing that a lot lately."

"We're under a great deal of stress," Luis answered. "And while that is rarely a good excuse, you show signs of recognizing the mistake, and thus are worthy of forgiveness for it."

Morgan smiled. "Smithers is right, you are a lot smarter and wiser than you let on."

"Part of my charm," Luis returned her smile.

They sat in silence for a while until a nurse came in. Upon seeing Morgan sitting up in bed, the woman smiled.

"Ah, glad to see you're awake," the nurse said. "How do you feel?"

"I'm feeling okay," Morgan said. "A bit battered, but I suppose the rest did me well."

"Amazing the healing powers of our own bodies," the nurse responded, and Luis had to turn his face to the window to avoid smirking too obviously in the woman's presence.

"Anyway," the nurse continued. "Since you're up, how about we go through a few questions quickly. Just to be sure everything is doing just fine upstairs."

"Well wouldn't you need to talk to the people upstairs about that?" Morgan asked. "I'm sure they would know better than me."

The nurse turned and gave a look to Luis, who just continued smirking and shrugged.

"I mean, she makes a very good point," Luis said, grinning broadly at the woman and tilting his head to one side. .

"Right," the nurse nodded at him, a slight blush spreading across her cheeks, before turning her attention back towards Morgan. "Anyway, how about we start with what day it is?"

"Well, last I remember it was Monday," Morgan said, cupping her chin in her hand and focusing hard on her answer. "But according to Luis I've been asleep for over ten hours, and it was the afternoon when we entered the mall in the first place, so I suppose that it's probably now Tuesday. The twelfth, I believe?"

"Very good," the nurse said with genuine pride. "Now I'll give you an easy one, who is the president?"

"Oh! I know this one," Morgan said excitedly. "Some asshole."

The nurse looked shocked by the answer.

"I mean…" she said, looking at a sheaf of papers. "You're not technically wrong. So I'll accept it."

The questions went on like this for a while, and after about a quarter of an hour the nurse nodded her approval.

"It seems you're doing quite well," she said, almost shocked by her own results. "Are you feeling up to a visitor?"

Morgan gestured to Luis. "I already have one."

"Well," the nurse said, looking between her and Luis. "This one is a bit more official in capacity. The authorities just want to get a statement about what you saw inside the Center before the bombs went off. Usually we'd make them wait until the morning, but considering the nature of the attack, they're quite insistent that they get the information as quickly as possible."

"Any particular reason why the nature of the attack is making them so insistent?" Luis asked. His trust for the local authorities of this world was limited, and the fact that they were so determined to speak to Morgan that they were bending protocol made him even more suspicious.

"Considering it is being labeled as a terrorist attack, they're worried that more people could get hurt if there's another subsequent attack," the woman explained. "They're not sure of the motives, but the more information they have going into the investigation, the better chance they have of preventing future loss of life and reducing injuries."

Luis looked at Morgan and knew what her answer was going to be almost before she said it. There was a fire burning in her eyes, a fire he'd seen all too often in those of fresh recruits to the temple. She wanted to do everything she could to help people, even if it meant putting herself in danger, but she wouldn't risk putting the others in danger without their permission. He saw the battle raging in her thoughts as she fought to do the right thing, but couldn't determine what the right thing was.

Luis smiled. He was willing to take the risk to protect the people of this world, but more importantly, he was willing to take the risk to protect Morgan's conscience. The others would just have to trust his judgment and assume the risk as well. The knight looked at Morgan and gave her a nod.

"Yes," Morgan said, smiling at Luis before turning to face the nurse. "I'd be happy to help in any way I can."

"Very well," the nurse said. "I'll let them know and you should be hearing from them soon."

After about twenty minutes, there was a knock at the door and Luis looked up to see a familiar woman standing in the door frame. She wore her short reddish-brown hair down in a wavy bob that framed the sharp angles of her face, though the wild curls that had once begun to form around the edges had been cut back and tamed. A pair of steely grey eyes pierced into Luis' own with deadly intelligence. On her waist was the same leather wallet that Luis knew held her badge directly opposite her pistol, which she wore openly under the neatly pressed suit jacket.

As she approached, Luis realized that in spite of her well toned frame and powerful build, Special Agent Temperance Fulmer stood a solid half head shorter than he did, but carried herself as though she towered over him. He hadn't noticed how small she really was in their last meeting due to the chaotic environment of the job fair, but he didn't allow that to color his expectations. He'd known too many people whose small stature belied devastating power.

"Fulmer," Luis addressed her. "What are you doing here?"

"It's 'Special Agent Fulmer' or 'Agent,' Luis," Fulmer said, walking into the room without curbing her stride. "Address me as such or not at all."

Luis felt his body tense as her attitude knocked something loose in his memory of the early days he spent at the Temple of Nike. There were many masters and knights who held themselves with the same authority. Luis may not have been able to recall their names or faces, but the attitude remained the same regardless of world. The only difference here was that Fulmer's authoritative tone never slipped into condescension as was often the slippery slope those in positions of power fell readily and head first down. She was exerting her authority, but asked no more than the respect that authority demanded, and so, stepping back, Luis granted her that respect and allowed Fulmer to pass. The agent gave him an approving nod and moved to take the seat by Morgan's bed.

"Good morning, Morgan. I hope you are feeling better," Fulmer said, her tone instantly becoming softer. Luis grit his teeth in irritation at the transformation, but bit back any comment that he may have wanted to shoot her way. "I know you've been through a lot lately and I just wanted to come in and check on you."

"Liar," Morgan said, echoing Luis' thoughts, though her voice did so in a much more diplomatic way than he would have. "But thank you for your concern, be it real or false."

Surprisingly, Fulmer smiled.

"Okay, you caught me," Fulmer said, her tone changing yet again, the steel returning, but with an edge of amusement. "I'm here for more. As you know I work for the Federal Bureau of Investigation. The attack on the mall today falls under several jurisdictions, one of which is mine. So I came in to question people about what happened today. I saw your name on my list and heard the nurses talking about Luis, so I decided to take this interview for myself."

"I don't know if anything I know can really help," Morgan said, shrugging. "But I'll do what I can."

"Thank you," Fulmer said as she took out a pad of yellow paper and pen. "Now, in your own words, tell me what happened."

"We were at the mall because Luis wanted to get some new shoes, and we all wanted to explore a bit..." Morgan started to explain.

"We?" Fulmer asked. Luis looked over her shoulder as she wrote Morgan and Luis' names down. "Who all is 'we'?"

"Luis and myself," Morgan said. "Then our friends, Smithers, Lee, and... and Timm." Morgan said, staggering over Timm's name. Luis felt a pang of guilt.

"I see," Fulmer said, writing those names down as well. "And where are they?"

"Lee and Smithers are safe," Morgan said. "But Timm... we don't know where he is."

"Is there any chance he'd join the others?" Fulmer asked, seemingly obtuse to Morgan's meaning, but Luis doubted it. "I know if I was separated from my team, or in this case, 'friends,' I would want to reconvene where I knew things were safe."

"He may have gone back to the church!" Morgan said, excitedly turning to Luis, who gritted his teeth in response. Morgan realized what she said a moment after and turned to see Fulmer writing down the word 'church' on her pad.

"Why are you writing that down?" Luis asked Fulmer, not bothering to keep the irritation out of his voice.

"Because as an investigator my job is to look into leads," Fulmer said, coolly. "And if your injured friend is taking refuge in the church, he could be in danger from subsequent attacks."

"Bullshit," Luis said, knowing that Fulmer wasn't worried about Timm in the slightest.

"Luis, you realize the fact you're still in this room is a courtesy extended by me," Fulmer said without turning to face him. "Reading the notes of an FBI Agent over her shoulder could constitute obstruction of justice, which carries quite a bit of jail time. The fact that this is about a domestic terrorist attack can only add years, so either stand there like a good dog or step outside."

Luis felt his blood beginning to boil as this woman sat calmly by and insulted him. She was digging into their lives, not into the terrorist attack, and Luis was sure it wasn't for the purpose of protecting others. She was suspicious of them, and had probably been since the job fair, if Smithers was right. Guilt dug at his heart again, remembering how he'd been a large part of why she was looking into them in the first place.

The knight dug his heels in, but quietly leaned back on the cold stone wall, staring daggers at the back of Fulmer's head.

"I'll take your silence for compliance," she said, looking up from her pad and back at Morgan, the tell-tale note of condescension starting to trickle into her voice. "I just have a few more questions.

Fulmer stayed for another hour and a half, asking question after question that seemed innocuous enough, but Luis and Morgan learned quickly that each word was a possible snare meant to hoist them over a pit of snakes. Luis tried to guide Morgan's answers, but Fulmer's watchful eye seemed to pick up just as much from a lack of an answer than from an actual one. By the time she'd packed up her pad and bid her good byes, the knight felt exhausted. He couldn't even imagine how Morgan felt.

"That was exhausting," Morgan said, laying back against the stiff pillows of the hospital bed.

Luis laughed and picked up the pitcher to pour her another glass of water, but there was no humor in it.

"I'm sure you're glad you got all that rest Lee insisted on now," he said, passing it to her.

She glowered at him, but accepted the cup regardless.

"Let's not go too far with that," she said, sipping at the straw. She pursed her lips and looked off thoughtfully into empty air. Morgan sat like that for a few minutes, and Luis did not interrupt her thoughts. Finally, she turned back to him and asked, "Do you think she may have been right? Do you think Timm would have returned to the church?"

"I think Lee would have contacted us somehow if he had," Luis said, knowing the honesty of the statement would hurt, but he did not have the heart to lie.

He saw immediately that he was right. Morgan looked crestfallen and close to tears. Luis bit his lip and stood up.

"Hold on a moment," Luis said, standing up. He exited the room and made his way to the nursing station he'd passed on the way to Morgan's room in the first place. The nurse who had taken Morgan's information earlier was not currently there, but there was a frazzled looking man in a similar outfit sitting at a computer working frantically on something.

"Excuse me," Luis said quietly, not wanting to startle the man. The knight could not make out any features well considering the mask he wore covering the bottom half of his face, but it was clear that he was irritated when Luis addressed him.

"Yes sir, how can I help you?" The man asked, though Luis could sense that he had no real desire to help.

"I don't mean to take up too much of your time," Luis said, appealing to the man's sense of isolation. "However, my friend and I were at the mall this afternoon and we were wondering if there's been any luck locating a friend of ours."

The man stopped typing and stared at the screen for a moment. Luis could see that he was controlling his breathing, as if calming or preparing himself. Slowly, the man turned to face Luis.

"We have very little information," the man said, calmly standing up to face Luis. He seemed to be measuring his words carefully. "People are still being brought in, however most are in critical condition or worse. If you have a name I can check the rosters..."

"He doesn't have identification on him," Luis said, cutting him off. "I am under no illusion he may be dead. Is there any chance my friend and I can see if his body has been brought in?"

The man seemed taken aback.

"That's pretty pragmatic of you," he said, demeanor changing entirely, back to the impatient man he'd been moments before.

"You're busy and I need to know," Luis said, shrugging. "No sense wasting our time dancing around the issue. I will do such a performance in front of her for her sake, but I've lost friends in the past, I mourn when I know I have to and not before."

The man nodded. "Okay, I can respect that. If you want, you can head down to the morgue. They'll let you know about any bodies still needing ID-ing and bring you around. If your friend's not there, it is possible that he could be at a different hospital, but not entirely likely. But it's something that may be able to keep her hope alive a little longer."

Luis nodded his thanks. "Then I shall collect her and do so. Where are Morgan Betony's personal effects?"

The man handed Luis a bag containing everything Morgan had on her when she was brought in before handing him a wooden square that had what was apparently called 'discharge papers' clipped to the front. That done, Luis left the man to his work and walked back to Morgan's room.

"Get dressed," Luis said, passing her the bag. "I'm going to fill out this paperwork, then we're going to see if we can find Timm."

Excitedly, Morgan tore open the bag and began dressing as Luis stepped out into the hallway and mentally prepared himself for what they may find. He didn't have the heart to tell her where they were to begin their search. Not yet. He couldn't take that hope away from her just yet.

~ 47 ~

SMITHERS

Smithers opened his eyes to the blinding lights and piercing sounds that shoved hot blades of pain into the very core of his being. His mouth was dry and his stomach roiled like the sea during a hurricane. He wasn't sure if he would throw up upon standing or simply come crashing down when his hubris finally told him to give it a shot. This was an affliction he knew all too well.

"Well," he said, his own voice raspy and painful to both his throat and ears. "I'm pretty sure I brought this on myself."

"You certainly did," came a booming voice that seemed to completely envelop Smithers' being.

"God? Is that you?" Smithers asked, closing his eyes against the assault of too many sensory afflictions to handle at one time. "Are you here to punish me?"

"No," Lee's voice came to him clearer now, causing him to open his eyes again. The priest stepped into view over him, mercifully blotting out the light. "On both accounts."

Smithers looked up at the priest. One thing he'd learned about Lee through the week or so of knowing him was that the man took good care of his appearance. It didn't seem to be a vanity thing, but more of a ritual. Something he did as a part of meditative practices. His appearance was as orderly as his thoughts, and by that logic, Smithers felt that Lee's thoughts may not be all that calm and level at the moment.

The priest's shirt was rumpled, and the tattoos he usually had hidden beneath peeked out, though not enough for Smithers to fully grasp what he was looking at. The long, platinum blond hair that was always perfectly combed and affixed back in a tail was now unkempt and escaping from its bonds. Dark circles cast shadows under Lee's eyes, making them seem deeper and darker than Smithers had ever seen them, like pools leading to the abyss.

"I could take it away, you know," Lee said to Smithers.

Suddenly, laying helpless in this bed, Smithers felt fear. What could Lee take away? What more could be taken from him that hadn't been already? Was he threatening to end his life? And with a hangover like this, was that really a punishment.

"What exactly," Smithers asked. "Would you be taking away?"

"Your hangover," Lee answered simply. "It is a simple spell to remove such a miserable effect on you."

"Oh," Smithers said, feeling slightly relieved, slightly foolish, and exceptionally nauseous. "No, I think I'll wear this badge."

"Badge of honor?" Lee asked, stepping away, his voice seeming to be a bit more judgemental than normal.

Smithers slowly pushed himself into a sitting position. It took about fifty years for the room to stop spinning afterwards, but eventually it was clear enough that he could make out they were in the basement of the church. The last thing Smithers remembered from the day before was going to the bar after...

Smithers shuddered and felt his stomach roll again.

"Badge of dumbass," Smithers said, slowly moving his head from side to side, as a true shake of it may send the world reeling again. "Letting myself get that trashed, putting myself in a vulnerable position after what happened."

Smithers looked up at Lee across the room from him. The priest sat in a chair flipping through a book whose name Smithers could not make out due to the double vision. He shook his head, trying to clear it, then instantly regretted that decision.

"Putting you in that position too, I suppose," Smithers said, resting his head in his clammy palm. "Sorry about that."

"I did not drink, so I was in no such position," Lee answered, and Smithers noticed the judgmental tone was gone as quickly as it had cropped up. He looked up from the book he was reading. "But yes, your indulgence in wallowing did put me in danger as I was the only one available to defend you and would have no backup to come to my aid had we been attacked. I appreciate that you recognize that and would appreciate you not putting me in such a position again."

"Yeah, sorry," Smithers said, somewhat more sheepishly than he'd expected. "I haven't done something like that in..."

In his mind's eye Smithers saw the flashing red and blue lights, the river, and heard the words repeated over and over again. The words that had forever changed him. The words on the day his old life had ended.

"Years," Smithers finished his sentence, pushing the thought from his mind. He kept his eyes down, not willing to look at Lee. "Haven't drunk like that in years."

The silence hung in the air for a few minutes and Smithers was positive the priest knew there was something more to the comment than he'd intended. Smithers cursed himself for saying anything at all. He tried to just sit still, ignore his own words until hopefully they'd dissipate like smoke.

The sound of footsteps booming down the stairs broke the tension, and Smithers turned to see Father Mitchell coming down them gingerly. He looked up and met Smithers' eyes.

"Ah, Smithers," Father Mitchell said. "Glad to see you're up. It's nearly eleven, I was getting worried."

"Take more than a fifth of whiskey to kill me," Smithers said, waving his hand dismissively. "How can I help you, padre?"

Father Mitchell shifted uncomfortably.

"Actually, I'm not here for you," Father Mitchell said, shifting his eyes towards Lee. "I'm afraid that you have a visitor, Lee."

Lee looked surprised.

"Why would I have a visitor?" Lee asked. He turned to Smithers. "Who would be visiting me?"

Smithers shrugged. "I don't know. You make any new friends at the bar last night?"

"I don't think we're 'friends' exactly," said the cool voice of a woman descending the stairs behind Father Mitchell.

The Father sidestepped, allowing the woman to step past him into the basement. Smithers felt the bottom drop out of his stomach as he recognized Special Agent Temperance Fulmer from the job fair at Boston University smiling at Lee.

"But a few of yours helped me find you," Fulmer said, staring at Lee, her smile growing wolfish and wide. "I have a few questions I would like to ask you."

Smithers looked between the FBI huntress and Lee, who sat before her calm and calculating. The old man couldn't help but imagine a mountain lion staring down a bison. One thing was for certain: he was in the middle of the whole thing.

"So what'll it be?" Smithers muttered to himself. "Trampled to death, or ripped apart?"

SIGN OFF

I wasn't sure how I wanted to do this at first, but I knew that when this book ended I wanted to address you, my readers, once again.

I started writing this book in late September 2020 and have completed it in late November 2020. I took some time to write other books, then came back and finished the edits for this book in January of 2026. Much of that is possible thanks to very supportive friends and the impeccable note taking skills of our very own Morgan Betony. When I finished the last two chapters, I knew that there was more I wanted to say, but wasn't sure exactly what that was.

The end of this book leaves our characters in a position of desperation and despair. Luis and Morgan are headed off to the morgue in hopes to find (or not find) the missing Timm, Smithers is hungover and tortured by his unknown past, while Lee is facing down the most dangerous authority figure they've encountered in their few days in our world. While I feel that makes for a great story, I also feel that with 2026 going the way that it has, it's kind of a crummy thing to leave readers hanging on to.

I've grown very aware of that effect on people the past few years, and if you talk to my players you'll hear the phrase "Death is *not* the worst thing he can do to you" in regards to our games quite often. It's a dark joke that refers to a lot of the ways I run my games, with levels of emotional turmoil that I put their characters through in order to push them to become amazing, like I know they can be.

And it feels to me that the 2020s have been that to many people. Things that just kept pushing and pushing, and even as we move forward into the second half of this decade we're going to be feeling those ripple effects coming and seeking nothing more than to knock our feet out from under us, and it is going to suck.

But much like what we see from our five friends here in these pages, we will press on. Death is not the end, and it's not the worst thing that can happen, that's true, but there will be a crest to this wave we're on as well. Life will have high points and low points, and there will always be a ripple to lift you up if you let it, even if it comes from someone we've lost.

The story continues, and while sometimes it will be hard for us to turn the page ourselves, it will be there when we're ready for it. Just be sure to bookmark the best parts and look back on them from time to time. Believe me, it helps.